Hungarian-O

First Part

33 Castles, Battles, Legends

Written by:

Gábor Szántai

Edited by:

Suzanna King

Copyright © 2020 by Gábor Szántai

Table of Contents

1. Some notes about the history of the land 6
2. Trencsén Castle   GPS: 48.895152, 18.051279 21
3. The Well of Lovers (1477) 24
4. Budatin Castle   GPS: 49.235852, 18.734340 27
5. The walled-in maid (1487) 27
6. Besztercebánya City   GPS: 48.723522, 19.130850 30
7. Gold from copper (1490) 32
8. Csicsva Castle   GPS: 48.921806, 21.663575 35
9. The Book of Lies (1526) 36
10. Tokaj Castle   GPS: 48.112440, 21.409302 39
11. King János Szapolyai in Tokaj – the Battle of Tarcal (1527) 41
12. Korlátkő Castle   GPS: 48.584064, 17.379272 44
13. The Devil`s Plough (1527) 45
14. Dévény Castle   GPS: 48.174965, 16.983475 48
15. The Strength of Love (1529) 50
16. Késmárk City   GPS: 49.135312, 20.420309 52
17. The Cheese Battle (1536) 54
18. Szitnya Castle   GPS: 48.401336, 18.885629 56
19. Lord Balassa's victory at Szalka (1544) 58
20. Kékkő Castle   GPS: 48.243644, 19.333233 69
21. The Blue Stone (1545) 70
22. Drégelypalánk Castle GPS: 48.016501, 19.036117 73
23. The Siege of Drégely Castle (1552) 76
24. Csábrág Castle   GPS: 48.243883, 19.106022 83
25. The Battle of Palást (9-10 August 1552) 85
26. Eger Castle   GPS: 47.905782, 20.375939 94
27. The Siege of Eger Castle (1552) 98
28. Salgó Castle   GPS: 48.144546, 19.846735 106
29. The Siege of Salgó Castle (1554) 108
30. Nagyida Castle   GPS: 48.591733, 21.169861 109
31. The Gypsy warriors of Nagyida Castle (1556) 110
32. Tarkő Castle   GPS: 49.194736, 20.967818 112
33. The Black Flags of Tarkő Castle (1558) 113
34. Komárom Castle   GPS: 47.755602, 18.108737 115
35. Battle on the Danube (1583) 119
36. Korpona Castle   GPS: 48.348025, 19.068727 122

37. The Duel at Korpona's Haversack Castle (1588)   126
38. Szikszó City   GPS: 48.197363, 20.930082   128
39. The Battle of Szikszó (08. October 1588)   130
40. Diósgyőr Castle   GPS: 48.097702, 20.689474   136
41. The Battle of Mezőkeresztes (1596)   139
42. Tiszolc Castle   GPS: 48.676916, 19.942191   151
43. The Wasps of Tiszolc Castle (1597)   153
44. The Castle of Osgyán   GPS: 48.374675, 19.890918   156
45. The Battle of Osgyán (1604)   158
46. Pozsony Castle   GPS: 48.144147, 17.108708   160
47. The Transylvanian Prince takes Pozsony (1619)   163
48. Murány Castle   GPS: 48.734282, 20.045237   165
49. The story of the Venus of Murány (1644)   168
50. Revistye Castle   GPS: 48.521318, 18.722730   171
51. The Sword with the Precious Stone (1646)   173
52. Nyitra Castle   GPS: 48.300032, 18.066939   178
53. The Battle of Vezekény (25 August 1652)   180
54. Érsekújvár Castle   GPS: 47.985466, 18.157982   184
55. The Taking of Érsekújvár Castle (1663)   185
56. Léva Castle   GPS: 48.215030, 18.600427   188
57. The White Geese of Léva Castle (1664)   190
58. Zsarnóca Castle   GPS: 48.481612, 18.721584   191
59. The Battle of Zsarnóca (16 May 1664)   192
60. Likava Castle   GPS: 49.104787, 19.311307   198
61. The Treasure of the Thököly family (1670)   199
62. Kassa   GPS: 48.710167, 21.222256   203
63. The Battle of Enyicke (14 September 1672)   209
64. Fülek Castle   GPS: 48.269974, 19.823365   215
65. Prince Thököly and Fülek Castle (1682)   217
66. Munkács Castle   GPS: 48.437224, 22.719615   220
67. The Legend of Munkács Castle (1685)   224

Foreword

Nam tua res agitur, paries cum proximus ardet Ucalegon.

(Your own safety is in danger when the neighboring wall blazes. In: Count Miklós Zrínyi`s letter to Emperor Leopold I, 1664)

Europe was being torn apart by religious and dynastic wars in the 16th century while the mighty Ottoman Empire was preparing to conquer the countries of the Christian world. So why did the Ottomans not achieve their goal? Why could not the Sultan water his horses in the Seine and in the Rhine? Was not Hungary praised by the West as the Bastion of Christendom?

This period is commonly considered as the most valiant historical age of the Hungarians. The Hungarians had contributed vastly more than their share to the steady development of the European civilization in this time. Hungary was a battlefield for two hundred years and 64% of its settlements perished. An entire spoken Hungarian dialect became extinct and tens of thousands were sold into slavery. Approximately one million people died, and one million new settlers arrived from the Balkans to replace them, which had consequences in later centuries when national states were established.

Unfortunately, the Hungarian's role in the Ottoman Wars is quite underrepresented and neglected in popular history publications, along with TV networks. This Hungarian-Ottoman War Series aims to fill the gap by making this age more popular and available in the English language.

Let us meet and pay tribute to the generations of long-forgotten heroes. Their struggles largely took place between 1372 and 1699 enabling safe prosperity for the luckier part of Western Europe.

This is the first book of a series which will offer a glimpse into the life of the castles of the 1,000-mile Hungarian-Croatian-Transylvanian Borderland beginning with some of the northern castles of the old Hungarian Kingdom.

As for the Borderland, there was a second, and sometimes a third, line of these fortifications behind the Frontier castles because the borders were quite flexible. This wonderous Frontier was the longest structure in the defense system of Europe which had worked for the longest period. Depending on the historical period, it was partly financed and maintained by the Austrian Habsburgs, the Hungarian nobles, and by the warriors called the Valiant Order.

There are many beautiful castles and many ruins on hilltops with stories and legends attached to them all along this long frontier. They have

witnessed larger or smaller raids, battles and sieges, and have seen cowardice, bloodshed and cruelty. The stories in this book are based on the records of contemporary historians and on the tales of the local folk. Some of them are just fairy tales or family-legends made up by the imagination of the following generations, but there is always a little truth in them. In order to describe some battles and sieges in a more entertaining manner, sometimes I have tried to apply the rules of historical fiction, adding details from my own imagination.

There are hundreds of wonderful castles from the Croatian seaside of the Adriatic Sea through the Trans-Danubian Region up to the northern Carpathian Mountains. There were also Borderland castles between the Transylvanian Principality and the Ottoman Occupied Land of Hungary. Many of them will be described in the coming series, including the major battles and sieges in their proximity.

All of these castles had been a part of the Kingdom of Hungary, Croatia or Transylvania, but now they can be found in the eight modern day countries which presently share the Carpathian Basin.

These countries are Austria, Slovenia, Serbia, Croatia, Romania, Ukraine, Slovakia and Hungary.

In the age of the Ottoman Wars, the Kingdom of Hungary was divided into three parts, namely Royal Hungary, Transylvania and the Ottoman Occupied Lands. In this book, I have chosen thirty-three castles from those which had guarded the northern part of the Hungarian Kingdom against the Ottoman Empire. The westernmost castle of these is Dévény Castle which is located in Slovakia near the Austrian border while the easternmost is Munkács Castle which is now in Ukraine.

Their old Hungarian name is commonly used in the stories and in their historical descriptions, however, I have given the modern names and the GPS coordinates as well so as to find them easier on modern maps because these fabulous places are worth visiting. Also, I have included some pictures in this book and more can be seen by visiting my Facebook page, the Hungaries-1632, where more information can be found about the castles and the historical period.

Please, visit: https://www.facebook.com/hungarianturkishwars/ and https://www.hungarianottomanwars.com/

I would like to express my deepest appreciation for the great work of my friend, Suzanna Lahner King who proofread and edited my writing. Please, excuse the eventual quirks I may have made. I hope you will enjoy this book.

Gábor Szántai

The map of the 33 castles and cities discussed in this book:

1. Some notes about the history of the land

Some Hungarian history must be told in order to draw a simplified picture of the events of this difficult period.

As the Hungarians are not Indo-Europeans, most of their habits, dress, food, language and warfare were quite different from that of the neighboring German, Italian, Wallachian and Slavic people. It is said that while the Hungarians are the easternmost Roman Catholics, they preserved many unique customs from their former nomadic lifestyle including the military traditions of light cavalry warfare.

They successfully blocked the attacks of the intruding eastern tribes, the Kumans and the Pechenegs. Even the Mongolians were stuck here in 1241-42, albeit destroying half of the kingdom. After their retreat, King Béla IV was the first ruler to begin building stone castles by the hundreds. The story of the Ottoman-Hungarian clashes is long, but at least an attempt should be made to summarize it.

King Louis I and King Zsigmond

The Ottoman-Hungarian wars began in the reign of our King Louis I, an Anjou king who was also King of Poland. History claims him to be the first European ruler to fight the Ottomans and to beat them in a significant battle. Also, we can begin to count the number of Turkish raids into southern Hungary from this period on.

King Louis I got into a conflict with Venice in 1372 and alas, the Venetians were allied with the Turks. They together, defeated the Hungarian and Paduan army at Treviso. After this, King Louis' attention turned to the Turks. He moved into Wallachia where he was ambushed in the hills by the Wallachians who were allied with the Turks. He could barely flee the battle. Yet, he was able to defeat the raiding Turks invading Transylvania. During his Bulgarian campaign, he defeated the Turks in a major battle in 1377. Sadly, the Hungarian politics of this age can be made to be partly responsible for the weakening of the Balkan people against the invaders. Many smaller Balkan nations had to seek the help of the Turks against the expansion of the Hungarian Kingdom which tried to use them as buffer-states. The Muslims soon attacked Serbia and defeated the Serbian army at Rigómező (now Kosovo Polje) in 1389.

The Kingdom of Hungary had been a middle-power of Europe, and during this time, its population is usually compared to that of England's. The Ottoman Turks took the first Hungarian Frontier castle of Galambóc (Golubac, Taubenberg) in 1391. Five years later the Hungarian King, Zsigmond (Sigismund) of Luxembourg, set out against the Turks. In his army, there were many European knights and soldiers of Czech, Spanish, Italian and French origin. Sadly, they were utterly defeated in the large-scale Battle of Nicopolis in 1396.

King Louis (1326-1382) fighting against the Turks in Bulgaria

Drawing conclusions from this, King Zsigmond decided to focus on building up his southern lines of defense in Hungary which became the first chain of frontier castles. He paved the way for János (John) Hunyadi's success by making a law that demanded the financing of one horse-archer per twenty households. As a result of this, Hungary could keep an 80,000-man strong army to defend the country and also be able to send 40,000 men when campaigning abroad, according to a report from Venice, 1423. When Sultan Mehmed I reunited the Sultanate between 1413 and 1422, he allied with Bosnia and together they attacked Hungary and Croatia in 1415. Mehmed was able to make Bosnia a Sanjak, an Ottoman province, and kept sending armies against Wallachia and Hungary, without success. In the end, it was he who asked for peace in 1419.

The Wars of the Lower Danube

This was the time of Ottoman wars in the Balkans. Sultan Murad II tried to conquer the whole of the Balkans, but was pushed back by the Hungarian-Italian General, Pipo of Ozora, in 1423. He had two more successful campaigns against the Ottomans before he died in 1426.
After some smaller raids, the Turks broke into Transylvania with a mighty army in 1432. The enemy crushed King Zsigmond's 2000-strong unit which was guarding the mountain passes. The Turks pillaged all over southern Transylvania taking thousands of slaves. There were many raids in Transylvania between 1435 and 1436, and two years later they tried to take the castle of Szendrő (Smederovo) in 1438 but the Hungarian-Serbian-Czech reinforcements chased them away.
Yet, the Turks returned a year later, broke into Transylvania, and took Szendrő by surprise. They could do so because the Hungarian armies were weakened and held up by fighting a major peasant uprising which had started in 1437.

The Hunyadi Clan

This was when our greatest hero began his career: János (John) Hunyadi. His first campaign took him deep into Serbia in 1441 and the following year he defeated the Begler-Bey of Rumelia in Transylvania.

Because of Pope Eugenius' IV incentive, János Hunyadi led his famous „Long Campaign" (1442-1444) against the Ottoman Empire. He was reinforced by Polish, Serbian, Wallachian and Bulgarian soldiers and he had German and Czech mercenaries as well. He almost reached Edirne, the capital of the Ottoman Empire.

Hunyadi successfully applied the Bohemian Hussites' warfare technique; the combination of armored wagons with firearms. The successful advancement of Christian forces into Ottoman territory encouraged the Balkan peoples to revolt. In the end, the Sultan was made to plead for peace which was made in 1444 at Várad, Transylvania. King Ulászló I aka Wladyslaw III, ruler of Hungary and Poland made the truce with the sultan.

Unfortunately, the Italian Cardinal, Cesarini, absolved King Ulászló from his oath in order to continue the Ottoman war. This war of 1444 had ended in a disaster at the Battle of Várna in Bulgaria when the great European coalition was crushed in an open battle by the Ottomans.

In fact, Hunyadi won the battle against the twice-stronger enemy and advised the king not to attack the Janissaries headlong, but it was in vain. The king was slain, some say it was the penalty for breaking his oath. After the battle, Hunyadi became the Governor of Hungary. It had also become obvious that the traditional knightly warfare style was of little use against the Ottomans.

János (John) Hunyadi (1407-1456)

The practice of tolling the bells at noon in Europe is traditionally attributed to the international commemoration of the Nándorfehérvár (aka Belgrade) victory and to the order of Pope Callixtus III as a call for believers to pray for the Christian defenders of the city.

The Battle of Nándorfehérvár was one of the most significant events of the Ottoman-Hungarian Wars. The Hungarian and Serbian warriors were defending the castle under the flag of Mihály Szilágyi in 1456 against the immense army of Sultan Mehmed II. János Hunyadi joined the defenders with his 10,000 men along with the help of the 30-35,000 peasant Crusaders of János Kapisztrán (Capistrano) they caused a crushing defeat to the Ottomans on 22 June 1456. After the siege, a plague broke out and killed many people in the Crusader's camp, including János Hunyadi and János Kapisztrán (John of Capistrano).

Hunyadi's son was elected to be our next king, King Matthias Corvinus. He was our greatest king, a real Renaissance ruler when Hungary was in its heyday. When he died, our proverb was born: „Matthias died, so did justice." Today, he is being criticized for not focusing enough on the Ottoman threat.

King Matthias Corvinus (1443-1490)

Yet others say that he made war against the West in order to become strong enough to fight the East. In fact, Matthias had been fighting the Ottomans for almost ten years taking back the Castle of Galambóc (Golubac) and later Jajca in 1463. This way he could control the rest of Bosnia. He could clearly see that however strong Hungary could be, its strength alone would not be enough against the Ottoman Empire. It was for this reason that Matthias led his campaigns against the Germans and the Czechs, because

Hunyadi successfully applied the Bohemian Hussites' warfare technique; the combination of armored wagons with firearms. The successful advancement of Christian forces into Ottoman territory encouraged the Balkan peoples to revolt. In the end, the Sultan was made to plead for peace which was made in 1444 at Várad, Transylvania. King Ulászló I aka Wladyslaw III, ruler of Hungary and Poland made the truce with the sultan.

Unfortunately, the Italian Cardinal, Cesarini, absolved King Ulászló from his oath in order to continue the Ottoman war. This war of 1444 had ended in a disaster at the Battle of Várna in Bulgaria when the great European coalition was crushed in an open battle by the Ottomans.
In fact, Hunyadi won the battle against the twice-stronger enemy and advised the king not to attack the Janissaries headlong, but it was in vain. The king was slain, some say it was the penalty for breaking his oath. After the battle, Hunyadi became the Governor of Hungary. It had also become obvious that the traditional knightly warfare style was of little use against the Ottomans.

János (John) Hunyadi (1407-1456)

The practice of tolling the bells at noon in Europe is traditionally attributed to the international commemoration of the Nándorfehérvár (aka Belgrade) victory and to the order of Pope Callixtus III as a call for believers to pray for the Christian defenders of the city.
The Battle of Nándorfehérvár was one of the most significant events of the Ottoman-Hungarian Wars. The Hungarian and Serbian warriors were defending the castle under the flag of Mihály Szilágyi in 1456 against the immense army of Sultan Mehmed II. János Hunyadi joined the defenders

with his 10,000 men along with the help of the 30-35,000 peasant Crusaders of János Kapisztrán (Capistrano) they caused a crushing defeat to the Ottomans on 22 June 1456. After the siege, a plague broke out and killed many people in the Crusader's camp, including János Hunyadi and János Kapisztrán (John of Capistrano).

Hunyadi's son was elected to be our next king, King Matthias Corvinus. He was our greatest king, a real Renaissance ruler when Hungary was in its heyday. When he died, our proverb was born: „Matthias died, so did justice." Today, he is being criticized for not focusing enough on the Ottoman threat.

King Matthias Corvinus (1443-1490)

Yet others say that he made war against the West in order to become strong enough to fight the East. In fact, Matthias had been fighting the Ottomans for almost ten years taking back the Castle of Galambóc (Golubac) and later Jajca in 1463. This way he could control the rest of Bosnia. He could clearly see that however strong Hungary could be, its strength alone would not be enough against the Ottoman Empire. It was for this reason that Matthias led his campaigns against the Germans and the Czechs, because he wanted to become Emperor of the Holy Roman Empire as King Zsigmond had been.

Yet, in spite of his western plans, King Matthias had consistently supported the wars against the real enemy, the Ottomans. The king had the first standing army in Europe, made up of mercenaries, famously called the „Black Army". Besides which, he adopted the most modern artillery units and tactics of the age, using armored wagons with musketeers in them in the Czech Hussite fashion as his father did.

The Turks attacked Hungary in 1475 and could break in as far as Nagyvárad (Oradea) but they were driven out. The army of King Matthias proved superior and soon the Turks lost the castle of Szabács (Sabac) on our southern border. In 1480, they suffered a sobering defeat at Kenyérmező (Breadfield), Transylvania, when General Pál Kinizsi scattered their larger army. He chased them deep into Serbia gaining back large territories.

Campaigns of the Black Army

An Ottoman army took away the City of Otranto from Naples in 1480 so as to build a beachhead against Italy. The Neapolitan King, Ferdinand II, the brother-in-law of King Matthias, asked for his help. Matthias sent him 2,100 soldiers led by his General, Balázs Magyar, who successfully re-captured Otranto. Italy was saved.

When King Matthias took the City of Vienna in 1485, he was not very far away from achieving his goal of becoming Holy Roman Emperor but he was poisoned and died in 1490.

The years before the Battle of Mohács

Not much later, the role of saving Christendom from the Ottomans went to the Habsburgs dynasty because of the decline of the Hungarian Kingdom. Some Hungarian historians claim the Habsburgs were inadequate in their protection of Hungary saying they just wanted to take possession of it rather than defend it from the Ottoman Empire.

The Hungarian Kingdom fell into a severe economic crisis after King Matthias' death. Vladislaus II, the king after Matthias, sent the Black Army against the Turks without paying them. The mercenaries rebelled and their former general, General Kinizsi, had to defeat them. Seeing this, the Turks made an attempt to take Nándorfehérvár in 1492, however General Kinizsi routed them and led his army to Serbia. He continued beating the intruding enemy back repeatedly in the following years, and succeeded in keeping Nándorfehérvár again in 1494 when its unpaid defenders wanted to surrender the fort. He led one more campaign against the Ottoman Empire that year but died soon afterward. Yet, his efforts were rewarded with the 3-year peace treaty of 1495 which was sealed between the King and the Sultan.

János Corvinus, King Matthias' illegitimate son, defeated the Turks in 1499 in Bosnia and he was able to relieve Jajca Castle in 1501. He was also recognized as Duke of Slavonia and Opava and as the Ban (Duke) of Croatia. From 1499 to 1502, he successfully defended the unconquered parts of Bosnia against the Turks.

Pope Alexander VI organized an anti-Ottoman alliance between Hungary, France, Poland and Venice in the year 1500. The Hungarian army was able to reach Bulgaria, but it was resultless, except for the capture of the city of Vidin. This war ended with a peace treaty in 1504 that was promulgated in 1510.

Unfortunately, the Hungarian Cardinal, Tamás Bakócz, was given the task by Pope Leo X (Giovanni Medici) in 1514 to organize a peasant crusade against the Turks in Hungary. The unpaid, hungry peasants rebelled, and led by György Dózsa caused a great deal of harm in the Kingdom there by alienating the commoners from the noblemen just before the greatest Ottoman threat.

The next set of Ottoman-Hungarian wars was fought near the Bosnian and Croatian Frontier castles. The Croatian armies defeated the enemy in the battles of Dubica, Jajca and Korenica. The hero of these fights was Petar Berislavic whose victories ended with his death in 1520. Things got worse when Nándorfehérvár (Belgrade) was taken in 1521, giving theTurks a freeway into the country. At this time, Hungary was ruled by the Jagiellonian King Louis II, who died in the Battle of Mohács in 1526 when his army was defeated by Sultan Suleiman I.

The Battle of Mohács, 1526

The huge Ottoman Empire was many times stronger and better organized than the Kingdom of Hungary, but as this battle was a milestone in the Ottoman-Hungarian wars its background is worth telling in a few sentences.

We can witness how during these years the southern chain of the Hungarian frontier castles, established by King Zsigmond in the 15th century, perished mostly because the garrisons were not paid. The Hungarian barons and noblemen had always hated the Jagiellonian kings and would have wanted to limit the King's power by any and all means. They needed a weak monarch and King Louis II of Hungary was said to be a prodigal youngster who realized the Turk danger too late. Moreover, George von Brandenburg, the Queen's relative and tutor to the young king, supported his bad habits.

There were two parties in the King's court, one of them was around his Queen, Maria von Habsburg, while the Hungarian party was led by Lord János Szapolyai. The barons, in general, can be made responsible for the disastrous financial situation of the otherwise wealthy kingdom. One of them was Palatine István Báthori, the second most powerful lord, who had been accused of fraud. Later, he managed to escape from the Battle of Mohács and became one of the leaders of the pro-Austrian party, allowing the army of Habsburg Ferdinand, Queen Maria's brother to enter the country by offering him free passage at Pozsony (Bratislava, Pressburg).

János Szapolyai, Voivode of Transylvania, was the greatest opponent of the Austrian party. He fought, together with Báthori, against the Turks in the southern borderland and even defeated them in Wallachia in 1522, thus gaining a little time for the country.

Gossip says that Szapolyai's father may have had a hand in the poisoning of King Matthias in 1490. The Voivode is blamed for not coming soon enough to King Louis II`s camp at Mohács with his Transylvanian army which was almost as big as the King`s. On top of that, Szapolyai`s younger brother, György, was accused of killing the King and his General, Pál Tomori, while fleeing from the battle. We will never know for sure because György disappeared in the battle. It is a fact, though, that later János Szapolyai became King of Hungary, right after the Battle of Mohács.

János Szapolyai

As for the financial crisis, even the Jewish historians agree that Imre Szerencsés (Fortunatus aka Snéor ben Efraim), the Vice-Treasurer, had been involved in the financial chaos of the country. When Fortunatus was accused in 1525 of fraud, he blamed it on the Fugger banking family, the makers of emperors, popes, and kings. It is true, that the Fuggers wanted to recover the mining rights of the rich Hungarian Mining Towns that King Louis had taken away from them. It is also true, that after returning the fabulous mines to the King`s care in 1525, the Fuggers removed all of their mining equipment, and even the local miners, just to make mining impossible for years to come.

Let us include here Emperor Charles V who was indebted to the Fuggers up to his knees. It was lucky for him that Habsburg Ferdinand, his younger brother (and brother of the Hungarian Queen, as well), wanted the Hungarian throne for himself. When Ferdinand seized the Hungarian throne in 1526, with the help of his sister, Emperor Charles V was happy to lend him mercenaries. With their help, Ferdinand could fight against King Szapolyai and soon he re-established the Fuggers in the mining towns. The German peasant war between 1524 and 1526 contributed to the hostile international environment, not to mention the lack of aid from Rome. Although the Pope sent 50,000 Ducats to King Louis II to hire mercenaries, it was nothing compared to the 10 million Ducat worth of booty that Emperor Charles V and his men stole from there a year later during the Sack of Rome, not to mention the ransom of the Pope.

Queen Mary Habsburg

Having some sense of reality, many Hungarian noblemen wanted to make a truce with Sultan Suleiman. In order to gain some strength and time, they may have agreed to open a corridor to the Sultan and let him go and attack Vienna if he wanted to. Not surprisingly, Habsburg Maria was against all peace negotiations with the Ottomans.

Taking all participants into consideration, let us next add Francis I, King of France, and his mother Louise of Savoy. Desperate for allies after the French defeat at Pavia (1525) in Northern Italy, it was they who encouraged Suleiman to invade Hungary in order to threaten the eastern borders of Charles V's Holy Roman Empire.

Sultan Suleiman found an excuse for war against Hungary because his envoy, Bey Behram, was imprisoned in Buda in 1521 by those who did not want peace with the Turks.

The Great Sultan led seven of his twelve wars against Hungary. His first campaign was aimed at Nándorfehérvár (Belgrade) which he took after a hard won siege in 1521. We will see that his last campaign also brought him to Hungary in 1566 where he died during the siege of Szigetvár Castle.

King Louis II of Hungary

Suleiman set out with his immense and well-equipped army again in 1526 and took the castle of Pétervárad while the Hungarians were very slowly gathering at Buda as the Hungarian noblemen were willing to follow their monarch only if he was leading the army in person into the war.

King Louis II and his General, Pál Tomori, decided to set out with their 24,000-strong army to beat the Turks while the Sultan's 80,000-strong army was on the march. Further, Czech mercenary units were supposed to come along with the Slavonian and the Transylvanian troops, but they were late. The Battle of Mohács took place on 29 August and resulted in a major defeat and in the King's death.After the Battle of Mohács, came the Dual Kingship of Szapolyai and Ferdinand which led to the partition of the country. During the Dual Kingship, King Ferdinand fought against King János Szapolyai who had to rely on the support of the Sultan against him.

In fact, the Ottomans were not strong enough to seize Eastern Hungary and Transylvania. However, the division of the Kingdom served their interests as it had in 1529 when the Turks defeated the army of Ferdinand at Buda, placing János Szapolyai on the throne.

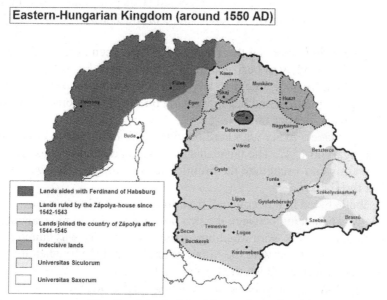

The Partition of the Hungarian Kingdom

King János Szapolyai evaded lending Hungarian auxiliary forces to Suleiman when the Sultan led wars against Ferdinand, but did not hesitate in borrowing help from the Turks when he needed some. Szapolyai died in 1540 leaving behind an infant son who was born in that same year. His widow, Queen Isabella, was able to rule because Sultan Suleiman allowed her to do so.

The Sultan arrived at Buda in 1541 to beat back Ferdinand`s army which was besieging it, and to greet the child. He decided to take Buda Castle which he gained with a trick. Then, he allowed Queen Isabella and her son, King János Zsigmond II, to leave freely and „gifted" them the control over the territories over on the far side of the Tisza River and Transylvania, in exchange for an annual tax. Although those lands were not in Turkish hands, Suleiman thought that he could gain them in the years to come.

The fall of Buda, 1541

Although the Kingdom of Hungary did not cease to exist, the taking of Buda in 1541 caused the partition of the country into three parts: the Ottoman Occupied Lands of Hungary, the eastern part that slowly became the Transylvanian Principality and the Habsburg-ruled Hungarian Kingdom with Croatia.

The Sultan had to be disappointed in the loyalty of his new "vassals", at least as far as Prior György Martinuzzi (1482-1551) the Guardian of the young King János Zsigmond II was concerned. This priest, the late king's innermost advisor, laid down the foundations of the Transylvanian Principality.

He had a great role in creating the Truce of 1538 between Ferdinand and Szapolyai. When Buda was besieged in 1541 by the Habsburgs he defended it valiantly until Suleiman arrived. He very quickly became disappointed in Suleiman and began working on the unification of Hungary under the Habsburgs after this.

Prior György made a treaty with Ferdinand in 1541 and began to organize Eastern Hungary in 1542. The talented statesman made tremendous efforts to raise an army and strengthen the Frontier against the Ottomans as well as against the Habsburgs.

Queen Isabella hated him deeply and tried to cross him wherever she could. He was balancing between the two powers and it led to his downfall. With dismay, the Turks were watching as Eastern Hungary was gaining strength and the next war with the Muslims broke out in 1550 when they came in force to further widen their occupied territories.

Prior György forced Queen Isabella and János Zsigmond II to resign in 1551 and Pope Iulius III appointed him as a Cardinal. In answer to that, the Ottomans made Ilie II Rareș, Voivode of Moldavia and the Wallachian Voivode attacked Transylvania to punish him, but the Prior led an army against them and defeated the attackers.

While Prior György was busily fighting off the enemy in Transylvania, Ferdinand sent him a 9,000-strong army, led by the Italian mercenary commander, Count Giovanni Battista Castaldo, to aid in the battle. Together, they succeeded in making the Turks withdraw. While doing so, the Prior (he was nicknamed "the White Prior" after his Paulinian robe) promised the Turkish garrison of Lippa Castle safe conduct. When Castaldo saw the Turks marching away undisturbed he was very surprised and began to accuse the Prior of treason.

Castaldo wrote a letter to King Ferdinand and to Emperor Charles V and reported Prior György as a traitor. As a result of this, Ferdinand gave the order to have the Prior assassinated. The mercenaries killed the 69 year old priest with two musket shots and 75 knife stabs. After dishonoring his corpse, the body was left unburied where it had fallen for 70 days. The Pope forgave King Ferdinand and nobody received any punishment for the crime.

The War of the Frontier Castles

This is a particularly significant part of the 300 years of the Ottoman war-period because the Hungarian warriors defended their castles with amazing heroism. Unfortunately, the Habsburgs did not give enough provisions or military help towards the upkeep of the chain of Borderland Castles which stood between them and the Ottoman Empire. After the death of Prior György, the Turks launched a campaign in 1552 because of the Transylvanians' disobedience and gained more than 25 castles and defeating the Habsburg army at Palást. Fortunately, they were delayed by the heroic siege of Eger and Drégely castles in that year.

Many more military actions of a similar kind happened throughout the 16th and 17th centuries, like the siege of Szigetvár in 1556, or the siege of Várpalota ten years later. It was during this period that the new Borderland was created. The larger and smaller forts and castles of the Borderland blocked the passable roads very effectively because the terrain was marshy and mountainous.

There were 100-120 larger castles and many smaller palisade forts and guard-houses, half of their garrison was infantry and half of them were heavy or light hussar cavalry. It was true of both the large and small fortifications. There were about 22-25,000 men serving in the Borderland, generation after generation.

These underpaid Hungarian and Croatian warriors had to develop very flexible hit-and-run warfare techniques against the enemy because this was how they could obtain the necessary income for their survival. It included sudden ambushes, night-attacks, raids, the sacks of markets in Ottoman territory, the hunt for captives, and the ransom-business flourished. In the battles, the Hungarians and Turks equally collected heads and sent them to Istanbul or to Vienna where rewards were paid for them.

Although half of their upkeep was supposed to come from the non-Hungarian parts of the Habsburg's Empire their pay arrived sometimes only long years later. While foreign mercenaries received twice or three times more pay, the local warriors who regarded themselves as members of the so-called Valiant Order had to find their own food as well as fodder for their horses. Their warfare was very effective against the Ottoman forces who opposed them in the line of the Turk chain of Borderland castles. There were twice as many Ottoman warriors who had a force twice as large and who were well fed and properly paid, not to mention the irregular Ottoman troops. According to the pay lists, 94% of the Ottoman garrisons in the Occupied Land of Hungary consisted of Serbian or Albanian soldiers. They were either Orthodox Christians or new converts to Islam.

Mobile warfare enabled very small Hungarian units to defeat a ten times larger troop of Ottoman soldiers. Even in times of „peace", there were raids and sieges all along the Frontier. Dueling became a favorite past-time between Hungarian and Ottoman warriors.

As for Hussars, the heavily armed „winged hussars" of Poland were almost identical to their Hungarian brothers. It was partly because of the Transylvanian Prince István Báthory who became King of Poland and Prince of Lithuania between 1575 and 1586.

The Hungarians and the Polish learned a lot from each other. The „Hussar castles" were being built during this time, these were extensions of existing older castles, usually a large yard surrounded by a palisade that the cavalry could easily use.

During the 1560s there had been constant war between the Habsburgs, Turks, and the Hungarians of Transylvania until they agreed to a truce in 1564.

The siege of Szigetvár was the seventh campaign that the aged Sultan Suleiman the Magnificent had led into Hungary in the distant hope of taking Vienna. It was during the siege that he died in 1566, along with Captain Miklós Zrínyi aka Nikola Šubić Zrinski, the famous defender of the fort.

The Treaty of Adrianople in 1568 finished this set of wars. The fall of Szigetvár was followed by a period of 25 years of relative peace between both empires. In the meantime, Transylvania was separated from Royal Hungary and gradually became more or less independent from the Ottomans as well.

Here, we must remark that King János Zsigmond II belonged to the Unitarian Church. He was the single Unitarian ruler in world history and his historically famous deed was the introduction of freedom of religion in 1568, the first in the world. After his death in 1571, Prince István Báthory was elected to rule in Transylvania. Fortunately, the Transylvanian Principality was equally as far from Vienna as from Istanbul and so managed to keep more independence than the other Ottoman satellite states of the region.

The period before the 15-Year-War can be described as the age of raids and ambushes. The Hungarian warriors achieved many smaller victories during this period and there were two greater ones at Szikszó, one in 1577 and the second in 1588, both times the troops of Captain Zsigmond Rákóczi were the victors.

The 15-Year-War (1591-1606)

The 15-Year-War between the Ottomans and the Habsburgs and Royal Hungary began between 1591 and 1593. The Holy Roman Empire, the

Habsburgs, and Royal Hungary allied themselves with Spain and the Pope, and the Cossacks and Persians were included as well. During the war, several castles were taken back in Hungary from the Ottomans. Transylvanians also joined in against the Turks.

The Hungarian, Transylvanian and Wallachian armies defeated the Ottomans on their lands at Gyurgyevo (Giurgiu) in 1595 but the Sultan defeated the Christian army the next year at Mezőkeresztes, near Diósgyőr Castle.

Hungarian-Ottoman battle

Transylvania had a very hard time during the rule of Prince Zsigmond Báthory. The intruding Habsburg, Turkish and Wallachian armies were contesting with the local Székelys and other Hungarian noblemen to gain power. There were many Crimean Tatar raids and their destruction was twice that of the Turks.

The Long War was finally ended in 1606 by Prince István Bocskai of Transylvania, the victor of Gyurgyevo (Giorgiu), who dictated the terms of the Peace of Zsitvatorok (Zitava). He became the first Transylvanian prince who could stop the Habsburgs' intentions because they had tried to seize the properties of Hungarian nobles by accusing them of treason.

Bocskai led a war by leading his Hajdú soldiers (armed herdsmen) against Vienna, conquering almost the entirety of Royal Hungary. He was also the first one who was able to effectively defend the Protestant faith from the Habsburgs. The Sultan sent him a crown but he did not accept it.

The Transylvanian situation (1611-1614)

The Transylvanian Principality was gaining strength and in the days of Prince Gábor Bethlen and later, the country was far from being a vassal of the Ottoman Empire. The first Ottoman-Transylvanian war took place between 1612 and 1613.

GABRIEL BETHLEN D. G. PRINCEPS TRANS.
SYLVANIÆ., PART, REGNI HVNGARLÆ. DOMINVS
ET SICVLORVM COMES. ETC.

Prince Gábor Bethlen

Prince Gábor Báthory gained the throne in 1608 with the help of the Hajdu soldiers and the Sultan accepted him as well. His rule was chaos and in five years he managed to anger everybody around him, including the Ottomans. Finally, in 1613 the Prince allied himself with the Habsburgs which was the last straw for the Sultan. Huge Ottoman and Tatar armies entered Transylvania in 1613 and Báthory asked for help from the Austrians in vain. In the meantime, Gábor Bethlen was elected as prince under the order of Sultan Achmed I. Prince Báthory was murdered by some Hajdú soldiers.

It was Prince Gábor Bethlen who turned Transylvania into the rich, tolerant and strong „Fairy Garden" of Europe. His rule began under the shadow of Turkish blades but his state enjoyed greater independence than did a mere satellite state of the Ottomans. Bethlen also led several successful campaigns against the Habsburgs. He was even elected as King of Hungary between 1620 and 1621.

Prince György I Rákóczi of Transylvania (1630-1648)

The Principality of Transylvania

The second Ottoman-Transylvanian war took place in 1636 when Prince György I Rákóczi defeated the Pasha of Buda. Four years later he made a coalition with the Polish King Sigismund III against the Turks.

Prince Rákóczi I was also involved in the 30-Year-War siding with the Swedes against the Habsburgs.

His anti-Turk war shows how little he was a friend of the Ottoman Empire and how independent Transylvania was from the Sultan. Rákóczi attacked and occupied the whole Hungarian Upper Land from the Habsburgs just as Bocskai and Bethlen had done because he gained the support of the Hungarian noblemen there.

Rákóczi's army outsmarted superior western forces without a major defeat. He didn't really want to bring the Austrian ruled Hungarian Kingdom down before dealing properly with the Ottomans since the Habsburgs represented at least some kind of an opposing power against the Sultan.

In the end, Emperor Ferdinand recognized György's rule over the seven eastern counties of the Kingdom of Hungary and reaffirmed the religious liberties of Transylvania in the Treaty of Linz in 1645.

Prince György II Rákóczi and the decline of Transylvania

Unfortunately, Prince György Rákóczi II, son of Rákóczi I, was not so fortunate. In alliance with the Swedes, he attacked Poland in 1657, hoping to gain the Polish crown. His campaign had not been welcomed by the Ottomans and his entire army was very unfortunately captured by the Crimean Tatars.

Soon, Transylvania was overrun by the Tatars and their terrible harvest sacked the „Fairy Garden" bare. The Prince died after being defeated again by the enemy in 1660. The newly elected Prince Apafi tried to regain the past power of the Principality but its days began to decline.

Count Miklós Zrínyi aka Nikola Zrinski (1620-1664)

Miklós Zrínyi aka Nikola Zrinski

Count Miklós Zrínyi was the descendant of Captain Miklós Zrínyi (1508-1566), the hero of Szigetvár.

He was an outstanding Hungarian-Croatian military leader, statesman, and poet, loyal to the Kingdom of Hungary and the Habsburgs to his death. His younger brother, Péter, fought against the Ottomans all his lifelong, too. In 1645, during the closing stages of the Thirty Years War, Count Zrínyi acted against the Swedish troops in Moravia, equipping an army corps at his own expense.

At Eger, he saved the life of King Habsburg Ferdinand III, who had been surprised at night in his camp by the offensive of Carl Gustaf Wrangel. Although not enthusiastic about having to fight against the Hungarians of Transylvania, Zrínyi subsequently routed the army of Prince György I Rákóczi on the Upper Tisza river, without shedding a drop of Hungarian blood.

For his services, the Emperor appointed him Captain of Croatia. In 1646 he distinguished himself in actions against the Ottomans and he was made a „Bán" (Duke), and the Captain-General of Croatia. During 1652–1653, Zrínyi was continually fighting against the Ottomans. In 1663, the Turkish army, led by Grand Vizier Köprülü Ahmed, launched an overwhelming offensive against Royal Hungary, aiming for Vienna. The Imperial army failed to put up any notable resistance and the Ottoman army was eventually stopped by bad weather conditions.

In preparation for the new Turkish onslaught due next year, German troops were recruited from the Holy Roman Empire and aid was also called for from France. Zrínyi, under the overall command of the Italian Montecuccoli, leader of the Imperial army, was named commander-in-chief of the Hungarian army.

In 1664, Zrínyi set out to destroy the strongly fortified Suleiman Bridge of Eszék (Osijek) over the Dráva River. The destruction of the bridge would cut off the retreat of the Ottoman Army and make any Turkish reinforcement impossible for several months and would have enabled the re-taking of the strategically important Kanizsa Castle. Zrínyi advanced 240 kilometers in winter, in enemy territory, and destroyed the bridge. He was frustrated by the refusal of the Imperial generals to cooperate.

The Court remained suspicious of Zrínyi all the way, regarding him as a promoter of Hungarian separatist ideas. It was why Zrínyi's siege of Kanizsa, the most important Turkish fortress in Southern Hungary, failed, as the beginning of the siege was seriously delayed by the machinations of the overly jealous General Montecuccoli. Later the Emperor's military commanders, unwilling to combat the Grand Vizier's Army hastily coming to the aid of Kanizsa, retreated and concentrated on the Austrian border, sacrificing Zrinyi to hold back the Ottoman army.

Zrínyi did not take part in the Battle of Szentgotthárd (Saint Gotthard) where the Turks suffered a crushing defeat in1664. In spite of the victory, the infamous Peace of Vasvár was made with the Ottoman Turks. It was negotiated by Zrínyi's adversary, General Montecuccoli. The peace treaty laid down unfavorable terms for the Hungarians by not only giving up recent conquests but also offering a tribute to the Ottomans.

Zrínyi ran to Vienna to protest against the treaty, but he was ignored so he left the city in disgust. He returned to his home, Csáktornya (Cakovec) and on November 18, 1664, he was killed in a hunting accident by a wounded boar. To this day, legend maintains that he was killed at the order of the Habsburg Court and "that boar spoke German".

No conclusive evidence has ever been found to support this claim, though. However, it remained true that the Habsburgs lost their mightiest potential adversary with his death. Gossip says that the Ottomans had offered him the throne of Hungary not much before his death.

Prince Imre Thököly

Following Miklós Zrínyi's death, his brother Péter rebelled against the Emperor with some very high-ranking Hungarian aristocrats. The plot was named after their leader the „Wesselényi Conspiracy" but was strictly put down by the Habsburgs. Péter Zrínyi was arrested and executed. The Emperor jumped on the possibility of taking away the wealth of the wealthier Hungarian noblemen, regardless of their involvement in the plot.

The Hungarians were becoming more and more rebellious against Vienna and in 1678 began the Thököly-uprising in Upper Hungary. They had realized that their real enemy was the Habsburgs. This was mainly due to the politics of King Leopold I (1657 and 1705) who had intended to crush the remnants of the Hungarian feudal constitution and privileges as well as Protestantism with one blow. King Leopold I dismissed two-thirds of the Frontier-castle warriors in 1671 and stopped governing Hungary by calling together the Diet. Moreover, he ceased giving the highest feudal offices to Hungarian nobles as had been the custom. And at the same time, he stopped the tolerance of religions which had been granted to the nobles by the Treaty of Vienna in 1606.

No wonder that Imre Thököly became more and more popular. This high-born general, later to become Prince of Transylvania and Hungary, put up a fierce fight against the Austrians and he was not shy in asking the Turks for aid. During the summer of 1683, the majority of the western Trans-Danubian counties swore fealty to him.

Imre Thököly didn't directly take part in the siege of Vienna on the Turk's side, but without his involvement, the Ottoman army could not have even reached the city.

Pozsony (Bratislava, Pressburg) was the key to Vienna and Thököly's troops were able to capture it because it opened its gates to them. He helped the Ottomans get safe passage to Vienna in 1683 in order to receive a similar status – or stronger - from the Sultan as the Transylvanian Principality had enjoyed. He thought Hungary would be able to gain greater independence than it had under Habsburg rule.

The „Liberation" of Hungary

In a way, the liberation of Hungary was triggered by Thököly. After Vienna was saved by the Hussars of the Polish King Sobieski in 1683, the Habsburgs drew the conclusion quite quickly: Hungary must be liberated and the Ottomans must be dealt with for good. They could not have afforded a new Ottoman attack nor a new Hungarian uprising. Besides, there would be no more Polish help in case of a new Turkish siege.

They had to attack in order to survive. Thus, Pope Innocent XI organized the Holy League in 1684 with the Papal States, the Holy Roman Empire, Poland, Venice and later on, with Russia. It was called a Crusade and many soldiers, mercenaries and nobles joined it from countries all over Europe. Of course, Hungarian Hajdú soldiers, all kinds of dismissed castle-warriors, and other soldiers from all over Hungary, had been of tremendous help to the Crusaders – not only because of their valiant warfare, but also because they knew the land like the back of their hands. Almost all of Thököly's soldiers abandoned their leader and joined the Crusaders. During the next 15 years, the Ottomans lost all of the decisive battles because of the disadvantages of their old-fashioned army. The key battles and sieges were at Párkány and Esztergom in 1683, then at Érsekújvár in 1685 and finally at Buda in 1686.
The battle of Nagyharsány in 1687 commenced the taking of Transylvania and finally, the siege of Nándorfehérvár (Belgrade) in 1688.
Although the Turks fought back in 1690 led by the excellent leader Grand Vizier Köprülü (Kara) Mustafa. They took back Nándorfehérvár, Lippa, and Törökkanizsa. The Vizier was encouraged by the French King, Louis XIV, in his actions.
Yet, the Grand Vizier was defeated and lost his life in the Battle of Szalánkemén.
The war went on between 1691 and 1697 with victories and losses.
Fortunately, Prince Eugene of Savoy took leadership in 1697 and after defeating the last rebels of Thököly at Hegyalja, he won a decisive victory at Zenta.

The „Liberation of Hungary" was so devastating that contemporary sources estimate the Christian mercenaries' destruction of the recaptured lands was worse than the many years of Muslim rule.

As the Ottomans suffered further defeats in Poland, Venice, and Russia, the war ended with the Treaty of Karlóca (Karlowitz) in 1699. As there were no Hungarians present at the negotiations it was decided „sine nobis de nobis" - decided about us, without us.

The taking of Buda in 1686 (by Gyula Benczúr)

The peace was disadvantageous to Hungary as it left vast Hungarian lands in Ottoman hands and the Principality of Transylvania was not accepted as a sovereign state anymore. Hungary was treated as a province of the Habsburgs which eventually led to the War of Independence of Prince Ferenc II Rákóczi between 1704 and 1711. It was a time when most of the castles of the Hungarian Borderland were destroyed primarily by orders from the Habsburgs.

The last Tatar raids took place after 1717 in Transylvania. The Crimean Tatars pillaged the lands around Beszterce and then they attacked the town of Szék and killed 90% of the population. The locals commemorate the massacre every year on 24 August to this day. The Habsburgs did not let the Hungarian soldiers fight the intruders because they were afraid of a new uprising, so the Tatars were freely looting and destroying in Transylvania for a long time. When they started riding into East-Hungary, the Habsburgs grudgingly let the Hungarians fight against them. Many thousands of captives were freed, but by then Northern-Transylvania, was already devastated. This war largely contributed to the profound ethnic change in Northern-Transylvania. It was the last, and the greatest, Crimean Tatar invasion there, later only a few smaller raids occurred. The fortified churches of the German Saxons and the Székely people offered some shelter against the raiders during this time.

Finally, Emperor Leopold II made peace with the Ottomans and allied himself with them against the Prussians in 1791. According to this treaty, Austria ceded Belgrade to the Turks. This was the last treaty that finished wars between the Turks and Hungarians, forever. Here, I have to remark that the Turkish people have become true friends of the Hungarians over the last couple of hundred years.

A Tribute to the heroes

As a result of these wars, Europe's ultimate disaster was evaded only because of the deeds of the Valiant Order who could make wonders under impossible circumstances. Their names are to be cherished, whether they be Hungarians or their fellow Croatians, Austrians, Wallachians, Serbians, Slovakians or sons of any other local or western nation who fought shoulder to shoulder under Spanish, Italian, Polish or any Christian flag from all over Europe.

2. Trencsén Castle   GPS: 48.895152, 18.051279

The castle of Trencsén (Trencin) was an important fortification in the Vág Valley, near the old Polish border. The first Hungarians took it from the hands of the Polish knight, Bolislo the Brave, in 1017 along with the rest of Trencsén County. The great Hungarian chronicle writer, Anonymous, Notary of King Béla, thought Trencsén was worth mentioning in his work in the late 12th century.

Thanks to its stone walls the fort was one of the few lucky castles that withstood the Mongol siege in 1241. It is no wonder that it was kept in high esteem in the future. It served as a frontier stronghold which guarded over the valley of the Vág River.

When royal power was declining, the castle became the headquarters of the Hungarian Baron Máté Csák whose power was broken only when he died in 1321. In spite of his death, King Károly Róbert was only able to take the fort after a long siege. Károly Róbert strengthened his ruling power by breaking down the authority and control of the feudal lords all over the country. He took care to appoint the Chief Comes of Temes County as his castellan of Trencsén Castle.

After this time, the fort was always given to the actual Chief Comes of Temes County which proves the importance of the position. Trencsén lay in a strategic location and it was considered accordingly. King Károly Róbert recognized this and it was at Trencsén where he received the monarchs of Poland and the Czech Kingdom in 1335. This Anjou king prepared the country for the next strong handed Hungarian king, Louis I the Great.

King Louis did not neglect Trencsén Castle. Having rebuilt it, he gave it to his daughter, Maria. King Louis received Sigismund of Luxembourg in

Trencsén castle and they agreed there that Sigismund would marry Maria. Consequently, King Louis' candidate for the throne of Hungary was the young Sigismund.

When Sigismund (Zsigmond) became king of Hungary, he had Trencsén reinforced against the cannons of the heretic Hussites and shortly after he gave it to his queen, Borbála. Had King Sigismund known what troubles the Hussites would stir in his realm he would not have permitted the burning at the stake of Jan Hus in 1415.

But it was too late: the followers of the church reformer were gaining more and more ground. It did not take them much time to reach the walls of Trencsén. They did not hesitate to besiege it in 1431, but they were repulsed by the defenders. The Czech mercenaries were furious at this and quit the siege. On their way home they set the town on fire burning it down to the ground.

However, they never gave up and were waiting for their chance. Their desire was fulfilled in 1440 when Trencsén came into the possession of the Hussite leader, Jan Giskra. He had originally been hired by Queen Erzsébet to aid in her attempts to seize the throne, but the Hussites took themselves into Upper Hungary and soon became their own masters. The famous János Hunyadi led many campaigns against them and eventually he managed to get Trencsén back in 1450. Yet, the Hussites were persistent and were in control of large areas. The folks of the Upper Lands suffered a lot because of them.

Giskra finally made an agreement with János Hunyadi's son, the young King Matthias of Hungary. According to their treaty, the remaining Hussite owned castles returned to the king in 1462. It was a very good decision for the king because Giskra became his most faithful mercenary captain. These Czech mercenaries were the core of the first standing army of Europe, the king's Black Army.

King Matthias started staying in Trencsén for longer periods of time and it was his headquarters when he led his campaigns against the Czech and Moravian lands. Some years later in 1475, he sold Trencsén to Baron Szapolyai for 15,000 gold coins in exchange for his faithful services. This sum was considered a very low price and was rather a token payment. The castle remained the king's property and he could buy it back at anytime.

A heart-breaking legend about the well of the castle dates back to those years.When Matthias, the last great king of the Hungarians died in 1490, the Szapolyai family left Szepes Castle and moved to Trencsén Castle to live. They enlarged the fort and people began to call them "Trencséni" aka Szapolyai of Trencsén. Their fame and power grew every day. There was no question that their loyalty was much needed by the weak-handed King

Ulászló II, who quickly reinforced them in their ownership in 1499. It was during this time when the outer walls of the town were built.

The most perilous of times were approaching the country. The Ottomans defeated the Hungarian army at Mohács in 1526. This was why Trencsén Castle and its town became more significant, because its owner, János Szapolyai, became the king of Hungary during the same year. The Dual Kingship began when Habsburg Ferdinand announced his claims to the throne and was crowned as another Hungarian king. His formidable mercenary army, the one which had sacked Rome in 1527, was steadily pushing Szapolyai out of the country.

King János was able to keep his castle until the usurper's commander, General Katzianer, besieged it in 1528. The siege lasted for a month and the defenders fought valiantly, but a cannonball set a roof on fire and the flames spread over the whole castle. The inferno blew up gunpowder at many places in it and the warriors in the fort suffered great losses. The artillerymen of General Katzianer had deadly aim and it was impossible to extinguish the fire. There was nothing else to do, the castle had to be surrendered.

King János Szapolyai fled to Poland and stayed there for a while. He later resumed his fight against King Ferdinand. The wars of the Dual Kingship served no-one better than Sultan Suleiman who was quietly biting off chunks from the lands of the two rival kings.

Eventually, the new lord of Trencsén was Ferdinand who sold it to Elek Thurzó for 40,000 gold Forints in 1534 but it returned to the Court in 1548. The damages from the previous siege were being very slowly rebuilt. Later in 1586, the castle went to the Illésházy family under the condition that they would rebuild it. They kept their word and made major constructions on it with the help of Italian masters.

When the fort was nicely rebuilt, the Habsburgs became so fond of it that they wanted to have it at any cost. Cunningly, they accused István Illésházy of treason and deprived him of his domains. This was a general method employed by the Court and Illésházy was not the only one whose property was taken in this manner.

Soon, all the deprived nobles were alienated from the king and they began to support the rebellion of István Bocskai. Prince Bocskai and his savage Hajdu soldiers finally forced the king to give Trencsén back to István Illésházy.

It was at this time that the Transylvanian princes led their wars against the Habsburgs. Illésházy's heir, Gáspár, joined the Transylvanian Prince Gábor Bethlen and fought alongside him against Vienna. After these wars, Gáspár Illésházy was able to enjoy some peace in Trencsén Castle from 1627 until his death in 1648.

Let us not forget the Turks who were not idle either. They attacked Trencsén and set the settlement on fire in 1663 but they did not dare to attack the high walls of the castle. Unlike the Ottomans, the German troops were more successful and were able to occupy the proud fort in 1670. Thirty-three years later the German garrison fled in advance of the soldiers of Prince Ferenc II Rákóczi.

The castle burned down in 1790 and has been under renovation from 1954 to the present.

3. The Well of Lovers (1477)

The heydays of the proud castle of Trencsén were those of the great Baron István Szapolyai, the father of a future king of Hungary. It was a time when the mighty Ottoman Empire reached its hands farther and farther into the north and the Hungarians were swaying under the weight of their attacks. The armies of the Sultan used the Hungarian river valleys to advance and gain ground. They followed the Dráva or the Temes rivers up from the south then destroyed everything along the rivers of the Maros and the Olt in the East as well. Strong hands were needed to beat them back every time. While good King Matthias was alive, the intruders, as a rule, had always been repulsed.

István Szapolyai, the lord of Trencsén Castle was a commander of the king's who gained the addition of the title of Vitez (Valiant) added to his name by defeating the Ottomans with his hardened men in the most dangerous places. One day, he proudly returned to his eagle's nest with a huge booty and numerous Turkish captives carried on his wagons. He was greeted at home with music and merry celebration. The only thing that spoiled his happiness was that he could never give fresh water to the many people in his castle as there was no well in it. All the water they needed for drinking and washing had to be carried up from the Vág River on wagons in barrels and in bison-hides. Although, it had not been for the lack of trying.

The lord had summoned wise German engineers and famous Italian masons along with jack-of-all-trade Székely craftsmen from Transylvania. But it was all in vain. None of them could get water off the cliff. Lord Szapolyai saw that the more prisoners, soldiers and servants he had, the less water he had within the walls.

He was puzzled and tormented by this problem as he walked along the ramparts. Suddenly, he glanced down at the Turkish captives who were sitting in the yard silently waiting for what life might have in store for them. He discovered a veiled face young girl among them who was wearing a silk dress decorated with gold flowers. The lord ordered her to remove her veil. Though grudgingly, the girl obeyed. When she lifted up her face, everybody cried with amazement. The young maid had wonderful looks. The ray of her black eyes didn't torch anyone though because she cast her eyes sadly to the ground. Princess Hedvig, Lord Szapolyai's wife was also there and saw her tears. Hedvig began pleading with her husband. "My good lord, please gift me this beautiful Turkish girl with sorrow in her eyes. I need nothing else from the booty." Szapolyai nodded in agreement. "Let her be your captive, maid, or whatever you would like to call her." He turned to the girl and addressed her in her language: "Come here. What is your name?"

"Fatima," said the girl quietly. "I am the daughter of Pasha Ibrahim, my lord."

Princess Hedvig was very happy and she ordered her maids to have Fatima dressed in the nicest clothes at once. Soon, Fatima was dressed in gold and silver finery and her beauty was shone ten-fold. The Princess and Fatima spent many hours together and one day the Princess asked Fatima to her tell about her life.

"I have not much to say" answered Fatima. "I am still very young and your lord husband's soldiers took me as a prisoner while I was traveling to visit my father, Ibrahim, the Pasha of Rumelia. I have a fianceé called Omar, a nice and valiant young man, the son of a rich merchant from the town of Smyrna."

Recalling her former life, the young girl broke out in bitter tears. Princess Hedwig had come to like the girl almost as if she was her own sweet daughter. Even Lord Szapolyai had taken delight in his wife's maid.

It was not two months later when the guards of the gate reported the arrival of a group of noble Turkish guests who were coming to visit them. They had come from far away Asia with many servants, bringing gifts to the lord of Trencsén Castle. A richly dressed young man introduced himself as their leader:

"I am Bey Omar. I have been informed that you have some Turkish prisoners of war. I have come to ransom them."

"If you have the money, you can take them." replied lord Szapolyai and had his Turk prisoners lined up in the yard at once. Omár was carefully looking at them all.

"Fatima, my bride is not among them." he declared sadly.

"I gave Fatima to my lady wife. She is the only one I cannot give to you. It is not my habit to take my gifts back from anyone. We have come to like Fatima, she has to stay."

"I would offer one-thousand gold coins for her."

"No, I have more than that on half of my palm. I have money like the sea."

"I will give you one-hundred Arabian steeds, then."

"I own plenty of noble horses which are just as good."

"My lord, then tell me what should I give you for her?" Omar desperately asked the heartless nobleman.

"What? Drill a well into the cliff and find water in it and the girl is yours."

"But you have water, Lord Szapolyai! The river Vág is flowing just beneath the castle and your peasants can dig as many wells on the riverbank as you want! Would you rather make Fatima shed more tears?"

"I need the water up here, in the castle. Dig a well here, and take the girl." repeated the lord stubbornly.

"I don't care about tears. I need saltless fresh water."

Omar could say nothing, but he began tearing at the cliff with his own hand immediately. He ordered all of his men to help him and Szapolyai let all the Turkish prisoners labor with them. They had been toiling there, cutting, breaking the hard stone for one-thousand, one-hundred and eleven days and nights when a cry from Omar came up from the depths of the well:

"May Allah be praised, honor to the Prophet, the water has sprung up!"

Omar was pulled up by the long rope and he happily showed his men the fresh water in his bucket. It was crystal clear and tasted good. Omár hurried to Szapolyai and offered a handful of it to the lord.

"Here is your water, high lord. I have kept my word, now it is your turn."

Upon saying this, he collapsed, exhausted by the horrible tiredness. Fatima was right there and she embraced the lad.

"My true love, I thank you for your steadiness," she whispered.

Lord Szapolyai, seeing this scene, also wanted to hug the young man. But Omar pushed him away with bitter words:

"Now you have water, István Szapolyai, but your heart is harder than the hardest cliff." With these words, Omár achieved one more impossible deed, he made the high lord shed a tear.

Szapolyai gave freedom to all of his prisoners without collecting the ransom. He even gifted them with decent clothes and silver coins. The Turks and Hungarians celebrated together that evening and the next day, the Muslims departed back home, led by Omar and Fatima.

Up high in Trencsén Castle, the well in the cliff can still be seen there today. It is still called the Well of Lovers.

Budatin Castle

4. Budatin Castle   GPS: 49.235852, 18.734340

The castle of Budatin is located one kilometer away from Zsolna, next to the River Vág. It was built in the second part of the 13th century by the Balassa family. Originally it was on an island. In the beginning, there was only a stone tower and later in the 14th century a palace wing was built next to it. During his campaign along the valley of the River Vág in 1397, King Sigismund had the castle pulled down; but it was rebuilt soon after this.

Budatin Castle went to the Szúnyogh family in 1487 and around the mid 16th century, the Gothic castle was rebuilt in the comfortable Renaissance style. The Turkish threat from the south and more uprisings at the beginning of the 17th century forced the Szúnyogh family to fortify the castle.

During the Baroque period in the 17th century, efforts were concentrated on building a chapel and finishing various outbuildings of the castle and surrounding it with a park. Later, the Csáky family became its owners. It remained in their hands until 1944.

The pleasant castle is worth taking a look because of its six-story-high medieval tower.

5. The walled-in maid (1487)

The castle of Budatin used to be the eagle's nest of the noble Szunyogh family. Gáspár Szunyogh was the strict lord of the castle and he was such a commander that even his thoughts were orders that his servants had to figure out if they wanted to avoid punishment. The lord did not suffer contradiction from anyone and had no respect for any lord above him.

Lord Gáspár had a daughter named Katalin who was famous for her beauty. Everybody praised her for her good looks. But Katalin didn't care much about it, for she had decided in her childhood that her husband would be no-one else but István Forgách. Yet, her father had different plans. He wanted her to marry István Jakusits, the Lord of the neighboring Oroszlánkő Castle. One day, Lord Gáspár turned to his wife Zsuzsanna and let her know of his decision.

„But our daughter is in love with István Forgách!" said Zsuzsanna. Lord Gáspár furrowed his brows at this and exclaimed in a thundering voice:

„She should love the one who is led to her by her father!"

What could poor Lady Zsuzsanna do? She told Katalin what her father had ordered. Upon hearing this, the girl ran to plead with her father, throwing herself at his feet and begging him not to force her to marry a man she does not love. But all the tears and pleadings were in vain. Lord Gáspár Szunyogh would not go back on his word. The day of the wedding approached. All the tears of the beautiful bride were shed, but the father and his knights paid little attention to her behavior. Even the women folk were telling Katalin that there is no need to cry because the couple would eventually grow to love each other once they shared a common table and bed.

When István Forgách heard of the wedding, he devised a daring plan. He used a small boat and crossed the white waters of the Vág river that flowed beneath the castle and with the use of a rope-ladder, he climbed up to the towering walls of Budatin Castle. There he met Katalin and the lovers spent the evening together. But, their time was cut short at midnight when the watchful father discovered them. The young man barely escaped with his life.

Lord Gáspár could not forgive Katalin and wanted to take revenge on her for the dishonor caused to his family name whose reputation was now smeared because the wedding could not now be held. He planned an evil punishment for his daughter. The masons were summoned and Lord Gáspár had them build a stone cabin in which only one person could fit and he had the girl walled in it. She was given food and water for three days and left with just a small gap for her to get some air.

The news of this ugly crime quickly spread over the neighboring lands and also to István Forgách's ears. Upon hearing this terrible news, the young knight jumped onto his horse and with all of his good men they soon rode up to Budatin Castle. He wanted to break the gate down, but it was not needed as the soldiers of Lord Gáspár loved Katalin more than their cruel captain, so they had left the gates ajar. Upon seeing this, Lord Gáspár became so frightened that he fled up into the highest tower and closed its doors fast behind him. But nobody cared about him, the attackers ran to free Katalin from her captivity.

When the stone wall was broken and the girl was recovered, she was in a weakened condition, but she was alive. István Forgách put her on his saddle and they rode out of the castle immediately. They had hardly left the walls of Budatin when they met the men of István Jakusits. Jakusits had heard of the plight of Katalin as well and was heading to Budatin to free her. But, what now? Both Jakusits and Forgách drew their swords and the two riders rushed at each other. Forgách had no time to put Katalin down from the saddle. As they rode towards each other, he was protecting the girl and was unable to parry the lethal blow which would kill him.

Jakusits lifted Katalin into his own saddle and rode away, not stopping until he brought her to Oroszlánkő Castle. In the meantime, Lord Gáspár had recovered from his fright and demanded Jakusits send his daughter back because her punishment was not finished with.

What was to be done? Katalin was crying in despair and sent a message to her mother, Lady Zsuzsanna, asking for her advice. The Lady was thinking hard then she answered like this:
„My sweet daughter, I know your father all too well. You can never return home because he will wall you in again. You cannot do anything except take the hand of Jakusits because he will protect you from your father."
Katalin took her mother's advice and married Knight Jakusits and she bore her fate with patience.

To this day, the stone cabin of Budetin Castle has been shown to many people to see the proof of how cruel a father can be.

6. Besztercebánya City   **GPS: 48.723522, 19.130850**

Besztercebánya, Neusohl or Banská Bystrica, the famous mining town of the Hungarian Kingdom, is located in the middle of the Upper Lands, next to the River Garam.

The town is 208 kilometers north-east of Pozsony (Bratislava, Pressburg) and 217 kilometers west of Kassa (Košice, Kaschau). It was perhaps the most famous and important copper mining town of the Carpathian Basin. The town acquired its present picturesque look in the Late Middle Ages when the prosperous Burghers built its central churches, mansions, and fortifications.

The settlement was founded by German settlers in the 12th century. It was first destroyed by the Mongols in 1241 but soon King Béla IV brought in a new colony of German miners to settle there from Thuringia and he made it a town in 1255. The town prospered because of the abundant copper ore in its mines. The copper business began to thrive when Count Elek Thurzó and his descendants were in charge of the city. They gained their enormous wealth from the mining towns of the Upper Lands of Hungary.

The Thurzós' success was multiplied when they intermarried with the Fugger banker family. The affluent Fugger and Thurzo families founded the prosperous Ungarischer Handel Company (German for "Hungarian Trade") in 1494 which became a leading world producer of copper by the 16th century. With the most sophisticated mining technologies in Europe, an advanced accounting system, and benefits including medical care for its 1,000 employees, Ungarischer Handel was one of the largest and most modern of the early-capitalist firms.

The Fuggers leased many more Hungarian mines and they traded precious metals all over Europe. They were the makers of kings, popes and emperors in the continent and the mines of the Carpathian Mountains produced immense profit for them. They were also involved in the selling of gray cattle herds to feed Germany but later they decided to invest their money into the slave trade in North America.

An early record of the miners' industrial action in Besztercebánya is from 1526 when the City Council needed to take refuge within the confines of the city castle. Before the Battle of Mohács in 1526, the Fuggers retained 80% of the mining profit, 10% went to the Thurzó family and 10% arrived in the treasury of the king, if the Vice-Treasurer failed to steal it. When King Louis II deprived them of the mining rights in 1525, the Fuggers removed all of the mining equipment from the mines of Besztercebánya as well as from the other mines. They even withdrew all of the professional local miners so that the king could not raise funds for his wars against the Ottoman invasion. Nobody was allowed to mess with the Fuggers without punishment.

During the Dual Kingship, King Habsburg Ferdinand took control of the mining cities and the Fugger's men returned to Besztercebánya and copper production was resumed. Let us not forget, that Emperor Charles V, the brother of Habsburg Ferdinand was in great debt to the Fuggers because the Fuggers had bought him his imperial title.

The town prospered, its famous clock tower was built in 1552 in its main square. It is a leaning tower and the top is 40 centimeters off of the perpendicular like the famous leaning tower of Pisa, Italy. Most of the buildings enclosing the square, and those in the nearby streets, are well-preserved Gothic, Renaissance, and Baroque noblemens' mansions and wealthy Burghers' residences. The most interesting among them are the Benicky House and the Thurzó House, the latter hosting a museum with a regional archaeological collection and remarkable Gothic frescos. The City has an inner castle that consists of a barbican protecting the main gate, three bastions, and part of the walls.

There are two wonderful churches and Matthias House built in 1479 as a five-story late-Gothic structure with a Gothic portal and stone console balcony. It served as a temporary residence for King Matthias Corvinus and his Queen Beatrix. The Renaissance Old Town Hall, dating from 1500, has been transformed into an art museum.

Besztercebánya was one of the richest towns in the Mining Towns District and it is no wonder that the Ottomans yearned for it. The Magistrate had the town fortified in 1589 and the Turks could never get close to its walls. The first Hungarian Diet was held in this fortified city after the taking of Buda in 1541. Later, in 1620, it was the city where the Diet elected Prince Bethlen to be King of Hungary. The troops of Prince Thököly took the town in 1678 and in 1680.

The copper mines around the town were rented by the Fugger family throughout the period. The city was renowned for its rich gold, silver, mercury and lead mines as well. Prince Ferenc II Rákóczi took it in 1703 and turned it into the industrial center of his War of Independence.

7. Gold from copper (1490)

The Thurzó family of Besztercebánya became one of the mightiest noble families of Royal Hungary, a stable cornerstone of the kingdom. Many storms threatened to swallow the remaining domains of the king during the Ottoman wars but they all broke on the rock of the Thurzós' loyalty. The story behind their wealth is worth telling.

Besztercebánya boasted the best copper mines and after the death of King Matthias, it was Count János Thurzó who was in charge of them. The Count made a contract with the mighty Fugger banking family who distributed and sold the good quality copper ore all over Europe. Was there ever a greater demand for copper in a time when more and more cannons were cast?

The miners had to continuously dig new tunnels because the traders never ceased in asking for more copper. Especially Venice, which tripled their order.

Count Thurzó was not very happy about this, though. Venice has always been a great rival of the Hungarian Kingdom as far as Hungary's Dalmatian seaside was concerned. However, Thurzó knew that Saint Mark's Republic was secretly trafficking with the Ottoman Empire. The Sultan needed excellent quality copper for his cannons and he paid the

Venetians well. This was not to his liking. One day he was drinking with an agent of the Fuggers and expressed his dislike:

"One day the copper produced in Besztercebánya will return to Hungary in the metal of the Sultan's cannons" he sighed. The good wine of Tokaj made the merchant of the Fuggers talkative and he blurted out:

"Sir, selling copper to the Sultan is a good business, indeed. But the Italians know something that is even better than that."

The Count became curious and he kept refilling his guest's goblet with the melted gold of Tokaj hill. Finally, the truth was made known. The raw copper ore contained much gold as well and the Venetians had the knowledge of how to separate the two precious metals. They guarded this secret technology above all because it was a source of tremendous wealth for them.

The next day, the Count summoned his elder son, György, a quick-witted and high spirited merry lad. The young man liked those things that the sons of the well-off are fond of: fast horses, nice clothes, and pretty women. His fashionable long brown hair and wavy beard spoke of elegance and wealth. György almost jumped out of his skin with joy when his task was assigned by his father. He was to go to Venice and spend some time there so as to find out the secret alchemy of separating gold from copper.

Who does not want to be a secret spy under a different name? Spending gold, having parties and meeting the fabulous Italian maidens in the best place in Europe for merriment? He could hardly wait to set out with his retinues on his Grand Tour to Italy like other noble young men did at that time. Except, his Grand Tour was special. As if he was traveling at random, György visited the Northern Italian towns that were in the heyday of their renaissance pomp and the summer found him in the city once built on the islands in fear of the Hunnish Attila.

He rented a nice palace for himself and jumped headlong into the joys of the city, embracing all its wonders. Our young man was acting like a savage Hungarian barbarian from the time of Attila, throwing money around carelessly for courtesans and freshly acquired drinking friends equally. Soon, he spoke like an Italian and danced like a local, entirely blending into the Venetian life. In the meantime, he was carefully trying to track the copper forgery down but even its location was shadowed from foreign eyes. It was well known that the Venetians were the best in the world at keeping secrets and their police were just as famous in their close-mouthedness. It was no wonder then, that the coins of György's father rolled all over the city in vain.

After a time, the Italians began to sniff around him and his real identity was revealed. All he could manage to achieve was to learn the language and find the factory where the copper was transported. Not to mention the good time he had. One morning, after a wild and lecherous night, György opened his eyes and saw a man in a black robe standing at the foot of his bed. The man looked him up and down with contempt and told him:

"Signore, so far we have allowed you to spend your gold in our city. But everything comes to an end. Now, you must take your leave and return to your barbarous land. You had better thank God that I was sent to you from the Grand Council with these kind words, warning you so bluntly so as to avoid dying in an alley without even understanding why."

Saying no more, the man was off.

György was left alone with his shame and bitter thoughts. The next day he left the city of islands, feeling outwitted and humiliated. He and his men did not hurry home with the news of his failure, they instead took a detour to Styria, Austria and visited the mines of Tirol. György was learning a lot from these excursions but he was growing more and more desperate about his original plan. Finally, he visited a holy hermit in the hills of Tyrol and confessed to him all of his wrongdoings with a sea of tears.

Having shriven and absolved, the old monk said the words that changed his life:

"The humble ones will have the Country of Heaven, the conceited ones cannot stand before the Lord."

Now he had a plan and knew what he should do. He told his retinue to go home without him and tell his father not to worry about him. They were strictly ordered to keep his departure in deep secret from anyone else. He obtained some drab clothes, patched trousers, and a raggy cloak and dressed in them. He had his elegant beard and long hair shaved as if he had been a fugitive slave from the galleys, bid farewell to his men and set out on foot towards Venice. György took no money with him and traveled from village to village, working for his food and sleeping under the sky until he found himself in the proud city of the most cunning merchants of the Mediterranean Sea.

This time he was nobody, and his features were so different. During his trip, he had lost much surplus weight and his toughened, strong hands had gotten used to hard work for everybody to see. Who would have recognized the frivolous rich youngster he had been in this sunburned, dirty lounger who was aimlessly wandering around in the busy harbor of Venice.

He was sometimes a beggar or a vagabond who entertained the crowd with dirty jokes or with ungainly tricks. He was begging with the beggars and running with the pickpockets before the guards, drinking with the whores and howling with the dogs in the filthy streets and alleys. György became Giorgio, one of the unique scum of the noble town of Saint Mark. One who can be given simple errands, one who was grinning like a simpleton. He was always available if an extra hand was needed and after some months he was a busy and accepted thug who was considered a grinning idiot who asked no questions and was willing to work for half price.

Soon, the young man found himself working among the dockers who were carrying coal to the factory where the copper was being processed. Some time passed and it seemed not suspicious to the foremen that Giorgio was given some dull tasks inside the forgery. He was working hard and did his job with utter precision so he was allowed to complete more and more superior tasks that require steady hands and strong muscles.

There was no suspicion around him and drop by drop, Giorgio learned the phases of how to extract gold from copper ore. Almost a full year was spent and the knowledge became his. When the master of the forgery realized that the slow-witted Giorgio was not there working with them, he just shrugged and jerked to another servant with his hand to take his place. No-one shed a tear for the poor villain, perhaps he was rotting in a canal or was eaten by the fish.

György was a different man when he reached the gate of Besztercebánya, after months of rambling. The hajdu soldiers of his father needed some persuasion before they grudgingly led him to old János Thurzó. You can imagine how happy his father was when he met his lost son again. It was not only the secret of making gold that he had been yearning for so long that made him so proud and happy.

It was that his son, György had become a man with a character that was purer than the finest gold.

8. Csicsva Castle   GPS: 48.921806, 21.663575

The castle of Csicsva is above Csicsvaalja (Podčičva). It belongs to the village of Telekháza (Sedliska) and it is not too far from Eperjes (Presov). The castle guarded the important trade route that came from Zemplén County and went to the north to reach Poland. Lots of the wine barrels of Tokaj traveled there to quench the thirst of our northern neighbor.

The first mention of the place is from 1270 when King István V gave it to Palatine Rénold of Básztély who was probably of French descent. Either he or his son, Gyulas, built the castle during the time when most of the Hungarian stone forts were erected.

This French family was the ancestor of the famous Rozgonyi family whose members dwelled in Csicsva Castle according to the sources of 1316. They became mighty barons of Hungary because they had supported King Anjou

Róbert Károly (Charles Robert) from the very beginning helping him to fight his enemies.

The castle was significantly enlarged and the noble Estates of Zemplén County held their meetings within its walls. Csicsva was far from the Turkish frontier so it remained peaceful for a longer time. After the Rozgonyies, the Báthory family inherited it in 1523, then it went to the Drugeth family. King Szapolyai laid siege to it after 1526 and gained it. Unfortunately, the king had set it on fire during the siege.

The Castle of Csicsva in 1686

The whole library of the County was consumed by the flames, including irreplaceable documents from the earliest times. After this, the castle was returned to the Drugeth family.

Csicsva played some role in the campaigns of the Transylvanian princes in the 17th century as it was located on a strategic road. It had been besieged several times by Prince Gábor Bethlen between 1619 and 1623 and by Prince György I Rákóczi I in 1644. As the castle was favored by the local nobility in which to hold their meetings, it was the place where the Hungarian nobles joined the rebellion of Prince Imre Thököly against the Habsburgs in 1683.

The castle of Csicsva was owned by the Barkóczy and the Csáky families after 1691. Their garrison ceded the castle to the troops of Prince Ferenc II Rákóczi in 1703. The castle was doomed in 1711 when the Austrian General Lauken had it exploded at the end of Rákóczi's War of Independence.

There had not been any archaeological excavation until 2011. But the trees were cut at least and some wooden rails were constructed for the tourists so now they can revel in the landscape without falling into the abyss.

9. The Book of Lies (1526)

Csicsva Castle silently guarded the road between Poland and Zemplén County but its halls were noisy from time to time. The sound of loud arguments and debates was heard all of the time when the lords of the county assembled in the castle to decide where their loyalty should be placed. Would King Habsburg Ferdinand shelter them from the Ottoman peril, or should the Hungarian King Szapolyai be trusted?

Day after day, the noblemen were reasoning and tried to make a guess as to which king would take away more money from their pockets. Only a few of them saw farther than the end of their noses and felt sorry for the fate of the kingdom which was bleeding from a thousand wounds. No wonder they were exhausted at the end of the day and they needed to refresh themselves at the white linen covered tables. The good wine of Eger served their merriment, and their mood was greatly improved by a special book which was brought out every evening and laid on a scribe's desk. It was the famous Book of Lies which was held in the treasury-vault of Csicsva. The book was said to have contained the list of all the lies of the Kingdom of Hungary since its foundation by King Saint Stephan.

The noble guests were recalling all the recent gossip and the most outrageous lies of their time and they debated which one was worthy of being penned into the book. As Hungarians are very talented at fighting against each other, only the most auspicious lies were noted which everybody voted on. At least, debating over the lies conciliated them and it was great entertainment until morning. Had they ever been able to agree on the affairs of the kingdom, the enemy perhaps would have never defeated them.

Their host, the owner of Csicsva Castle, was the powerful Chief Comes of Zemplén County, István Drugeth. He insisted that Ferdinand was a good Christian ruler, backed by the mighty Holy Roman Empire. Surely he would chase the Turks back to Asia. Sir István was annoyed beyond measure because his younger brother, Ferenc Drugeth argued that King János Szapolyai was the one to bring back the heyday of the country. After all, Szapolyai was sitting in Buda and not in Vienna.

The noblemen of the county could hardly separate the two of them when they confronted each other with their fists.

"You are the egg of the Emperor's double-headed eagle!" Ferenc shouted at his elder brother.

"And you are hiding in the shadow of the Turks kaftan!" cried István.

They just could not come to terms and they carried on debating who was a better Hungarian and a better man. Finally, István struck the table and had the meeting dispersed. The noblemen were sent home and were left alone with their dilemma. The next day found István Drugeth on the road to Vienna, he was heading to Ferdinand's coronation.

Not many days after he had left the castle, his brother Ferenc reappeared at the gate of Csicsva with some of his trusted men and two wagons behind him. The chain-bridge was down but the gates were shut fast. He drove his two wagons onto the chain-bridge and called for the opening of the gate.

"Let me in, I have come to make a family visit," he told his brother's castellan. He added: "I have brought some nice presents for my dear brother to send to Vienna because I want to take the side of King Ferdinand, too."

The castellan was shaking his head. He had seen the brothers fighting and nobody can teach an old dog new tricks. The warrior was not a slow-witted man and he realized that Ferenc Drugeth was up to no good.

"Let me be cursed if I open the gate for you, Sir!" he replied and sounded the alarm. But Ferenc was prepared for this answer, was not he coming from an ancient Italian family who was famous for their cunning nature? He gave a sign and his men pulled one of the wagons up to the strong oak wooden gate. It was packed full with barrels of gunpowder and Ferenc lit the short fuse. They quickly freed the horses from the harness and all backed off, leaving the second wagon on the bridge. The guards tried to pull the bridge up but the wagon was full of heavy rocks in bags. Half a minute later, the gunpowder exploded with a terrible roar and the gate was broken in. Only a big smoking hole was left. The bridge had fallen into the moat and the gate's tower was burning with great, angry flames. Ladders were quickly placed over the moat and broad planks were thrown on top of them. Running legs and screams increased the noise amongst the chaos and a musket was fired.

There was no serious resistance when the defenders saw the old castellan fall under the cuts of the attackers. He was the only one who paid with his blood for Sir István. All the rest knew the "young lord" and would have hated to kill him accidentally. Or, to be killed in trying to do so. Anyway, they knew it is no good interfering with the lords' game. Swords were laid down and men were bowing their heads in reverence.

Sir Ferenc accepted the easy victory, but he did not plan to take Csicsva Castle over for good. Knowing that his brother would not rest until he could take the castle back from him, he decided that he would take away his brotherly share from the treasure-vault, and destroy the castle. The guards of the castle had no choice, they had to join in the plundering. They made such a thorough job of it that no Turks or Germans could ever do better. When the halls and the rooms were swept empty and all the carpets and cartable pieces of furniture were torn out, they knew that there was no way back. They had to leave Csicsva and follow Sir Ferenc Drugeth to join King Szapolyai.

The castle was burning behind them when they all left, except for two of them who were forgotten. The wine cellars had been broken into and two heavily drunk Hussars were swaying up the stairs.

"Why did Sir Ferenc order us to destroy this nice castle?" the younger warrior asked his grey-haired soldier accomplice. "Boy, the Drugeth lords are high ranked folks and bear it in mind, now they both serve the homeland, one brother in Vienna, the other one in Buda. They will always be on the right side."
"Let the devil take them, it is the greatest lie I have ever heard. It should be written into their big book."
But it was never recorded into that five-hundred-year old book because these two hussars stumbled upon the book's wooden box that was accidentally left behind.
"Son, we do not need the lies of the high lords any longer." said the old hussar and kicked the Book of Lies into the fire.

10. Tokaj Castle   GPS: 48.112440, 21.409302

Everybody knows the famous wine of Tokaj; now here is the story of its castle. This castle guarded the most important and world-famous wine region of the country. It was also a junction of trade routes coming from the eastern part of Royal Hungary and Transylvania. The only other similarly significant crossing place over the Tisza River was at Szolnok which was in Ottoman hands in the 16th and 17th centuries.

The first fort of Tokaj was built by Chief Árpád in the 9th century on the right bank of the Bodrog River. It was destroyed during the Mongol invasion in 1241. King László IV permitted the noblemen of the Nyírség area to build a castle in 1283. When the stone castle was built, the king laid siege to it when fighting the Aba Amádé family in 1290. The castle was utterly ruined and instead of rebuilding it, a completely new one was built on the left bank of the Bodrog River in the 14th century.

It was mentioned in a document in 1410 and its value at that time was 12,000 gold Forints. Around 1422, the castle was given to the Serbian Despot Stefan Lazarevics and later it was inherited by his heir, György Brankovics.

The next owner was János Hunyadi in 1451 and later his son, King Matthias Corvinus took ownership of it. The noblemen of the area assembled in Tokaj in 1458 to aid the freshly elected king against the Hussites. Tokaj was given to Imre Szapolyai in 1469 and it became an important center for the family and was the place where János Szapolyai was nominated king of Hungary in 1526, after the battle of Mohács.

The troops of the usurper King Ferdinand I defeated his army at Tokaj, ruining the walls of the castle. Ferdinand gave the castle to István Báthory in 1527, but Szapolyai re-took it the following year.

The castle changed hands several times until 1530. Finally, it went to Ferdinand who gave it to Gáspár Serédi who had to beat Szapolyai back many times again. Yet, King Szapolyai took it back in 1537 for a short time.

I think it is very strange what happened next: in 1538, the two kings agreed to own the castle together. They split the garrison and each paid an equal number of guards. In reality, the Serédi family regarded the castle as theirs and they were in charge instead of the kings. They had the captaincy of the castle officially between 1541 and 1555.

Tokaj Castle in 1595

The Ottoman peril was imminent, so a new bastion was built to prepare for this. When Benedek Serédi died, his widow, Zsófia Dobó did not hand over the castle to György Serédi. Instead, the widow and her captain, Ferenc Németi, beat back his assault. Németi managed to become the foster father of the young István Serédi and soon sided with King Szapolyai. Németi continued the reinforcement of the castle and built further bastions. The king sent him 1,000 Hussars and 600 infantrymen. The army of Emperor Maximilian took the castle by siege in 1565 with the help of his General, Lázár Schwendi. Németi died during the siege.

The damages were repaired soon after by Captain Jakab Raminger and Tokaj became one of the most important fortifications of the Habsburgs in Hungary. The castle was modernized by Italian military engineers including Francesco del Pozzo, Ottavio Baldigara and his brother Giulio Baldigara as well as Cristodoro della Stella. Their work proceeded very slowly because of financial hardship and also because the river flooded their bridge of boats, a passageway resting on boats moored abreast across a stretch of water in 1591.

The Hajdú soldiers of Prince Bocskai took Tokaj back from the Habsburgs in 1605 with a year-long siege. The defenders eventually surrendered because they ran out of food. After Bocskai's death, the castle returned to the Habsburgs in 1607 who sold it to Palatine György Thurzó for 71,590 gold Forints.

The Diet of 1609 ordered free labor from the peasants of eight counties to repair the castle. Thurzó's son inherited the fort in 1616, but he happened to be loyal to Prince Gábor Bethlen. The prince had to take the castle by force in 1619. The Holy Crown of Hungary was held in Tokaj at that time. Finally, in 1622, Bethlen agreed with the Emperor who let him have Tokaj in exchange for 300,000 gold Forints. The Prince oversaw further reconstructions and even held his wedding there in 1628. The castle was later the dwelling place of his widow, Katalin of Brandenburg, who gave Tokaj back to the Habsburgs.

The castle on Tokaj hill was witness to the Habsburg army's defeat in 1630 by the Transylvanians and their Hajdú soldiers. The fort was in very poor condition even though the Diet of Pozsony had issued several orders for its renovation. It was said to be "not good enough for a pigsty if it wasn't surrounded by water. One could easily ride straight into the middle of it through its gentle slopes". Its captain was Miklós Abaffy, who had sided with Prince Bethlen aiding him with soldiers. Yet, it was again in Habsburg hands in 1630.

The city of Tokaj was an agricultural settlement and according to a list from 1640, 73 peasant families lived in it, including their judge. There were an additional 22 stately homes with 16 noble families in them. Only six people served as ferryman at the important military and trade crossing of the Tisza River. The castle fell into Prince György I Rakoczi's hand in

1644 after a short siege and he was allowed to keep it according to the Peace of Linz. After the death of Prince György II Rákóczi, the fort went to the Emperor.

General De Souches camped under the castle for a year in 1660 before attacking Transylvania.

The Austrians employed famous engineers to build the fort: Jakob Holst, Battmayer, Scicha and Strasoldo. The men of Prince Ferenc I Rákóczi captured the Captain of Tokaj, Starhemberg Rüdiger, in 1670. The prince's army of 12,000 men besieged the fort. They were led by Mátyás Szuhai and Pál Szepesi but they could not take it. The rebels could not take the castle in 1678, either. Yet, the rebel Prince Thököly took it in 1682 and kept it for three years. The rebels attacked the castle again in 1697 with 500 Hussars of Ferenc Tokaji and they were successful. General Vaudemont paid a high price when he attacked the fort during the same year. It was Prince Ferenc II Rákóczi who finally took it by siege in 1703 and it was he who had it destroyed in 1705 because he realized he would not be able to keep it.

11. King János Szapolyai in Tokaj – the Battle of Tarcal (1527)

When King János Szapolyai arrived in Tokaj Castle one evening he was informed that not far away, in Tarcal, there were German mercenary troops of King Ferdinand.

"Well, once they are there, I'll smoke them out," he told himself and he ordered the officers of his warriors to set out against Tarcal.

Ferenc Bodó and Lukács Marjai had their horses saddled at once because they were leading the cavalrymen. Imre Czibak, the officer of the Hajdú infantrymen followed suit without delay. Then they all hurried away despite the late hour. They were hoping to catch the Germans unaware, however this was in vain. The mercenaries were watchful and when the sentries raised the alarm, the mercenaries appeared before the Hungarians in the blink of an eye. Suddenly, there was a bright light everywhere around. The Germans had set the houses of Tarcal village ablaze to see well. They arranged the light on purpose so their cannons could find their targets easier.

The mercenaries must have been expecting the Hungarian's attack because their cannons were all lined up and began to throw lethal fire at the cavalry, causing terrible damage amid their ranks. Lukács Marjai, the first officer of the Hussars was one of the first men struck by the cannonballs and the best warriors fell one by one. Yet, the riders did not want to retreat shamefully. However, they could not reach the terrible source of the fire. With the horses bewildered and out of control, the seasoned Hussars had to turn and flee. The battle had been lost.

Imre Czibak made one more attempt to attack with his savage Hajdú footmen, but they were scattered by the heavy fire. The remnants of the beaten army returned to Tokaj Castle after midnight.

The lords of the king were worriedly awaiting the outcome of the battle because many of them were unsteady in their loyalty. They wanted to find out which king was the stronger. When they heard the bad news, they came together in the City Hall of the town of Tokaj and made council there. But it turned into a rather angry debate. The noblemen were shouting and couldn't hear each other. They had been raging for a long time until one of them with the strongest voice demanded silence and exclaimed:

"My lords, we are not on the right side. Now I daresay, let us go and take King János Szapolyai captive. Let us tie him up and take him to Buda and hand him to King Ferdinand. He will surely have mercy on us if we do so."

A good many of them welcomed and praised this plan, but there were some who just made a sour face and disliked it. But it never occurred to any of them that there was a smart Hajdú soldier serving wine among them, who had pledged his life to King János and would not have forsaken his oath.

The Hajdú hurried with the news to the house of the king. But, in his great haste, he was unable to find the entrance in the dark. Ferenc Körösy, the guard of the king, heard him and shouted at him:

"Who are you? What are you doing in the king's court entrance at night?" The Hajdú answered him excitedly:

"Dear Lord, lead me to the king at once before they come and capture him."

"Tell me the case and I will let His Highness know about it," answered Körösy.

"I will not tell it to you. Only into the ear of His Highness. Because you noble lords are not faithful to him."

"If it cannot be otherwise, then come and follow me." agreed Körösy grudgingly and led him straight to the king.

The poor king was wide awake and all dressed up in his armor when he received them. The Hajdú addressed him, bowing deeply:

"Listen, my merciful king. You will be taken into captivity before the sun rises if you do not take care of yourself. All of your chief advisors have lost heart and in their despair, they want to join the Germans."

The king was not frightened, though. He replied to the man:

"Listen to me good brother in the arm; just do not think of anything bad because we are going to set out against the Germans soon." Then, he summoned his Treasurer, telling him:

"Open the box Bence, and give ten gold Forints to this Hajdú here, he should not be waiting around here empty-handed for long." The Hajdú got his reward and the king asked him:
"How many Hajdú soldiers like you are in the castle of Tokaj?"
"Two-hundred."
"Go at once and call them to attention with their arms ready. I will reward all of your Hajdú night guards by granting nobility to all of you."
The Hajdú ran away like the wind and not much later he returned with the soldiers. Altogether, three hundred Hajdús were surrounding the king until sunrise. When the noblemen arrived and saw that the king was alert and sober, they were afraid to lay their hands on their king.

The king kept his word and rewarded each of the Hajdú soldiers just as he had promised them.

12. Korlátkő Castle GPS: 48.584064, 17.379272

Korlátkő (Cerová) is a village which used to be in Nyitra County in the western part of the Upper Lands. The castle is situated on a 455 meter high hilltop above the village and it was already guarding the trade route to the Czech Kingdom in the 11th century.

Korlátkő Castle / Korlátsky Hrad

Korlátkő Castle was defending the northern pass of the Little Carpathian Mountains and blocked the road towards the city of Nagyszombat (Trnava). The castle was named after its first owner, Konrád Korláth. After the Mongolian invasion of 1241-43, the castle went to the Aba family and it was rebuilt as a royal fortress.

The great oligarch of the Upper Lands, Máté Csák tried to get it in 1320 but the king's man, Hascendorfer Wulfing (aka Farkas) beat him back, losing 13 soldiers in the siege, receiving a severe wound himself. There was a contest for this strategically important castle and the heirs of Máté Csák took it back from him. It was Farkas Hascendorfer who returned and besieged it in 1324 and gave it back to King Anjou Róbert Károly. The king gave them the task of collecting taxes from the merchants at the bridge belonging to Korlátkő in 1336. At this time, the castle was under the command of Márton Treutel, the Comes of Pozsony.

The Czech Count Prokop took it as a token in exchange for his military help in 1385 but King Zsigmond fought for its return some years later because he had cheated the king. The king passed it on to Voivode Stíbor in 1394 and when the proud oligarch who called himself the "Lord of the Vág River" died, Korlátkő returned to the crown. The upstart Miklós Újlaki, the Voivode of Transylvania became its lord but the Czech Hussites beat him out from Korlátkő Castle in 1443. We are fortunate to know three Hussite captains' names who were in charge of the castle at this time. They were Henrik of Schomberg, Tomek of Knienicz and Gaspar Nydrsspeuger. Újlaki gave the castle to Osvát Bucsányi three years later who paid four thousand gold Ducats to the Hussites to cede him Korlátkő. King László V confirmed his ownership in 1453 and Osvát began to call himself Osvát of Korlátkő, thus establishing a second family with this name. (The first family with this name used to be Konrád Korláth.)

The Bánfi family was its next owner but they were unfaithful to King Matthias Corvinus who took the castle away from them. King Matthias gifted Korlátkő in 1485 to his soldier, a German knight called János Planker. Yet, neither Planker nor his heirs could move into the castle because the Korlátkői family had occupied it before them. This old family remained in the castle into the 16th century.

Péter Korlátkői, the Chief Chamberlain of the king, lost his life in the battle of Mohács in 1526. He had only daughters so the castle went to the Pongrátz and the Nyáry families. The Apponyi family followed suit and the fortress was reinforced with a cannon-bastion and with an outer castle during this century. It was a lesser private castle, though, and whoever owned Nagyszombat (Trnava) or Pozsony (Bratislava, Pressburg), came to own Korlátkő as well. As the lords of the castle were loyal to the

Habsburgs, it was not exploded by the Austrians after the War of
Independence of Prince Ferenc II Rákóczi in 1711.
The Renaissance palace of the castle was still inhabited in the 18th century.
The owners later had a stately late-renaissance home built in the village of
Lészkó and the old castle was gradually abandoned. The cellars of
Korlátkő were in use in 1740 because they were guarded by some Hajdú
soldiers but later the fortress was left alone and the locals used its stones
for other constructions.
Today, you can still see the several stories high remains of the Renaissance
palace and the huge parts of the outer castle's walls. The inner castle
contains the walls of the old Gothic palace and there stands the ancient
tower in its middle. There was no archeological excavation or renovation
before 2004 at all.

13. The Devil's Plough (1527)

The tale of Korlátkő Castle is about two brothers. And, the Devil.
One of the brothers was called Ozsvald, the other's name was Péter. They
lived together in peace in the castle as long as their father and mother lived.
They had no reason to quarrel with each other. Both of them received
enough food, good clothes and love.

One day, their father went on a hunt into the dark forests of the Carpathian
Mountains and his men brought him home dead. A huge boar had killed
him with its tusks. Ozsvald was the elder brother and he wanted to split the
heritage up but Péter told him not to do so.
"Let us not make our mother sad with this, Ozsvald. She would not like it
if we happened to quarrel on something. Rather, let us keep the good
feelings between each other. Now, I am going to join the king against the
Turks and we can arrange everything when I will return." said Péter.
Indeed, the bloody sword was being carried around the kingdom; it had
been the habit for five hundred years in a case of war. Soldiers rode to the
villages with a red, naked blade. Its message was clear to everyone:
"Come and join the king's army, the homeland is in peril. The southern
borderland is on fire, the Turks are killing and destroying the land, herding
away the young men and women to the slave markets of Istanbul. Only one
man can stay behind from each family. All the others must take up arms
under the penalty of death."
Did the Hungarian lords pay heed to the young king's call? Many of them
said that it was the king's trouble and went after their own business. Why
did he execute the envoy of the Sultan? Now, he should eat what he had
cooked. Yet, there were many who answered to the king's summons and
Péter was among them.

The Battle of Mohács was fought on a hot day in August, King Louis II died and the kingdom was lost.

At home, Ozsvald thought that his brother had perished because he did not show up. Thinking him dead, the elder brother took command of their domains into his hands and he became the sole lord of Korlátkő Castle. His mother also passed away and still no news came about Péter. Or had there been? In fact, the younger brother had been taken as a prisoner of war and was carried all the way to Istanbul. He was thrown into the deepest dungeon of the seven-towered fort, the Yedikule and was waiting to be ransomed. Had he not tried to send word home? Yes, he had, and not just once. The castellan of Korlátkő Castle once led a pilgrim to Ozsvald who claimed to have come from the Ottoman capital, but nobody saw him leave the castle.

It took a few years for Péter to raise enough money through his friends and benefactors in order to buy his freedom back. When he appeared at the gate of Korlátkő on a cold autumn day, the guards could not recognize him in his half-Turkish, half-Hungarian rags. Finally, it was the old inner servant of his late father who realized who he was. He was joyfully ushered before his brother, Ozsvald. Did not his brother go pale upon seeing him?

He had already thought himself the master, and now he would have to divide the inheritance. Peter was given his old room but he felt himself as an unwanted guest rather than the owner of half of the castle. All the servants were happy to see him home and tried to please him by all means, but the mood in the castle's hall did not improve.

Ozsvald kept sending dark glances towards him and did not want to sit down with him to discuss the last will of their father. There was an old hag in the castle, she was called Zsuzsanna. After the death of their mother, she was in charge of the household and she gained the hatred of the cooks and the maids for she was a strict and bad-tempered woman. One could hear her screeching voice quarreling with everybody who was so unlucky as to cross her way. This hag was secretly feeding the greediness of Ozsvald and she was the one whose poison had gotten rid of the pilgrim a few years before. At night, the witch was trying to brew magic potions to make her young again and another potion to poison Péter. She wanted to become the wife of Ozsvald after the younger brother's death. One time, Péter was about to enter the vaulted knightly hall of Korlátkő Castle when his ears were struck by the old woman's screech:

"How many times have I told you that there is no other way, except the death of Péter!"

Péter opened the door on them and exclaimed angrily:

"How is it that you are plotting against me who has done no harm to you? Ozsvald, was it the last will of our father?"

Ozsvald just turned away, the old woman ran out of the hall. From that day on, the brothers regarded each other with anger and suspicion. Finally, Zsuzsanna was able to persuade Ozsvald to agree in the poisoning of his own brother. He said to her:

"Do, whatever you want with my younger brother just give me peace and stop annoying me."

The hag was merrily salting Péter's food with the lethal potion powder and right after this, she drank the magic drink she had made for herself.

Who says we have no guardian angels? In her haste, the ugly witch accidentally exchanged the powders and swallowed the poison she had concocted for Péter. She died at that moment. On the other hand, Péter felt young again and his whole body was refreshed, as if he had never spent a single day in the damp Turkish dungeons. Péter could stay not a minute more in the castle. He jumped on his horse and rode straight up to the new king and told him everything. King Szapolyai had known of the valor of Péter of Korlátkő and it was time to declare justice. The king made his verdict:

"You have been faithful to your late king and fought alongside with him until the end in the Battle of Mohács. Our decision is that half of the castle of Korlátkő be given to you and half of everything your father had owned. Now, return home and tell your brother to come before us at once."

Péter was escorted home by the king's men but alas, when they drew near to Korlátkő, Ozsvald and his soldiers had laid a trap and ambushed them in a valley. Péter was chained and the king's men were given a beating. When they protested that the king would make him an outcast and the church would excommunicate him for that, Ozsvald was just laughing into their faces and answered proudly:

"What do I care for the king and the church? I just laugh at them. No-one can demand me anything of me, I know no lord above myself. Nobody can limit my will or my desire except the Devil. I swear it on my eternal soul!"

He had hardly shut his mouth, when in an instant the Devil appeared in front of them once he had been invoked so boldly. Sulfurous smoke broke out from the gaps between the rocks of the narrow valley and soot painted the white limestone black. The sky went dark and they heard thunder, but saw no lightning. The wind began to blow vehemently and the trees swayed. A dense fog descended on them and freezing rain fell on the frightened people. They could barely see how the Devil took out from a cave an enormous plough, tied a shadowy figure before it and snapping his whip, made the womanly figure drag the red-hot plough across the terrain.

Many of the observers believed to have made out the features of Zsuzsanna in the moaning figure tied into the yoke. The terrible plough furrowed a long trench into the soil and split the domain of the two brothers into two exactly equal parts. When the Devil was finished, he turned his glowing eyes to them and said in a deep, terrible sound:

"Now, now, the left side of the ditch is yours, Sir Ozsvald, and the right side is yours, Sir Péter."

With this, he was gone. The rain stopped and the mist was dispersed and the sun came tentatively out. Only the rainbow was not appearing for the Devil does not like the rainbow.

The deep ditch brought peace. The castle was also divided into two. Indeed, it was told that the Devil himself was needed to make peace between two Hungarians.

14. Dévény Castle   GPS: 48.174965, 16.983475

Dévény Castle and the Danube River

Dévény (Devín, Theben) Castle used to guard the western border of the Hungarian Kingdom where the Danube and the Morva rivers meet on the summit of a 212-meter high cliff. Now it is located eight kilometers from the city center of Pozsony (Bratislava, Pressburg), the capital of Slovakia. You can see the Castle of Hainburg from the walls opposing Dévény on the Austrian side of the Danube River. Its palisade castle was mentioned under the name of „Dowina" as early as 864 AD. The fort saw the famous Battle of Pozsony in 907 when the Hungarians defeated the huge army of Louis the Child.

The royal stone fortress was built between 1242 and 1271 and it was called Dyven in 1288. As for the village that used to serve the castle, it was first mentioned as Villa Thebyn in 1237. There is a gothic church there from the early 1300s as well.

The castle was the gateway between Hungary and Austria so it witnessed lots of contests. The Austrian Frederick of Badenberg, assaulted and took it in 1234 though he gave it back to King Béla IV soon after. The fortress used to be encircled by outer walls that reached down to the Danube River but those cannot be seen now. As for the size of the castle, even the remains are quite impressive. Dévény was attacked by the Bohemian King Ottokar II in 1271 who held it for a while. The area was frequently attacked by Czech troops in the next period because Dévény Castle had a strategic role in defending the border against them.

All of Pozsony County was under Austrian rule between 1301 and 1323 in order to pay the expenses of Ágnes von Habsburg who used this income for her upkeep in her nunnery. The area returned to the crown in 1323 but it had Czech owners again between 1386 and 1389. King Zsigmond was always short of money so he pledged Dévény to the Austrian Baron, Lessel Hering, for eight thousand gold Forints. It was Palatine Miklós Garai who bought it back in 1414 and began major construction works in the castle. He had the middle castle built and the Garai palace within it. The German King, Frederick III, occupied the western counties in 1444, Dévény included. He owned it until 1450 when, according to the peace treaty, Dévény returned to the Garai family. As Baron Jób Garai left no male-child behind, the oligarch's domains were inherited by the Royal Treasury in 1481.

King Matthias Corvinus reinforced his rule by gifting Dévény Castle to the greatest landlords of the Little Carpathian Mountain Area, the Bazini and the Szentgyörgyi families. They had the huge lower castle built which defended the harbor of the fortress. As Dévény was very close to Pozsony Castle, it was always used as a private fort and as a result of this; it was not properly updated so as to answer the challenges of the developing firearms.

Dévény was obtained by the wealthy Báthori family in the first part of the 16th century. Palatine István Báthori, the foster-father of late King Louis II, played a shameful part in the putting down of the Peasant War in 1514 and he was also accused of fraud some years later. He is blamed for his role in the Battle of Mohács as well and on top of this, he sided with

Archduke Habsburg Ferdinand in 1527. The „lame" Báthori allowed the troops of Ferdinand to pass undisturbed below the cannons of Dévény Castle when the usurper had his army march against King Szapolyai of Hungary.

Dévény Castle was not besieged by the Ottoman army in 1529 when they wanted to take Vienna. The ill-reputed Báthori died in Dévény in 1530. Emperor Maximilian granted some privileges to it in 1568 and it boasts a palace from the 17th century which became a monastery of the Jesuits. The defenders of the castle remained faithful to King Habsburg Rudolf in 1605 when Prince Bocskai led his troops against the Austrians.

The Báthori family owned the castle until 1609. Shortly after this, the Habsburgs pledged Dévény to Count Keglevich for 400,000 gold Forints. When the army of Prince Gábor Bethlen of Transylvania took Pozsony with an ambush in 1619, the small garrison of Dévény surrendered the fort. It has changed owners quite often in these struggles because its walls were not adequate against the more advanced artillery of the age. General Buquoy took it back easily for the Habsburgs in 1621. Count Keglevich sold it immediately to the Palocsai family for a nice profit in the same year. The owner of the pledge-right over the castle became the Pálffy family in 1635.

The Ottomans attacked Vienna in 1683 and they tried to take Dévény, too, but all their efforts were in vain. The Pálffy family was perhaps the wealthiest and the most loyal family to the Habsburgs. This was the reason why Dévény was not exploded after the War of Independence of Prince Ferenc II Rákóczi. The castle lost its military importance in 1711. Nevertheless, the troops of Napoleon Bonaparte had Dévény Castle destroyed, along with the castles of Győr and Borostyánkő in 1809. The French also buried the well of the castle by filling it with stones.

Now, the armies of tourists are besieging the majestic ruins of Dévény Castle.

15. The Strength of Love (1529)

Dévény was the western gate of Hungary where the Danube breaks through the Little Carpathian Mountains and meets the waters of the Morva River. An ancient legend says that the guardian spirit of lovers, the Goddess Devina, still dwells among the walls of the castle. She must have been the one who came to the rescue of the two lovers living in Dévény in the first century of Turkish peril.

Once upon a time, the Turks set out to take Vienna with a great army. No matter how much they tried to get close to the Golden Apple as they called the Austrians' capital, they could come no closer because Dévény Castle blocked their way. Bey Achmed, their leader, deployed all of his wall-breaching cannons and was bombarding the castle for many weeks but it was all to no avail.

There were just a handful of frontier warriors defending the walls but they were defiant and repelled every assault one by one. Their captain was György Dévényi, fighting valiantly on the first line. His young wife, Júlia was fighting at his side. She would never have left her lover for a minute, so she covered her golden hair with a steel helmet and dressed in chainmail. It was a time when wielding a saber was a common enough skill among the Hungarian women. Fighting beside their mate was considered as a natural routine of life, too.

One day, Bey Achmed had had enough and got mightily angry. He decided to take the castle by cunning if there was no other way. The cannons ceased to throw fire and a Turkish envoy appeared in front of the castle's gate in shining golden dress, saying:

"You are all valiant and brave fighters, may Allah make you rich. To make you even richer and happier, let me tell you the joyful news, you valiant Ghiaurs. Behold, Bey Achmed accepted that Allah would not want to give him this castle so he would leave tomorrow morning. All he asks for, that he would like to see the brave captain, György Dévényi in his tent tonight as a guest for dinner. He would like to meet him in person and say farewell to him."

"I will be there," answered Sir Dévényi. The captain knew the ways of the enemy and before going to the Bey's tent which stood on the bank of the Danube, warned his beautiful wife.

"Now I have to go and dine with the Bey. I bid you never surrender the castle, not even if you see a letter with my signature. They might take me as a captive but the castle must not fall."

Lady Júlia was crying and begging him not to go, but it was in vain. Sir Dévényi took two of his good men with him and rode to the Turkish camp. He was well received and well fed, ate lamb-chops and pilaf, drank sherbet and black coffee, tasted oranges from Jaffa and dates from Arabia. When he was about to go home, Bey Achmed demanded him:

"Yield the castle for mercy at once."

"I would die sooner than that. If you try to force me to write a letter, my men would not trust it because I have warned them. Bey Achmed, you have brought dishonor to your name by breaking the golden rule of hospitality."

"The Prophet has ordered me to occupy this castle and his order is stronger than any hospitality." replied the Bey and signaled to his servants to tie the captain up.

The next day, they tried to assault the walls again but they were beaten back. There was nothing to do, as the cold weather was on them, they had to return to Istanbul. Sir Dévényi was dragged after them and he was closed into the deepest dungeon of the Yedikule. Lady Júlia was inconsolable. The months went by and one day, she received word about his husband's fate from a warrior who was ransomed from captivity. She jumped up and pulled together all of her jewelry and precious stones emptied the treasure vault of the castle and hurried to Istanbul at once to find her dearest love. When she got there, she looked Bey Achmed up and begged him to help get her husband ransomed.

Alas, it was of no use, there was not enough money that could buy Sir Dévényi out of prison. The Turks were very angry at him for they blamed their Viennese campaign's failure on him. Yet, Lady Julia did not give up and in the evening when the muezzins finished their song in the minarets, she sneaked up next to the wall of the Sultan's Palace. She brought along her harp because she could play it wonderfully, and began to stroke the strings gently. Silver sounds were born under her fingers and her sad song flew up to the terraced tower of Sultan Suleiman.

The second and the third evening found her there again and even the heart of the grim Sultan was touched by the fabulous sounds.

"Who is that woman who is singing like a lark below the window of my palace?" asked the Sultan from his inner servant.

"She is a Hungarian woman from far away lands."

"Go and fetch her, let me listen to her in here."

After a few minutes, Lady Julia was standing before the mighty Padisah.

"Your sound is beautiful; your music is like the Houris' play from Paradise. Play and sing for us, you Hungarian woman." ordered the Sultan, "Sing to the women of my harem."

Julia bowed low and placed her harp before her. She started to sing. There was so much hope and joy coming from her song that they were amazed and listened to it until sunrise.

It was repeated three more nights and in the dawn of the fourth day the Sultan addressed her like this:

"You Hungarian woman, teach your song and music to my favorite wife, Fatima and I will gift you richly."

Fatima also had skill with the harp and after three days she had learned the tunes and the songs, too. She had a nice voice and the Sultan was utterly fascinated by their singing.

"Like a lark and a nightingale!" he exclaimed and he added, lifting up his bejeweled fingers: "Ask for anything, it will be granted."

Lady Julia fell to her knees.

"Powerful Sultan, I want to ask for my greatest treasure, my husband, György Dévényi who is your prisoner of war."
"Go and bring him here." said the Sultan, clapping his hands three times. His servants hurried to find the poor captain at once. Sir Dévényi was in a very bad state, his thin body was covered by rags and his eyes could hardly blink when he was made to stand before the Sultan of the Ottomans. He thought he was dreaming when he discovered his wife, Julia there.
"My dear Lord, György" hugged she him tightly "I have come to take you home."
The Sultan nodded and the chains were taken off his legs, he told him:
"Honor this woman above everything. For not only her throat is made of gold but her heart and faithfulness are more invaluable than all of the precious stones on the Earth."
They were given two good horses that flew them home like magic steeds. It was Christmas Day when they entered Dévény Castle above the waters of the Danube and the Morva rivers.

16. Késmárk City   GPS: 49.135312, 20.420309

Késmárk (Kezmarok, Käsmark) was the famous city owned by the Hungarian aristocrat Imre Thököly, it is on the bank of the Poprád River, amid huge forests. The settlement was founded by German Saxons and Tyroleans between 1120 and 1150. They were skilled miners and they were excellent traders as well. The first large building was a nunnery that was built in 1190. The Mongols destroyed both the nunnery and the place in 1241 but the town was soon rebuilt. King Béla IV invited German settlers to come in 1251 and it was again a prospering city by 1269.

It was surrounded by walls in 1368 but these walls could not defend it from the Hussites who were pillaging the town between 1431 and 1441, burning and destroying the nearby settlements of Szentmihály and Szenterzsébet as well. The town went to the Szapolyai family in 1440 and it was the beginning of their free trade with the nearby Polish towns. There was a violent debate between Késmárk and Lőcse during the 15-16th centuries. The cities contested over the right to hold markets. They did this by stopping the incoming trade. The two towns regarded each other as lethal enemies and fought wars frequently.
The castle of Késmárk was built to oppose the Polish and the Hussites in the 15th century from the stones of the destroyed nunnery of Szenterzsébet. Then, it was rebuilt in 1570, and in 1620 as well as in 1650. When King Ferdinand forced King Szapolyai to flee to Poland after 1526, Késmárk became the property of the Habsburgs. King Szapolyai was able to get it

back only when he returned in 1530. He gave the town and the castle to the Polish Jeromos Laszky in exchange for his help.

It was a rich northern town, the birthplace of Dávid Frölich (1595-1648), a great geographer, calendar-maker, astronomer and mathematician who had an extended knowledge of physics.

Sir Sebestyén Thököly got his wealth from trade and this was how his family eventually rose to be among the greatest Hungarian aristocrats. He purchased Késmárk and it belonged to the Thököly family between 1583 and 1656. He had an elegant palace built in the castle that his son, István Thököly, rebuilt in the renaissance fashion.

The city became a Free Royal Town only in 1656 and Imre Thököly had to take it back by force in 1684 from the Habsburgs. Imre Thököly, Prince of Upper Hungary and Transylvania, was born in Késmárk, on 25 September 1657. He also often called himself Imre Thököly of Késmárk. We can see the tombs of the Laszki and the Thököly family in the city's gothic chapel. After the fall of Prince Thököly, Késmárk went to the Emperor, but the Burghers of the city joined forces and bought the town from him for 80,000 gold Forints in 1703. During the War of Independence, Késmárk sided with the rebels of Prince Ferenc II Rákóczi. General Heister punished the town severely for this in 1709. Unfortunately, the splendid palace of the castle burned down twice in the 18th century and most of the old buildings were pulled down.

It is pure luck that all of the splendid pieces of furniture and all of the luxurious ornaments of the Thököly family had been confiscated and taken to Vienna by the Habsburgs in the first years of the 18th century.

17. The Cheese Battle (1536)

Three thousand good German Burghers of Késmárk had been fighting a bitter and bloody private war against the three thousand good German Burghers of Lőcse City for more than two centuries.

Both King Ferdinand and King Szapolyai took part in this war during the chaotic years of the Dual Kingship of Hungary. The question was: Who should have the right to carry the linen, iron ore, and the boots to the markets of Gdansk and Warsaw?

On top of that, the German name of the city, Kasemarkt, stood for "cheese market". Where can they sell their famous cheese if not in Poland? The enmities never seemed to cease. There was always an ambush, a murder or arson between them. The merchants were clever in both cities and hired mercenaries instead of wasting the lives of their own children.

There were always errant German or Bohemian soldiers and cut-throats, who offered their services to willingly kill the Hungarian hajdu soldiers or the Cossacks from Poland in Lőcse, or vice-versa, whoever paid more. The good Burghers cared only about their war. The baleful news from the rest of the kingdom did not even penetrate their ears. News like "The kingdom was lost at Mohács, King Louis is dead" and "The Turks are heading to Buda" or "The Sultan is lurking around the Mining Cities already", "We have two kings, Ferdinand and Szapolyai".

Késmárk in the 17th century

Mihály Braxatórisz was the Judge of Késmárk city when Mihály Prezsenszky, the Hetman of the Cossacks of Poltava, visited him on a nice spring day, saying:

"Sir, I have four hundred brave riders, picked and seasoned Cossacks, why don't you hire us?"

Sir Braxatórisz quickly took the offer and agreed to pay them in salt cubes and in silver. There were twenty-five wagon loads of cheese to sell and the roads to Poland were blocked by the Burghers of Lőcse. The Hetman had arrived just at the best time. The next week, the Cossacks were merrily riding out against the enemy.

Hearing this, Márton Lányi, the Judge of Lőcse, immediately sent his envoy to Kassa so as to hire two-hundred Hussars from Captain Gáspár Serédy. The captain's hussars arrived quickly because they were paid in gold.

The Burghers of the cities withdrew behind their city walls and watched with satisfaction as the Cossacks and the Hussars were slaying each other. Everything was going on as it had always been going until real life interfered and their hirelings left them standing. Alas, the Hungarian Hussars were heading off to fight against the Turks and the Cossacks' swords were needed against the Lithuanian prince. As a result of this, the good Saxon Burghers grudgingly had to take up arms themselves. Márton Lányi immediately armed one thousand men with spears and blunderbusses and sent them against Késmárk. They were not coming through the hills as the bird flew, but they rather came around where the Poprád River meandered.

This was the luck of Késmárk city because they were informed in good time so they could be prepared. The Burghers were headlessly arming themselves and were digging deeper moats and higher trenches. When the Saxons of Lőcse got there, all able-bodied Saxons of Késmárk were on the ramparts with their cannons, bows and guns. There was a great commotion taking place. The Burghers of Lőcse were valiantly attacking, and the Burghers of Késmárk were even more valiantly defending themselves. The fighting had lasted for four days when the millers, locksmiths, and smiths, who were around the cannons of the castle, ran desperately to Judge Mihály Braxatórisz, saying:

"Sir, we have run out of cannon balls. We have gunpowder but there is nothing to feed the cannons!"

"Then, use stone cannonballs and canister shot."

"We do not have any of that, either, Sir. What if the Burghers of Lőcse heard of this? They will kill us all."

Judge Braxatórisz was scratching his head but could not come up with a good idea. He knew that the enemy would go home in a day because they had had enough of soldiering.

They needed just one more day but how . . . ?

Outside, the eight canons of the city became silent one-by-one. Then, the youngest man of the City Council, the shrewd Edmund Loysch, came to him, saying:

"Sir, worry not, I have got the solution. We will have enough good missiles in a couple of hours."

"What will you use as missiles?"

"The name of our town, Sir."

"Well," exclaimed the Judge with a sour smile "Lőcse will surely be frightened if you shout at them: Késmárk!"

Edmund Loysch just shook his head and continued his talk confidentially: "Sir, just give me some wagons and good horses, and the keys to the storehouses. We will go and take care of everything with Andreas Bergh and Abraham Kuszmann."

As there was nothing left to trust, Sir Braxatórisz let young Edmund do as he would wish. Not much time later, the Chief Judge of Lőcse, Sir Márton Lányi, became aware that the cannons of the castle began throwing fire at them again. Strangely, a great black smoke and a terrible odor engulfed the attackers who were just about to scale the walls with ladders.

The good Saxons were being hit with volleys of some new and formidable missiles. Weird, frightening cannon balls hit them which exploded with a white splash. Mouths, noses, and ears were full of this strange substance and the people were spitting it out confusedly. They could neither see nor breath, so the attack faltered. They threw away the ladders and shields and ran home with the deep conviction of being lethally poisoned. A strong smell covered them as though it had come from the depths of hell. Sir Lányi was shocked, made the sign of the cross, and had the drums sound the retreat. The Burghers of Lőcse left behind their tents and wagons trampling each other as they ran home right away. Nobody should fight with demons, after all.

Edmund Loysch sent a last smelly cannonball after the fleeing enemy, and then turned his gunpowder-smeared face to Sir Braxatórisz, grinning:

"Have not I told you, Sir, that we would chase them away with the name of our city, Késmárk? Remember that we had twenty-five wagon loads of cheese to sell. That came in handy."

The Judge was smiling with relief:

"It is all very well and good, but now we have nothing left to sell in Poland."

18. Szitnya Castle   GPS: 48.401336, 18.885629

Szitnya Castle crowns the top of the huge Szitnya Hill above the village of Illés (Ilija), it is only four kilometers away from the rich mining town, Selmecbánya (Banská Štiavnica, Schemnitz). It takes one and a half hours to climb the steep path that leads to the castle which is one of the highest built forts of the Upper Lands or „Horná zem" in Slovakian. The view is magnificent from 1009 meters although the walls and the buildings of the inner and the lower castles have been mostly ruined by the forces of nature and by human destruction.

Old Royal Hungary used to have 72 counties. From the summit, one can see 18 of them, from the blue line of the Danube up to the snowy Tátra Mountains of the immense Carpathians.

The fortress was divided into a lower and an upper castle. The servants and the soldiers lived in the lower castle and stairs were carved into the steep cliffs that led up to the inner castle's tower where the lord of the fortress lived with his family.

It is not recorded who built Szitnya Castle, but it is assumed that it was built after the Mongolian invasion of 1241-42 when King Béla IV feverishly raised castle after castle in fear of the horse-archer nomads.

Szitnya's role was to defend the area of the Mining Towns District of Upper Hungary, the area which supplied Europe with huge quantities of gold and silver.

The village of the castle can boast a church built in the first part of the 13th century in Romanesque style. Inside, there are statues from the 14th century and the altar is from the 17th century. Its Gothic paintings are treasured in the Museum of Túrócszentmárton (Martin, Sankt Martin). The owners of the castle from the early centuries are not listed anywhere. All we know is, that the high-ranking Lévai Cseh family became its owner before 1542. Baron Gábor of Lévai Cseh lost his life while defending the City of Pest against the Turks in 1542 and his only son, János inherited Szitnya Castle.

The infamous but valiant robber knight, Menyhárt Balassa, got Szitnya Castle by marriage. He was the uncle of the most famous Hungarian poet-warrior of the Renaissance, Bálint Balassa. Lord Menyhárt Balassa was a renowned warrior; his father fell in the Battle of Mohács in defense of the king. He defended the Castle of Léva from the night-attack of the Turks in 1544 and then he helped the Hussars of Ferenc Nyáry and György Thury to defeat the Turks at the City of Szalka, on the banks of the Iploy River.

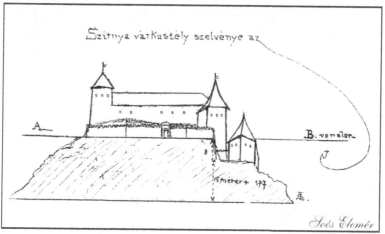

A heroic song was composed about Balassa's victory at Szalka by the greatest troubadour of the age, Sebestyén Tinódi Lantos. Balassa also became the lord of Léva and Csábrág castles at the same time and he was appointed by King Ferdinand I as Comes of Bars County as well.

However, he was not satisfied with the king and tried to take advantage of the unstable situation of the kingdom. From time to time he pillaged and robbed the properties of the petty nobility in the area, claiming they were not loyal to the king. When he stole the gold-plates brought from Selmecbánya, he reasoned that he needed the money to fight the Turks.

Finally, the Habsburg king had had enough of him and he ordered the arrest of Balassa in 1549.

General Nikolaus Salm, the Chief Captain of Hungary was sent against him with almost 6,000 men. Salm's second task was to fight another robber knight called Mátyás Basó who was the lord of Tiszolc and Murány castles. The General laid siege on Léva, Szitnya and Csábrág castles and took them one by one. Lord Balassa was smart enough not to defend his forts in person and he left for Transylvania giving the command of Szityna Castle over to Captain Lukács Makri. Captain Makri heroically defended the fort on the steep cliff and repelled the assault of the Habsburg's Spanish mercenaries.

According to the records, there were 300 Spanish troops, led by Ebestorf and his subordinate, Horvátinuvity. The besiegers lost seven infantrymen, one artilleryman and twenty-five soldiers were injured on the first day. A hajdú Captain, Orbán Bak, tried to relieve Szitnya Castle by attacking the Spanish mercenaries with his 100 Hajdu soldiers but he and 56 of his men were captured by Horvátinuvity. Seeing the reinforcement defeated, the defenders made Captain Makri surrender the eagle's nest under the term of receiving a pardon. The Hungarians were free to go and they left Szitnya Castle. They were more than welcome in other places of the Borderland to fight the Turks. Salm's men did not destroy the castle because they thought it would serve them well against the raiding Turks.

Szitnya remained part of the castle-chain that protected the Mining Towns, but it was never rebuilt to withstand the more advanced artillery weapons of the age. The Turks visited the area because they wanted to gain access to the gold and silver mines. They destroyed the village of Szitnyatő right below the castle in 1571. Szitnya was in the hands of the Illésházy and the Pálffy families but somehow, the Balassa family always regained ownership of the castle.

Szitnya Castle was not in the best condition in the time of Prince Thököly between 1678 and 1683 when it was defended by the rebel troops against the Emperor's army.

The last soldiers in the castle were the Germans of the Emperor during the War of Independence of Prince Ferenc II Rákóczi in the first decade of the 18th century. When they heard the approach of General László Ocskay's rebels, the mercenaries hastily had the whole castle exploded before running away.

When the wars ceased to blacken the ruins anymore, the first sight-seeing tower of Hungary was built on top of them in 1727.

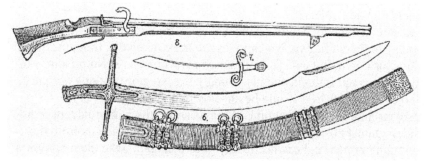

Hungarian weapons in the 16th century

19. Lord Balassa's victory at Szalka (1544)

It was the spring of 1544 and the Turks of Esztergom were growing restless as they watched nature turn green and seeing their horses gain strength again from the sweet fresh grass. Pasha Saban was in charge of the Turkish troops of this northernmost garrison of the Sultan's Empire. His, and his warrior's bravery were acknowledged by Sultan Suleiman himself and the Pasha was eager to prove his worth. He was a wiry and sunburnt warrior and fought in the first lines with his Sipahis. Now, he summoned his five best men, the fierce Agha Ramadán of the Janissaries, the cunning leader of the irregular Deli riders, Agha Kubát and the three Sipahis, the old Agha Ajvát, the invincible Agha Musz and Agha Naszuf, the fearsome duelist from Arabia.

"Listen to me, true followers of the Faith. We will set out against the city of Léva and pick the infidels' tree bare. Our Janissaries are going to climb the clay-plastered palisade of the city and the wretched Ghiaur captain, Balassa, will be taken as prisoner easily once we are there.

His ransom will be huge; we might get Szitnya Castle in exchange for him. My "pribék" spy from Léva said he had only one-hundred guards in the castle. But lend me an ear, oh, great bearers of the green flag of the Prophet. Those infidel warriors in their pitiful sheep-pens they call "castles" are like angry wasps and when they see us coming, they will swarm out just to annoy us.

This is why we must set out tomorrow at dusk, cross the Danube and travel at night following the Garam River to the north, so as to reach the walls of Léva city, unexpectedly, before the first light of dawn. No musicians we will take and no instruments this time.

We will sit our eight-hundred Janissary heroes on wagons and carts on the other side of the river so they can travel quicker and can save their strength. The wagons will wait for us along with the spare Sipahis from the garrison of Vác castle.

Those carts will come handy on the way back for carrying the booty from the rich Burghers of Léva. No captives are to be taken this time; they must not slow us down. Put everyone to the sword who resists. No prisoners to burden us, except Balassa and his young wife. No more playing around with the maidens than it would be absolutely necessary.

Our seven-hundred brave mounted Sipahis and Delis will protect us from all sides against possible reinforcements which might reach us from the surrounding borderland castles. Ready your men and make them rest for a full day before we start. May the merciful Allah aid us. We will crush them like a bug, like this." said Pasha Saban and snapped with his strong brown fingers.

A shot woke him up. A musket? No. He could recognize the sound of a Janissary rifle even in a half-dream. The robust young man sat up in his bed and looked out of the window. Screams. Two more shots. He felt the nails of his young wife, Anna, sink in his upper arm. She was up. "Menyhárt, what is it?" she asked but received no answer. Lord Balassa jumped out of his feather bed in a trice, snatching his broad-bladed cavalry saber from the corner, leaving its scabbard and his bewildered wife behind. He ran up to the castle's ramparts in frenzy and grabbed the first man's neck he met and shouted into his face: "Sound the alarm! To arms! Hussars into the saddle and Hajdus to the walls with burning fuse and loaded rifles! Shoot at will."

The soldier first did not recognize his commander in a nightshirt, but the enormous black mustache and the Hussar-style, half-shaven skull, decorated with scars from old battles quickly reassured him who it was shaking him as if he were a rag-doll.

The Hajdú saluted and, picking up the captain's speed, ran away. Orange light spread from the city below, the air was filled with smoke. Soldiers appeared and horses were being led out, orders were being obeyed. Two minutes later Lord Balassa was making his stallion dance in front of the locked gate, some seventy riders were hastily adjusting their saddles and clambering up onto them. Many were half-dressed, just a few of them had helmets and breastplates on and the servants were busily handing them weapons and the spiky Hussar-shields.

Somebody grabbed the bridle of the Captain's black horse, steadied the beast and two invisible servants struggled to pull his riding boots on Balassa's bare feet. He was just in his long nightshirt and was angrily waiting for the gate to be opened. His Hajdú lieutenant, Amborus Nagy, caught up with him and reported, panting:

"The Turks . . . they had cut the city gate in with axes and climbed the walls. The whole palisade is burning around the city . . . the Turks are looting and killing the city folks."

"Killing, not capturing? They must be in a hurry. Follow me in one group and do not spread out. We start with the city gate. Kill them, the sneaky bastards, hujj-hujj, hajrá!" he roared with bulging eyes and when the gate was opened, at last, he was the first to spur his mount into a crazy gallop, aiming at the city gate at the end of the steep street that led them down there. The fearsome, ancient Hungarian battle-cry was sounded behind him:

"Hujj, hujj, hajrá! At it, at it!"

What seemed like minutes to the surprised and bewildered Hungarian warriors was, in reality, more than an hour. Plenty of time for the experienced pillagers to fill the wagons with booty, be it cutlery or textiles, strong-boxes full of silver or whatever they could lay their hands on. They spared the time to find joy in the prettiest girls before slitting their throats while their comrades slaughtered anybody else who was pitifully running up and down. A man in black Hungarian dolman, wearing a red turban, was showing the way to the Janissaries. The "pribék" lead them to the nicest houses of the richest Saxon Burghers and helped them shatter the doors. The rest of the buildings were set on fire with long torches they had brought for this very purpose. Busy hands emptied the stables and herded the animals of the burghers out of town.

Wealth, piled up by generations of prosperous decades were hoarded onto the Turk's wagons and hastened through the gate before Balassa's Hussars rushed into the dense lines of the Janissary unit that served as a rearguard. The Janissaries were elite infantryman with a reputation of standing firm against every storm that attempted to break them. They despised death and never stepped back in retreat regardless of whatever calamity befell them. More were joining them from behind as they finished the looting and killing at the sound of a bugle. After the first clash, Balassa reined in and bellowed:

"Back to the gate and line up again! Wait for my sign before the new attack!"

The sun rose behind them and its beams shone into the eyes of the enemy who were getting ready to receive the second assault with an indifferent face. The moment Balassa made some room between his riders and the Janissaries, a terrible explosion was heard from above. It was Amborus Nagy who had all the old guns brought out and placed his remaining thirty men and all the servants and even the children on the ramparts to give him a hand.

A well-aimed volley of muskets, cannons and big old hooked guns spat lead, iron balls and nails into the face of the blinking Turks. Death was harvesting among them, but although they were shaken, they stood their ground. Balassa gave the sign and his men charged again. And three times again before they slowly pushed the stubborn Janissaries out of the city gate. The enemy was withdrawing, triumphantly, with wagons filled up high with plunder, herding away horses and cattle.

Stepping out of the gate, the Hussars received strong rifle fire that stopped them and covered the disciplined retreat of the Janissaries. Heavy Sipahi riders appeared and Balassa heard the savage cries of the irregular light cavalry, the Delis. He cursed.

"Back to the castle, men. Amborus, set the alarm-tree on fire and pass the warning signals on. Send a lad to Ipolyság and bring the whole garrison here. Word must reach Komárom Castle, too. Tell my inner servant, Godocsi to warn Selmecbánya city, the rich Burghers must give some help. After Selmecbánya, he is to go to Sellye, up the Vág River. On the way, alarm the nobles in the stately homes, they are to obey my summons, I am Comes of this county, damn them."

When they returned to the castle's gate and all of them dismounted, Sir Balassa glanced back at the corpses of the Janissaries. A Saxon girl was staggering among them. Her skirt was stained with blood. She held a broken yatagan. A Turk was stirring and she struck him once, twice, ten times before somebody jerked her away.

He turned and saw his men run with buckets to put out the fires and the women pouring out of the castle to tend the wounded. His lady wife was among them and came to him straight away with a jar of diluted wine. While he drank, he thought that the enemy had set the palisade on fire just to hinder the chase. The wine got into his nose and he was coughing and choking. "They expect me to sit and lick my wounds until reinforcement arrives many hours later." he thought.

"No. Not me," he said aloud and turned to his soldiers and shouted at the top of his voice:

"All able-bodied men are to don armor, chain mail and shields, fetch their lances and get fully ready and come to the castle gate in the time one says a Holy Rosary. We will give chase."

Anna Thurzó looked at her man, at his strong, bull-like muscles that showed under the nightshirt which had been torn into tatters in the combat. Smiled at him, and said:

"Give them twice as much time, my Lord. And now I bid you come to your chambers. You must break your fast and change clothes. Think of yourself.

And of me." she said proudly and shook her blond, uncombed hair that was freely falling down below her hips. Sir Balassa grinned and followed her. He knew that even the conflagration of Léva town would not stop her having her way. Life is too short to waste.

Ninety-six well fed, rested and angry men sat in the saddle, dressed in the flexible steel armor of the Hussars, armed with sabers and long swords, battle-axes that pierced plate armor, holding sixteen-feet long lances which were hollowed out inside for the sake of lighter weight. There was a wooden ball on the lances' grip to provide good balance and to protect the steel-gloved hands which could aim the long metal spearheads with deadly precision. The helmets looked like the Persian conical helmets of the Ottomans, with a long piece of iron hanging down to protect the nose.

Sir Balassa gave way to Father Balázs, the Franciscan monk who carried a long cross in his hands.

"Dismount, salute the cross. To prayers" he shouted and jumped off his stallion. Legs fell from the saddle and all the soldiers were on their knees. They received Father Balázs blessing and heard his Latin words of the public absolution of their sins. They made the sign of the cross and re-mounted. Sir Balassa gave his instructions:

"Once we catch up with them, spread out in groups of three and four. We have to slow them down until the reinforcements from Selmecbánya and from the Borderland arrive. Challenge them and play around, provoke duels but do not hold a battle. Taunt them, pinch them and be noisy. Now, we must make haste, we can rest in the bird's stomach which is the proper cemetery for the brave warriors of this Homeland's Frontier." he paused and thrust his sword up to the sky and cried:

"Jesus, Mary!"

"Jesus, Mary!" roared the Catholic warriors while the Protestants cried "Jesus, Jesus!"

The wasps were out.

Pasha Saban was glad to have put some miles between him and Léva city which was marked by a black smoke pillar behind them. On the other hand, he was dismayed by sighting the enemy appearing from the bend of the gentle hills and bushes. The Hussars immediately spread out and began circling the Turks' rearguard. The light Deli riders spurred their horses into a gallop and with screaming and yelling, led by the cunning Agha Kubát they fell headlong on the auspicious infidels.

As the terrain generously allowed it, the green fields were soon filled with riders who clashed at each other with their long lances. The heavier Hussars were easily knocking the Deli horsemen out of their saddles so the

Delis scattered to the left and to the right, dancing around the Christians. Half an hour was hardly spent when Saban's keen eyes discovered a dust cloud from the south. A small Hussar unit appeared and the Pasha sent one hundred and fifty iron-clad Sipahis to trample them down. He was annoyed because even from this distance he quickly recognized their leader, György Thury, a Hussar lieutenant from the small Palisade Castle of Ipolyság. He had less than thirty men but he was said to be a promising duelist.

The tombstone of Lord Menyhárt Balassa

Sir Balassa was through his third opponent and the Deli riders jumped away from his proximity. He was happy when a giant Sipahi warrior answered his challenge and rushed at him with drawn scimitar. Balassa had thrown away his broken lance a few minutes ago and he was wielding his beloved cavalry saber.

"Rá, at it, Pejkó!" he cried at his horse who was clearly having fun in the combat he had been trained for. Pejkó shook his clever head and neighed up aloud, rolling his eyes menacingly. Balassa loosened the reins and trusted his warhorse to do his job without interfering. The Sipahi was rushing straight at them, crying "Allahu Akbar!" and his scimitar rose to sever the infidel's head. Pejkó slyly side-jumped and was already prancing on his hind-legs. The two iron-covered heavy hooves were wickedly flinging about the head of the Sipahi's mount.

The Turkish horse jerked back and his legs lost the rhythm. This was when Pejkó played his second trick by turning tail and kicking out with his strong hind-legs. Balassa was anticipating it and swung his saber from below and caught the face of the warrior with its razor sharp tip. Blood covered his enemy's eyes and by the time Balassa spun his horse back, the Turkish horse was running away with an empty saddle. Balassa reined in and stroked the sweaty head of his animal.

He saw his Hajdú lieutenant, Amborus Nagy rushing past him with four Hussars and he instinctively joined them. His two Hajdú lads were following suit. In a blink of an eye, they found themselves attacking the side of a Sipahi unit which was heading to the south to trample down some thirty Hungarian warriors coming from there.

"Sweet Jesus, they must be more than a hundred . . ." he thought but there was no time to turn back. The eight riders threw themselves on the Sipahies like wolves attacking a herd of bison's. They used their long shafted battle-axes which were clacking on the Turks' armor, opening holes on breastplates and helmets.

"Allah! Jetisin! Help!" The surprise attack cost several lives to the Turk heavy cavalry but they soon realized the power of their numbers. It was Balassa's Hajdú lad who went down first. Amborus fought against two enemies and Balassa saw his lieutenant receive a spear-thrust in his waist. The Hajdú sank on the neck of his horse, embraced it and the scimitars hacked him to pieces. Balassa tore himself from the shocking sight and saw they were surrounded and pushed by all sides.

Only three Hussars were dancing their horses around him.

"Make a star, come on, lads!" he cried and the four riders took up a star-formation where the rumps of their horses touched each other. It was a very effective defensive stand and they could evade the strikes of the circling Sipahis with ease. Balassa knew they cannot stay like this for a long time but he needed to take a breath and waited for the chance to break out. When he was just about to give the command he saw an enormous horseman penetrate himself into the Sipahies line with terrible shouts and cries. He was wielding a long sword and used it with such lethal elegance that it left bloody gushes behind at each strike or thrust. The Sipahis yielded the ground and reined in with frightened cries: "Thury! It is Thury, the Djinni!"

Lord Balassa so far had never seen a more robust and formidable looking man than his own reflection in the mirror. Now, he had come to know

György Thury, the young Lieutenant of Ipolyság. It was this twenty-two-year-old lad's reputation as a duelist and not his thirty hussars who made the Sipahis ride back to the wagons waiting on the country road. The Janissaries climbed on the wagons and white smoke appeared at the end of their long-barreled rifles. A horse whinnied and collapsed and another Hussar cursed when a bullet caught his arm.

"Fifty paces back! Back!" Balassa cried and they skipped away from the danger zone.

"Thank you, son, for coming so quickly. Take my hand. You are a man, indeed."

"Sir Balassa, the honor is mine to meet you." answered Thury and they warmly shook hands. Thury looked at the dueling riders throughout the field and pointed at a Hussar with a white-red striped spiky shield covering his left side.

"Who is he, Sir?"

The Hussar was nicely maneuvering his horse beside a Deli rider and took his head with a sweeping strike of his saber.

"That is Godocsi, my trusted servant." answered Balassa and added, "His horse is called Ráró."

Now, another Deli rider appeared next to Godocsi, a warrior in shining chain mail, obviously an officer. His painted horse was dancing around like a deer and he was swinging a thin-bladed scimitar. The swords crossed each other not once, with a terrible speed. Both riders received cuts and blood colored their clothes. They jumped their horses against each other again and then again. Blades rose and fell, the muscles pumped more blood from the wounds and the warriors' blows were weakened and feeble but none of them wanted to give up. The Turkish and the Hungarian warriors withdrew and made a circle. Everybody was watching the spectacular duel. The onlooking Turks shouted their encouragement: "Agha Kubat! Agha Kubat!"

Finally, the opponents were swaying in their saddles and just looked at each other. They had no strength to raise their hands. It was Ráró who saved the situation. He snorted, shook his head and began to nose the painted Arabian horse with interest. Then, the mounts seemed to have agreed and both turned tail and jogged back to their own people.

Busy hands grabbed Godocsi and helped him off the saddle and the same was done with Agha Kubat, the leader of the Deli riders on the other side. In a pause of the skirmish, Balassa looked around and assessed their position. He decided quickly:

"There are too many of them, they will push us down. We have too many wounded. It was a nice fight but there is no sense in letting the injured men die and perishing along with them. Collect them and let us return to Léva until reinforcement from Selmecbánya arrives."

Pasha Saban allowed the infidel riders to leave for Léva. He sighed and now he was sure they could make it home to Esztergom without further troubles. His men were not that merry, though, the wasps had stung too many of them dead. He carefully had Agha Kubát laid on a wagon and gave a sign to proceed following the Ipoly River to the south. When the Ipoly reaches the Danube, they will be very close to the safety of Esztergom's walls. So far he had lost two dozen Janissaries and almost seventy riders and would not have liked to push the limits of his luck.
It was the middle of the afternoon when they reached the small town of Szalka where the Ipoly's confluence with the Danube was just a couple of miles away. He was about to give an order to cross the Ipoly and start the last phase of their trip home when his scouts rode up to him from the riverbank and reported that a whole Hungarian army of Hussar riders was silently waiting for them hiding behind the trees above the ford of the river. Only the small Ipoly River separated them from each other. Saban immediately had the wagons halted and sent the Janissaries with their rifles to line up along the riverbank in two groups. He was soon told that the Hussars had come from Komárom, Surány, Morva and Sellye castles, according to their flags. Saban knew that it meant some nine-hundred infidel riders, very likely led by Ferenc Nyáry of Surány, or perhaps by Bertalan Horváth of Komárom Castle.
"They had to leave behind their infantry so as to reach us this soon. It means, they have no firearms and will not dare to face our muskets and rifles while crossing the Ipoly. Yet, make your men known that however close we are to home, they cannot make it alone without the cover of the cavalry. In case of being scattered, the infantrymen will be hunted down one by one." he told Agha Ramadan, the commander of the Janissaries.
Saban summoned his officers and sent the old and wise Agha Ajvát with his Sipahis to the left of the Janissaries while placing the invincible Agha Musz on their right. He kept the remaining Deli riders under his command and turned to his most trusted man, the fearsome duelist of Arabia, Agha Naszuf:
"It is a pity that almost all of our soldiers are from the hills of the Balkan and there are so few noble born Arabian and Anatolian warriors like you or me. The Devil brought here that György Thury."
"I will bathe my saber in his blood if the infidel dog shows up," said Naszuf, grinding his teeth. Saban summoned a Deli rider and told him:
"Hussein, I make you the commander of the Deli riders. Take a patrol and go around but be back soon."

Pasha Saban rose in his high Turkish saddle and looked at his well-deployed small army on the field of Szalka, protected by the line of the Ipoly River from the left. He was not worried; he was still outnumbering the infidels almost two to one.

Ferenc Nyáry was a bandy-legged, fidgeting small man with a quick temper. He saw his scout, the daredevil Lőrinc Zoltai, return with his three men. Captain Nyáry did not know that the severed Turkish head, still running with blood, at the tip of Zoltai's spearhead had once belonged to Agha Hussein. Zoltai saluted him and gave his report:

"Lord Captain, the approaching men of Sir Balassa can be made out. I sent a lad to greet him and inform him of our plans," said Zoltai and he carefully rolled Hussein's head before the hooves of his commander's horse.

"With compliments, Sir," he added shyly.

"Had I not told you to avoid duels?" the captain scolded him with a little smile. Lord Nyáry turned towards his officers and gave his orders:

"When Sir Balassa's sixty-seventy men are in ear-shot, I will give the sign to charge. Now, go and deploy our army into three groups. When you see my flag waved, you, Gáspár Gerei attack the left wing and you, Zoltai the right wing. I will wade over the river right here and if God grants us victory, with Sir Balassa's help from their rear, we can win the day before sunset. There is no taking captives and no looting until the end of the battle. Whoever disobeys must die on the spot. Without Sir Balassa, we have nine-hundred and thirty horses so the odds are with us. God and all His creatures know that ten Hussars can outman fifty riff-raff riders of the Sultan."

His orders were carried out at once and the Hussars began adjusting their equipment, watering their horses, talking merrily or praying before the battle. Not much time later they saw Captain Nyáry's flag waved three times in the air. The warriors cried "Jesus, Jesus" as most of them were Protestants, and they jumped their horses, amid a great splashing and clattering, into the shallow water of the Ipoly River. It was a mile-long frontal attack with a forest of lowered lances aimed at the enemy waiting for them on the field of Szalka. The volley of the Janissaries swept many riders off their saddles, but Lord Nyáry got through the water and pushed the infantry back. The Turks fought for each step and gave their ground grudgingly, making the Christians pay with their blood for their advance. As a rule, four Janissaries lived in a tent, three seasoned warriors were training the fourth, a youngster who made their soup and cleaned their clothes. They were not allowed to bring women into their camp, so the young trainees were often the lovers of the three older men. Now, three elite warriors were desperately defending the fourth and died without a word if it was needed. They were orphans brought up by the Sultan, loved by no-one except the Padisah and their own comrades. No wonder that they despised death. Their leader, Agha Ramadan was fighting like a lion of the desert in their front lines.

The Hussar assault was slowed down by the stubborn infantrymen yet, it struck the Turkish cavalry like a thunder-bolt. Agha Ajvát lost his life in the first minute and his opponent, Gáspár Kerei followed his fate some seconds later. The Sipahis became confused because of the Agha's loss while the Hussars tripled their efforts and gripped the shafts of their battle-axes harder after seeing Kerei fall.

The Hussars pushed the Turkish riders into the middle of the field at Szalka as if they were feathers. A tremendous "Jesus, Mary" battle-cry from the other side announced the arrival of Lord Balassa and György Thury which spread more havoc. The Sipahis were wavering but Pasha Saban and Agha Naszuf rode to and fro to give them heart. It was then when the Arabian Agha met his fate through nobody else but György Thury.

"Allah Akbar!" he cried and he at once attacked the giant infidel whom he had recognized.

In the middle: Captain György Thury

Despite his size, Thury moved with the swiftness of a beast and his long sword parried the scimitar with a loud clanging sound. The onlookers were not familiar with the teaching of the Italian fencing genius called Maestro Fiore and knew nothing of his elegant tricks. All of the Turkish and Hungarian spectators who lowered their swords for the moments of the duel cried out in awe. For all they saw was that the scimitar flew into the air in a wide arc and Naszuf was gazing at his missing left fist that landed in the grass. "Inshallah!" he cried and Thury finished him off with a stab under his second rib.

It was enough for the Sipahis. Nobody is obliged to fight against djinnies, after all. They fled. Agha Musz grabbed the reins of the stupefied Pasha Saban's mount and dragged it out of peril with a huge force.

"Spare yourself, great Pasha, we must flee!" he shouted and Saban did not reject the will of Allah. By now, the Ottoman cavalry was running away, abandoning the infantry to their fate. Which fate was cruel to them.

While most of the Hussars gave chase and killed as many Turks as they could, Balassa and Thury were joined by the savage Hajdú horsemen of Zoltai and began to charge the Janissaries. The long-hats of the elite troops of the Sultan did not waver for a second. They stood their ground against the cavalry and their long lances and defended each other with a stubborn determination. Some Hajdu soldiers dismounted and joined György Thury who preferred fighting infantrymen on foot. He opened a bloody path with his long, two-handed blade and the Hajdus followed on his heels. The Janissaries kept on fighting and refused to surrender when in the end it was offered to them with a good heart.

Agha Ramadan was one of the last ones to die by the sword of Lord Balassa. More than five hundred Janissaries entered the Paradise of their Allah on that day in May, in the year of 1544, eighteen years after the Battle of Mohács and three years after the fall of Buda Castle. The Hungarians took no captives until the end of the fight. No one plundered the dead.

Dusk came and the tired warriors returned from the chase. The wagons of the Turks, and the horses, and cattle were collected along with the weapons and valuables of the fallen enemy. There stood a group of captured Deli and Sipahis, too. A precious ransom was anticipated in exchange for them. Lord Balassa spotted a man in a black Hungarian dolman among them. He recognized the "pribék" of Léva, the spy who guided the Janissaries into the city. He sent two Hajdús to fetch him. The man threw himself before his legs and wept. He begged not to be hanged.

"Hanging a 'pribék ''"? By no means. It is not in our habit to hang them, be assured, poor man. We have different treatment for them," and the Captain of Léva turned to the Hajdus "Go and cut off a young tree and sharpen its top. Impale this "pribék" before the sun goes down."

While his men dragged the screaming traitor away, Balassa thought of the Saxon girl in the blood-stained skirt with her broken yatagan and his heart sank.

Great bonfires were lit and the booty was quickly divided into the usual three parts under the watching eyes of Lőrinc Nyáry who said:

"As custom and habit demand it, one-third is given to His Majesty, King Ferdinand. The second third will be given to the widows and orphans of the fallen warriors. We will have the third part divided among ourselves according to rank and valor."

The Hussars and the Hajdus roared with delight and orders were given to prepare a feast on the battlefield from the cattle and food taken back from the enemy. The dead bodies were gathered and piled up, Turks and Hungarians lay peacefully next to each other. The corpses were covered by thorny branches so as to keep away the meat-eaters. Only the ravens and eagles could reach them from above, hence the saying that the proper cemetery of the borderland warriors was the stomach of birds. Esztergom was too close and there was no other way to bury them. A Turkish raiding party could show up at any time.

Lord Balassa could not escape the memory of the poor dishonored maiden of Léva. A black mood engulfed him and he sought out Lord Nyáry with a darkened face.

"My Lord, what of the Burghers of Léva? Everything here had been robbed of them. Should they not get their property back?"

Lőrinc Nyáry was a jumpy and ill-tempered warrior which suited him well in times of war but served him not in dealing with his fellow-captains. He looked at Balassa scornfully and thought to himself how true it was what was said about the Captain of Léva behind his back:

"He has never-ever obeyed any orders coming from rulers, religion or anybody in his entire life." Aloud, he said this much:

"Sir Balassa, the Burghers should have protected themselves better, now they can look at themselves. Tell them to go and plead before the king, not from us who saved them."

Balassa was near to a blood-stroke.

He replied:

"The king?! You know what sort of help the king sent me from his Selmecbánya city and what support I got from the petty nobles who call themselves the feet-lickers of Ferdinand? Nothing! Nobody came to my aid and the king sent me not a single soldier . . . !" he added: "Now, now, listen to me you little man." Balassa leaned down and peered into the eyes of Nyáry from two inches away:

"I swear to God Almighty a solemn oath that I will re-collect every single Thaller and Penny from this King Ferdinand of yours and I will squeeze the neck of all the petty nobles until they cough up the money they should have given to the aid of the weak and the innocent. Let me be called a robber knight, I will not rest and no wagons carrying silver and gold to your king's treasury can safely reach Vienna anymore. And if you dislike it, my small lord, so much the worse, you may stamp your feet."

Turning abruptly, he jumped on his horse and rode back to his wife. And this was how Sir Balassa became an enemy of the king, a robber knight, stealing the king's gold and silver . . .

20. Kékkő Castle   GPS: 48.243644, 19.333233

The castle of Kékkő (Modrý Kameň), was the famous castle of the poet and warrior Bálint Balassi. Kékkő, in the Hungarian language means "bluestone", is near Besztercebánya (Banská Bystrica, Neusohl). It is in the middle of the Upper Lands, right in the historic Mining Towns District of the Hungarian Kingdom, now called „Horná zem" in Slovakian.

Kékkő Castle

According to the family legend of the Balassa clan, once there was a dragon which was guarding a huge blue diamond. The ancestor of the Balassa family slayed the dragon and gave the stone to the king who let them build a castle in exchange for it. Additionally, the king gifted them with the half of the blue stone which was to be guarded in the castle. Eventually, when the Turk Bey Ali took the castle, the stone rolled away into the grass because it did not want to be in the Bey's hand.

With good luck, anybody can find it now, without having to fight the dragon.

In truth, it was King Béla IV who permitted the building of the castle to Péter, son of Mikó in the 1250s who was the ancestor of the Balassa family. The castle - without the dragon - was first mentioned as „Keykkw" in 1290. The name of the Balassa family has often appeared in the pages of history. They were famous for their valor and talent but they also had a reckless reputation. The greatest Hungarian warrior-poet wore his name as Bálint Balassa of Kékkő.

Later it was taken by the oligarch of the Upper Land, Máté Csák. Then the Zólyomi family owned it for a short time in the 16th century. Except for a few years during the course of seven hundred years, the Balassa family has been the owners of Kékkő Castle, until the 1930s.

János Balassa was the Chief Comes of Hont and Zólyom counties in the 1570s and he was often sallying at the Turks from the castle. Pasha Mustapha of Buda finally had enough of him and ordered Bey Ali to take Kékkő in 1576. The Turks met no resistance because the castle's garrison had fled before them. The castellan of János Balassa, Imre Temesi, fled to Dévény (Divin) but could not escape his death, the Turks tracked him down and killed him. Bey Ali had the castle carefully renovated and erected a new tower and a gate.

Kékkő was taken back in 1593 but the Ottomans had it exploded before fleeing from the army of Kristóf Tieffenbach and Miklós Pálffy.

The castle became such an important borderland fortress that it was rebuilt by Zsigmond Balassa between 1603 and 1612 who even persuaded the Treasury of the Kingdom to contribute to his expenses. Many attacks were aimed at it, and during the 17th century it had been destroyed repeatedly. Besides the Turks, it once was set on fire by the man of the Transylvanian Prince Rákóczi, called Kókay.

Emperor Leopold gave the settlement of the castle a privilege and allowed it to keep markets in 1658. Gábor Balassa had a nice palace built next to the ruins of the old castle in 1750.

If you climb the Calvary Hill above the palace, you can visit the remaining bastions and walls and can enjoy a magnificent view of the land where the Turks had deployed their troops so many times.

21. The Blue Stone (1545)

The lords of Kékkő Castle had many troubles with the Turks, even during the period of truce. There was never peace on the one-thousand mile long Borderland. Larger and smaller Turkish units were always ambushing the

Hungarians and tried to take the castles by surprise. Not as if the Hungarians were not doing the same thing.

Was it not a Turkish army coming in broad daylight with flutes and drums, waving lances with horse-tail flags on their ends? The guard in the tower of Kékkő Castle rubbed his eyes and ran to the dining room of his lord, Sir Balassa.

"The Turks are coming!" the guard was panting.

"How many?" asked the captain of the castle because he never was frightened by a couple hundred of them.

"They can not be more than twenty-twenty five of them. The rest could be hiding in the forest, though, to entice us into a trap." answered the guard.

To their amazement, the Turks arrived at the gate and their trumpeter signaled that they had come in peace. Their leader and his retinue were wearing brightly colored clothes and no armor.

"Who are you and what do you want?" shouted the guard from the tower.

"I am the mighty Bey of Fülek Castle, Mehemed, the most loyal subject of the Bright Faced Sultan. I have come with a peaceful heart to your lord, the valiant Sir Balassa. I wish to speak with him in person."

Bálint Balassi, the Poet and Warrior

"Three of you may enter because we had seen such a trick before. It was how the Turks had walked into Buda Castle peacefully then they stayed there forever."

Bey Mehemed got angry and began banging the gate with his fist.

"I repeat, infidel, that we have come with peace."

But there was nothing to do, the Bey had to bid his men withdraw. Having seen this, the guards opened the heavy gate, and Bey Mehemed could ride proudly in with three of his servants. On his right rode his flag-bearer and two musicians were playing their instrument next to him. The Turks traveled nowhere without music. The Bey had inserted a shining blue stone in his turban, out of courtesy towards the lord of Kékkő. They dismounted in the inner castle yard and went up to the knightly reception hall where Sir Balassa was waiting for them with three men at his side, the castellan, and his two lieutenants. Soon, the Bey stood before him and bowed in eastern fashion, putting his hand to his forehead.

"Honorable and valiant Sir Balassa, may my Allah and your Jesus both bless you because Jesus is a respected prophet of our faith as well. I am bringing you the white flowers of peace and doves speak out of my soul and the sounds of love are played on my zither."

"Just tell me plainly, respectable Bey Mehemed what you want because we Hungarians are not used to this ornamented talk."

Yet, the Bey of Fülek was hard to be diverted from his bird-singing style and he continued his speech all the same way:

"I have come into a garden where only miraculous flowers are growing and where the bülbül or nightingale bird is singing on a silvery sound." Sir Balassa waved his hand in a resignation and said:

"Then, we had better sit down because as I see it, it will not come to an end for a while. Please, take a seat and let us smoke a pipe together before going on with it."

The Bey liked this peaceful reception because it was not the way they used to communicate on the battlefield. He was given a big leather pillow where he sat crossed-legged and his host did not sit higher than him out of politeness. As it is befitting to meditate while smoking, they had not said a word until they had finished. Then, the Bey resumed his talk.

"Valiant Sir Balassa, sometimes my friend, sometimes my enemy. There is a fire-red rose growing in the tulip garden of Kékkő Castle."

"Your talk is still like a nightingale's, respectable Bey, so please, accept a little drink as it is befitting after the pipe."

"Allah permits us only the honey flavored water or sherbet but you are talking about wine. For the Prophet's name, it will not be good." The Bey was blinking with embarrassment.

"Now, valiant Mehemed, you are in my house and you must obey the laws of my home. Alas, I tell you that you will drink that wine if I told you so. It has just been brought from Putnok the other day."

Bey Mehemed opened his arms and pretended as if he was forced but finally, he gave in.

"If Allah sees it is inevitable, then I will do your bidding but please, in this case, let my servants drink, too."

The wine was quickly served in huge tin cups. When the host saw that his guest's eyes were gleaming, told him to carry on with his speech. Now, the Bey was able to draw some courage from the wine and spoke more fluently.

"Sir, I will make it short, then. The red rose I was talking about is no-one else than your own lady wife. She is a beauty of beauties. A flower fitting only into the seventh heaven of Allah. It was a month ago when I took the sight of her on the road to Léva Castle when we were traveling there. The glimpse of my eyes touched her only for a moment but she enchanted and charmed me, cast a spell over me. Give her to me, my respectable Sir, you can have all my treasures in exchange for her."

Sir Balassa was a quick-tempered man and he wanted to slay the auspicious Turk in the heat of the moment. There has never been such a scandalous thing in the chronicles of the Balassi family. But he surpassed his anger and made a straight face.

"And what about the woman? Had she seen you, too? Were you to her liking?"

"No, she did not see me, she just had her horses whipped and fled as fast as she could before me. Is it not enough that I did see her?"

"No, not enough" answered the host grimly "but know that she had seen you and she came to like you as well."

"By Allah and the prophet!" exclaimed the Bey "So you can give her to me, can't you?"

"Really, what had you offered for her?" asked Balassa.

The Bey leaned forward and quickly listed:

"All my treasure, my gold and silver and all my lands."

"Not enough."

"I promise you that I will not attack your castles for three full years."

"Not enough."

"I can offer you only three years because I will be in Istanbul in the fourth year already. I will take your wife there, she is going to be the most beautiful flower of my garden, my first wife."

"Not enough."

"I have a small castle, next to Rimaszombat, Szabatka."

"Not enough."

The Bey bit his lips. What else should he offer?

"I give you a paper that my soul will be yours when it goes up to heaven."

"Well-well, why did you not begin with this? It would be just enough."

"Then, are you going to give her to me right now? Where is that fiery, sweet rose?"

"She is at the gate of heaven. I threw her out of the window. She admitted that she had fallen in love with you and wished to become the nicest flower of your harem. I could not do otherwise, I sent her to heaven."

The Bey jumped to his feet, swaying because of the wine.

"You have done it to her and with me? How could you do it?" he was stammering with a bitter surprise.

"Like this," roared Balassa with dense rage and grabbed the Turk by his waist and dragged him to the window and flung him out of it. The Bey ended up in the muddy moat, his turban with the blue stone was rolling after him. The two servants were fleeing headlessly from the castle and they fished the disgracefully dirty Bey out of the moat. Nobody chased them except the laughter of the soldiers from the ramparts.

Lady Balassa all the while had been silently eavesdropping behind the door but now she entered the room and hugged her husband. Sir Balassa shouted after the Turks from the window:

"This is how a guest ends up if his intention is not honorable. Nobody may dare to cast an eye on my lady wife!"

With this, the lord of Kékkő ordered the turban of Mehemed to be fetched and be the blue diamond stripped from it.

The blue stone was to be given to Lady Balassa.

22. Drégelypalánk Castle   GPS: 48.016501, 19.036117

Drégely Castle is located in northern Hungary near the Slovakian border. Its ruins are on a hilltop guarding the basin of the Ipoly river where it meets the Börzsöny Mountains. Many Hungarians have heard of the valiant siege of Drégely and the heroic death of its captain, György Szondi. Because of this, it is present in the historical consciousness of the nation. Drégely Castle's fortress was erected by the Bozóky line of the Hont-Pázmány clan between 1275 and 1285, in the golden age of Hungarian castle building. Drégely's name first appeared in 1285. The small castle was taken by Máté Csák, the notorious oligarch who was the lord of northwest Hungary at the beginning of the 14th century. After his death (1321), Drégely became a royal estate in the middle of the 14th century under the rule of the Anjou dynasty. It was seized by a Moravian marquis in 1388, then King Sigismund took it back from him and donated it to the Tari family in 1390.

After a generation's time, it became a royal estate once again. Though only for fifteen years, as King Albert Habsburg gave it to the archbishopric in Esztergom as a present. The small fort was kept as a hunting palace for the bishops of Esztergom. Pál Várday, Archbishop of Esztergom, had been a supporter of King Szapolyai, but he fled to Drégely Castleand later sided with King Ferdinand. The consequences of his betrayal of Szapolyai hit the inhabitants of Drégely hard. Three years later, the Serbian, Turkish and Hungarian soldiers of Szapolyai set the small agricultural town on fire and herded their cattle away. Ottoman troops arrived to pillage the area in 1536 and Drégely was amongst the sacked places.

After Buda fell into the hands of the Muslims in 1541, King Ferdinand had to create a new chain of defenses in the north. This frontier line was designed by Archbishop Várday and by Count Nicholas Salm, Chief Commander of the Habsburgs. North of the Danube River the castles worth renovating were Drégely, Ság, Pásztó, Szécsény, Buják, and Léva. Nógrád Castle was taken by the Pasha Mehmed in 1544 and this important castle in the neighborhood of Drégely became their base for raiding the Upper Lands of Hungary. During the winter of 1543-44, the Turks burned a village called Oroszi next to Drégely. This was the year that Drégely became a frontier castle, guarding the gate to the mining towns of Upper Hungary, especially towards Selmecbánya.

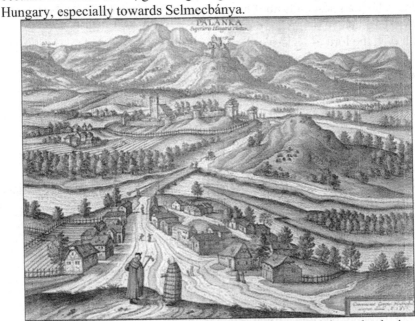

The weak truce between King Ferdinand and Sultan Suleiman broke in 1551. Suleiman sent three armies against Ferdinand. His aim was to divide the western and eastern parts of Hungary so as to separate Transylvania from Ferdinand and to open a border with Poland. It was the third, the smallest army with 10-12,000 men that turned towards the mining cities of the Upper Lands. This army`s leader was Hádim Ali, the Pasha of Buda who was also known as 'Hádim, the Gelded'.

The first roadblock for this army was Drégely Castle with Captain György Szondi in command. The Fort was in rather poor condition as a lightning bolt had exploded its gunpowder-storage, and there was not enough ammunition or soldiers in it to mount a proper defense. Captain Szondi had been in the service of Archbishop Várday, but after the priest`s death, the castle went under the command of the king as the Treasury took over the Archbishop`s income. As a result of this, the pay of the soldiers became even worse than it had been before. When Gergely Bekefalvy, the vice-captain of György Szondi in Drégely, heard that Pasha Ali was coming, he abandoned the castle. He complained that he did this because of the lack of money and said he had a family and children to take care of.

At Ság, in the fortified monastery, there were twice as many defenders as in Drégely, but when the Turks came near, its commander, Captain Ferenc Jakosits, burned the castle and fled to nearby Léva Castle. He joined the camp of General Erasmus Teuffel who was observing the events with his 10,000 strong German-Italian mercenary army.

At Drégely Castle there had been only sixty soldiers in Captain Szondi and his co-captain, Lőrinc Zoltay`s, service. The king allowed the hiring of only a further 40 soldiers. The rich town of Selmecbánya sent 24 men, but no gunpowder. The repairs to the castle had not been finished, and Szondi had just a few cannons and 22 more men. Szondi and his 146 men swore to defend the old-fashioned castle to the end, knowing that General Teuffel denied sending reinforcements.

They were only able to resist the Turks for four days, but these few days were legendary. They caused great losses to the enemy and their example gave encouragement to the Hungarian warriors all along the Borderland. Ten injured Hungarian warriors were taken as captives, but Szondi and the rest of his men died. The Pasha had Szondi buried with military honors on 9 July 1552 in recognition of his bravery.

The Turks went on and took the frontier castles of Gyarmat, Szécsény and finally, Ali defeated General Teuffel in the Battle of Palást, two months later. Only the small castle of Bussa followed the example of Drégely hindering the Turks in their victorious campaign which was stopped only at the unsuccessful siege of Eger Castle.

Two years later, with Fülek and Salgó being occupied by the Turks, the first system of castles along the border was established. In 1575, Új-Drégely (New-Drégely) aka Palánk (Palisade) was built by the fortification of the church in Drégely. The Turks did not renovate the old castle on the hilltop, instead, they built a strong palisade which was capable of holding 2,000 riders. This kind of palisade-extension was called "huszárvár" or Hussar castle in that time.

The new castle became the headquarters of the raids aimed at the mining towns. This was also the center where taxes imposed on the population of the region were collected. The population of the medieval borough of Drégely probably did not reach one thousand. Some more German settlers arrived at the beginning of the 16th century. They, however, left the settlement during the Turkish rule and escaped to better-protected areas. South-Slavic people came to the settlement during the years of the occupation.

This palisade castle was taken back by General Pálffy in 1593 at the beginning of the so-called Long War which lasted for 15 years. Hungarian military command once again considered it a border fortress for two decades. General Pálffy left Ferenc Nagy in charge of the fort as a castellan. It remained the target of constant Turkish attacks which were beaten back repeatedly.

Due to the lack of payment, the number of defenders at Drégely decreased to a mere ten soldiers in December 1595. These were not enough to protect the surrounding villages and the settlements eventually fell into Turks hands to whom they paid taxes. Fortunately, the garrison's number was increased the following year and with these they withheld the renewed Ottoman attacks.

The castle, repaired and strengthened after the Tatar raid of 1599, was subdued by the commanders reporting to the princes of Transylvania at the time of the Thirty Year War. During the military campaign of Köprülü Ahmed, the Grand Vizier in 1663, Érsekújvár (Nove Zámky) fell and hearing the news, the guards of Drégelypalánk set the castle on fire and escaped.

The palisade was beyond repair but it was somewhat rebuilt in 1615. During the Habsburg-Transylvanian wars, Prince Gábor Bethlen`s army was camping next to Drégely castle in 1626, waiting for the chance to fight General Wallenstein. After the liberation from Ottoman rule, the two legally separated villages could start their new lives, Drégely and Palánk. Drégely, which was mentioned as a borough in sources from the 16-17th centuries, degraded to the status of a serf village owned by the church. Palánk (meaning 'palisade' in the Hungarian language), was born in the middle of the 16th century, managed to preserve some of its freedom as a border castle. The leading authority in the settlement was a lieutenant and not a judge. Its population, mostly craftsmen were exempted from socage and tithe. They worked as escorts to the lords and delivered the post and collected and safeguarded the tithe.

In the first thirty years of the 18th century, German settlers arrived to populate Drégely and Palánk, which were then organized into a single village and called Drégelypalánk.

23. The Siege of Drégely Castle (1552)

György Szondi put down his quill pen after signing his name to the last letter he was going to send to Archduke Maximilian asking for reinforcements.

"At least he should send some powder and bullets if nothing else." he thought to himself as he looked out of the window. There was not much to see. The blackened walls of the old tower of Drégely Castle were pointing accusingly towards the summer sky. The castle had been struck by a lightning bolt three months ago which had exploded the gunpowder which was stored there. Four people had died and it was a wonder that the tower did not collapse. The carpenters tried to repair the cracks and gaps with makeshift scaffolding, but Szondi was sure that even a mild storm would finish it, let alone a cannonball of the enemy. Bishop Thurzó visited last month to assess the damage and sent a few masons to salvage whatever was possible.

"It is fortunate that His Majesty, Archduke Maximilian, had not paid me his debt so that I had no money to buy more ammunition. Had the tower been fully packed with good black power, the whole decrepit castle would have gone up in smoke," he added to himself. Indeed, the Archduke owed him 322 Gold Forints on behalf of the king.

Drégely used to be well paid from the priests' pocket but since Bishop Pál Várday died a few years before the Habsburgs had been in charge of this stronghold. The stream of their regular pay began to flow through the desert of the Treasury which swallowed it thirstily. Stronghold? The delicately carved thin walls with their elegant gothic pillar heads had served the needs of the hunting bishops in the forests of the Börzsöny Mountain. It was rather a reinforced palace from a peaceful age when cannons were regarded as a laughing stock. The captain shook his head. "Sebestyén! Give this letter to a messenger and have it sent to Pozsony right away. And fetch some wine," he said to his young page, a lad who was learning in his court with his friend, Libardy. They were both typical mischievous 16-year-olds, with long dark hair and with a mustache-like shadow under their noses.

The lads were good at singing and could play the lute, but Szondi was not content with their horsemanship just yet. As for their knowledge of the sword, Szondi himself was teaching them the Art of the Longsword, according to the school of the great Italian master, Fiore dei Liberi. He recalled his days as a page in the court of his liege-lord and benefactor, Ferenc Révay, the Vice-Palatine of the Kingdom. In those days, he was not called Szondi but was known as Szuhó. Szond was just his home, a small agricultural border town in the south. Lord Révay found him there and decided he was talented. Why, even burgher boys could rise in rank if they rode a horse decently enough and had a way with the saber. In his court there was a great demand for youngsters to defend the southern borders of the kingdom. The young Szuhó was given a knightly education and was taught by the same Italian fencing masters as his lord's sons. Szondi sighed and threw himself into the bishop's armchair. Yes, that was a different time and age, hundreds of miles away. Hungary had just one king instead of two and the Turks were just getting ready to invade the country in the not-far-away Serbia, occasionally sinking their teeth into the flesh of the Borderland.

Sebestyén entered with the big copper jar and poured the cool red liquid into a goblet for him.

"My son, I was just four years older than you when I rode out beside my Liege-lord Révay to the field of Mohács. That was my first big battle, if we do not count the small raids and counter-raids on the borderland before that. Alas, I saw young King Louis with my very eyes."

The page listened attentively to him and thought "Sweet God, now the old lion is going to tell me the entire battle story all over again. How he saved his lord's life, and how they escaped miraculously, and arrived in the north in Szklabinya Castle, where he was rewarded."

He looked at the captain. The almost fifty-year-old warrior was smoothing his enormous mustache in order to swallow the wine decently. Szondi was a broad-shouldered, bull-like man with seasoned wrinkles on his face and indeed, he dreamily told the lad the whole story.

". . . and Lord Révay made me a knight and this is how I became a nobleman and I am no longer called Szuhó. King Ferdinand gave me my hometown, Szond near the Serbian border. One day, I might be able to take it into my possession when we chase the Turks out from there." "Yes, my Lord," said the page. Both of them knew it would not happen soon. Since Mohács in 1526, the Ottomans came even farther into the north and took Buda in 1541. Now, eleven years later, they were here in the northern hills trying to cut the remaining country into two. Just Drégely and some other pitifully weak Palisades and makeshift forts were blocking their way.

"But enough of this. Go and take your friend Libardy to the cellar and issue wine to the soldiers. Here are the keys. Tonight they can have a double portion."

No wonder the captain was so talkative to the lad. He had nobody to talk to since his co-captain, Gergely Bekefalvy had left the castle before the Turks began their march here. He was complaining because of his lack of pay and said he had three unraised children to take care of at home. So who could he share his worries with? Szondi admittedly would have fled, too, but he could not endure the shame in front of his liege-lord and the king. He was torn by despair. To whom could he say that he had only sixty footmen and sixteen hussars, one artilleryman and three castle guards under his pay, altogether eighty souls. That the king allowed him to hire only forty more men and the wealthy Selmecbánya city sent him a mere 26 soldiers.

It is said that each Burgher in that town had a share in a silver or copper mine and they stored fabulous fortunes, enclosed in strong barrels, in their cellars. Was he not defending them? The short-sighted, tight-fisted bastards. The road which went through Drégely headed toward Selmecbánya via the stone bridge at the Ipoly River and guarded by another small castle called Ság. The fat-headed Burghers knew that Drégely blocked the road that would lead to their treasure vaults. But they were just rolling their eyes and gave no real help. Last month Szondi sent one of his two cannons to Körmöcbánya, the gold minting town belonging to the crown, to have the old battle-snake repaired. He was expecting it back this week. A letter had only just arrived stating that the town needed the king's approval before carrying out the repairs. The Turks were a mere half days march away and Szondi knew the cannon would not come home in time.

A few years before, Szondi had recommended to the Military Council to have Drégely and Ság castles pulled down and instead of the two old castles, have a new fort erected on the nearby marshland, studded by earthen bastions in the Italian fashion. The Council liked the concept, but claimed they had no money. There was a knock on the door and Sebestyén ushered a dust-covered soldier into the room. It was János Zoltay, his youngest officer. His blond hair was wet and his clothes were soaked through because of the heat.

"At ease, my son. Drink this before you tell your news." Szondi poured some wine with his own hands and while the young man quenched his thirst, the captain dismissed his page with a glance.

"Sir, I have come all the way from Ság Castle. The castle is on fire and has been abandoned."

"The Turks . . . ?"

"No Sir, not them. Sir Captain Jakusits believed he could not withstand Pasha Ali's twelve thousand strong army. So he took his three hundred

men and joined the forces of General Erasmus Teuffel at Léva Castle. The general's army is camping a couple of miles further to the north."
"Are they coming to our rescue? How many troops does he have?"
"General Ördög, or Devil, as we call him, has ten-thousand good German, Italian and Spanish mercenaries under his command. But, he has no authorization from the king to attack the Turks, Sir. Although, he has sent a messenger to Vienna to ask for permission." Zoltay wiped his mustache and put the cup back on the table. He added with a half smile:
"He promised to light great bonfires on hilltops to frighten the enemy and to give us hope."
Szondi pursed his mouth so that his delicate, uniquely Hungarian curse would not leave his lips but the full attention of all the Saints of the Heavens and all the demons of Hell were suddenly focused on General Teuffel. Nobody knew at this time that the curse would eventually hit the coward German a month later when, after having been shamefully defeated by Hámid Ali at the Battle of Palást, he would be taken to Istanbul where he would finish his life gruesomely, impaled in front of the Sultan's very eyes.

The next morning Szondi and his 146 men were watching as Pasha Hádim Ali of Buda was arranging his troops into three camps, deploying them to block the road to Selmecbánya and Teuffel's army. The Pasha was convinced that the Germans had left this toy castle in his way just as bait. He had an earthen rampart built and lined up his cannons there.
Ali the Gelded, was not a bloodthirsty man. Soon, the Pasha sent an envoy to the captain of the Ghiaurs to surrender the castle. To his great surprise, the envoy returned at once. The moment the messenger left the gate, three Hussars rode out and set the hay piles in front of the walls on fire. A few light riders, the Akinjis rode there to salvage some of the fodder but they were shot at from the towers.
The envoy bowed before the old Pasha and waited to be addressed.
"Tell me the answer of the infidel's leader as it was told."
"Great Pasha, may Allah adorn your way to victory with Ghiaur heads. The captain of this small place is called György Szondi and he looks as if he has lost his senses. For he refused your merciful offer and said he had got up this morning too late to surrender the castle. He firmly decided to die with honor rather than throw himself into the yoke of slavery. He would not like to be dragged around as a slave with a chain on his neck to be sold."
Ali was slightly amused by the reply. He turned to the Agha of the Topcu soldiers, the officer of his artillery.

"Bismillah, let it be as Allah wants it. Show me how your men can handle the new French cannons."

The Topcus bent over their long bronze bombardiers and aimed them at the tower at the main gate of the castle. Three wall-breaching cannons and six howitzers broke both the peaceful summer afternoon and the stones of the tower to shreds.

Cranes flew up from the roof of the inner castle that lay on the hilltop. The birds circled in the air before flying away to the east. The Turks thought it was a good sign because the tame cranes of the borderland castles were always regarded with superstition. After the third volley, the whole construction suddenly collapsed in a huge cloud of dust, burying some of the Ghiaurs under the rubble. The Pasha had been expecting it and signaled the Agha of the Janissaries to proceed. The Agha cast a contemptuous look at the small castle and flourished the green flag of the Prophet. Three-thousand throats bellowed "Allahu Akbar!" and the tall white-hatted disciplined Janissaries rose and began their menacing march towards the pile of broken stones that only moments before used to be the tower. The musical band was playing victorious tunes and the grim soldiers were singing loudly. Inside the castle, nothing stirred.

Szondi saw the red feathers of Zoltay's helmet flicker, and then his officer was buried under the flying stones and shreds of timbers of the falling gate tower. He made the sign of the cross then motioned with his hand to his men in the lower castle's yard. The big old arquebuses crackled and spat nails and small bullets as the white hats and faces showed up on the top of the stone pile. The long lances were immediately leveled, thrust at the Janissaries climbing above the rubble. The singing had gradually ceased, the cries to "Jesus" and "Maria" had subdued it when a green flag with Arabic letters was torn off and trampled into the blood-soaked dust under the defenders' legs.

After the Janissaries withdrew, the utterly surprised Pasha sent the dismounted Akinjies with ladders to scale the walls from all sides. Captain Szondi drew his razor-sharp longsword which he had cherished since 1526 and the death of King Louis. His men received the enemy with sabers and battle hammers along the walls. It was almost dark when the second assault was beaten back. Szondi had a dozen or so old arquebuses or hook guns from the time of King Matthias. These were added to the few muskets and shot volley after volley at the running Muslims. Amid a tremendous roar, the captain's only cannon sent an occasional carved marble ball from the height of the inner castle's tower.

The rising moon shed light on a much less conceited Turkish camp where Pasha Hádim Ali was given a report of many hundreds of casualties that he should not have afforded.

After this unlucky day had passed, Pasha Ali decided not to take any chances. He expected Teuffel's attack at any minute and did not want to waste more men nor break the Muslim warrior's morale. He acknowledged the defiant valor of this petty captain, however insane and suicidal it was. He smelled heroism here. All the same, Ali shrugged and issued his orders to the Agha of the Topcus.

"Shell the place to shreds."

The Topcus took delight in systematically turning the whole fort into burning embers, beginning with the palisade walls of the lower castle. Then, breaking the fragile gothic towers, and the buildings of the inner castle into fragments. After two days of terrible bombardment, no more shots issued forth from the pitiful remains. The defenders had either all died or had run out of gunpowder.

The fourth day of the siege had come. Bonfires were burning on the tops of the neighboring hills which betrayed to friend and foe that no reinforcement would dare to relieve the defenders.

Szondi knew they were doomed. The cannons were silent and there was really not much to shoot at except broken stones and fallen roofs. The captain had emptied the lower castle right after the first two assaults and hid his remaining warriors in the cellars of the inner castle among the women and children. He had only three dozen people left and no gunpowder with which to fight. His men were desperate, they had all sworn to fight to their last breath and would not forsake the king's house.

A lonely figure in a black robe approached the castle from the enemy's camp. The man stumbled through the loose stones of the outer wall and climbed up the hillside to the place that used to be the gate of the inner castle. Szondi could make him out now: it was Father Márton, the priest of Oroszi village. They all knew him well.

The priest was a good man. He said he was sent by Pasha Ali and begged the captain to surrender and save their lives, telling him that the Pasha seemed to be a reasonable man who valued their bravery and steadiness. Continuing on would be in vain. There would be no help arriving, why should they waste more blood? Father Márton pleaded with tears in his eyes.

"The Pasha will wait only until midday for me to go back with your answer, Sir."

"Well, then we have a couple of hours to get ready, don't we."

"To leave the castle?" asked Father Márton.

"No, Father, to prepare our souls. Would you give us the last rites? Please, shrive and absolve us, Father, as it is befitting."

Upon saying this, Szondi summoned his two pages, Sebestyén and Libárdy. They were there at once, in ragged and bloodstained clothes. The boys had taken their manly shares in the first fight and their Lord knighted them during the following night.

"Sebestyén, my son, go and open the secret tunnel for the womenfolk. Now they must depart and leave their husbands and sons. They have to reach safety while the Turks are waiting for our reply. Libardy, have the men bring out all the valuables we had hidden in the cellars. Build a pile and throw wood on it. Be dismissed."

While Father Márton was completing his priestly work among the soldiers, Szondi fetched the keys of the dungeon and opened its doors. Down there he had a dozen Ottoman prisoners of war. Marauders and rapists caught burning peasants' homes. Scum of the Earth riff-raff irregular villains from the Balkans. But, there were also two Turkish captives who were of noble kin, captured during a duel. He sought them out.

„Achmed, Ibrahim, get on your feet and follow me," he ordered in Turkish. When they went up to the yard, Szondi saw that his pages had done his bidding and were standing to attention. The captain felt pity for them, they were so young and talented. His plan was taking shape, though.

"Yes, they deserve a longer life," he thought and gave them his new orders: "Get yourselves washed and choose the best clothes from the valuable items piled up high in the middle of the yard. Then, make Ibrahim and Achmed do the same."

When they were ready, Szondi opened his strongbox which had been brought to the courtyard along with the silver and gold items from the chapel and from the treasury chamber of the palace. He measured two sizeable bags of gold to each page and to each young Turkish prisoner. "Now, Father Márton, listen to my words. We and our men are unable to leave here. But, I am sending my two good pages to Pasha Ali and these two Turkish noble lads as a ransom for their lives. Tell him to give my lads a valiant education and when grown, let them have their freedom to choose their fate. As for me, a decent burial of my remains would be much appreciated. Now, I ask for your blessing, Father, and then be off with you. Noon is almost here."

Pasha Ali, the Gelded, was smoothing his white beard but his face was dark. He was an honest man and silently nodded in agreement and accepted Szondi's last wish. The pages were ordered to join his retinue and they were made to stand in a good place to overlook the final assault against the castle. The Agha of the Janissaries was agitated and wanted to take revenge, he was nervously playing with the grip of his yataghan.

The assault was launched and the roaring crowd rushed up to the inner castle to finish the defenders off. There was no music this time. This final fight lasted for two full hours and Pasha Ali considered its outcome a miracle. He had to watch his best troops slaughtered and beaten again, turning tail, howling and fleeing down the slopes, bloodied and humiliated by a handful of raging daredevils. Shaking his head, Ali sent his officers with whips to turn the runners back. When they were beaten into submission and thronged up in the yard of the lower castle, Szondi and his few men sallied out. The Hungarians fell on them like scavengers, led by a figure in shining armor. The bulky man was wielding a longsword that easily outdid any Turkish saber or Persian scimitar. The throng yielded before the long blade. This was the last stand, the time of the bloody harvest.

"Shoot him." ordered the Agha of the Janissaries and it was obeyed.

The first bullet hit the captain's knee and brought him down. Two Akinjis threw themselves on him but he fought back on one knee and sliced them with an elegant sweeping move of his longsword. More Muslims were cut down, the man seemed invincible. The Janissaries loaded their guns again.

Several musket muzzles rose and the French-made gun's ammunition pierced his breastplate easily from this close distance. The angry Janissaries pushed into the inner castle but soon returned, even angrier. Their Agha rushed to Szondi's body and separated his head with his yataghan, spat in his eyes then thrust the severed head on a long spear. It was planted into the remains of the first tower for everyone to see.

Pasha Ali learned not much later that the Janissaries had rushed angrily back out because they had found no booty in the castle. No gold, no silver. No women to rape or children to sell. All they saw were the corpses of splendid Hungarian stallions slaughtered by their previous owners next to a huge bonfire that had consumed all of the precious things they wanted to have. Twelve Muslim prisoners were hanging from a makeshift gallows-tree and everything was sticky with decay.

A Jannissary from 1577

Ali let the spear stay where it was until he had Szondi's body carried to a proper place selected for his burial. The Pasha was a wise man and knew that his Janissaries needed to be taught a lesson, so he had his army aligned next to the Ghiaur captain's tomb. Ali felt a growing dislike towards the

Agha of the Janissaries so he ordered that he and no one else should fetch Szondi's head and fit it next to his body.

The Janissaries had to watch silently as the infidel priest called Márton finished the last rituals for the Captain who had humiliated them so much. Hádim Ali, the Gelded, Pasha of Buda Castle delivered the funeral speech in Szondi's honor.

"May Allah bless him who had fallen in an honorable fight and give him eternal peace in exchange for his virtue. Let this spear be struck in his tomb so the wind can blow the horse-tail on it to show the resting place of a true warrior. And you, you Janissaries, the elite troops of the Bright Faced Padishah, you bare in mind that respect for the enemy may bring you sweet victory, while pride is a sin before Allah. Why do you think this Captain was wearing no helmet when sallying out? He showed he was ready to die and not be taken alive. Ponder on it, before you meet the army of Erasmus Teuffel, the German Djinn. Learn this lesson that this valiant man called Szondi has taught you. You paid the price for this knowledge dearly. Inshallah."

24. Csábrág Castle   GPS: 48.243883, 19.106022

Csábrág or Csábrágvarbók (Čabradský Vrbovok) is 23 kilometers to the north-east from Ipolyság (Sahy) and it guarded the roads to the fabulous Mining Cities. It was mentioned first in 1276. King Róbert Károly built its castle after 1335 and gave it to the Dobrakutya family. The castle was called "Litva" for a while and 26 villages belonged to it with six places where taxes and tolls were collected.

Péter and Leukus of the Dobrakutya family became unfaithful to the king in 1342 so the king took away all their lands and properties. Csábrág Castle changed hands between Queen Maria and Frank of Szécsény, then between King Zsigmond and Leusta of Zsolna, between János Pásztói and László Kakas.

The Kakas family came to love the place and after 1394 they were able to hold it for a longer time. They would keep the castle until 1467 when Damján Horváth became its owner. Their descendants began calling themselves Csábrági and Lippai because of the castle. The Balassa family obtained a part in the property through a marriage in 1475.

Csábrág castle became better-fortified in the 16th century and was manned by royal guards. Orban Fáncsy owned Csábrág in 1511 until he sold it, and its villages, to Cardinal Tamás Bakócz for 1,000 gold Ducats. The high priest reinforced it in 1511. The Endrődy family inherited the castle from

him in 1517 and Péter Pálffy obtained it from them by a marriage. His son, Miklós Pálffy, was born in Csábrág who later became famous for his military deeds as a General against the Ottomans.

The castle and its villages suffered a lot during the Dual Kingship. Menyhárt Balassa took away Csábrág Castle from Péter Pálffy by force in 1547 because Pálffy was on King Ferdinand's side. Then, Count Salm, a General of Ferdinand managed to get the castle back two years later. He garrisoned it with the king's soldiers and Péter Pálffy was able to return.

Pálffy had a daughter, Katalin, who gave her hand to a valiant man from Dalmatia, János Krusich. He was a good owner who reinforced the castle and defended it from the assaults of the raiding Turks. When he died in 1582, the castle went to the care of Palatine István Illésházy. The Military Council of Vienna wanted to pull down Csábrág but instead of this, they decided to reinforce its walls in 1585. They sent an Italian architect, Giulio Ferrari, who had designed the forts of Korpona and Bakabánya. In addition to this, they supplied the castle with lots of gunpowder. The raiding Ottoman troops were never able to take the castle, unlike the soldiers of Prince István Bocskai who took it in the winter of 1604 along with Drégely.

CSÁBRÁG VÁRA

Csábrág Castle in the 19th century

When the widow of István Illésházy died, King Ferdinand II took back the castle and gave it to yeomen Péter Koháry in 1622. The members of the

Koháry family always remained loyal to the Habsburg kings because they thought that was best for the homeland. Nevertheless, the attacking Transylvanian princes always took Csábrág Castle from them by force. Yet, after the troops of Prince Bethlen, Princes György I and II Rákóczi, the army of Prince Thököly and the "kuruc" rebels of Prince Ferenc II Rákóczi had all gone, the Koháry family always returned and repaired the castle.

In the 18th century, they used it only as their summer resort. The family let the castle become abandoned in the 19th century when, for the sake of comfort, they moved to the village of Szentantal. Ferenc Koháry gave the order to burn Csábrág Castle in 1812 and it has been in ruins since that time.

The several story high walls are still very spectacular and they are presently being restored by a remarkably enthusiastic group of Slovakian people. When you travel there, take a look at the small settlement at the foot of the castle hill. The inhabitants of the village of Csábrágváralja are all gone and their houses are half-ruined, dreaming of visitors who would revive the old days of the ancient castle.

25. The Battle of Palást (9-10 August 1552)

Hádim Ali, the Gelded, Pasha of Buda Castle was deep in thought stroking his long beard which was slowly turning white. He was quite satisfied. His mission was to cut the two infidel countries, Royal Hungary and Transylvania, apart from each other to prevent their unification.

His army, albeit suffering painful losses at Drégely Castle was penetrating deep into the northern lands of the Christians. So far he has taken all of the smaller forts of Nógrád County and his raiders were plundering lands which had never seen Ottoman blades until now. It was a month ago when he took Drégely Castle and the two young pages of the late Captain Szondi were still with the Turk army just as he had promised that valiant infidel. Bey Achmed and Ibrahim, whom Szondi released from his dungeon before making his last stand, were guarding the lads. The pages, Libardy and Sebestyén, were free to walk only in the military camp, though.

"Even the heroism of Szondi served the interests of Allah," Ali thought "because the proud Agha Arslan, the leader of the Janissaries, was humiliated. Too many elite Janissary troops died by the swords of Szondi's 146 men. It was a sign to everybody that the infidels might fight back with a terrible rage."

Yet, Ali was a bit puzzled. He could clearly see that the approaching infidel army of General Teuffel two hills away from him wanted to crush him now.

"Were not General Teuffel and his 11,000 men idly watching the peril of Szondi? The cowards lit bonfires on the hilltops but did not dare to attack me. He must have received reinforcements and wants to improve his reputation by taking Drégely Castle back." Ali concluded.

As if Allah had peered into his mind, a messenger appeared in his tent, deeply bowing. He came from Agha Arslan. Ali made him report without allowing him any ceremonial niceties.

"Great Pasha, the infidel army is making camp for the night at the village of Egyeg and seemingly they have no idea that we are so close."

"Could the noble Agha Arslan count their number?"

"Noble Blade of the Padisah, the Agha captured a few tongues. After some gentle prompting, they hurried to tell everything they knew. We learned that Erasmus Teuffel von Goundersdorf has 3,000 German and Spanish heavy cavalry under his flag and further 3,000 German landsknechts, led by Dietrich von Marcel. Half of the Germans have long pikes and half of them have muskets. The best troops are the Italian mercenaries, 4,500 men, freshly recruited in Rome. Their commander is the wicked Sforza Pallavicini who had poisoned Cardinal Martinuzzi by order of King Ferdinand. They have only six cannons altogether."

"What about the Hungarian warriors?"

"They are there, too. Previously, some 300 Hajdú soldiers of Captain Jakusits fled to General Teuffel's camp, abandoning the Castle of Ság to us some weeks ago. Now, the heavy Hussar units have arrived, 200 from Győr and 500 from the castles of Léva and Zólyom, their captains are Keglevich, Rátkay, Dessewffy and the riders of Dombay and Sándory. The number of the lighter Hussars is 500 and their captains are Sárkándy, Székely, Rácz."

"Are they renowned warriors?"

"All of them are infamous murderers of the true warriors of the Bright Faced Padisah, especially Takositch and Matasnay."

"Is Captain György Thury among them or Captain Balassa?"

"No, great Pasha, those rabid dogs are not here this time."

"Anybody else?"

"There are 800 Czech mercenaries and 800 hajdu footmen of little value as well. We are informed that there are 7,000 Hungarian noblemen assembled in Fülek Castle who can set out at anytime to join General Teuffel or Devil Matthias, as the Hungarians call him. He is so conceited that he has not even placed sentries on the hilltops around his camp."

The Pasha dismissed the messenger and ordered his water-pipe to be lit. While inhaling the cold smoke he was thinking hard about how he would attack the enemy before further 7,000 horsemen arrived from Fülek. His men were greatly outnumbered already but he had his staunch Janissary units and his Sipahis who were panting for revenge after their losses back at Drégely Castle.

Not to forget his excellent Topcus with their splendid cannons. There was a crescent moon rising in the clear sky which filled his heart with hope.

Csábrág Castle today (photo: Pe-Jo)

"God has brought you, my dear son, I am gladdened to see you. Now that you have arrived I can see we will send the shaven-headed folks back to Asia."

Lord Bishop János Bardelatti-Dudics was an old iron-clad knight who was in charge of the provisions in the camp of Devil Matthias. He was shaking the other man's hand, squeezing it with his powerful grip as if he had wanted to break his fingers. Anybody's fingers would have been crushed, but not György Thury's. He stood out from the crowded camp by his height, and his massive muscles made him look twice his size. Genuine joy sparkled in his blue eyes when he received the old priest's welcome.

"But look, Father, I am also shaven like them." and he was playing with his long tuft that was growing above his forehead and hung down below his huge shoulders. Further jokes were exchanged about how his horizontally waxed mustache looked different from the Turkish fashion who wore their mustache hanging down as a rule. Finally, the young captain came to the point.

"Father Dudics, I have to tell you that you cannot enlist the cannons of Zólyom Castle for a week. The roads are flooded with mud there. I rode here with the two hundred Hussars of Farkas Puchaim from Zólyom leaving my five-hundred men at Bozók Castle to drag those bronze-monsters as best as they can. On the way here, I met the riders of Gáspár Csuthy and János Krusits from Korpona. I saw Menyhárt Macska coming also from Végles, he had more than two hundred horsemen with him."

"So you could not resist missing the dance, my son, well done. Once you are here, we won't need those cannons. Anyway, who has ever heard of making good use of them in an open battle?"

"Times are changing, Father. Alas, cannons were skillfully used by Suleiman at Mohács."

"And how many decent priests died the martyr's death with saber in their hands there." sighed the Bishop "Which saber did you bring here? The scimitar you took from that Arabic Bey in your last duel?"

"Nay, Father, that is a toy. You know that I prefer the good old two-handed Italian swords in the melee," said Thury. He climbed up on a wagon and looked around the forest of tents and the sea of soldiers completing their morning tasks like noisy, enormous ants. He remarked to Bishop Dudics: "I can see some decent warriors from here. Are they any good?"

"Except for the Hussars and the heavy Germans, son, there are no experienced soldiers here. The Czech and the Hungarian footmen are badly supplied with pitiful weapons. They will run at the first cannon shot. Fortunately, His Holiness, the Pope had recruited the Italians for us and they are cunning old foxes, but the rest have never seen Turks in their lives. The landsknechts are formidable with their pikes and muskets but they are green, too. I hope the Hungarian lords can catch up with us, I do not know why they are sitting around so long. Fülek is just a stone's throw from here."

"But we have the Devil Matthias with us." Thury grinned.

"God save us, we have the Devil as our commander." shuddered the old priest, crossing himself. Both of them knew that the Turks had not been beaten in a grand-scale battle since Mohács happened. And that was twenty-six years ago. They would have been chatting about it, but frightened cries disturbed them.

The alarm was hardly sounded when one-thousand hand-picked Sipahi riders appeared in a long line at the edge of the forest without any warning. Green flags were unfurled and the iron-clad horsemen bellowed a terrible battle-cry of „Allahu Akbar" and loosened the reins of their horses making them fly against the Christians. Many of the surprised mercenaries were spiked on spearhead or slain before the units stood up to answer the cavalry charge. Thury immediately hurried to see to his men. Commands in many languages filled the air.

The Sipahis turned and attacked three times before the German cavalry thundered out to trample them with their sheer weight. After some minutes, the Turks turned the heads of their horses and withdrew into the forest. The Germans rushed headlong into the trees where they were greeted by the musket-fire and the spiky halberds of the Janissaries who were hiding among the trees in their usual groups of four warriors. The German heavy cavalry had to come back and while returning, the Sipahis were behind them again. When the Germans chased them angrily back into the woods, everything started again. Then, the Hungarian Hussars decided it was time to join in the game.

vn SPAHIS. 433

The fight went on all morning long in this manner. Many German knights and armored men-at-arms had to bitterly realize a few seconds before their death that the heavily armored Sipahis, despite their smaller numbers, were a perfect match to them. The cuirassed mercenary cavalry had never met with the fury of the Ottoman Sipahis, and now they were heavily tolled. They also paid a high price until they learned not to chase the enemy into the woods. Whoever ventured beyond the tree line was shot from close distance by the Janissaries, or was pulled down from the saddle with halberds and their blood painted the dry fallen leaves crimson.

The arrival of the Hungarian Hussars saved the situation because they knew one or two tricks about the Turks as even their great-grandfathers had learned their warfare. Individual duelists filled the terrain who circled around their opponents like hundreds of whirling mythical beasts. The helmets of the Sipahis and the Hussars were hard to distinguish from each other, but unlike the Germans, they both wore flexible armor with wings attached. The Turk horses wore chain-mail blankets and their bodies were painted in bright colors while the long and spiky shields of the Hungarians were usually decorated with red and white stripes. As their lances had long been broken, the Christians used battle-axes and heavy sabers against the Muslim scimitars.

There was less pushing and shoving when Captain Desewffy went under because of a nasty cut and his men tried to salvage the injured body. Luckily, he was carried away, but many Hussar officers died. Captain Sándory and Dombay were wounded and captured by the enemy. The Sipahis were not able to bear the overpowering Christians and began to weaken. Their officers fought in the front lines, but more and more were slain. The Bey Defterdar was among them.

Meanwhile, the Christian infantry could not get any nearer to the fight so they spread out in the valley which widened into the field at Palást village. The air of confusion was almost palpable but they stood firm in their square formations until the Turkish cannons began to play their dark music from the surrounding hilltops.

There were two high barren ridges on the left and right side of the valley where the Topcus managed to deploy their batteries while the Sipahis and the Janissaries of Agha Arslan distracted the attention of General Teuffel. Fourteen French-made cannons shelled the mercenaries from both sides of the valley. The Topcus were excellent marksmen and were able to see their target clearly from above marveling how precise and fast the new French cannons were. Hot iron missiles cut corridors into the packed formations of the pike men. The dense forest of lances swayed to and fro in the savage storm of artillery fire. This was when Sforza Pallavicini and Dietrich von

Marcel were finally able to make Teuffel accept that he had been snared in a trap. Valuable minutes were spent until they sounded the retreat and began to move inch by inch back behind the cover of the small hills behind them, exposed to the killing bullets and grape-shot for an hour. The Italian pike-musket tercio was especially caught in a cross-fire so they had to spread out and hurry to the left side of the field of Palást where thick bushes and ditches offered some little protection.

Suddenly, Captain Sforza's tercio found themselves separated from the main army by a thicket. He began to give thanks to the Virgin Mary because the Ottoman guns shifted their aim from them and began shelling the landsknechts with full force. He was wrong. The Turks stopped firing at them only because a strong Janissary unit appeared from the left hillside of the valley and hoards of them ambushed the surprised Italians.

The strength of a tercio lay in the smooth and skilled cooperation of the pike men and the musket-men. While they were together in their thick square-formation, the forest of the long pikes could keep any attackers away until the musket-men reloaded and were able to fire their volleys.

Now, they had to spread out because of the terrain and the heavy cannonade. It was exactly what the Janissaries were waiting for. Bitter hand-to-hand combat developed but Sforza knew that without their formation they would not be able to resist for long.

Rapiers were drawn and musket-butts were swung, yatagans and halberds rose and fell. They were doomed.

"Hujj, hujj, hajrá! At them, at them!" cried Captain Thury who noticing the Italians' plight, pulled together some loose Hussars and attacked the side of the Janissaries, sweepingly. Seeing his charge, the men of Captain Jakositch joined him, crying "Jesus, Mary".

Sforza Pallavicini (1519-1585)

The heavy cavalry knocked the elite troops of the Sultan off their feet and trampled them into a pulp in a few minutes. Thury was swinging his double-handed sword with delight, making a harvest of the thronged enemy. He was proud to show these Italians the skills he had learned from the school of Maestro Fiore.

The Janissaries fled to the forest leaving behind their wounded. Captain Sforza crossed himself and his people greeted the Hungarians with cheers and loud applause. But the day was lost. Beaten by inferior numbers, humiliated and outwitted by the Muslims, the army could barely withdraw behind the Krupina Creek that flows from the low hills into the field of Palást.

György Thury was cursing furiously. As furiously as only a Hungarian Hussar officer could or even worse. Hearing it, Bishop Dudics did not stop crossing himself, the old priest could barely refill the wine cups with his left hand.

"Let the Devil take this Devil Matthias for not having posted sentries. How many more valiant soldiers must perish because of his pride and cowardice."

He stopped only to drain his cup and nervously motioned for some more wine.

"My son, you are the hero of the day, everybody talks about how you have saved those Italians. Perhaps, tomorrow morning we can shame this pagan Hadim Ali. Why is he called the 'Gelded', I wonder?"

"Ali was made a eunuch and he is a full-blooded Turk, unlike that cunning Albanian renegade, Pasha Achmed. This Hádim Ali is said to be a cruel man. Did not he make bloodshed in Szeged in March? Did he not take the Castle of Veszprém in June? Did he not promise safe conduct to the handful of surviving defenders? Were they not slain or enslaved immediately after opening the gates? A liar, he is, I tell you, Father. May the Devil take him and fry him together with Devil Matthias. Any more wine you have, Lord Dudics?"

"Drink, son, tonight you have to regain your strength. Gossip has it that after taking Drégely Castle, he gave a decent burial to Captain Szondi, may God rest him."

"The Turk pig did it just to humiliate his Janissaries, a captive said that. Father, Temesvár Castle is currently under siege. Pasha Achmed, the Second Vizier, the leader of the other Ottoman army may take it any minute. They say there are three thousand foreign mercenaries with good Captain Losonczy in the castle. I hope they are better than these landsknechts here. Father, what is next? Eger? Or Kassa? The Mining Towns?"

"My son, let us pray to God that we can stop them tomorrow. Or slow them down, at least . . . Even those four days which were bought with the price of Szondi's blood are precious because the Turks never make war after the 17th day of October. They cannot stand the cold."

They sank into their thoughts and drank on under the shining crescent moon.

"Great Pasha, the infidels are already up and ready. They have been standing in battle formation since dawn all along the field of Palást." Hadim Ali, the Gelded, yawned and stretched his oversized body, his bones creaked. He knew that his troops were also deployed and eager to repeat the success of the previous day.

"Let them stand and sweat in terror for a while. We have to attend the morning prayers before scattering their bones in the field for the feast of the ravens."

So saying, he completed his divine morning chores, then broke his fast. From his tent, he was able to see clearly the deployment of the enemy. He saw the German and Italian squares standing in the middle. Six cannons were placed in front of them, guarded by the Hungarian Hajdús and the Czech footmen. At first glance, he could recognize the flags of the Hungarian cavalry of Győr and Léva on the right wing and saw the German and Spanish cruassiered horsemen on the left. He had hardly finished his coffee when he noticed the enemy stir. As slowly as the pike men could move in close formation, the entire enemy army came into motion. Ali smiled.

"After all, Devil Matthias has at least as much wits as to attack. It is the only way to give some spirit to his men after yesterday's fiasco." he thought and gave the order to answer the attack.

The Topcus fired their beloved cannons with lethal precision and smoke engulfed the field. Dozens of bloody paths were carved into the pike men units. When the thunder ceased, a mighty "Allahu Akbar!" roar went up and a confident, rested army rushed headlong into the midst of the disheartened enemy.

Captain Thury was in a dark mood and after a few clashes the Sipahis superstitiously gave way to him. No scimitar or saber was strong enough against his powerful two-handed blows which fell with the speed of lightning from the most unexpected directions. His men could not follow him so quickly and he had to rein in from time to time so as not to get entangled into the Sipahis's throng. He fought like a berserker, seeing the world in slow motion and his stallion was biting and kicking in the same manner. His flexible Hussar armor and his cloak hanging on his shoulder deflected the accidental hits and cuts he received but he knew that his lads kept an eye on him when his mad fury was on him. Time was not measured and perhaps hours or just minutes had passed, he had no sense. Death arrived among the Sipahis upon his cuts and thrusts whenever he could catch one unaware. The enemy was losing ground and Thury pushed on harder.

An explosion was heard. A huge one, somewhere from the middle where the Hajdús and the Czech fought. Screams of fright and further explosions followed suit. Thury felt his warriors pulling back his horse and saw the gladdened faces of the enemy. Something was wrong. Very wrong. He shook his head and cleared his vision from the killer's frame of mind and he rose in his saddle. Being a head taller than the rest, he could see the Hungarian and the Czech infantry fleeing headlessly, throwing away their rusty swords and makeshift spears. Black pillars rose from where the supply wagons for the cannons used to be.

The enemy roared and attacked with renewed frenzy and the morale of the Christians shrank. Thury was not in control of his men, not even over his horse. The Turks sensed his wavering and closed on him angrily. Miklós Borsán, a Hussar officer threw himself bodily to receive the cut aimed at his leader's head and slid off of his saddle. Farkas Suly, Thury's trusted man was the second to give his life for him. He lost one more lieutenant, Kristóf Rozsony, before realizing the end.

"It is enough!" Thury cried and turned the head of his horse back and added: "Sound the retreat."

The cavalry units quit the battle one by one, galloping past the tercios of the mercenaries who were equally shaken but still standing. Dietrich von Marcel managed to keep his landsknechts together for a while but some soldiers in the rear ranks dropped their long pikes and sneaked away. Von Marcel cursed and shot one of them. The Janissaries were breaking the pikes with their halberds and some of them fell on all-fours and were creeping under the pikes, with their short, inward-curved yatagans between their teeth. When they reached the Germans, the yatagans sliced ankles, sinews, causing terrible destruction and havoc. Before long, they all threw away their pikes and muskets and began to run madly toward the forest, with the savagely screaming Turkish riders at their heels, slaughtering them without mercy.

The Italians saw this and they knew what would befall them if they gave in to panic. The seasoned mercenaries from Rome gritted their teeth but stood their ground. Captain Sforza Pallavicini saw that they were the last tercio still fighting. "Virgin Mary, as only if we could retreat until the fringe of the forest in an intact formation." he thought and gave out the orders to inch backward. These were the Italian units which survived the battle at Buda Castle ten years ago when the Ottomans defeated the German army. Then, Sforza could only survive it by keeping their discipline firm and endure the artillery fire with cold blood.

The forest was still painfully far away when the Topcus rolled out the cannons and took aim. The first volley killed his nephew, Hipolit Pallavicini. He saw his two officers fall, Mark Tiburtino and Albert Castro. Sforza prayed like an Italian and cursed like a Hungarian at the same time. The second volley killed his friend, Vincent Altimori and people began to drop their pikes. The forest was just five-hundred yards away and the Italians suddenly broke and ran. Sforza was desperately looking around, waiting for the light Akinji riders to finish them off. In a second, the Akinjis did appear and Sforza, his thin rapier in hand, faced them alone because he preferred to receive the killing blow, not from the back. Then, he dropped his jaw in surprise because miracles usually do not happen twice.

"Mio Dio, it is that daredevil Thury again," he muttered and watched with cow-eyes how a small unit of no more than hundred Hussars cut in the side of the Akinji riders, beating them back with ease.

Sforza quickly made after his men and they reached the shelter of the "green fortress" where they had enough brains to reassemble. The Hussars stayed not a minute longer and slid away when seeing a Sipahi contingent turning against them. Among the trees, he was surprised to meet General Erasmus von Teuffel, busily changing into clothes he had pulled from the corpse of a landsknecht.

"I am not going to tell the rotten pagans who I am when they take me into captivity. They will not get rich from my ransom . . . " Teuffel was raging. Sforza turned away from him with contempt and shot his last orders to his mercenaries:

"Make a circle, musket-men are in the second rank, fire at my command. Lads, we can negotiate for a better condition only if we can demonstrate at least some strength. The Pope will ransom us, His Holiness had promised it. Avanti, move your asses."

The next morning the field of Palást was covered with the bodies of the dead and the injured. Asabs and Akinjis were browsing the land and collecting their wounded and finishing off the infidels still breathing. Some renegade pribéks accompanied them to sever the heads of the dead Ghiaurs. It was a greasy job, disliked by a true Muslim, but the heads had to be collected, salted and thrown on wagons. Sultan Suleiman the Magnificent was anticipating these kinds of trophies in Istanbul. Besides, he paid a gold coin for each one. It was all right, King Ferdinand of the Ghiaurs paid the same price for Turkish heads in Vienna.

So the job had to be done. Bey Achmed and Bey Ibrahim, the two former captives of Captain Szondi, were in charge of a small unit of pribéks. They had long staffs and punished the pribéks who tried to steal a gold ring or a necklace from the corpses. The booty belonged to Pasha Ali and he had strict orders about it.

Libardi and Sebestyén, the pages of Captain Szondi, had to come along as they were put under the control of the two beys. The boys followed the pribeks with sullen faces, bloody up to their knees. They arrived at the camp of the Christians the wagons had long been pillaged. Corpses and garbage covered everything.

"Look, Sebestyén," cried Libardi "It is Father Dudics!"

Horrified, they saw the old Bishop of Vác lying on his back, his white mustache red. His fist was gripping a broken saber and six dead Janissaries surrounded him. One of the pribéks stepped to him and probed him with his leg. When he proved to be no dangerous anymore, he grinned, spat on him and raised his saber to cut the priest's head off. Libardi jumped. Oh yes, he had learned how to disarm a soldier with his bare hands. The pribék screamed and the young lad brought the wretch to the ground, breaking his arm with a loud crack. In the meantime, Sebestyén threw himself on the body of Father Dudics and was shouting in Turkish:

"No, you cannot take his head, except you take mine, too. I appeal to Pasha Ali!"

Bey Ibrahim and Achmed had to use their wooden staffs and all their authority to keep away the angry Asabs who wanted to cut the lads into mince-meat. The boys were ushered to the Pasha of Buda at once. Hádim Ali was annoyed to see the two kneeling troublemakers in front of his tent. He ordered a slight punishment, twenty beating with a stick on their bare soles but being righteous, he heard the pages out.

"Do you have anything to say?"

"Yes, noble Pasha" Libardi replied, "First, I thank for your lenient judgment and the light punishment. The dead man I wanted to save was the priest who had buried my late father and the one who sent me to serve Captain Szondy. I owed this much to him. Please, merciful and just Pasha, allow the decent burial of this man with his head staying on his neck. In return, I can tell you a secret."

"What secret may you have? Be quick," asked Ali, annoyedly.

"Great Pasha, everybody is looking for the corpse of General Teuffel or as we call him, Devil Matthias. The one who had been cowardly afraid to help my good lord Szondi. I happen to know that this enemy of yours is still alive, moreover, he is hiding in a mercenary's disguise among the 4,000 captives you had taken, victorious Pasha, because he does not want to pay a high ransom for himself. Everybody knows that Captain Sforza's ransom is between 16-20,000 gold Ducats and Devil Matthias wants to cheat you and the Sultan with approximately the same amount. "

Hádim Ali was a cunning man, indeed. He grinned and told the page:

"Find him and show him to Bey Ibrahim but let Devil Matthias think he had misled us. Bey Ibrahim, I order you to follow Devil Matthias and Sforza and beat them with your long staff all the way until you reach the Sublime Porte in Istanbul. There, he may uncover his identity before His Majesty, the Magnificent Padisah and save his life from the slow and painful impalement."

Libardi and Sebestyén were dismissed and after their punishment, they could not walk for a day but soon they limped with Bey Ibrahim to the camp of the prisoners. Not much later, Libardi pointed at a man who had a long, distinctive red beard and was sitting apart from the Italians who sent despising looks towards him.

"He is Devil Matthias, the real murderer of my poor lord György Szondi, his pride and cowardice has caused the perishing of many thousand good Christian soldiers. May he burn in hell."

26. Eger Castle   GPS: 47.905782, 20.375939

The castle of Eger (Erlau in German) is in North Hungary where the Bükk Mountains meet the Great Hungarian Plain. It was guarding roads toward the mining cities in the west of Upper Hungary and to the east, to the great city of Kassa (Kosice, Kaschau).

Eger became world famous for its good red wine and for the victorious siege against the Ottomans in 1552.
The castle dates back to the 6th century AD. And already in the 11th century it could boast stone walls that were six meters tall and two meters wide. The city became a center of a bishopric in King Saint Stephen's age of 1009. According to legend, it was Saint Stephan himself who personally oversaw the construction of the cathedral of the town. The masons finished the great church ten years later and they built a stone wall around the town, too. It was during this time that the first moat and drawbridge were built. They also dug a 75-meter-deep well into the cliff inside the castle that was 2.5 meters wide. The whole construction work was not finished when in 1047 the rebelling troops of the pagan Chief Vata took the castle and caused great damage to it. The Mongols were the next to take it in 1241 and destroyed it along with the town.

The castle's rebuilding began only after 1248 and it was Bishop Lambert who finished it in 1261. The peaceful days lasted until 1271 when the beloved nomadic Kuman warriors of King László IV destroyed it. The castle was given into the Bishop of Eger's charge in 1275 and it was

Bishop Csanád Teleghdy who restarted the construction. All the bishops added something to it and finally, it was Bishop Miklós II who completed it in 1350. A tower wears his name above the Old Gate of the castle. The famous wine production of Eger dates back to the 14th century. There is a document from 1379 which mentions the castle as the property of "Saint John, the Apostle". After the death of King Louis I (1382), the bishop of Eger, Tamás Ludányi, got hold of the castle. Ludányi was unlucky to have sided with the opposers of the new king, Sigismund (who ruled between 1387 and 1437), so he had to flee to Poland. Bishop Simon Rozgonyi was the new lord after him.

Eger Castle

Not much time later, in 1446, a shameful event happened during the visit of a noble Polish guest called Peter Ozdrovácz. A part of the castle's garrison celebrated his arrival with the Polish knight's men by drinking the famous wine cellars dry around the city of Eger so their duty of guarding the walls was neglected. The Czech Hussite leader, Telefusz, was lurking nearby with his mercenaries and they quickly took advantage of the situation. The Hussites ambushed the castle and killed everyone who could not hide, and then they set the castle and the town on fire. Loaded with rich booty, they hastily left. The Hussites had also captured the Polish Péter Ozdrovácz and took him with them. But they did not get far because the Hungarian and Polish troops sobered up and quickly made after them defeating them in a roadside battle. Most of the mercenaries were slaughtered and now it was Ozdrovácz who took the Czech Telefusz prisoner and closed him in the dungeons of Eger castle.

Bishop Rozgonyi learned a lesson from the ambush and had a stand-alone 20 meter high bastion built in the middle section of the southern wall of the castle. They called it the Szépbásyta (Nice Bastion) and it became the armory and storage for military equipment.

The Bishop's castle went to László Héderváry then it was given to Orbán Dóczy, the Chief Treasurer and Guardian of the Crown of King Matthias.

After the death of our greatest king, Matthias Corvinus, in 1490 the Austrian Duke Habsburg Albert tried to take Eger. When he failed to do so, he set the town on fire before going away. It was the Italian Ipolito d'Este who had the burned cathedral repaired and equipped the garrison with proper weapons.

Unfortunately, the well-supplied garrison opened the castle's gates in 1514 before Barabás, a commander of the rebelling peasant army of György Dózsa.

After the Battle of Mohács in 1526, the Dual Kingship tore the country in two and Eger was either in the hands of King János Szapolyai or in King Habsburg Ferdinand I's. Ferenc Bodó, a commander of King Szapolyai took it in 1527 and he cruelly slaughtered the greater part of its garrison. King Ferdinand I sent a big reinforcing army, but instead of enduring a siege, Bodó attacked them at Keresztes where he was beaten. The few remaining soldiers of Eger surrendered the castle to the king after this.

King Szapolyai took the castle back in 1529 but it was in the hands of the enemy again in 1530 when Gáspár Serédi, a captain of Upper Hungary seized it. Eger changed hands in 1534 again when it went to the great lord Péter Perényi's possession. It was Perényi's man, Captain Tamás Varkoch, who, in 1542 began a grand-scale construction in the castle according to the plans of Alessandro da Vedano. He had the church of Orbán Dóczy pulled down and had the famous Sanctuary (Szentély) Bastion built on the top of the Nice Bastion. He had another massive bastion built, the Sándor Bastion. He had a huge moat dug which divided the castle into two, this is how the inner castle was separated from the outer castle. A new tower was erected on the southern wall which was guarding the southern gate. This tower got its name after the Captain and was called Varkoch. Moreover, the Tömlöc (Dungeon) Bastion was also built so the castle now looked like an enormous turtle. The walls were strengthened by numerous earthen structures which were five meters high and appeared every 200 meters in front of the walls.

King Ferdinand had Peter Perényi imprisoned, but Captain Varkoch was so fond of turning Eger into a fortress that he refused to cede the castle to the king. Finally, his faithfulness to his overlord paid off because Ferdinand had to release Perényi in exchange for getting his royal hands on the formidable stronghold of Eger in 1548. Unfortunately, Perényi couldn't enjoy his freedom for long because he died on his way home.

King Ferdinand, according to the military fashion of the age, appointed two captains to command Eger castle, István Dobó, and Ferenc Zay. They carried on with the rebuilding that had to be done because of the improvement in firearms. Dobó had the „Dobó" bastion built in the inner castle in the old-Italian fashion and had the living quarters of the officers and the pages built along the western walls. He added another bastion next to the Dungeon Bastion which was called Earth Bastion.

This was the situation right before the famous 39 day siege of Eger in 1552 when Captain István Dobó beat back the overwhelming Ottoman army who besieged its walls. The siege was significant because it was the first major defeat of the Turks after the Battle of Mohács and under the ruined walls of Eger their invincible reputation evaporated. After the victory, Dobó and his officers resigned in order to protest King Ferdinand's refusal to contribute any material help to the defense.

The king accepted Dobó's resignation and made him the Voivode of Transylvania, sending him to command Szamosújvár but his family had to live in the castle of Déva. The Court tended to distrust the wealthy Hungarian lords and at times the always empty Treasury was filled with the gold of those who were accused of treason. These victims were mostly innocent like Dobó who was arrested in 1556 for a similar reason. He was able to escape from his prison only a year later. However, King Miksa (Maximilian) decided to pardon him and granted him further lands and titles in 1558.

Gergely Bornemissza, Dobó's cleverest officer during the siege, was appointed to take over command in Eger. Some years later the Turks took revenge on him. The hot-headed Captain rode out with a small unit that was insufficient to beat the Turk raiders of Hatvan castle. In the battle, he was captured and taken to Istanbul. It was Pasha Achmed, the unsuccessful besieger of Eger Castle who gave the order to hang him.

The new Captain became the other famous officer of the siege, István Zoltay. He carried on with the repairs that Bornemissza had begun earlier. Two Italian architects, Francesco Pozzo and Martino Remiglio were in charge of the reconstruction. A third Italian engineer, Ottavio Baldigara, continued their work between 1572 and 1583. He had planned five new bastions but could build only four of them, the last one remained unfinished. The famous Hungarian knight and poet, Bálint Balassi, also served here for a few years beginning in April 1578.

The fortress of Eger remained defiant of Ottoman attacks until 1596 when 7,000 defenders, mostly foreign mercenaries, capitulated to the Ottoman forces personally commanded by the Sultan Mehmed III, after three weeks of siege. The Turks immediately had the walls repaired and they also reinforced the main entrance with a new fortification that is now known as the Turkish Garden. The town remained in Ottoman hands for 91 years. The minaret, which was built at the end of the 17th century, preserves the memory of this period. Among all the buildings of this type, the minaret of Eger is found in the northernmost point of the former Ottoman Empire. During the Turkish occupation, Eger became the seat of a Vilayet which is a Turkish domain including several Sanjaks. Churches were converted into mosques and other structures were erected, including public baths.

The castle of Eger was surrendered by Pasha Rusztem to the Christian army led by Count János Doria in 1687. The Pasha ran out of food during the 6 month long siege. His troops were starved out and the town fell into a very poor state. According to the records, there were only 413 houses in the area within the town walls which were habitable and most of these were occupied by Turkish families. These Turks later became Hungarians and settled around the castle of the nearby Szarvaskő.

Emperor Lipót I (Leopold) sent a military engineer called Dumont to Eger in 1702 who was instructed to have the whole outer castle blown up which he obediently did.

During the War of Independence of Prince Ferenc II Rákóczi in 1704, the rebelling Kuruc forces laid a 408-day-long siege on the fort until the imperial soldiers opened its gates. General Cuseni could take Eger back only in 1710 and it marked the end of the castle's military importance.

27. The Siege of Eger Castle (1552)

Pasha Hádim Ali of Buda, the Gelded, was the first to arrive at the Castle of Eger on 11 September. The forces of the Serdar, Kara Ali and the third army of Begler Bey Szokolu Mehmed had not arrived yet and it filled Ali's heart with joy. After building his camp on the northern side of the city he immediately had his four huge siege cannons positioned against the well-fortified walls of Eger which looked like an enormous turtle. He knew that the war season would come to its end on 26 October. It was the final payday, the day of Kaszim for the true Muslims and the day of Saint Demetrius for the Orthodox Serbian mercenaries who served in the Sultan's army in great numbers. The unwritten custom of the Janissaries, who hated the cold weather, demanded the leaving of the frosty land of the infidels behind so he wanted to finish his successful campaign with the taking of this strategic city.

The pasha watched as his Topcu artillerymen adjusted their beloved western-made cannons which had served them so well at the siege of Drégely Castle and on the battlefield of Palást. He thought of his costly victory at Drégely and recalled how Captain Szondi humiliated the Janissaries by repelling their fiercest attacks for four days with his mere 146 men before his death.

"Praise be to Allah," he thought "the Janissaries were so ashamed that they could hardly wait to make amends in the battle over the infidel Teuffel's army a month later." While he looked at how his Topcus fired their cannons for the first time to measure the right distance correctly he recalled the pleasant victories of this summer. How he and Kara Achmed had taken Veszprém and Temesvár, not to forget Szolnok and Lippa as well as some twenty-five Hungarian strongholds. Thinking of Kara Achmed, he winced. The mighty Serdar's troops were due to arrive anytime now. He disliked him for his pride, but the third commander, Begler Bey Szokolu Mehmed of Rumelia, was not to his liking, either. As Ali, the Gelded was a true noble Anatolian he despised the Croatian renegade Szokoli who was an upstart regardless of his martial deeds.

The Sultan's army had to take Eger so as to open the road to the fabulous mining towns to the northwest. Eger was their only obstacle towards Kassa, the great town which was the key city of the eastern part of the Hungarian Upper Lands. Eger was doomed to fall.

Within two days, Kara Achmed and Szokoli Mehmed arrived and made their camps on the western and eastern sides of Eger. All the other beys and pashas managed to obey the order of the Serdar in time and the commanders from the Ottoman Occupied Lands of Hungary joined them. Pasha Hanivár came from Belgrade, Pasha Arslan arrived from Székesfehérvár along with Bey Dervis from Pécs and Pasha Mehemed from Szendrő.

By the evening of 13 September, Bey Mustafa from Szeged and Bey Veli from Hatvan saluted the Serdar but they did not have to wait for Bey Kamber from Illyria and for Bey Uláma from Bosnia, either. As a whole, they could boast almost 45,000 warriors. The Ottomans had 16 Zarbuzans, which were very large siege cannons, as well as 150 medium and smaller pieces of artillery. They had a fleet of two thousand camels, which proved to be highly useful in the collection and transportation of wood to the site used for the construction of temporary siege platforms.

Serdar Kara Achmed contributed twice as many troops to the united army, but he appreciated Hádim Ali's wise strategic talent and his skill in artillery. The Serdar received him and Szokoli Mehmed in his recently erected tent and asked Ali:

"Wise Pasha of Buda, as you were able to arrive here first you must know the details of this miserable sheep-pen that we will take easily and quickly for the Glory of the Bright Faced Padisah. Enlighten me and the noble Begler Bey with the report you most likely have made for us."

Eger Castle

Hádim Ali bowed and hid his smile. Everybody knew he had the best network of spies and renegade 'pribéks'.

"Most valiant Serdar, may Allah pave your way to the seventh Heaven with joy. Indeed, I have a 'pribék' who can come and go between us and the infidels' castle like a ghost. Although the number of the defenders is just 2,364 men, their commander is a cunning enemy of the Islam, a certain Lord István Dobó. He has filled the stores and chambers of his castle with provisions and supplies that would feed them until winter. Then, he sent away all of the people whom he thought would burden him and made the remaining men and women alike swear a terrible oath to hold Eger to their last dying breath. Dobó desperately asked for help from his king, but it was mostly in vain. Some reinforcement arrived only from the other castles near Eger and from the villages."

"Will the Habsburg king send him reinforcement?" Szokuli Mehmed interrupted.

"Great Begler Bey, the Imperial troops are idly waiting for the order of their cowardly king at Győr, which will never be issued. They are allowed to block the way to Vienna, but they are strictly banned from taking any action."

"If they knew how many good Janissaries you lost during the summer they would certainly make haste, oh, victor of the Sultan," remarked Szokuli Mehmed. Kara Achmed furrowed his brows and investigated further:

"It is most likely that those landsknechts in Győr will run whiningly to their master, King Ferdinand, in fear of our swords. Tell me, Pasha Ali, how many cannons are in this sheep-pen?"

"The defenders have only six large and about a dozen smaller cannon and additionally, about three-hundred trench guns which are also called "hook-guns" or Arquebuses. The cannons are said to have been wisely deployed even behind the inner castle's walls so as to cover the entire fort with their fire. As for gunpowder, they have two dry mills which can produce ample supplies of ammunition. Glorious Serdar, the sheep of this pen have rather desperately prepared to face us."

"What makes you think so?"

"Their morale is high because the defender of Drégely Castle, György Szondi, provided them an example of valor. On the other hand, they recall how your forces, mighty commander, slaughtered Captain István Losonczy when they surrendered the Castle of Temesvár to you in exchange for safe conduct."

"By the holiest beard of the Prophet, you are trying to accuse me of cruelty with your honeyed words? Did you not do the same thing when you took Szeged and Veszprém Castles? We both know that the oaths given to the infidels can be changed anytime a true Muslim would think it proper. Instead of this talk, go and aim the church towers of the castle with your renowned cannons so as to prevent them to see into our camp. Besides, we could have started the siege a lot earlier if you hadn't wasted your time by going back to Buda Castle after the Battle of Palást. You wanted to sell the German captives in the slave market of Buda and in your greed you neglected the duty to the Padisah. Now, be dismissed."

Hádim Ali was choking with fury because the Serdar was right. On top of this reproach he could not boast of a huge income from the captured landsknechts because those cunning traders pushed down the price so much that even a sack of flour was too much for a healthy German infantryman. Seeing the flabby eunuch gone the Serdar summoned a clerk. He turned to Bey Mehmed, saying:

"Have the following letter delivered to this Captain Dobó and let us see whether he would make his pants dirty in fear for his life, or not. Write him the next. I, Serdar of the Bright Faced Padisah, Kara Achmed, demand you and warn you to seek for the mercy of the mighty and righteous Sultan Suleiman instead of experiencing the edge of his weapons and surrender Eger Castle at once. In this case, I will grant you your lives and properties and even give you all the old privileges you used to have at the time of your former king. Yet, if you want to stubbornly insist on defending your castle, you will lose not only your property but also your children and your own lives."

The letter was quickly sent and Dobó's answer did not make the Turks wait a long time. A black coffin was hung out from two spears in front of the southern wall to show how he and his men were all prepared to die a decent warrior's death. The cannons of Hádim Ali began to roar . . .

The bombardment lasted for two full weeks and paused only for a couple of days when they ran out of cannon balls which were carved out of marble and weighed 100 pounds. The lack of supply was unusual in the well-organized Ottoman army and tensions grew between Hádim Ali and the Serdar who mutually blamed each other for the lack. The eunuch proved himself superior in commanding his Topcu soldiers, though. Each night Ali had his Zarbuzans deploy closer to the walls. As a result of this, his four cannons caused greater damage than the twelve Zarbuzans of Achmed and Mehmed altogether. The walls were so ruined that toward the end of the bombardment even a rider could climb through them in many places. To Ali's annoyance, Captain Dobó had the breaches repaired during the night as if he commanded hundreds of Djinnies. He had the gaps and breaches filled with earth and timber. Luckily, the makeshift masonry was easy to destroy.

To hinder the cannonade, the officers of Dobó would break out of the castle with their picked Hussar warriors at the most unexpected times during the siege and caused great harm and confusion, especially when they sallied out at night. Ali's pribék informed the Pasha that Vice-Captain István Mecskey and other officers like Fügedy and Zoltay were leading these heroic assaults. Soon, there were enough breaches and Kara Achmed gave the order to launch the first general attack on 29 September which was regarded as the day of Saint Michael amid the Christians.

Thousands ran against the throats of the infidel's cannons and hundreds never reached the foot of the walls. The castle was assaulted from all sides. The Turks scaled the walls and the breaches by wide ladders which enabled six-seven soldiers to climb up next to each other. The main attack was aimed at the outer castle and at the two bastions of the inner castle which lay on the north-west. According to the report of his pribék, Hádim Ali knew that their defense was in the hands of the four Chief-Lieutenants, namely the cunning Gergely Bornemissza and János Fügedy as well as Gáspár Pethő and István Zoltay. He knew that Dobó and his Vice-Captain Mecskey were overseeing the fight from the inner castle.

Terrible hand-to-hand combat raged on the ramparts all around the turtle-shaped fort. The Ottomans wore no heavy armor just a shield in order to climb swiftly but the Hungarians were clad in iron from tip to toe and received them with long spears and battle-axes. The Angel of Death harvested among the Turks but they managed to seize a tower where the first green flags of the Prophet were being unfolded. A huge cry to Allah arose from the thronged troops which oppressed the frightened "Jesus, Jesus" calls of the defenders. The tower was in the Turk's hands and hundreds pushed themselves inside of it. Hádim Ali watched the assault from his tent and a bad feeling crept up his spine. And that very thing happened in the next minute; just what he would have done himself. Dobó had cleverly deployed his biggest guns in the inner fort exactly for such incidents. All these guns were turned towards the occupied tower and sent a deadly volley into the weakest lower inner part of the building. The massive tower swayed and collapsed in a cloud of dust and gunpowder, burying the victorious Turks under the rubble. It was the end of the assault. The Ottoman warriors' morale broke and nobody could stop their retreat to the camp.

The bombardment of the castle went on and the cold fog of autumn mixed with the white cloud of smoke coming from the Zarbuzans and the smaller battle-snakes. Hádim Ali paid only the most necessary of visits to the Serdar and ignored Szokoli Mehmed at large. He was deeply hurt and told Kara Achmed that his artillery skills would perhaps speak less sweetly, but much louder than his words. The Pasha of Buda worked hard and seemingly had lost some weight while instructing his beloved Topcu soldiers in person. He had keen eyesight and was not shy to dirty his kaftan by adjusting the barrel of his Zarbuzans himself, aiming at the Cathedral of the inner castle where the infidels were storing their gunpowder according to his "pribék". It was already the fourth day of October and some progress had to be made because the soldier's morale was very low.

The Zarbuzans were fired and Ali wiped the blackened sweat from his eyes. To his great surprise, the roar of cannons was suddenly overpowered by a huge explosion coming from the castle. The Cathedral was gone, rubble showered on them even in the Turk camp and a terrible white smoke cloud engulfed the castle of Eger. Deadly silence commenced. Then, a huge shout of Allah went up and the entire Ottoman army rushed against the walls, not waiting for the orders of the officers.

Indeed, it was a red-hot cannonball of Hádim Ali which blew up the greater part of the gunpowder supplies of the defenders, causing damage in lives and walls, while shaking their morale at the same time. The Turks ran against the ruined bastions of the turtle and assaulted the great gate as well. It was Dobó's smartest officer, Gergely Bornemissza, who saved the Christians from this peril. He had devised primitive, but lethal, grenades and powder keg sized bombs to use against the attackers as well as a water-mill wheel packed with gunpowder which he rolled into the Ottoman ranks. His secret lay in the gunpowder not simply exploding but sparking even more fire. He loaded these weapons with oil, sulfur, and flint in order to shower the enemy with burning missiles.

Even after the storage tower containing 24 tons of black gunpowder exploded and caused extensive structural damage the invaders still could not find a way into the castle compound and they had to retreat again. The bombardment went on and Kara Achmed tried to outdo Hádim Ali. He tried to dig tunnels in order to collapse the walls using mines. Yet, Dobó had counter tunnels dug and all his attempts failed. Bey Szokoli had a different plan in mind. He borrowed Hádim Ali's "pribék" and tried to bribe István Hegedűs, one of the officers, but his plot was revealed and Dobó had Hegedűs hanged along with the "pribék".

The Turks had expected an easy victory, but the bravery of the castle's defenders, as well as Dobó's inspired leadership, resisted and repulsed the repeated Ottoman assaults. Despite the difference in troop numbers, Eger's strong walls and the steadiness of its defenders allowed the fortress to withstand five major assaults and continuous cannon fire. Excluding the ones stuck in the walls of the stronghold, almost 12,000 cannon balls landed inside the fortress.

This was how 12 October came about. There was frost inside the tents at night and the soldiers suffered from epidemics. The Pasha of Buda and the Serdar agreed that they have to force victory by launching a great overall assault. Although the Ottoman warriors proved an unearthly heroism in fighting from early morning until late at night their efforts were put down by the desperate defenders. The women of Eger took part in a sizable portion of fighting on the walls, pouring boiling water or tar over the advancing Turks or taking up sabers and spears themselves. Helping their men in combat was not uncommon among the women folk of the Borderland, but for the women of Eger, their heroism has become legendary. It was all the more humiliating for the Muslims having been beaten by women.

After the unsuccessful assault new gossip began to spread among the soldiers. Ali knew the source of it, but he was unable to fight against the legend that the Hungarians were fighting with the strength of bulls because they were drinking the blood of bulls. Ali knew it was not true, the Hungarians were only consuming huge quantities of good red wine during the fight which turned the soldier's beards the color red. The mood of the Muslims was sinking every day with the coming of the freezing nights and the heavy rains of autumn. They complained to their officers and the Janissaries were close to mutiny claiming that Allah was on the Hungarians' side and they would not fight against God.

Indeed, the Turk's casualties were innumerable. In addition to this, the reduced rice rations and allegations of corruption among the officers caused further discontent. Kara Achmed was raging and gave a strict order to repeat the assault the next day. In the morning, the Ottoman officers had to put aside their whips and use their naked blades to herd the tired soldiers to launch the assault.

Several bastions and gates were attacked at the same time, but the losses were very high and they were beaten back. The following three days were spent in collecting the dead and burying them.

The fighting mood of the troops in the irregular units had been decreasing for many days, but the Serdar wanted to force them to launch a final attack. He reasoned that the Hungarians had also lost one-third of their number and they were fatigued enough having given up faith that King Ferdinand would send them reinforcements. To his dismay, even the most disciplined Janissaries refused to continue the fight and they plainly refused the orders from their own Agha officers. It meant the end of the siege, and of the campaign, because the irregular troops would have never fought without the Janissaries.

After forty days of bloody fighting, after this brutal and intense struggle, the Ottoman Army withdrew, beaten and humiliated. The troops of the Serdar and the units of Szokoli Mehmed left the camp on 17 October. Hádim Ali, the Gelded, followed them a day later. He was the first to arrive and the last to leave. Ali felt his position as the Pasha of Buda quite stable, but he thought he should blame this last failure of an otherwise very successful campaign on the Serdar and on the Rumelian Begler Bey. Ali had a good friend in Istanbul, Pasha Dzselálzáde Mustapha. He had a high-ranking position near the Sultan's ear as his poet and historian.

Before the Serdar could reach the Sublime Porte in Istanbul, Pasha Dzelálzáde Mustapha had already read the letter of the Pasha of Buda. Among other things, Hádim Ali wrote him the following:
"The number of the fallen martyrs who died at the walls of the castle is countless. The fight had been going on for forty days but it was impossible for the Serdar to take the fort easily because its bastions were towering into the sky and the foundation of its walls was in the sea. The defenders were perfect masters of preventing their disaster and they were briskly applying all the tricks and snares of the martial arts. Furthermore, this matchless castle was built on an extremely inaccessible location. As Allah had ordered, the winter season and the cold weather have arrived and the patience and calmness have disappeared due to the rain and snow. There was a shortage of food supplies, which has made the troops worried and the cold has disturbed the patience of the animals. As the time of taking this castle had been destined and postponed to a later date by Allah, the Serdar thought it reasonable and better if he withdrew the army from the castle and give up the fight and the siege."

28. Salgó Castle   GPS: 48.144546, 19.846735

Salgó castle is located in Hungary on the northern border. It is silently facing Somoskő castle on the top of a 625-meter-high hill. The small castle was built after the Mongolian invasion of 1242 by the Kacsics family. We know that in 1246 its lord was called Péter; he was the ancestor of the Salgói family. When he died, his brother Simon inherited it. Simon had been involved in the murder of Queen Gertrudis, the wife of King András II, in 1213. It is rather interesting to note that neither King András II nor his son, King Béla IV could take revenge on this high ranked nobleman. The members of the Salgói family passed the castle on from generation to generation. We know that after Simon's ownership, his sons, Miklós and Simon followed suit. It was Miklós who had the castle rebuilt.

Salgó castle started as a small tower according to the fashion of early medieval castles and it had a small castle-yard. It is thought that the cellar of the tower was used as a prison. Obtaining a good water-supply was difficult on this volcanic rock, therefore on the lower level of the peak, under the tower, they constructed a water-collecting cistern. This rock-castle had two cisterns, a huge one and a smaller one. The water was essential, as it served not only for drinking but also for firefighting in case of a siege.

The next heirs were Illés and his brother, another Miklós in 1327. The first document that mentions the castle is from 1331. The castle was still in the hands of the Salgói family in 1348, but later in 1387, it is referred to as a royal castle. King Sigismund gave it to a chief bodyguard of his in 1399. This bodyguard was called Simon and was from the Szécsi family whose descendants were later also called Salgói. When Simon died, his son Miklós took the castle over, but the king took the castle back from him because of his villainous lifestyle. Then, the king passed the castle on to László of Szécsi, the Chief Comes of Nógrád County.

The fortification was controlled by the Czech Hussites in 1450 for ten years until King Matthias beat them out. According to legend, the king was personally leading the siege and was injured by an arrow that struck him in his face. He was so angered by this that he had the previously occupied castle of Zagyvafő, which stood nearby Salgó castle, pulled down.

Perhaps King Matthias did not want to keep Salgó Castle due to the bad experience because in 1470 he gave it to László Cseh of Léva and Palatine Mihály Országh of Guth. Not much later, Salgó Castle was gifted to Imre Szapolyai, a great lord of the king. Rumor says that the Szapolyai family had a hand in the poisoning of poor King Matthias in 1490.

We will never know for sure, but it is a fact that the Szapolyai family provided the next king of Hungary after the tragic Battle of Mohács in 1526. There is hearsay whispered that János Szapolyai let the young King Louis II die on the battlefield so as to gain the throne for himself.

King János Szapolyai did not keep Salgó Castle either but gifted it to Mihály Szobi, then it ended up in the hands of the Palatine István Werbőczy in 1527. At this time, the lower castle-yard was built in and the upper castle-yard became roofed over. This part of the yard became a living space. The lord of the castle, István Werbőczy did not live in Salgó but his substitute the castellan lived in the upper yard living quarters. In the lower castle yard there were stables and storehouses.

Salgó Castle today (Photo: Civertan Grafik)

Later, the castle was owned by the infamous robber knight, Ferenc Bebek in 1542. He was perhaps one of the most interesting characters of the medieval Upper Lands of Hungary he was a villain yet a valiant knight against the Turks at the same time. Lord Bebek got the king's permission to sell Salgó Castle for 8,000 gold Forints to Farkas Derencsényi in 1548. King Ferdinand I accepted Derencsényi as the captain of the castle, but at the same time, the king imprisoned the former owner, Ferenc Bebek in Salgó Castle for forging money in secret. It is not known how Derencsényi handled the situation and how he treated the seller of his castle. They may have even become friends.

During the Dual Kingship, many Hungarian noblemen changed sides, sometimes annually. Many of them looked only at their personal interests and this was not considered immoral according to contemporary public opinion. Yet, there were many who could not decide which king could protect the country better from the Ottomans, Ferdinand or Szapolyai.

The Turks were threatening from all sides so Captain Derencsényi tried to reinforce the castle against them and had a pentagonal bastion built on the east side of the rock at the old tower. Salgó Castle was officially enlisted as a Borderland Castle and was waiting for the advancing enemy.

Ferenc Zagyva, its next captain in 1554, was the one who surrendered the castle to Bey Kara (Black) Hamza of Szécsény and Hatvan Castle. The legend of the castle tells its tale with different names. Unlike as described in the legend, the fortress was shelled into ruins by the Turks. They set artillery on top of the neighboring hill, called Kis-Salgó (Small-Salgó) or Boszorkánykő (The cliff of witches) opposite to Salgó.

The father of Bálint Balassi, the great Hungarian poet, was given the fortress in spite of the fact that the Turkish were in it. In this period, monarchs liked to gift places that were in the Ottoman Occupied Lands. More surprising is that that the new landlord was accepted by the locals who even tried to send him taxes.

The Turks owned Salgó Castle until the beginning of the 15-Year-War. The Christians, led by Kristóf Tiefenbach and Miklós Pálffy, set out in 1593 and during their first successful campaign they took back many Hungarian castles from the Muslims. They seized the nearby Fülek Castle as well and a smaller contingent was sent from there to liberate Salgó and Somoskő castles. It was Bálint Prépostvári who led them and the warrior-poet Bálint Balassa was riding in his company.

According to some sources, both Salgó and Somoskő castles were surrendered without a fight, but it is also said that at Salgó, the fortress was taken by using heavy cannons and that the occupying army utterly destroyed it. Unfortunately, Bálint Balassi only had Salgó in his possession for a very short time because he died a heroic death at the siege of Esztergom in 1594. The nephew of Bálint inherited the ruins of Salgó and he left it to the Jesuits.

After the Ottomans had gone from the country the Court got its hands on this small fort that had no military role anymore. Soon, the king gave it to a loyal nobleman, Count Kristóf Otto Volkra. Finally, after all of its landlords had abandoned the fort, the ruins became overgrown with grass and shrubs.

When Sándor Petőfi, another great and famous poet of Hungary, climbed up to the ruins of Salgó in 1845, the atmosphere of the ruins inspired him to write his romantic poem: „Salgó". This is the tragic story about Kompolti family, the lords of Salgó who tyrannized the region which was under their power. The story is based on a traditional legend.

It was the first castle I visited in my life; my father took me up there. The white clouds covered everything below, and nothing except the opposite castle of Somoskő could be seen. The place deserves a visit.

29. The Siege of Salgó Castle (1554)

The small castle of Salgó stood on such a high summit that even the birds grew tired flying up there. The castle was not in need of weapons or military supplies. It was not worth much because the castle's Captain, Simon Ságivári was not very clever in the knowledge of war-craft.

When Pasha Arszlán arrived with his huge army and made camp beneath the legs of the high cliffs the Hungarian soldiers just laughed at his efforts. How would he climb the steep slope of the hill without wings, they were jesting around. Even if he could get to the foot of the walls, how would he take a cannon there to open a breach?
Pasha Arszlán was wondering the very same thing. It was bad enough that he didn't have a single cannon. Even if he had one, how would he be able to have one towed up the hillside?

Ottoman cannon from the 15th century
The Pasha was not famous for his shrewdness without reason. Finally, he came up with a cunning plan. The clever Pasha had a great tree cut down and its branches chopped off. His carpenters worked on it until it looked like an enormous, six-meter-long cannon. Having painted it pitch black, he had the strange cannon laid on two huge wheels. Pasha Arszlán had six oxen tied in front of it to make it appear as if it was very heavy. Slowly, he began to have his wooden cannon pulled up the slopes of the hill next to Salgó castle amid great noise and whip-rattling. The herders were prompting the poor oxen loudly so the soldiers in the castle could well hear how hard they were toiling.
The foggy weather also contributed to the success of the Pasha's plot. The dense fog was restricting the visibility from Salgó castle. This was why the defenders were deceived and took the trunk as a formidable firearm of the enemy. They became even more frightened when a few riders of Pasha Arszlán appeared at the walls and began to cry in the Hungarian language,

"The cannon is here! The cannon has arrived! Surrender the castle and you will have the mercy of the Pasha! Save yourselves and receive pardon!" The borderland warriors were so frightened by the trunk-cannon and shouting that they fled from the castle during the following night.

When the truth about the cannon became known, the whole Valiant Order of the Borderland was laughing at the slow-wittedness of Lord Ságivári.

30. Nagyida Castle   GPS: 48.591733, 21.169861

Nagyida (Velká Ida) was named after the small Ida River or rather stream which flows next to it. The village is 16 kilometers to the southwest of Kassa (Kosice, Kaschau). In the old times, this distance was regarded as short so that the inhabitants could sell their products in the big town easily. The settlement was famous for its agricultural goods and for its fertile lands. It was no wonder that they held great markets there which helped the settlement to prosper.
The name of Ida first appeared in the document of King Béla IV in 1251 and once more in 1275. The castle was built in 1406 by the Chief Judge of the Kingdom, Péter Perényi. All we know is that this high lord was signing his letters in the castle of Ida in 1417.
When the Bohemian Hussites broke into the Upper Lands, they took many prisoners of war and in the fashion of medieval warfare, they demanded a ransom for them. This was how Jan Giskra, their leader got Ida Castle; it was ceded to him as a ransom. When the Bohemian Czech mercenaries were fought by King Matthias, the castle was returned to the Perényi family.
The legend of Nagyida is connected to the 20-day-long siege in 1556 when King Ferdinand`s army took the castle. After slaughtering the Gypsies and the Hungarians of the castle, Ferdinand`s men utterly destroyed the castle as revenge for their losses during the particularly bloody siege. Yet, the trenches and the moat of the castle can be clearly seen today.
There was a stately home in the small town in 1671, but ten years later it was in ruins. The Csáky family had their huge palace there in the 18th century.
Today, there are still many Gypsies in the settlement but they deservedly have a most heroic tale which made them and Nagyida famous.

31. The Gypsy warriors of Nagyida Castle (1556)

Nagyida Castle was inherited by the two Perényi brothers; Mihály was the older and Ferenc the younger. They could have lived in peace but they could not agree about the castle. They kept on arguing until a day came when Mihály had heard enough and set out hunting for a change.

Nagyida (photo: Gergely Fábián)

When he returned, the gate of the castle was shut before him and nobody would open it. Finally, his younger brother came out to the wall and shouted down to him:

"Now, Mihály you can hit the road because you won't find a dwelling place here anymore. Find a new home for yourself."

Mihály Perényi became very angry but there was nothing he could do. He had to go and find his luck in the court of King Ferdinand, while Ferenc remained in the service of Queen Isabella, the widow of late King János Szapolyai.

Mihály ended up in Kassa and joined the army of General Puchheim who was about to take the castles of Upper Hungary for King Ferdinand. Mihály Perényi and his men were most welcome and the General needed very little persuasion to set out against the castle of Nagyida. In the meantime, Ferenc Perényi had the castle fortified and appointed Mihály Gerendai as his Castellan.

When the army of Puchheim marched to the castle, they were received by such a fierce volley of cannons and arquebuses that they could hardly withdraw beyond their range. The General was not idle and arranged his own cannons at once and he poured out a terrible fire both from the south and from the north at the bastions. He tried to breach the palisade that went down to the Ida River but the defenders aimed twice as well as his artillerymen and the Germans suffered great losses. However, Puchheim had 4,000 infantrymen and 600 heavy cavalry, in addition to his 600 light Hussar cavalry.

Who were these excellent marksmen? Soon they found out what Captain Gerendai had done. As his soldiers were falling one by one, he had to make do with other men who had taken shelter in the fort. These were the Gypsies whose number was between 500 and 1,000 and they were led by their Voivode, Csóri. Gerendai gave them all the rusted armor, helmets and old swords he found around the castle's attic and in the cellars.

They were valiantly fighting on the walls and repulsed Puchaim's assaults amid great shooting and shouting. In the old armor that was left from the time of King Matthias, they looked like savage Saracens as they were shaking their fists and their sabers towards the Germans,

"Good riddance, Germans. You had better get away from here while you can. We are going to send the lightning and thunder of Devla (Devil) against you, with double-charged cannons and muskets!"

They were not just boasting, they handled the firearms with deadly precision as if they were the Devils themselves. What's more, when the Germans did not expect it, they sallied out day and night, led by the brave Voivode Csóri.

Not much later, the morale of Puchhaim's army was broken. The General was most annoyed that he was being beaten by mere Gypsies. The Folks of the Pharaoh, as they were called in Hungary, merrily sent volley after volley whenever a German soldier showed up near enough to the walls. The first rains of autumn were beginning and Puchhaim did not know what Gerendai and his men knew. Namely, that there was not more than a handful of gunpowder left in the entire castle of Nagyida. Some of the Hajdu soldiers of the Castellan took it in mind and left the Gypsies alone and fled during the night.

Puchheim decided to leave too. He gritted his teeth, and to the greatest sorrow of Mihály Perényi, he made his mercenaries march away. Seeing the victory, the Gypsies were so happy, that never before or after could a Gypsy man be that happy. Dancing and singing they all ran to the ramparts and were shouting and screaming after the disgracefully retreating Germans.

"Run for your life! Lucky you, save your skins, if we had not run out of powder and balls, you would all be dead now."

The scorning and cursing were clearly heard amongst the ranks of the enemy. Even Puchheim turned his head to one of his officers who spoke the Hungarian language.

"What are they shouting?" he asked him.

"My Lord, they keep crying that we would lose our lives if they had more gunpowder."

Puchheim turned the reins of his horse immediately, drew his sword and gave the order to attack the castle. It was the twenty-first attack but it was the last one.

"Forward! Give mercy to no-one!"

It was the end of the Gypsy soldiers. The mercenaries of Puchheim left not a soul alive in the whole castle as the general was so ashamed.

There are many songs among the Gypsies which preserve the valor of their folk in the castle of Nagyida and it is said that while Puchheim is being tormented in Hell, the Devil is playing him Gypsy music.

German Landsknechts from 1530

32. Tarkő Castle   GPS: 49.194736, 20.967818

Tarkő Castle (Kamenica) sits on top of a 725-meter-high summit. It was divided into two parts which were separated by a narrow cliff ridge. By now, you can see only a few remnants of them. The castle is in the Valley of the Tarca and it is 14 kilometers from Kisszeben to the north-west, near the Polish border.

Tarkő has always been a private castle and was never updated to answer the challenges of the more advanced artillery. During its long history its owners had always belonged to one family.

Rikalf, son of Rikalf, the ancestor of the Hungarian Berzeviczy and Tarkőy families was given the surrounding land in 1296 from the Kercsi family. They built the castle before 1306 to supervise the trade route between Kassa (Kosice, Kaschau) and Poland. The Sztáray family had ownership of the village since the beginning, too. The castle was first mentioned as "Thorkw" and it controlled ten villages from 1296. The church of the village was built by Count of Szepes, Rikalf Berzeviczy in 1300. There were 41 tax-paying houses in the village in 1427. János Fogas Tarkői became unfaithful to the king in 1436, so the king's army laid siege to the castle and chased him away.

According to sources, Baron Péter Tarcay (aka Tarkői) was loyal to Queen Erzsébet in 1442 and he was loyal to her son, to King László V. as well. Queen Erzsébet was the employer of the Bohemian Czech Hussite mercenaries, led by Jan Giskra. Giskra was given the Castle of Zólyom (Zvolen) and was made the Captain of Kassa (Kosice, Kaschau) and his task was to block the traffic towards Poland. This is how Giskra's men got control over the fort in 1444. During the Hussite wars they burned its village in 1456. At this time, the castellan of the fort was György Hototini, the castellan of the Tarkői family. The other branch of the Tarkői family, namely Henrik and Kelemen were the owners between 1436 and 1458.

Tarkő Castle today (Photo: Jerzy Opiola)

King Matthias sent his Treasurer, Imre Szapolyai to drive the Hussites out of the Upper Lands of Hungary in 1462. When Jan Giskra lost control over the Szepesség (Zips Lands) and King Habsburg Frederick III quit the war, the Hussite leader became loyal to King Matthias.

Tarkő Castle remained in the hands of the Tarkői family. There were 13 villages serving the castle at that time. Tarkő was reconstructed in the Renaissance style during the first part of the 16th century. We know that Miklós Tarkői died in the Battle of Mohács in 1526. As King Ferdinand defeated King Szapolyai again in 1528 near Kassa, it is quite surprising how Tarkő Castle was able to remain on King Szapolyai's side for a further

28 years. Queen Isabella, the widow of King Szapolyai often dwelled in Tarkő during her trips to Poland.

The troops of the Holy Roman Empire besieged the three castles of the Tarkői family, Tarkő Castle, Újvár and Pécsújfalu in 1557 or 1558. Tarkő was defended by Anna Tarkői, the wife of the powerful Lord György Drugeth. She had to surrender the castle after a week-long fight and she and her men were given safe conduct. She died in a nearby village, Orsóc, in deep poverty in 1567. After the siege, the mercenaries had the walls undermined and exploded by gunpowder and nobody has ever rebuilt Tarkő Castle since that time. King Ferdinand I gifted the ruins of Tarkő Castle and the village to the Tarczay and the Dessewffy families in 1558. We know of 31 houses in the village from 1600 which were of the Reformed faith at this time, but the Catholics got the Gothic church back in 1672.

The extensive destruction of the castle is mainly due to a man called Tahy, a nobleman who had the stones carried away to build his distillery in 1816. As far as we know, there have never been archaeological excavations.

Yet, the heroism of Anna Tarkői is cherished by the locals and commemorated by castle festivals.

The tombstone of Tamás Tarcay from 1493 (Héthárs)

33. The Black Flags of Tarkő Castle (1558)

White limestone cliffs stand next to each other and reach to the sky guarding the Valley of the Tarca River. Two castles sat on either side of the long rock ridge, Tarkő Castle and Újvár Castle which was also known as Hönig Castle.

Let the lords of Tarkő call themselves either Tarkői or Tarcay, they had been firm and loyal to the Hungarian kings since the Mongolian invasion of 1241. Balázs, one of the first ancestors of the family, fought alongside King Béla IV in the Battle of Muhi and when the king had to flee the fearsome Mongol's attack, he was defending him with his body. The king never forgot his faithful soldier's injuries and granted him permission to build Tarkő Castle, as the family legend recalls it.

Time went on and the heyday of the Hungarian Kingdom was shadowed by dark clouds. The Turks crushed the Hungarian army at Mohács, the young King Louis and the flower of the nobility died on the battlefield. Alas, Miklós Tarcay was among the thousands of fallen knights. He left behind only an adopted son, György.

György kept the family tradition and remained faithful and steady to King Szapolyai and later to his widow, Queen Isabella.

These were the merriest days of Tarkő Castle because Queen Isabella had often stayed within the walls when she was visiting Poland. The Queen was always warmly welcomed and could rest there. The Tarcay family tried to chase away the burden of the state from her with their pleasant hospitality. Her son, János Zsigmond was with her and the young prince took delight in the scenic landscape and in the hunting. They needed this little peace in this hidden eagle-nest of the Carpathian Mountains because the Kingdom was in constant peril. It was the sad time of the Dual Kingship when the country was ruled by two competing rulers. The Habsburg King Ferdinand thought himself the rightful claimant of the Holy Crown of Hungary and did his best to drive out the men of late King Szapolyai and his widow.

In the meantime, the Sultan of the Turks was the laughing third monarch who could only gain on the discord of the Christian rulers.

As there was the limitless resource of the Holy Roman Empire behind King Ferdinand's back where the sun never set, he could employ plenty of mercenaries who were giving a hard time to the army of Queen Isabella. There came the Battle of Nagyszőlős where the Hungarians had to flee with bloodied heads. It was the fight where the faithful György Tarcay lost his life in defense of his Queen. The knight left behind a widow, Lady Dóra Bánffy and a daughter, Anna Tarcay. Their hatred against King

Ferdinand had not changed and they remained faithful to their beloved Queen Isabella.

As there was not a male heir to inherit the four castles of the family, King Ferdinand wanted to wrest the castles of Tarkő, Újvár, Pécsújfalu, and Homonna from the weak womanly hands. Dozens of villages, huge forests and immense lands belonged to these forts and the king badly needed money.

Anna Tarcay, by this time the widow of György Drugeth, refused to cede all her properties to the king who was regarded as a foreign usurper of the throne. She collected all her faithful men and took courage from her love of Queen Isabella and from the rage she felt against the Habsburgs. She and her mother decided to close the gates of all four castles in front of the approaching mercenary army and repel the attacks as it would befit a fierce Hungarian Lady. They recalled the heroic example of the women of Eger Castle, how bravely they fought back the storms of the pagan Muslims just a few years before. Now, they were facing the pagan Austrians with the same determination. Let the cannons come!

The German soldiers arrived in due time and besieged Tarkő Castle and their cannons began the ruin of its old-fashioned, thin walls. The General of the mercenaries was a gentleman and after demonstrating the power of his mighty cannons he sent a message to the castle:

"Surrender the castle and hoist a white flag into the tower!"

And waited three days for the answer.

To his great surprise, it was a black flag which was set out on the third day's morning. And not just a single flag. Lady Anna was so desperate that she had the castle's walls draped in black so as to show she would rather die with her handful of defenders. The gates, the bastions, and the windows were covered by the woeful black clothes of death. Even the mouths of the canons were yawning darkly. The General was wondering where Lady Anna had gotten so many black clothes from. Nobody could say. Soon, a messenger arrived at the camp and reported,

"The castles of Pécsújfalu, Újhely, and Homonna are all dressed in black, too!"

Only a soldier sent from the castle had a white flag in his hand with the answer from Lady Anna,

"The reply of Her Ladyship, Mrs. György Drugeth Anna Tarcay is as follows: the castle and the entire kingdom have fallen into mourning. If you want to know its reason, it is because Ferdinand was elected as the king."

The General lost his patience and exclaimed:

"Well, then you had better go on mourning, I will give you even more reasons."

The bombardment of Tarkő Castle continued until the gate was broken in. The last attack took place on the seventh day of the siege. The mighty army of the Emperor managed to break down the resistance of one more Hungarian woman who had the courage to take up arms against the oppressor.

It happened in the year 1558, thirty-two years after the Battle of Mohács and seventeen years after the fall of Buda Castle.

34. Komárom Castle   GPS: 47.755602, 18.108737

Komárom is at the confluence of the Danube and the Vág rivers, half of the city is located in the Upper lands (Horná zem, Felvidék) which is now in Slovakia and called Komarno. The other part is still in Hungary and it is known as Komárom.

Whoever owned Komárom, could control three large regions of Hungary, namely the Dunántúl (Trans-Danubian Region) the Csallóköz and the Mátyusföld. Komárom Castle was a formidable fortress, blocking the Danube before Vienna and Pozsony (Bratislava, Pressburg), making all river passage impossible and it was a very good crossing place. The city has a system of forts, bastions, and fortifications on both banks of the river Danube.

Its history dates back to the time of the Hungarian Chieftain Árpád's Home Taking in the 9th century when he gave this area to his man, Ketel. After Ketel's son Alaptolma built the first earthen-castle, Komárom was established from the three villages of Komáromfalva, Andrásfalva, and Keszifalva. The settlement became the center of Komárom County, one of the earliest counties of the Kingdom. The Mongols could not destroy it in 1241 because of the rivers which protected the castle well enough. King Béla IV gifted the town with a privilege and turned it into a royal town, a "regis civitatis" in 1265 because of the city's great market and busy harbor and the ferry. It was at this time that the stone castle was built. Later it fell into the hands of Máté Csák, the mighty oligarch. Máté gave further privileges to the town in 1307 which were confirmed later by King Zsigmond.

King Albert of Hungary died near Komárom, at Neszmély in 1439 and his widow took refuge in the castle of Komárom. She gave birth to King László V there in 1440 and there she plotted with Baron Cillei so as to steal the Holy Crown of Hungary from Visegrád. Queen Elisabeth stayed in Komárom until the summer of 1440. Later, King László V awarded his birthplace with four letters of privilege. The role of the city grew in the period of the Hunyadi family. King Matthias visited there first in 1465 when he led his campaign against the Czech lands. The king and his wife, Queen Beatrix liked to stay in their palace in Komárom. They had a game reserve park and a royal pleasure boat there.

King Ulászló II fled to Komárom from cholera in 1520 hoping that the rivers would keep the epidemic away. After the Battle of Mohács, the role of Komárom became more significant than ever before because the castle's cannons were able to block the Ottoman fleet on the Danube.

The first siege took place in 1527 when King Ferdinand's army took it after a day long bombardment. Two years later, his garrison surrendered the castle to Sultan Suleiman, but the Turks did not leave guards in it so it was retaken without a fight. Regarding Komárom's central location, the Ottoman attacks had been continuous until 1683.

There was a river battle at Komárom during the Dual Kingship in 1532 when Sultan Suleiman was on his way to take Vienna, but his army was delayed by the heroic defenders of Kőszeg Castle. In the meantime, King Szapolyai's sloops were successful against the German ships. Szapolyai had 68 vessels and attacked King Ferdinand's fleet of 49 sloops. The Hungarians sank 36 German ships but Szapolyai had no troops with which to take Komárom Castle.

After the fall of Buda in 1542, King Ferdinand realized the importance of Komárom and had it fortified. The Italian Pietro Terbosco designed the first modern fort in 1550. Next year, the Turks tried to take the fort with a surprise attack at dawn but were repelled.

Soon, the Ottomans took themselves into Esztergom, which was very close to Komárom. This was a great threat because the Ottoman warriors of Esztergom were renowned for their raids against the Mining Towns and at the same time they controlled the water of the Danube with their well-supplied fleet. In 1583, the sloopers of Komárom had their black day because they ran into the snare of the Turks. The Turks considered this victory a major one. Habsburg Rudolf sent a message to the Pasha of Buda that this time it was the Turks who had broken the Truce and thus demanded the release of all the captured soldiers, which was not granted.

The famous Count Miklós Pálffy (1552-1600) was appointed as the Captain of Komárom in 1584. His first deed was to lead his warriors to Esztergom Castle where they challenged the Turks to duels. A famous Ottoman warrior, Deli Halil, was said to have been slain there. Raids and counter-raids frequently followed each other and the Turks were often seen at the walls of Komárom. It is worth noting that during the first three years of Captain Pálffy's leadership, the Turks attacked the city thirty times. Not all of his raids were successful, though. Pálffy was beaten and lost 278 men during his ill-fortuned raid in 1587.

Pálffy's Vice Captain, Márton Thury reported to the king in 1586 that the enemy was building a boat-bridge across the Danube between Esztergom and the Palisade Castle of Párkány. In answer to this, Archduke Ernő Habsburg ordered that Captain Pálffy to also build a bridge. Pálffy, who had had two small Palisades made on the bank of the Danube and of the Vág in 1585 was given all the supplies to have the bridge of boats built. A bridge of boats is a passageway resting on boats moored abreast across the river.

A certain bridge-master called Lajos Jurisich from Pozsony was in charge of the construction and in 1589 he was ready with the 500-step-longboat bridge over the Danube. Eighty boats and two big "old boats" or sloops were used for the building. Just to make sure, Miklós Pálffy had another small palisade fort erected to guard the bridge.

As Komárom was the most important castle in the chain of forts of the Hungarian Borderland, further forts were built there after 1592. The Szent Miklós (Saint Nicholas) Palisade (later it became the Star-Fort) was built on the right bank of the Danube while the Szent Fülöp (Saint Philip) Palisade was erected on the left.

Hardly had the Italian engineers finished the new fort system in the summer of 1594 that it was put to the test in the autumn. The Grand Vizier Sinan victoriously took the castles of Tata and Győr, then attacked Komárom with a huge army of 50,000 men. As Count Pálffy was fighting against the Pasha's huge army near Győr, the defenders were led by Captain Erasmus Braun and by Captain of the sloopers, Farkas Sztarcsics. They had only 300 German infantrymen and a couple of hundred Hungarians. Many sloopers chose to flee the castle before the siege, though. The Austrians were able to reinforce the castle with approximately 1,200 troops just before the siege began.

The Turks' cannonballs could not do much harm from the other side of the river so Tatar riders were sent to surround the city and soon the Turks could deploy 18 cannons near the walls. They herded Hungarian peasants to dig trenches so as to reach the walls. As the bombardment was not effective, Pasha Sinan tried to explode some mines under the walls but the Janissaries were ambushed and slain. Captain Braun was shot in his right knee at this time. Despite his injury, the Captain had himself taken onto the field the next day among his soldiers and encouraged them to sally out.

On 22 October, 400 men broke out, led by Farkas Stracsics and inflicted great harm on the enemy, bringing in lots of supplies and even a few cannons. The lieutenants of the sloopers, Márton Contrarius and Ferenc Zapata even destroyed several Turkish sloops. Three days later, the morale from the epidemic and cold-struck Turks became so low that Pasha Sinan quit the one month long siege, losing more than 800 of his men so far in vain. He did not know how little gunpowder and supplies were left within the walls. Fortunately, Count Pálffy, albeit injured himself, was bringing the reinforcements to his beloved Komárom Castle's relief.

Sinan's troops began to retreat and then they set the boat-bridge behind them on fire. Seeing this, the defenders took boarded their sloops and sent a volley of cannon fire after the hastily retreating enemy, then, they began to chase them.

Captain Braun died of his wounds in Vienna and Pasha Sinan went to Istanbul to receive the green silk string from the Sultan, and he was executed by strangulation. Miklós Pálffy was again appointed Captain of Komárom and Farkas Kiss became his Vice. In the meantime, the Tatars of Sinan caused horrible destruction in the area of the Csallóköz and went home undisturbed with their booty and slaves. The plight of the surviving population was worsened even more by the incoming German and Czech mercenaries who were furious because they had not been paid and pillaged the land as savagely as the Tatars had done.

Zsitvatő village is located next to Komárom and was the place where the Peace Treaty of Zsitvatorok was made in 1606 between King Rudolf and the Turkish Sultan at the conclusion of the 15 Year War. Komárom city had a Reformed College founded in this year and the Catholics had their high school established thirty-three years later. The next negotiations between the Christians and the Muslims took place on the island of Komárom in 1627 and these resulted in the Peace Treaty of Szőny.

Due to the new Turkish peril, the castle was improved further in 1663 and in 1673 by Italian and French engineers. Both the city and the forts were seriously damaged in the flood of 1682. After the Siege of Vienna in 1683, the withdrawing Ottoman troops were utterly beaten in the two day long

Battle of Párkány, located not far from Komárom. On the first day, the 5,000 Polish cavalry under King Sobieski were defeated by the 50,000-strong Ottoman army led by Kara Mehmed Pasha. More than 1,000 Polish Hussars and dragoons were slain.

The 28,000 strong Austrian forces of Charles V, Duke of Lorraine, arrived the next day and together they attacked the Turks who tried to withdraw their army via the boat-bridge between Esztergom and Párkány. The Austrians had the bridge bombarded to shreds, besieging and taking the Palisade of Párkány. The battle was not only a whole scale battle on the field, it raged also on the water and included a siege as well. Finally, the men of the Duke and of the Polish King Sobieski won a decisive victory over the Ottomans, killing 9,000 of them. Unfortunately, the troops of Prince Imre Thököly were on the Turk's side in this battle. After the defeat, the Austrians besieged Esztergom and Pasha Ibrahim ceded it to them.

Soon, the Ottomans were driven out of the country and Komárom's role diminished, although the city became the fifth largest town in the country by 1715. There were five major earthquakes during the 18th century which ruined the buildings. Yet, the Habsburgs decided to rebuild the forts and huge reinforcements were taking shape between 1827 and 1839. Later, Komárom had a heroic role in the Hungarian War of Independence in 1848-49.

Now, its huge brick walls give a home to festivals every summer to our greatest joy.

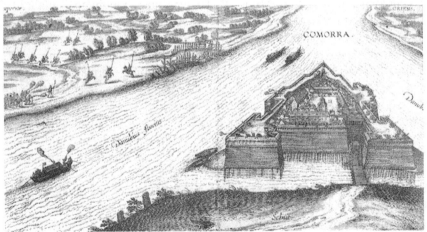

Komárom Castle

35. Battle on the Danube (1583)

The Austrian clerking officer was sitting on a comfortable chair behind a makeshift table as the last warm sunbeams of October were caressing his back. In front of him there stood the entire garrison of Komárom Castle eagerly watching him as he was trying to spell the barbarous sounding Hungarian names from a long, never-ending, list of names.

It was the long-awaited payday and the soldiers were relaxed in the knowledge that King Habsburg Rudolf would pay them at least a part of what he owed them. Were they not luckier than the other warriors of the thousand-mile-long Borderland where they had to wait three to four years to receive half of the full sum? Gossip had it that there was a God-forsaken far-away spot in the north-eastern part of the frontier where the poor devils had to wait nine years. Half of them perished from hunger and the rest became villains. Only eight Hussars remained behind those palisade walls. Komárom was lucky because it was blocking the Danube and the Viennese Court provided them with food and money relatively on time. The lords in Vienna knew that after taking Komárom, Pozsony would be the next and a gap would be opened to their city which was indefensible without the Hungarian circle of castles.

"Francois . . . Kudar . . . or Chudar . . . Chief Voivode of the Hungarian boaters, step right out."

Old Ferenc Czudar smiled sourly. He was close to his 80th winter and no German officer could ever pronounce his name.

"Jawohl, Herr Captain," he saluted and went to the clerk's table where one of the two paymasters handed him sixty Hungarian Forints in gold. It was half of his annual pay and the king remained in debt with the second half. He was well aware of the difference in how the Austrian officers in the same position earned twice his pay, but this was a general phenomenon among the simple soldiers as well. Foreign mercenaries everywhere got twice or three times higher pay and on top of that, they did not have to buy their own food.

"As if these neatly uniformed monkeys were better warriors with their muskets and laughably small swords," he muttered while returning to his men.

All of the artillerymen and infantrymen were Germans while there were Hungarian Hussars and boaters in equal numbers. Many of the sloopers were of Serbian origin whose grandparents had fled here in front of the Turks. Those who could not flee joined the Ottoman army and many of the Ottoman boaters also spoke Serbian. They were better paid on the Turkish side, this was no question to old Czudar.

The Turks did not often dare to come near to the formidable cannons of the three fortifications guarding the water from three sides. The real work was always done by the Hussars who rode out every day to trace down the eventual Turk and Tatar raiders. Similarly, the boaters rowed and sailed endlessly on the Danube doing the same. Except that the Hussars could always get a hold of some booty, at least from duels. The Turks of Esztergom were a reckless and dangerous enemy whose main desire was to torment the small garrisons of the nearby Hungarian castles with raids, snares and ambushes.

The clerk cleared his throat and began to struggle again with the next Hungarian or Serbian name when the alarm was sounded. The warriors cursed the Turks as if they had intentionally planned to disturb this most important act of payment with their appearance, but ran to arm themselves and wait for orders. Eight Ottoman sloops had been sighted, rowing straight against the forts which were packed with dozens of cannons. Chief Captain of Komárom, Andreas Kielman, was quick to respond and issued his orders. Most of the boaters took to their sloops and soon eighteen Hungarian vessels were hurrying towards the Turks in hopes of an easy victory. Ferenc Czudar was their Chief Voivode and he merrily told his sub-voivodes that whoever captured the first Ottoman sloop would receive a double share of the booty.

The weather was splendid and they took advantage of the small westerly breeze which flew their triangular sails downriver. Twenty lads were rowing on each side of the narrow ships and the sound of their singing was heard long distance away. Old Czudar was standing on the prow of the leading sloop, waiting patiently until he could fire the single cannon from it. To his annoyance, the small Ottoman flotilla turned tail and fled just before they were in his cannon's range. Scornful yells and catcalls came from the oarsmen and the Turks had to bear the shame forever. But Czudar did not want to let them slip away this easily. The chase had begun. It was so good to see the proud warriors from the famous Esztergom flee.

Just before the white walls of Esztergom Castle could be seen on the hilltop towering over the waters of the Danube, the river became narrower as the great curve between the mountains embraced it. Some movement caught the eye of the Voivode among the trees on the left bank. There was something shiny as well. He quickly looked at the right bank and his blood froze. White clouds of smoke puffed out on both banks.

"Bushfire?" he wondered. Then the unmistakable crackle of musket fire filled the air and a rain of bullets was knocking on the hulls of the sloops.

The Turkish ships were elegantly turning and there were others joining them from the harbor of Esztergom.

"It is a trap!" Czudar bellowed and he realized that the Turks were playing with them. Ashamed, he gave the order to turn and retreat. His Hajdú musketmen tried to return fire but Czudar angrily stopped them. The Ottoman marksmen could hide behind the willows and alder trees of the floodplain with ease offering a very small target to the Hajdus. On top of this, the Turks had well prepared their trap because they had brought out all of the small caliber cannons from the castle and deployed them along the two banks where the river was the narrowest. A musket was effective enough from this distance, but the small cannonballs caused fist-size holes in the ships' planks. Two or three Hajdú lads had already fallen from each vessel turning the blue water to red with their blood. Czudar estimated there were two to three hundred Janissaries on each riverbank. They began walking upriver when they saw the Hungarians flee.

Now, it became a real chase. Except that the newly arrived Turkish sloops were rested and they did not get tired rowing like the Hungarian oarsmen. Advancing upriver proved a lot harder and steady musket fire followed them from two directions. Occasionally, a cannonball splashed next to them, scaring the hell out of the rowers. Some of the vessels were already far from mint condition and the hailing musket fire tore splinters and shreds of wood from their hulls. There was no more singing. The wounded were laid down in the ship's hold and the crews were desperately rowing on with fewer and fewer strong hands to paddle. Smoke puffs appeared from the prows of the Turkish ships as they closed in. Czudar could do nothing for the four lagging boats which were unable to row hard enough.

Soon, they were flanked by Ottoman vessels, gangways were dropped and the Janissaries overran them from both sides. Knowing that they were being watched by their comrades the Hajdus were too proud to surrender. They took many Janissaries with them to the other world with loud and angry curses. Three voivodes of the boaters perished. These were men with whom Czudar had shared most of his life. They died proudly because the advance of the Turkish ships was slowed down for a few minutes.

The old voivode had not much time to watch their last stand because three of his sloops had begun to sink. He immediately maneuvered his vessel next to one of them and saw that sloops on his left and right hurried to save the other unfortunate boaters. They cared nothing for the whizzing bullets and fished the surviving crews on board. The newcomers were soon put to work. Komárom Castle and its yawing cannons were just too far away yet. Old Czudar had had many battles with the Ottoman raiders and he was one of King Szapolyai's sloopers back in 1532 when they defeated the fleet of King Ferdinand.

"It was fifty-one years ago, I swear I have never been tricked like this before." he exclaimed to his steersman. The man opened his mouth to say something reassuring to his voivode but a bullet hit off the boat. Voivode Czudar took over his job.

There were more boats beyond salvation by now and those who could not climb on a passing boat, tried to swim ashore. Even the wounded jumped into the water from the sinking vessels and let their bodies be carried by the current to the shore where the Janissaries herded all of them together. Good oarsmen had a high price in the slave market of Belgrade where they were sold to Italian or Turkish galleys.

Half of the Hungarian sloops had been sunk when old Czudar saw through his tears the reinforcements arriving from Komárom.

"God may bless Captain Andreas Kielman." cried the old man and new hope filled his heart seeing the five slow big ships coming towards them with three cannons placed in each of their prows. It was the end of the Ottoman attack. When some of the Christian's cannonballs hit home the Muslim vessels came to a halt. It was pointless to expose themselves to unnecessary damage as the canons of Komárom itself were not far away..

When Ferenc Czudar tied his boat in the harbor and clambered up to the parade ground he thought it was an eternity ago that they had all been standing there waiting for their pay. Now, more than a hundred women were made widows and their sons were orphaned. He knew that the captured will never return home from slavery and the king in Vienna will not care to ransom them. Yes, the Turks broke the Truce but it does not mean they will let the prisoners go.

Voivode Czudar squared his shoulders and approached the paymasters and clerks of the Vienese Court. Squeezing the share that was supposed to be habitually given to the orphans and widows out of these bureaucrats would be harder than fighting a thousand pagans on the river.

"Let us not allow the Military Chamber to save money on the dead and their family." he thought with tight lips.

36. Korpona Castle   GPS: 48.348025, 19.068727

Korpona (Krupina, Karpfen) is a town 27 km to the south of Zólyom (Zvolen) on the banks of the Korpona River. Its name may have come from the Saxon or Carpiani people. The city is surrounded by hills rich in gold, silver, copper and iron ore. The settlement lay on the route known as "via Magna" connecting the Baltic Sea with the Adriatic.

The Hungarian Hontpázmány clan founded the village in the 11th century and many Germans arrived in 1135 having been given privilege as reward for their military deeds by King Saint István. King András II invited more Saxon miners from Transylvania to move there in the 13th century. It was first mentioned in 1238 as „Corpona" in a document of King Béla IV who gifted it with "town privileges" which only had been given to the greatest towns of the Kingdom at that time. Cities like Buda, Pozsony or Brassó. The Mongolian invasion devastated the settlement in 1241. King Béla IV gave it the privilege of "Free Royal Town" to the surviving inhabitants in 1244.

CARPONA

1. La Madonna Chiesa del castello.
2. Torre alta con due cannoni.
3. Torre della poluere.
4. Quartiere del Commandante.
5. Torre armata di moschettoni.
6. Bastione de Turchi con un pezzo di cannone.
7. Bastione inferiore.
8. Bastione verso il Borgo.
9. Riuellino contro il Borgo.
10. Riuellino nelle mura della Città

11. Altro riuellino nelle sudette mura.
12. Porta de Turchi con 2 cannoni.
13. Borgo con 177 case.
14. Falsa braga con due batterie.
15. Porta superiore con due cannoni
16. Casa di Gaspero Baroli.
17. Casa del Boru
18. Casa del Visconte soluti
19. Porta del Borgo
20. Vedetta, ò sentinella.

21. Altra uedetta.
22. Strada di Schemiz
23. Strada uerso Sergin, et Offgrad.
24. Strada di Altsol.
25. Porta del Borgo.
26. Riuolo chiamato Erasniza.
27. Torre doue si fa la guardia.
28. Due montagne, che dominano la Città

Korpona's main square was the first paved square, built in German fashion, in the Kingdom of Hungary. The small town was given privilege to hold a market in 1393. Korpona was growing a great deal so many German families moved out and founded a new city, Dobsina, in Gömör County.

The old city was surrounded by a wall with bastions in the 15th century and their remains are still standing. After the attack of Giskra's Bohemian Hussites in 1440, the church was also fortified. The Hussites owned the town for 20 years and only King Matthias was able to take it back. The "Korpona law", based on the Magdeburg rights, was the basis for many towns in northern Hungary. The deposits of gold and silver ran out in the 14th century and thereafter the town's economy was based on handicraft and agriculture. Korpona used to be the city of the Hungarian Queens in the Middle Age because the taxes coming from the city went to the Queens as their "needle-money".

When the Ottoman threat increased, the walls of the city and the church were reinforced and a separate small stone tower was built on the hill next to the town in 1546. The locals called it a "haversack-castle" because the garrison used to take their food every week in sacks when they changed the guards. They built a second fortification in front of the town's gate in 1564 which was pulled down only in 1905.

Korpona became a Borderland castle and provided shelter to poor and rich in the neighboring area whenever the Turks were coming. It was during this time that many Hungarians moved into Korpona so the number of the city counselors was made up equally of Germans and Hungarians who had the same rights. The Turks besieged it in 1582 but could not take the fortress. The town was the center of Hont County during the 17th century because of the permanent Ottoman peril.

Ferenc Rhédey, the general of Prince Bocskai took the place in 1604. The Diet of 1605 took place in Korpona where Bocskai called together the representatives of 22 Hungarian Counties and the delegates of the Free Royal Towns of Northern Hungary. The envoys of Transylvania also took part in it. Bocskai made sure to call in 7,000 Hussars and 10,000 Hajdú troops for the sake of safety, too.

The verdicts of this Diet significantly influenced the legal order of Hungary until 1848. They decided that religion should be freely practiced and that the king would not be allowed to make war in Hungary without the agreement of the Diet. They reestablished the function of the Palatine. They ruled that the Holy Crown of Hungary must be kept only in Hungary, guarded by people who had to be native Hungarians. Instead of the Chamber of Vienna, the old Treasury institution was re-installed. The Jesuits were deprived of all their rights in Hungary. They were not allowed to own any properties there, either. Only Hungarians were allowed to be appointed to have offices in Hungary, regardless of their religion, and only Hungarian soldiers were permitted to guard the castles of the Borderland. The king was to live in Hungary otherwise the Palatine would reign on his behalf. People could not be judged without holding a court case. Additionally, Prince Bocskai issued the document in Korpona which gave nobility to his Hajdú soldiers.

Korpona was in the hands of Prince Bethlen during his western campaigns. The Turks sacked the city in 1626 but the defenders would beat them back in 1647. The defenders withstood two more sieges in 1678. Prince Thököly took it in 1682 and the troops of General Ocskay took it in 1703. The rebel

Kuruc troops of General István Andrássy set the town on fire in fifty places in 1708 before the Imperial army could take it back.

The haversack-castle or Warte in the German language is still standing and is a half hour's walk from the city. It offers a magnificent view of the oldest mining town of the Upper Lands of old Hungary.

Korpona's Haversack Castle

37. The Duel at Korpona's Haversack Castle (1588)

The time came when the Turks began to threaten the eight mining cities of the Upper Lands. The Burghers of Selmecbánya, Körmöcbánya, Bélabánya, and Újbánya were trembling with fear just like the inhabitants of Breznóbánya, Besztercebánya and Libetbánya, not forgetting the smallest of them, Bakabánya.

The turbaned warriors were lurking around Korpona as well and they took away men by the dozens and cattle by the hundreds. When they tried to break the gates in the Chief Captain of Esztergom ordered the Burghers of Korpona to erect a guard tower on the hill above the city. There was nothing to do but open their purses, and soon the stand-alone tower was built on the hill next to Korpona. It was just big enough to hold forty soldiers, not more. As it had neither a kitchen nor cooks in it, the garrison was fed from their haversacks week by week. Ever since, it was cleverly called Haversack Castle by everyone.

The Chief Captain of Esztergom also ordered that the cannons in the tower must be always loaded and ready to give signal day or night. The guards were told to light a bonfire if they saw the Turks coming from Bozók Castle or from Csábrág Castle's direction. A single shot was a sign of caution and two shots meant that the enemy was close. Three shots in quick succession meant that the Turks had already crossed the town's boundary. The Chief Captain added to his orders one sentence:

"The cocks walk together to scratch. This is what you should bear in mind, Burghers of Korpona."

It was Sir Mihaly Molitórisz, the Chief Notable in the city, who discovered its meaning;

"It means that we, the men, should keep together valiantly in order to defend the women."

The Burghers took this advice to heart but they were not always able to look after their womenfolk when they were cultivating the fields around the city's walls. Sometimes the Turks of Nógrád Castle ambushed them and took away the pretty ones for themselves, and their children for the Janissary schools. However, the warriors of the Haversack Castle improved the situation and rushed down from the tower to protect the women. They held the Turks up until the Burghers were up on their horses and had galloped out through the city gates. Now, together, they were able to overwhelm the enemy and scatter them, returning home with shaven bald heads on their spearheads.

Did the Turks become disheartened by the failures? Not in the least. They kept coming back always in greater numbers. The Burghers of Korpona had to send an envoy to Zólyom Castle to plead for the help of Captain János Balassa. There must have been some Turkish spies in Zólyom, though, who reported this to Bey Ali of Buda who became terribly angry with the Burghers. The Bey did not hesitate a minute but sent a letter to Korpona:

"You infidel pigs, do not dare to allow the dogs of Balassa within your walls unless you want to see yourself impaled and your heads drying on stakes."

This was the way the Hungarians, Turks, and Saxons were entertaining each other for one hundred and fifty years around Korpona.

One day, a small unit of Turkish warriors arrived at the gates of the city, no more than fifty Muslim soldiers, all dressed in their best clothes. They were followed by just as many musicians who were mercilessly banging their drums and sounding their war-whistles and instruments. The Burghers heard the warning shots from Haversack Castle and five hundred defenders were eyeing the enemy from the walls and bastions. They suspected more Turks were to come and nobody guessed what they were up to.

The Captain of Korpona was called György Fáncsy at this time. The spokesman of the Turks waved a flag, had a whistle sounded and knocked on the oak-wood gate with the shaft of his lance.

"Listen to me, Ghiaurs, you coward dogs! We declare your Captain, the hound-souled György Fáncsy a coward swaggerer as he is indeed. It cannot be otherwise since even in the coat of arms of your city is just a coward sheep bleating. Your castle can fit into a haversack but you do not have as much courage as can fit into a leaking haversack. Well, that is all we want to say."

With this, he tucked a turkey-feather into a crack of the gate. The Turk's bugles gave out scornful whining sounds. It was at that moment that the reddened face of Captain Fáncsy appeared in the gate tower's window. He shouted angrily at them;

"Are you running away, already, you dogs? You are insolent boasters, snakes, shameful weaklings of your Allah. Would none of you dare to face me, fight me with a spear or a sword?"

The Turkish unit reined in. Now, it was another Turk who spoke up, turning his horse back on its hind legs,

"This was why we have come here, do you really dare to accept my challenge? I am Agha Hassan, come and fight me, go ahead!"

Agha Hassan was a renowned warrior, the son of the Bey of Nógrád Castle. He was always riding up and down in the Borderland in search of military honor. György Fáncsy could hardly wait to try his sword with the famous Turkish warrior's saber.

Duels had their unwritten rules among the Valiant Order which were solemnly respected by both sides. Captain Fáncsy took no more than fifty warriors from the castle and they rode out to the field next to the city wall. Quickly they agreed to the rules, selected two judges from each unit, and marked the length and the width of the dueling field. It was all great fun and Turks and Hungarians were cordially chatting and mingling with each other. They knew not only each other's language and names, but even the names of their enemy's horses as well.

The Agha rode his Arabian stallion to the far side of the field and repeated his challenging words. Captain Fáncsy said nothing, just leaned forward in his saddle and when the bugle was sounded, he squeezed his horse into a gallop and sped toward the brave Agha at once. They were supposed to break three lances before unsheathing their swords but now it was not so. To the horror of the Turks, the lance-head of the captain caught the steel visor of the Agha in the middle, knocking him out of the saddle with a terrible jerk.

The Turks cried out seeing how their fallen leader was being dragged by the stirrup after the bewildered stallion.

Ottoman-Hungarian duel at Mohács, 1526

"Allahu Akbar, death to the Ghiaur dogs!" they screamed and they all fell on the Hungarian warriors with drawn sabers and yatagans. The Hussars of the Haversack Castle proved to be no boasters because they fought back and slew sixteen attackers in the bitter but short fight. The Hungarians lost no one. Seeing their warriors falling onto the green grass, the Turks turned tail and began to flee. The warriors of Korpona did not chase them, rather they called after them:

"Now, you do not need to run away! Come back and bury your dead in peace and let us keep the funeral feast together. We will not hurt you."

The Turks believed them and they returned sadly to collect their brother-in-arms from the field.

And what befell to Agha Hassan? Did he die or stay alive? Miraculously, he survived and now he was standing on his unsteady legs with a bleeding forehead.

As was the habit after duels, the warriors made peace after the good game and celebrated together, sharing their wine and food. The Burghers of Korpona were happy that they had suffered no harm so they sent eight heavy wagons pulled by oxen, loaded with food and wine barrels to the field. Bonfires were built and the musicians began to play each other's songs. They roasted meat and ate the soft white bread of the city. The fiery wine was flowing down their throats in great quantities and soon the Turks proposed a new contest, a horse race. In this game, they bested the Hungarians to their greatest merriment.

This was how the valiant warriors of Korpona were passing time with the brave and restless Turkish warriors in the year Anno Domini 1588.

8.

38. Szikszó City   GPS: 48.197363, 20.930082

The city of Szikszó is an agricultural town in Borsod County just 17 kilometers to the East of Miskolc. The first mention of the settlement is from 1280 when King László IV issued three documents. The next king who visited the place and issued a document was King Róbert Károly in 1307.

The area was owned by the Aba family at this time. King Zsigmond inherited it from them in 1391. He gave it to his wife, Queen Mária, just as with the castle of Diósgyőr. Szikszó was regarded as a "royal" city which meant it enjoyed various liberties and privileges.

The Gothic church and its 170 centimeter thick stone walls were built during this flourishing period of the town. Stones of previous churches were used for the construction of the new one, although the covering stone of the arched roof was completed only in 1500. We can see a stone in the northern part of the church which commemorates the victory of 1588 when Count Zsigmond Rákóczi defeated the Turks at Szikszó.

By the end of the 16th century the settlement was surrounded by an earthen wall with five bastions at each corner of the pentangular structure. Szikszó was part of the chain of castles of the Hungarian Borderland against the Ottoman Empire. Szikszó developed quickly due to its location as it was on the trade route between Kassa (Kosice, Kaschau) and Krakow. The wine production of the area was quite considerable. The lords of the city came from the Perényi family and the inhabitants converted to Protestantism in the 16th century and took the Gothic church for the Reformed faith.

While Szikszó lay on the Borderland it officially belonged to Royal Hungary. However, the Pasha of Buda often made the town pay taxes to the Ottoman Empire as well. When the taxes failed to arrive in Buda, the Turkish units always showed up at Szikszó. The first large conflict took place on 13 October 1558 when Bey Velican of Fülek Castle sacked and burned the city. When Bey Velican was on the way home with the booty, the Borderland warriors of György Bebek and Imre Telekessy ambushed him at the Sajó River and defeated his army. Although we know that the city began to pay its taxes more regularly to the Turks in 1564, the Turkish threat did not ceased to exist. There were Turkish looters in 1566, 1567 as well as in 1573 and in 1577. During such occasions the inhabitants found shelter behind the wall of the church, shooting the enemy from its tower.

The second major clash took place on 10 November 1577 when Bey Ferhát of Fülek Castle attacked the city right in the middle of the Sunday morning service interrupting the Reformed pastor's preaching. The Turks timed their surprise attack when there was a famous city fair with lots of traders from all over the country so they traveled at night to get there unnoticed. They managed to break through the low stone fence of the church but the denomination was stubbornly holding the building of the large gothic church. We can conclude from this fact that the Hungarians either visited the church with their weapons or there had to be an armory in the church. The fighting and looting were going on all day long and was not yet finished even into the late hours of the night when the sky was lit by the famous comet of 1577.

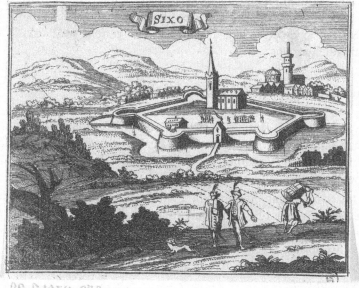

When Bey Ferhát was returning home on the following day he was again beaten at the same place, at the ford of the Sajó River at Sajószentpéter. Although the Turks vastly outnumbered the Borderland warriors of Szendrő Castle, led by Chief Captain Claudius Roussel and Captain Zsigmond Rákóczi and the Hussars of Ferenc Geszti and Bálint Prépostváry from Kassa (Kosice, Kaschau), the Hungarians defeated the enemy.

The inhabitants of Szikszó built a hedge-palisade with a moat around their city in 1586 against the looting marauders and the Turks, turning the old church into a heavily fortified building at the same time.

The third battle of Szikszó was in 1588 when an 11,000 men strong Turkish army attacked the city. Captain Zsigmond Rákóczi of Eger Castle defeated them with his 2,000 Hussars and 400-500 German infantrymen. Several hundred Hungarian and German soldiers died in this battle while the Turks lost more than 2,000 men. The next battle of Szikszó took place in 1679 when Prince Imre Thököly of Transylvania was victorious over the Imperial troops.

The Burghers joined the War of Independence of Prince Ferenc II Rákóczi in 1703. Three years later General Rabutin set the whole town on fire in revenge for that. Following another major fire in 1852, the city declined and became a rather large village.

Yet, if you ask them, the locals of Szikszó can show you the place called "Törökhalom" (Turkish pile) where the fallen soldiers of the famous battle of 1588 sleep together in their mass-grave, Hungarians and Turkish, side by side with Germans.

39. The Battle of Szikszó (08. October 1588)

Sir István Drugeth of Homonna, Chief Comes of Zemplén County, was a red-faced somewhat overweight man in his thirties who usually made jokes about everything in life rolling his round eyes merrily, but now he was green with envy.

It was his rival, Mihály Serényi, the Captain of Kassa, who was saddening his life again. Was not he richer and mightier, did not he come from a more ancient noble family than Serényi? Why did Emperor Rudolf need to pamper this upstart Serényi by giving him command over the most important captaincy of Upper Hungary? Had not he, István Drugeth deserved it more?

These kinds of thoughts chased each other in his mind while he was donning his Hussar armor. This armor, which was masterfully wrought together from steel straps and allowed him to wield his saber from his saddle in all directions. The young György Pethő was silently helping him with the buckles and clasps. Pethő, his Lieutenant, had just delivered the news about the Turkish peril of Szikszó city and he thought it better to keep his mouth shut.

"Why did you have to run with the message to Captain Serényi, why did not you hurry here instead at once? Did His Majesty Emperor Rudolf give you the order to notify Serényi before me, your liege-lord?"

"Sir, as I have told you there were no orders from the king. The peasant rider from Szikszó who brought the warning caught me on my way to Kassa. As time was pressing, I thought it proper to call Captain Serényi to arms and urge him to ride out."

"You, little whelp, thought it proper? What if his Hussars reach Szikszó before me? Serényi has already been over-glorified for his valor and speed. Pethő, Pethő, I will perhaps never forgive you if he gets there even a step before me. What are you waiting for? Are the men ready? Have you sent envoys to Captain Zsigmond Rákóczi in Eger? What about the two castellans of Szendrő Castle, János Rotthaler and Albert Raibicz? Be off with you, and pray for finding me in a better mood when you bring them after me to Szikszó. After me, you heard?"

György Pethő ran with haste. He knew that his lord would calm down as quickly as he became angry and paid little heed to his threats. He was more concerned about the poor folks of Szikszó city. The peasant riders had told him this morning that the Turks had had enough and set out from Székesfehérvár to collect the debt from the city. Szikszó was paying taxes equally to both Emperor Rudolf and the Ottoman Sultan, but the Turks were demanding 1,000 gold Forints now. Emphasizing their claim, the Pasha of Buda sent Bey Kara Ali from Székesfehérvár and Bey Mustapha from Széchény with six thousand Sipahi horsemen and six thousand Janissary infantry to remind their taxpayers of their duty. It was not a joke. Pethő gave thanks to the Almighty that the Turk army paused to take Putnok Castle and they were delayed for a little while. However, having been unsuccessful and humiliated by the Christian warriors of the small fort of Putnok, they pushed on towards Szikszó, covering the land in blood and smoke wherever they passed through.

The young knight did his best and rode from castle to castle. By noon, the signal-trees of the Borderland were set on fire one by one. The flames spread the warning: "The Turks are here! To arms, to arms!"
The poor folks herded their animals into the hills and they hid in caves and led their women and children to marshlands and into the shelter of the "green castle", the forest.
It was late afternoon when the Hungarian noblemen from Eger, Kassa, Szendrő and Homonna finally met in the village of Vadász, not far from Szikszó city and it was Captain Rákóczy who took over the leadership. Zsigmond Rákóczi smiled when he saw Chief Comes Drugeth, this round-headed funny man waiting for him already, sitting behind a hastily erected table. The Comes offered him wine and they drank to the health of the newly arrived Captain Serényi.
Rákóczi was famous for his quick decisions and as soon as the last units of Captain Heling arrived, he and his men mounted at once and he held a council of war on horseback, instructing his officers from the saddle:
"My dear friends; Sir Serényi, Sir Drugeth, and Captain Rothaler. Let your Hussars ride straight into the city of Szikszó and attack immediately the side of Kara Ali. According to the reports, he has been besieging the fortified church of the city for three hours by now and would not expect our arrival this soon. He is being occupied and annoyed by the stubborn Hajdú Burghers of Szikszó who had the wits to send away their women and children before the Turks got there. They have a huge Reformed

church with thick walls, surrounded by a stone wall and a deep moat. Knowing that we are on our way, they will not be likely to surrender their lives and valuables. We have good Hussars with us, two-thousand seasoned warriors of the Valiant Order. The five hundred German musket-men of Captain Heling have already marched out to take up positions near Szikszó. What are we waiting for? Let us surprise the pagans while we can. May Jesus and the Virgin Mary help us. Amen."

Zsigmond Rákóczi

It was five o'clock in the afternoon when the iron-clad Hussars of Zsigmond Rákóczi threw themselves at the Turks who had thronged around the Reformed church. The fifteen foot long lances easily picked their targets and Kara, or Black, Ali paid a bitter price before withdrawing his troops to arrange them in proper battle order. He was a true Ottoman from Africa and he utterly despised the local soldiers under his command, except for the faithful and loyal Janissaries, the fosterlings of the Sultan. To gain some time, he ordered all of the buildings of the town to be set on fire. He was satisfied seeing the flames engulf the roof of the Reformed church which had originally been a strongly built Cathedral of the Ghiaurs before the Protestant times.

He had not given this order earlier because he did not want the treasures of the infidels consumed by the inferno. Now he just shrugged and summoned Bey Mustapha to lead the Sipahis to the right wing, and told Bey Bajazid to place his Janissaries on the left, not leaving his four bronze cannons behind. He could carry these moves out easily since the Hussars had dismounted and tried to help the Hajdú Burghers put out the flames and salvage their property from the church, with seemingly pitiful success.

To his annoyance, it took him quite a long time to deploy his army even in this simple formation on the field below Szikszó city because the soil was muddy. Of course, it was slippery because it was a flood plain bordered by the rapid waters of the Hernád River and the Bársonyos Stream. He had no other choice as there was no other open place which would have been large enough to deploy his men. Not as if he cared much about the outcome of the clash, all of them knew that the Christians had never defeated them on the open field, in a larger battle, since the time of the wicked János Hunyadi.

Kara Ali did not want to expose his baggage and tents to any accidental damage so he had his camp surrounded by wagons behind his army. He ordered two-thousand infantrymen to guard the booty and especially the Christian prisoners they had collected so far because he wanted to get a good price for them in the slave market of Buda.

While the Ottoman commander was still struggling with the deployment of his soldiers, the Hungarian horsemen, mainly heavy cavalry, and a negligible German unit of no more than half-thousand soldiers appeared in front of them.

Captain Zsigmond Rákóczi stood with his black-dressed riders on the left and he had placed the Hussars of Serényi and Rotthaler under the flag of István Drugeth of Homonna who was proudly making his horse dance in front of the middle. The right wing was given to Captain Heling's musketmen who were aided by some Hajdú footmen from Szikszó. Their manly task was to hold the Janissaries who outnumbered them by four-to-one. Not as if the Hussars were not facing thrice as many Sipahis as their number.

The enemy was visibly not yet fully prepared for the battle. Rákóczi knew that his only advantage was his quickness so he drew his sword and ordered the charge. Two-thousand horses gathered speed and the forest of lances were leveled.

The shocking impact of the Hussar lances swept away the first line of the Sipahis and the "Jesus, Mary" and "Jesus, Jesus" battle cries dominated over the shouts of "Allahu Akbar". Drugeth of Homonnai raced with Captain Serényi to find the leader of the enemy. The Turks could be defeated easier if their commander was slain and Sir Drugeth wanted this triumph for himself. His prayers must have been answered because a black face appeared before him with great white bulging eyes. Drugeth recognized Kara Ali at once and his heavy saber rose and fell in a deadly pattern which usually worked against his opponents.

One does not fence in a battle just parry the blows instinctively trusting in his Patron Saint. Drugeth tried to fence but the African was a famous duelist in his home and a slight move of his scimitar was enough to deflect the Hungarian's blow. His body was twisting like a snake, and his scimitar knocked the saber out of the Hussar's fist, sending it to fall in the mud. Before the killing cut could reach Drugeth, a rider pushed his horse between them. It was young Pethő who followed his lord like a shadow. His left hand grabbed Kara Ali's right wrist and his horse stopped abruptly, and it was the terrible strength of the animal that jerked the Turk's sword arm backward. Ali turned in the saddle and exposed his torso and head to Pethő for a half second. It was enough for the lad to cut Ali's forehead. The delicately woven chain-mail pieces hanging down from his helmet were not enough to stop the brutal blow. To the greatest horror of his bodyguards, the Bey lifelessly fell from his high Turkish saddle.

Drugeth was taken away from the scene by his horse but he glanced back and saw that three Sipahis were hacking at Pethő with revengeful cries. The Chief Comes unhooked his battle-ax from his saddle and began to wield this long-shafted weapon whose steel beak was perfectly apt to pierce helmets, shields and armor alike.

The loss of Kara Ali happened in the first few minutes of the fight and it was regarded as a bad omen which weakened the hearts of the Muslims. It was Mustapha, the Bey of Szécsény Castle who took over control and encouraged his warriors to fight back in good order. There was a Hussar Lieutenant called Péter Széchy whose family had been driven out of Szécsény Castle so he did not spare himself and broke through the bodyguards of Mustapha. He was in frenzy and literally cut the Bey to pieces, not caring that he was pulled down under the shoes of the horses by the Sipahis while doing so. In a short time, the Ottomans saw two of their most respected Beys die.

The grim-looking black Hussars of Zsigmond Rákóczi were relentlessly pressing the wavering elite Ottoman cavalry, their battle-axes knocking on their armor like a bloody hailstorm. It was a small miracle that the Sipahis did not scatter towards the four directions of the Earth, but were disciplined enough to retreat behind the massive lines of the Janissaries to restore their order.

In the meantime, the Germans of Captain Heling and the Hajdú soldiers of Szikszó on the right wing worked hard to keep the war-machine of the Janissaries at bay. However fanatic the orphans of the Sultan had been, the combination of cold German discipline and savage Hajdú swords were still holding up the overpowering enemy. Not paying a small price for it, though. The German's feet were slipping in mud painted red by their fallen comrades.

When the Sipahis withdrew themselves it was Pasha Bajezid, the Pasha of the Janissaries, who took command firmly into his hands. He gave the order to roll out the four enormous cannons which had been hiding behind the front lines of his infantry thus far. The bronze battle-snakes with their long barrels were aimed at the black-clad Hussars who were turning towards their horses in this moment.
"Quickly, load them with double-charge and feed them with two bags of musket-balls per barrel." he gave the order to the Agha of the Topcus.
"Noble Bey, I am afraid the barrels will burst if I use double the amount of gunpowder," protested the Agha with a pale face.
"Allah ordered us not to fear anything. Obey or die." Bajezid reprimanded him and while the Topcus hurried to do his bidding he added:
"These cannons were cast from the first quality bronze which we had got from the idolizer infidel's king and saint statues from Nagyvárad. The bells of the pagan churches and their own kings have been used as materials for the honor of the Bright Faced Padisah. Are you ready, you lazy loungers?"
Bajezid mounted his Arab steed and drew his sword: "Fire!"

A fiery hell was loosened upon the onrushing Hussars from no more than thirty paces. Lines were swept away and terrible screaming and neighing covered the field where the cannon's white smoke was slowly engulfing everything.

Two volleys of the Janissaries joined the cacophony. First, the kneeling line, then those standing behind them shot as it was their habit. The cannons were turned towards the Germans and the hot barrels punished them with devastating fire too. Many Hussar units lost their leaders, and it was the end of some good officers like Lénárd Kerczi or Lukács Tarnóczy. Captain Rabitz from Szendrő Castle bitterly saw how his brother, Frigyes fell and his Lieutenant, Lukács Tarnóczy was taken away with a severe wound in the stomach. It was an age when the officers did not shy away from leading their men from the front line and now the Hungarians were heavily tolled.

A flag of Hajdú soldiers from 1605

Captain Heling gave the order to retreat half a mile, as slowly as they could, leaving behind his wounded. They stopped when they reached the fences of the village called Vadász and took up position behind some makeshift cover they pulled from the roofs. Fortunately, instead of the Germans, the attention of the Janissaries was focused on the middle of the Hungarian army where Sir Drugeth was desperately trying to pull together his horsemen with not much success.

Drugeth saw the sea of the white high-hats of the Janissaries swallowing them. This tough infantry was never afraid to attack any cavalry. Now, their halberds and sabers worked very effectively, they were attacking each Hussar in their usual units of four. The horsemen had no chance to fight them, their lines were broken through and the elite infantry was slaughtering them one by one. Triumphant "Allahu Akbar" cries froze the blood of the Christians. Captain Rákóczi sounded the half-retreat. When he saw the regrouped Sipahis join the attack, he was inwardly hesitating and was cherishing a thought to rescue his army towards Szerencs Castle and flee.

Sir Drugeth was losing his strength, so far he had been able to cut down all of his attackers, but he was getting out of breath. The Janissaries wanted him dead because they realized he was a kind of leader. Two more bodyguards paid with their lives to gain him some rest, János Nimtsch and Kristóf Prachich. Drugeth was gritting his teeth and killed a big-mustached Jannissar with his battle-ax. The curved beak got stuck into something and he had to lean down to free it. It was then that hands grabbed him and pulled him out of the saddle. A broad-faced Janissary knelt on his chest, pushing him into the mud while his two mates were tying his hands with skillful fingers. Yearning for ransom was burning in their eyes.

New shouts filled the air, this time coming from the left wing.

"Hujj, hujj, hajrá. At it, at it."

It was none other than the men of Captain Serényi who materialized from the fog and ran into the side of the Sipahis, pushing them abruptly aside. Drugeth saw the confusion in the eyes of his captors. They exchanged glances and did not know whether to kill him, or spare him for ransom, but seeing the new enemy the Janissary who was kneeling on him, raised his yatagan. Drugeth strained his muscles and rolled away. Screams were heard and the noise of falling sabers. Hooves were splashing around his head and horses were neighing. He was covered by bloody mud and desperately tried to spit it from his mouth when suddenly he was brought to his feet and he felt the ropes sliced off his wrists.

Captain Serényi was towering over him, looking down from the height of his saddle as if he was a worm having crept out of the soil. Drugeth blinked and cleaned his face, thus smearing it with unwanted materials. When he looked up again, Serényi was gone. One of his dismounted Hussars, the one who had cut his ropes, was respectfully cleaning the filthy coat of the nobleman. Drugeth jerked his coat away and shrieked at him:

"Your horse! Your saber!" and after taking hold of these items, he madly threw himself into the melee without saying thank you. It was woe to the poor Turks he encountered in the following minutes.

He joined the black riders of Rákóczi who took advantage of the confusion of the Janissaries and sallied against the cannons which could spit the third volley into their eyes but could not stop them anymore. The Topcus were slain in a second and some dismounted Hussars busied themselves with turning the cannons against their previous masters.

The men of Captain Heling rejoined the battle with the remaining three-hundred men and their volley decimated the Janissaries. Pasha Bajezid on his horse offered a decent target and soon he was hit by a German bullet. Not much later, Captain Heling was also hit. He sank to his knees and silently gave his spirit back to His Creator.

The battle had been decided but the fight was still going on. The Turks turned, and ran towards the shelter of their fortified camp with the Hungarian horsemen on their heels.

There were one-thousand rested Janissaries who were guarding the wagons and they covered the retreat with their volleys. The Hungarians began to besiege the camp but the enemy was fighting with teeth and claws for their sheer life, putting the captured Christian prisoners to the sword. The screams of the children and the women were terrible to hear.

The Sun set and the struggle reached deep into the evening. The fighters were lit by the inferno of Szikszó City which was burning to the ground in the meantime. It was eleven o'clock when the Turks gave up and fled. The Hussars chased them in the dark up to the waters of the Sajó River and took no captives, killing more than two-thousand of the enemy.

The next day Sir Drugeth was already clean and together with Rákóczi's officers, he gave thanks to God for the victory. After receiving a nice compliment from the Captain of Eger, he was reconciled with Captain Serényi.

They silently stood and watched as the Hajdú soldiers were collecting the dead in a pile and covered them with a hedge woven from thorny branches.

They counted 1744 Turks but there were 410 Hungarians lying next to them, not to mention the 220 German musketmen who had finished their lives so far away from home.

"My Lord, I have received the report of the gains recently," said István Drugeth to Rákóczi. "There are 400 Turks who were lucky enough to become our prisoners of war. Besides the four long bronze cannons, we captured 30 flags, 482 horses and 600 wagons with their baggage. The one-third of it will be sent to the king, the other third is the widow's share and the rest will be divided among the soldiers as the habit of the Valiant Order goes. I hope, Emperor Rudolf will take delight in the booty we had taken from the Truce-breaking pagans."

They smiled and exchanged a nod. Sadly, none of these lords gave even a fleeting thought to the question of who would help the once flourishing agricultural town, Szikszó, recover from the ashes it had been trampled into.

One more bone pile was built on the banks of the Hernád River to remind everyone that the real burial of the fallen warriors is in the stomach of the birds.

40. Diósgyőr Castle   GPS: 48.097702, 20.689474

The castle of Diósgyőr is in northern Hungary near Miskolc. Its importance lay in standing near the road leading to Poland. The Hungarian home-taker, Chief Árpád, gave the lands called Miskolc and its castle Győr to Böngér, the son of Bors. The land which became Borsod County remained in the hands of the Bors family until 1128. It was King István II who took it away from them.

The first castle was built in the 12th century but it was destroyed during the Mongolian invasion in 1241. The castle that stands today was probably built by the order of King Béla IV, who, after the Mongols left the country, had many castles built. The king gave the area to Duke Ernye of the Ákos clan who carried out the order and completed the construction of the second, stronger castle between 1262 and 1270. Ernye's son, István, continued his father's work in 1274. István's son János was already able to celebrate his marriage to a princess from Bayer in a great knightly castle in 1303.

After the end of the Hungarian dynasty of Árpád, the Ernye clan joined the wrong side in 1316 and tried to fight against King Robert Károly who had been an Anjou applicant for the throne. The king was the stronger and all of the grandsons of Duke Ernye were beheaded. The king gave Diósgyőr castle to the Voivode of Transylvania, Dózsa of Debrecen. We can find the castle in the hands of the Croatian Duke Miklós Széchy of the Balogh clan between 1319 and 1325 but then it returned to the king.

The castle's heydays were during the reign of King Louis I, a Hungarian king from the Anjou dynasty who often stayed within its walls. In 1364 the nearby town Miskolc was annexed to the Diósgyőr estate. The Peace Treaty of Turin was signed in the castle of Diósgyőr in 1381. In the treaty, the Italian town of Venice was compelled to raise the flag of the Anjou dynasty in St. Mark square every Sunday.

Diósgyőr Castle became the property of King Louis's Queen in 1340. When King Louis I died in 1382, King Zsigmond was its next owner and arrived there in 1387 with his Queen Maria and held a Diet in the castle. King Zsigmond gave the splendid castle to his second wife, Borbála of Czillei in 1424.

Diósgyőr Castle today (Photo: Hello Miskolc)

For the next few centuries, the castle was a holiday residence for queens. The last queen to own the castle was Habsburg Maria, wife of King Louis II. During the Dual Kingship, King Szapolyai gave it to the Balassa family of Gyarmat in 1536 and they were the ones who turned it into a large fortress.

Additionally, they had an Italian-style round bastion built to the north-western tower. King Ferdinand took Diósgyőr away from Lord Balassa but gave it back to him when the Lord became loyal to him instead of King Szapolyai. To make a good deal, Ferdinand made Balassa pay 20,000 gold Forints to get his castle back. When Balassa died, the castle returned to the Habsburg king.

The castle had been sacked and burned in 1544 by the raiding Turks. After 1564 the owners changed frequently but the Perényi, the Török, the Bedegy-Nyáry and the Haller families let the castle slowly deteriorate.

In 1596 the Ottoman army occupied the Castle of Eger and defeated the Christian army in the Battle of Mezőkeresztes which lay not too far from Diósgyőr. Diósgyőr became a Borderland Castle but it was rather an old-fashioned Gothic palace with nice but thin walls so it was almost impossible to defend. As the surrounding hills were high enough to deploy the enemy's artillery, the castle lost its military importance.

The Turks looted it in 1596 and it inevitably fell into the hands of the Ottomans in 1598. The Turks promptly burned it down. However, the damaged walls were soon taken back. There were many Turkish raids in the area in the following period, not to mention the destruction of the Imperial army of the Habsburg in 1600.

The Hungarian Diet ordered the renovation of Diósgyőr in 1618 but the work had not yet been finished in 1631. According to Gáspár Szentkereszti, the officer of the castle, the Turks raided it 27 times in 1641, killing 22 soldiers and the vice-captain, taking away 48 women and children, stealing the cattle herd four times and taking 20 horses as well. Chief-captain Samuel Haller died in fighting there in 1643.

The army of the Transylvanian Prince György I Rákóczi took it in 1644, but the Emperor took it back during that same year. It was a heroic deed that this castle could withstand a Turkish siege in 1650 in spite of its wall conditions. According to a contemporary survey from 1662, they could not have rebuilt the castle for even 4,000 gold Forints. In addition to this, the roof burned down in 1673.

During the War of Independence of Prince Imre Thököly, the garrison of the castle consisted of German and Hungarian troops, but the Hungarians rebelled in 1678 and drove the Germans out killing many of them. The arriving Habsburg army took revenge on the castle and after taking it, they burned it and then ruined it almost to the ground. The surrounding lands were ruled by the Pasha of Eger until 1687 when this part of the country was finally freed from Turkish rule. When Prince Ferenc I Rákóczi's army arrived there in 1704, the ruined castle lost all of its military importance. Now, the castle has been nicely renovated and there you can see in it the biggest knightly hall of Central Europe. Many concerts and festivals take place within its walls. It is home to the largest fighting arena in Hungary wherein re-enactors can hold their historical tournaments and championships.

41. The Battle of Mezőkeresztes (1596)

Sir Edward Barton, the Ambassador for Queen Elisabeth of England in the Sultan's Court, looked out of the window of his elegant residence which overlooked the Bay of Bosporus and took delight in the colorful fireworks which colored the capital of Sultan Mehmed III. His thoughts went to the latest poem which celebrated the Sultan's triumph in the Battle of Mezőkeresztes in Hungary. His keen memory recalled it at once:

"All the shops of the city became colored due to conquerors wishes. Each of which was decorated as if it were the kerchief of the sweetheart"
It was true, the town joyfully reveled in the victory, the greatest defeat of the Catholic idolizers since the battle of Mohács which was seventy years ago. And it was indeed a sweet victory because during these celebrations, four galleys full of state procured sugar from Egypt arrived in Istanbul harbor, which added "sweetness" to the news of a military victory. On top of this, Sultan Mehmed III was awarded the epithet of 'Conqueror of Eger Castle'.

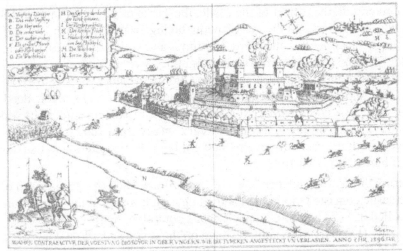

The siege of Diósgyőr in 1596

Sir Barton tore himself from the view and returned to his letter in which he tried to give a detailed report of this battle as was required of him. He decided to use the official styles and title of the Queen in his letter knowing that many spies would copy it before it could get to London.

"From Edward Barton, British Ambassador in the Court of the Ottoman Sultan to:

By the Grace of God, Queen Elisabeth of England, France, and Ireland, Defender of the Faith, and of the Church of England in Earth, under Jesus Christ, Supreme Head.

Your Majesty, as Your appointed Ambassador, I am to give you the account about the latest conflict between the Sultan and the Catholics. And if your Majesty may say that one must begin before one can finish, I hold it for very certain that by all that I have seen and heard of this clash of armies was a turning point in the recent war as the Ottomans proved themselves better again in a grand-scale battle than the western generals but only their good luck saved them from being defeated. And for my part (poor worm as

I am) if I had riches and more than the riches of Crœsus, I would dare to venture both property and life in assuring your Majesty that you will find my report true and necessary in order to assess the military potential of both the Sultan and the Catholic forces.

This is why I owe Your Majesty a more detailed description of this particular battle of Mezőkeresztes which I have carefully pieced together from hearing out many captured Catholic officers and by having been an eyewitness of the battle by my humble self. Let me be allowed to start at the beginning:

There had been a peace between the Habsburgs and the Ottomans since 1568 but Pasha Hassan broke the Truce in 1593 with his unfortunate private action to take Szikszó Castle. The Pasha lost his head in the fight and this was how Emperor Rudolf and Sultan Mehmed became enemies again, to the greatest advantage of the English Crown and of the Church of England on Earth.

So far, the war has been raging with largely equal success, the Catholics took back some Hungarian castles in the north, namely Fülek, Fehérvár, and Nógrád Castles while the Turks were able to take some very important forts in the Trans-Danubian Region. They gained Várpalota Castle, Veszprém and the Castle of Győr which is dangerously close to Vienna. Sadly, the Protestant interests had been betrayed last year when the Principality of Transylvania stabbed his brothers in the back by allying itself with the idolizer Catholic Emperor Rudolf, the enemy of the Church of England.

Sultan Mehmed III

Soon, Wallachia and Moldavia were made to rebel against their sworn lord, the Sultan, and this is how the balance of the war began to move in their favor. This was how the Catholics could take back Esztergom Castle in the

Bend of the Danube and the important forts of Lippa and Jenő which are the gates to Transylvania. On top of this, it is a shame that a Protestant lord, a certain Stephen Bocskai dared to defeat the Sultan's army in the battle of Gyurgyevo.

As I have hinted before to Your Majesty about the false-heartedness of the Transylvanians, now it has all come true. Their prince proved to be just as lenient towards the Catholics as he had been towards all the sinuous sects of the Protestant faith, including the polygamy Anabaptists. The alliance of the Protestant Transylvanians with the Catholic Austrians is a proof that any Muslim Sultans would be more trusted allies of England than the unreliable Transylvanians or Hungarians, let them call themselves Protestants or not.

Seeing these baleful signs, though, Sultan Mehmed III decided to lead his 150,000-strong-army in person and he set out against the Catholics on 23 June 1596. His strategic goal was to punish Transylvania and Wallachia and teach them obedience, not to dare ally themselves any more with the enemy of the Ottomans. I counted myself lucky to be allowed to join his retinue as Your Majesty is in high esteem before the Bright Faced Padisah. The army marched through Edirne, Filibe, Sofia, and Nis to arrive at Belgrade on 9 August. On 20 August, the army crossed the River Száva and entered the Hungarian territory of Siren.

A war council was called at Zalánkemén Castle, and it was decided that they would begin a siege on the Hungarian fort of Eger. This castle controlled the communication routes between Habsburg Austria through Royal Hungary towards Transylvania and Poland. The army got there only after a month, and meanwhile, the Catholic army, led by Archduke Maximilian, took Hatvan Castle by siege and killed all the Ottomans housed there, including the women and children. Hearing of our approach, they were forced to retreat when they realized the strength of our mighty army. The Great Sultan took advantage at once on their fright and seized the important fort of Eger, leaving not a soul alive in answer to the Austrian's cruelty.

The presence of the Sultan indicated that this campaign was more than a simple military clash between the two armies. It was the conflict of two great powers, two different political systems, two cultures and two religions, the battle between two worlds, the conflict between the West and the East. The enemy consisted of a European coalition, troops recruited by the Pope, units led by the princes of Lüneburg and Anhalt, the Transylvanians with their Wallachian and Moldavian allies, not to count the Polish and the Cossack contingents. Besides the troops of the Holy Roman Empire, there were mercenaries from France and from Bohemia but one could see many Walloon, Spanish and Serbian soldiers as well. It was a real Christian coalition albeit led by the idolizer Catholics. These many sons of several nations flocked under the flag of Archduke Maximilian von Habsburg against the warriors of the Sultan.

CONTERFACTVR WIE HATWAN MIT GESTVRMETER HANDT EROBERT VND EINGENOMEN WORDEN. DEN 3 SEPTEMBER. ANNO DMI 1596.

The taking of Hatvan Castle in 1596

The Archduke was the highest born ruler they all accepted as their leader. Since the Archduke did not have much experience in the art of Mars, a military council was established to help him. The two best soldiers in this council were Adolf Schwarzenberg, the Field Marschall, the "brain of the army" and the equally renowned Count Miklós Pálffy, the commander of the Trans-Danubian Hungarian troops from Royal Hungary.

General Schwarzenberg had gained lots of experience from the wars from France and the Low Countries and Count Pálffy had fought against the Ottoman Empire all in his life. It was the Chief Captain of Kassa City, Christoph Tieffenbach who was in charge of the Hungarian warriors from Upper Hungary while the Transylvanians were led by Prince Sigismund Báthory. The Transylvanian army consisted of the Székely frontier-guards, the Saxon troops, and the Hungarian noblemen's units. Their paramount contingent was actually under the strict command of a certain Albert Király who was a more seasoned soldier than his prince. This huge allied force of the Catholic and Protestant powers wanted to make a desperate attempt to liberate half of the Balkan from the Sultan's hand. The Sultan had to demonstrate his strength and break their spine or let his Empire fall into pieces.

It was already 13 October and the weather strongly limited the reach of the Ottoman army but the taking of Eger was an enormous success. No wonder that the Catholics wanted to take it back. As the mentioned fort had been greatly damaged during the siege, Sigismund Báthory, the Prince of Transylvania persuaded Archduke Maximilian to jerk it out from our hands. The combined Transylvanian-Austrian army could boast with more than 50,000 men and they set out from Diósgyőr Castle with the determination to meet the Sultan on the way to Eger. They were marching in a two-mile-long line and took up their position near the small town of Mezőkeresztes which had recently been destroyed to the ground during the war.

Maximilian III, Archduke of Austria

It was a wise choice to wait for the trice-larger army of the Sultan because the place, as it is hidden in the meaning of its Hungarian name which is "The crossing of the field" is located on a perfect strategic point.
Everybody must cross this 5 times 3 miles large field who wants to commute between Eger and Kassa city. To the North, the dense forests of the Bükk Mountains border it while it is blocked by the marshy lands of the Tisza River to the South. The slippery, steep banks of the Sályi Stream bordered the field to the West and the muddy valley of the Csincse Creek to the East made the field a natural stronghold.

Right before getting there, the Catholic forces organized themselves into four columns to prevent any ambushes because they had not have much idea about our position.

Hearing of their advance, a war council was conducted under Grand Vizier, Pasha Damat Ibrahim where I was allowed to be present as the

Ambassador of Your Majesty. It was decided that the Ottoman Army should march out of Eger castle so as to meet the Austrians at a more suitable battle terrain than the ruined fort. I must remark the fact to Your Majesty that during the meeting, the Sultan thought that the Ottoman army should disengage and return to Istanbul; it was with great difficulty that he was persuaded to engage the enemy forces. Yet, against the hopes of the infidels that the Sultan would turn back to his home, Mehmed's main army bravely continued their advance and the vanguards began their clashes with the enemy on 22 October.

The Ottoman army marched through several passageways of marshy terrain and finally reached the plains of Mezőkeresztes, exhausted after the previous long siege and a hard, long march. The Austrian-Transylvanian army was waiting for them in a better position, deployed in a delicately designed battle-order, leaving not much room for the Sultan's army to get properly deployed in full size.

It was the middle of the afternoon when I caught sight of the Catholics. A Hungarian "pribék", a renegade was assigned next to me and he proved himself to be useful in telling me the details as both of us spoke Turkish fluently.

Zsigmond Báthori, Prince of Transylvania

The enemy has just marched decently in by the tunes of a music band, although maintaining a nice order of this 50,000-strong multinational army must have been a challenge. The vanguard was led by Count Pálffy and his light Hungarian Hussars. Behind them, the column on the left side consisted of horsemen, proceeding steadily along the bank of a small river. They guarded the foreign mercenaries in the middle, footmen armed with their long lances and muskets. In front of them riding Archduke Maximilian, surrounded by the heavy cavalry of the princes of Lüneburg and Anhalt, their soldiers wearing full armor and their beasts were twice the size of a Turkish horse. Their right side was guarded by a column of a mixed unit of Hungarian riders and infantry. The "pribék" in my service pointed at the cannons deployed on both sides of the columns which guarded the train of wagons along with 4,000 Hajdú soldiers. I was told there were 97 cannons altogether, just half as many as the Sultan had. According to the spies, there were about 8,000 wagons behind the Catholic army, now being fastened together by chains. Their camp was full of servants and with the usual riff-raff camp-followers whose number was about 15,000.

Sultan Mehmed could boast with almost 150,000 Turk and Tatar troops and naturally, it was why the deployment of such an enormous army was slower than the enemy. Only a small part of the Ottoman army was lined up on the other side of the field where I stood.

The Sultan sent the Rumelian army led by Pasha Dzsigalazáde Sinan and Pasha Murad who was the Begler Bey of Diyarbekir to snare the infidels into a trap but they ran into the 300 Transylvanian lancers of Albert Király at a stream called Csincse. Soon, 600 German riders joined in the fight, led by Hermann Christoph Russwurm and Johann Baptist Pezzen. These cavalry officers immediately realized their weakness and sent for reinforcement. Field marshal Adolf Schwarzenberg hurried to their aid in person, bringing along 900 Austrian knights and about the same number of Transylvanian Hussars. He was supported by 300 Hungarian riders who were supplied with rifles and 400 Walloon pike-men who could offer stable defense in case of a retreat.

The Rumelian cavalry had been recruited in the Greek Vilayets of the Empire and they were bravely withholding the first clash for a while but they turned tail when noticed the entire Catholic army catching up with their vanguard. They jumped over the Kácsi Stream and left the Janissary infantry unit and the Topcus with their cannons alone to guard the stream, led by Bey Djafer. Shamefully, the bewildered Rumelians ran as far as Mezőkövesd which lies several miles behind the Ottoman army. It was hard to regroup them by the angry Ottomans officers who used their long whips for this purpose.

Fortunately, the volley of the Janissaries was enough to stop the Austrian and Hungarian riders who were chasing the Rumelians, as I can bear witness to this. The Janissaries used square-shaped bullets which they cut off from thin lead sticks with their sharp hanjars, curved daggers. These bullets penetrated an average breastplate better than the lead balls used by the enemy, although their range was shorter.

General Miklós Pálffy

Yet, the enemy kept trying to cross this stream and there were two passageways where bridges had served this function before the battle. One of these was the bridge of Mezőkeresztes village which could have been easily mended. Light troops, Transylvanian riflemen were sent to take it who unlike the western mercenaries, wore no helmets or armor and could move fast among the bushes of the stream. The Topcus aimed their cannons at them and the daredevil Transylvanians were punished from 43 angry iron throats. They skillfully spread out at once and took cover behind the ruined houses of Mezőkeresztes village. They were firing madly at the Janissaries but soon they received six smaller cannons and further troops hurried to their aid as well.

While their fire was intensified, we did not notice the elite bodyguard of the Transylvanian prince crossing the water a bit downstream. These blue-uniformed Hungarians are formidable and disciplined infantrymen, they are called the blue-drabants. Eight-hundred of them attacked the Janissaries in the side and their volleys decided the possession of the bridge. I saw the Janissaries glimpsing behind their backs and as they had been abandoned by the Rumelian cavalry, they quickly turned and fled.

The Battle of Mezőkeresztes on a Turkish miniature

My long legs prevented me from being captured and my "pribék" servant led me to the camp safely. I heard that a few light cavalry units managed to chase the poor Janissaries of Bey Djafar and slaughtered many of them. The falling darkness was a real blessing because the enemy stopped further troops to cross the stream and decided to make their camp for the night. They seemed to have been satisfied by the taking of our 43 cannons.

Their camp-makers had been working hard by erecting a proper military camp until the next day's afternoon. In the meantime, Sultan Mehmed held a war-council and the Sultan seemed to have wanted to flee from the battlefield. However, first, he asked for the opinion of his tutor, the high cleric Hoca Sadeddin Efendi. He told the Sultan that he should continue the battle till the end. Heeding this advice, Sultan Mehmed ordered that the battle should continue. Dammad Ibrahim, his Grand Vizier supported the advice of the Sultan's tutor. Soon, it was decided to force the infidels into a battle next day and as a result of this, the Ottoman troops crossed the marshy Csicsve Stream during the night to enter the field of Mezőkeresztes.

Székely flag from the 17th century

When the Sun rose on 25 October, the Catholics were surprised to see in front of them a tired but fully organized Ottoman army standing in battle order. Obviously, the enemy was in a better position but nevertheless, the Turks attacked the Austrian trenches, the Battle of Mezőkeresztes or Hacova in Turkish, commenced and continued for two days, from 25-26 October. There were 10,000 riders in the Sultan's vanguard detachment and 3,000 Tatar horsemen of them - or better call them mounted devils - were sent forward to disturb the enemy and assess their strength and position. They spread along the stream and tried to find fords in smaller units because the two proper passing places were severely guarded by the Catholics at the village of Mezőkeresztes and at Ábrány, which was the second place for an army's decent crossing.

Nevertheless, they managed to cross the creek farther to the south and tried to get close to the Catholic camp, riding past the Transylvanian troops. They were unlucky because they received a heavy cannon and howitzer fire from there so they had to find cover behind a small mound. Then, a few Transylvanian riders rode out and individual duels were developed, some men fell from saddles from each side. More and more Székely riders joined the fight and soon overpowered the Tatars. The Székely warriors, these seasoned frontier guards of Transylvania`s mountains, began to loot the fallen Tatars. Seeing this, the Tatars turned and fell on them. If the heavy cavalry of Archduke Maximilian had not thundered to their rescue, alas, these barbarous folks would have never returned to their lowly dwellings. Finally, the Tatars decided to get back behind the Ottoman lines where the cannons could not reach them.

The Ottoman warriors stood in a battle line which resembled the crescent moon while the Catholic lines were at a right angle to them. The Tatars stood in the first line with the horsemen from Diyárbekir and from Damascus, led by Dzsigalazáde. The cannons were deployed behind them and in the second line, the Janissaries and the bodyguard cavalry of the Sultan were standing. The Rumelian army was on the left wing and the Anatolians were on the right wing.

Being too early in the morning, the Catholics were slow to complete their battle-formation. The Hungarians from Upper Hungary were facing Mezőkeresztes village, standing between the burned church of the settlement and the Christian camp. At the northern end of the camp was the stream's second crossing, at a place called Alsóábrány which was guarded by the forces of Archduke Maximilian. The Transylvanian troops, reinforced by other forces, were standing on the field, turning towards the west towards Nagymihály village. Their right wing was supported by the Hungarian soldiers of General Tieffenbach and by the trenches built around the burned church of Mezőkeresztes. Their left wing was secured by a wagon-fort towards the east.

Initially, the advantage seemed to have been seized by the Sultan's forces. They were able to take the Catholic's trenches around the ruined church before the enemy could get fully deployed in their battle-line. These trenches above the ford had to be taken because the cannons placed over them were able to control the whole line of the creek from north to south. Any crossing of the water was only possible after silencing their fire. Having taken this important bridgehead, the Ottoman troops could enter the theatre of war which they bravely did. By the time some units got through to the eastern bank, the Habsburg and Transylvanian troops have been organized and their combined artillery fire severely hit the advancing Turks in the face. The Catholics and their Protestant Transylvanian allies took good use of all kinds of firearms, smaller and bigger cannons and muskets alike. They were supplied with these in great numbers and the swiftness of their cannons was worth recognizing. So far, the cannons have been quite fixed weapons in the Ottoman army and albeit used in quantities, after sending a few volleys they did not take further part in the course of the grand-scale battles. The Catholics moved their cannons on their wheels with a surprising speed and the artillery followed the advancing or retreating mercenaries as it was required by the moment. They sheltered their cannons by pike-men and tried to provoke the Sultan's troops to run into the fire and the forest of pikes again and again.

When the brave Muslim warriors were driven back by the savage and unusual bombardment, the wicked Hungarian Hussars were riding right behind their heels, slaughtering them. When the Turks turned on them with regained strength, these horsemen cowardly turned tail and galloped behind the pike-men and the artillerymen who had finished loading the cannons by that time. And it began, again and again, causing huge losses to the Sultan. To take full advantage of this tactic, the Catholics had to force the Ottoman army back behind the creek so the Hungarian troops, led by Christoph Tieffenbach, the Chief Captain of Kassa, attacked the church and the fortifications.

Grand Vizier Ibrahim had sent four cannons for the reinforcement of these trenches which proved to be most useful and cut bloody corridors into the warriors of Upper Hungary who got thronged under the trenches. It was the Rumelian Begler Bey who was defending the church and the combatants were amply aware of the strategic importance of the bridgehead. The Greek warriors of the Begler Bey fought valiantly but they were beaten out after a fierce struggle. Alas, the Hungarians took our four cannons and turned them against us and succeeded in driving back the Ottoman assaults with a barrage of cannon and musket fire.

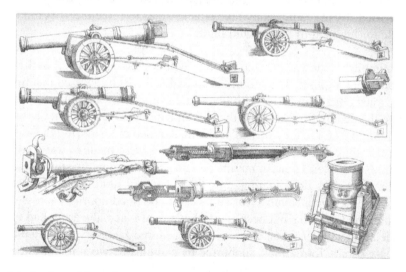

As this ford could not be taken back at Mezőkeresztes, smaller Turk units attempted to find other crossing places but their vain efforts were awarded only by heavy rifle fire. By noon, the Austrians carried more cannons to the hillock at the ruined church from where they could shoot not only the smaller units which were miserably attempting to cross the marshy creek but their missiles fell into the midst of the Sultan's battle line as well.

I was watching the progress of the battle from the close proximity of Sultan Mehmed himself and the cannonballs stroke the earth just a few yards next to His Brightness the Padisah, killing a few of his bodyguards. The wicked cannonball's range covered a full English mile and it was mainly the horses which suffered mightily because of the fiery and loud missiles.

In the afternoon it became clear that the Janissaries had failed to regain the crossing place, the entire battle line had to be withdrawn because of the cannonade. This precaution had to be made because most of the soldiers had been standing idly in readiness since dawn and they got totally exhausted. Yet, the work of making camp was still ahead of them and while they were toiling to erect the tents, the other half of the army remained in battle formation to protect them.

Allegedly, the war council of the Archduke agreed that evening that they should follow the successful tactic of this day and they should let half of the Ottoman army come to the field of Mezőkeresztes and shot them to shreds. They wanted to squeeze the Ottoman army between the Csincse Creek and the Lator Stream so the Turks could be forced to launch only a facial attack against the cannons. Despite his lack of military experience, the Archduke had the wisest opinion. He suggested keeping the whole Ottoman army in readiness by fake attacks so as to force the Turks in the saddle for hours until they would faint.

My humble person was invited again to witness the war council in the Sultan's tent at night. The bright Faced Padisah wisely realized that his army must engage in battle with the infidels otherwise it would fall apart due to the deadly tiredness and the lack of supplies. He gave out the order at midnight to force the army to cross the damned creek during the night wherever they can. The soldiers and the horses were made to use up the last morsel of their strength but the dawn found them on the southern end of Mezőkeresztes field again, facing the blackened stones of the church. The entire Ottoman cavalry was supposed to be lined up, right across the camp of the Catholics but because of the lack of place, the army had to be divided into smaller parts. There were three large Janissary units standing in dense square formations, supported by cannons between them. The rest of the cavalry was deployed to the south, turning towards north-east, behind the Tardi Stream. The Janissary and Sipahi bodyguard of the Sultan along with the rearguard stood between the Turk camp and the ruined village of Szentistván.

The first attack stubbornly targeted the ford at Mezőkeresztes. The mass of Ottoman horsemen began to approach its guards, the 2,000 Hungarian Hussars in slow steps. Some reinforcement was sent to the Hungarians but either they could not repel the mighty numbers of the Turks or they did not want to because they retreated and let the Sultan's forces cross the creek. The Catholics withdrew all their troops and cannons from behind the trenches of the ruined church so the entire Ottoman army was able to fight off the murderous creek without having to lose men.

In my humble opinion, Your Majesty, it should have been a warning. When half of the thronged Ottoman force could get over, the trap became obvious. The idolizer Catholics rolled out their wicked cannons and even the lighter and smaller ones made a great damage to our tightly packed ranks. The horses advanced twenty paces and were thrown back fifteen again and again. Behind the smoke of the one-hundred battle-snakes, the Christian coalition got masterfully deployed in a complicated pattern which allowed them to attack or defend themselves with equal ease.

Their battle order had to be organized so as to find the best position for the light- the half-heavy and the heavy cavalry just like the place for the squares of the western mercenary tercios and for the lighter Hungarian infantry. Each tercio consisted of several thousand of pike-men and musket-men who fought like unbreakable, living strongholds. They could move very slowly but the forests of pikes defended each bastion from all sides. The Italian, Walloon and German soldiers serving under the flags of their mercenary captains knew they can survive any battle if they keep discipline and obey the orders. As individual soldiers, they may have been the filth from the gutter but their battle-moral was excellent.

No wonder that the tercios were the strong backbone of the Archduke's army in this battle. Five of them stood firmly in the middle of the field while the light Hungarian infantry supported them on both wings. The bulk of the Catholic attack was given to the cavalry whose number was a lot fewer than the Sultan's. It was the reason why they were deployed between the tercios where they could have a chance to withdraw and regroup, any time it would be needed. Yet, the Archduke had a strong attacking wedge placed in the middle of his army. The core of this wedge was made up from 4,000 heavy Transylvanian Hussar warriors who were supported by 1,000 half-heavy German horsemen on their right and 1,300 of them on their left. Behind them came the heaviest 500 armored Vestfalian riders, clad in iron from top to toe. They all were supposed to tear the Ottoman battle-line into two.

Your Majesty may reprimand me for blaming the Ottoman cavalry for waiting idly until the Catholics have arranged their lines. Did the Turks really let the initiative action slip from their grasp so easily? Grand Vizier Dammad Ibrahim was as merciful as to find an answer to my question, saying that they had to wait for the assault of the infidel cavalry because the cannon-fire ceased only after this. The Archduke had to stop the cannons when his cavalry trotted out in the field in order to save them from their own fire.

Waiting idly in vain or not, the Ottoman cavalry paid a heavy price when the full force of the steel wedge hit them. The terrible weight had a loud impact on the Ottoman lines when the lances of the galloping Hussars shattered them. The Westphalian cuirassiers trod the fallen Sipahies into the soil and the rest of the infantry followed them suit. It took only a short but awful time and the whole Ottoman army was forced out from the field of Mezőkeresztes. The Tatars on the left wing tried to hold on for a while but then they fled. The 300 brave Janissaries of Bey Djafar were fighting steadily at the ruined church but their resistance was soon put down. The attackers could take away 40 cannons from them, along with ten wagon loads of ammunition.

The Ottoman army was not beaten, though. The Hungarian horsemen were stopped everywhere along the creek and the attacks of the Germans and the Transylvanian infantry were repeatedly fought off. Finally, it was the cannonade that helped the enemy, like so many times before. The musket-men and quickly deployed cannons tolled the Ottomans from the trenches around the ruined church so badly that they had no choice but to withdraw out of their range. Several German and Hungarian units crossed the creek and established bridge-heads for the entire Catholic army to cross the water.

The carefully designed battle formation of the Archduke had to be changed when 50,000 footmen crossed through the three narrow makeshift bridges they built. Their new formation consisted of only two lines on the other side of the creek and they had to get deployed quickly because this time, the Sultan did not wait for long to attack them. Unfortunately, the attack was repelled by the pike-men and because of the killing musket fire. Only two major fights were worth mentioning, the first took place in the north-eastern part of the Turk camp where the Sipahi and the Tatar riders were being re-grouped. They were unlucky enough to meet the steel wedge of the Catholic cavalry again.

The outcome was the same as in the morning. Later I met a captured French knight who recalled this clash like this:

"…we were attacking the right, the Saxons were galloping in the middle and the Transylvanian Hussars were running on the left side. We hit the enemy hard and chased them all the way through the field. After this, other riders joined us and we rode on with such ferocity, shooting and slaughtering the enemy's back that cannot be properly described . . ."

The second fight occurred on the south, near the eastern side of the Turk camp. Here, 4,000 Janissaries stood steadily, supported by cannons. Again, it was Bey Djafar who led them but his valiant soldiers were scattered totally in half-an-hour time by the first line of the enemy.

Hungarian cavalrymen

Meanwhile, the middle of the Catholic army pushed the Ottomans back beyond their camp. During the melee, the mercenary unit's formation spread out and they became utterly disorganized when it came to the chase. Alas, the whole Ottoman army around me seemed to have just one thought, how to flee the battlefield. Practically, the enemy was chasing the Turks in their own camp. For a brief moment, I was as paralyzed as them. In my despair, I believed that the dream of the combined Christian army might come true and the famous Ottoman army can be defeated in a grand scale battle. It would have brought about the loss of not only the Hungarian conquest of the Ottoman Empire but the Balkan Peninsula would have fallen into the hands of the Catholic idolizers and their heretic Protestant allies within a short time.

Yet, our Merciful God did not allow the victory of Your Majesty's enemy and the Battle of Mezőkeresztes has come to a turning point. The greed of the mercenaries and the Székely Hungarian riders caused the end of the Archduke's good fortune when they rushed into the two-miles-long Turk camp from the north.

Instead of turning the Turk's own cannons against them and continuing the chase, these soldiers began to loot the tents, eventually reaching the Sultan's tent which stood on the southern end. Bey Djafar, the Agha of the Janissaries told me the rest:

"The Christian soldiers attacked the tent where the chests of gold money of the Ottoman Exchequer were kept. They killed and otherwise eliminated the Janissary and household cavalry soldiers guarding the State Treasury. The Christian soldiers got on the Treasury chests of gold coin and put up their flags of cross over them and started to dance around them. After this, the troops from the Austrian army had reached the Sultan's tent, which was surrounded by the viziers and the teachers at the Palace Pages School for protection. While some troops were trying to enter the Sultan's tent, the other Austrian army's soldiers disengaged, in search of booty and plunder instead of continuing the engagement. The Ottoman horse groomers, cooks, tent makers, camel minders retaliated against the plunderers with whatever arms they could find, including cooks' spoons, blocks of wood, hammers. They also used other tools as weapons: adzes, and axes for cutting wood.

Of course, the strong attack of Pasha Yusuf Sinan's horsemen has helped to clear the camp, too. The Austrians were surprised and retreated in confusion. Soon, the Ottomans noticed that the number of their chasers has been significantly reduced. The cries of "the Christian enemy is fleeing" were heard by the Ottoman troops still fighting what seemed like a losing battle on the frontline. The boost of morale allowed them to recover the battle. With a major action from the artillery, the Ottoman forces started another attack on the Austrians across the front and outflanked the Austrian-Transylvanian army, routing them."

The noble Agha was right but my confidence in your Majesty's clemency giving me hope that you will not take amiss my poor writing and that your innate good disposition will lead you to be pleased to accept my addition to the Agha's report. As I have carefully investigated it, the bulk of the Catholic army began to flee not because of noticing the running mercenaries from the Turk camp. The second line of the Archduke was still intact and a couple of dozen of fleeing individual soldiers could not have broken their order so easily. According to their own report of Archduke

Maximilian himself that he wrote only a few weeks after the battle, his army was frightened and confused by a few hundred fleeing Christian riders.

The Sultan's chief spymaster managed to make a copy of this report so let me cite it to Your Majesty how the Archduke wrote about this: "... abruptly, in spite of the chief officer's hopes, a couple of hundred Hussars and a few hundred German horsemen returned from the enemy at once, without any visible reason because they did not seem to have been attacked by anyone. Then, they began to flee and all Hungarian and German riders followed them ..." The Archduke concluded that it was the result of a fatal military negligence because the vibrating bustle of the battle and the clouds of smoke had distracted the attention of the commanders from assessing the Ottoman forces which were still intact at the southern end of the Turk camp. Exposing the undefended left wing was the fault of the professional soldiers like the Transylvanian Albert Király and Miklós Pálffy. General Tieffenbach and Fieldmarshal Schwarzenberg had to bear the responsibility equally but curiously enough, later everybody blamed it on Archduke Maximilian who had the least role in it.

Obviously, the Catholics would not have launched their full attack towards the Ottoman camp if they had guessed that the Sultan's 10,000 Janissary bodyguards and the iron-clad Sipahis along with the rear-guard were waiting for the order to draw their swords. Not to mention the several thousands of Ottoman riders from their right-wing and the remains of the still fighting Turk units. The size of the total force which attacked the Archduke's army into the side was about 20-25,000 men. Why did the Ottoman army need to wait for the counter-attack more than an hour after the Christians had launched their overall assault?

Most sadly, it was not a cunningly timed action, the Ottoman army simply consumed this much time to react and organize the counter-attack of Pasha Cicala who lead the cavalry of the rear-guard. Their attack hit the left-wing of the Archduke and the Hussars along with the German riders had to dodge the sudden onslaught by turning to the right which was the only possible way to go. It was how they crashed into the second line of the Christians, throwing them into disorder. Pasha Cicala took the last intact Ottoman cavalry into the fight and it was only the good luck of the Sultan that the fleeing individuals and small groups running out of the Turkish camp showed up at the same time. The panic swept away the famous discipline of the landsknechts and the entire army began to rout.

Archduke Maximilian made a futile attempt to rescue the infantry by hurrying to their aid with three hundred riders but the maddened crowd simply scattered his riders like fallen leaves. Prince Bernhardt of Anhalt faced the chasing Ottoman cavalry with two hundred German riders but it has not changed the situation. It was due to the falling dusk and the miraculous valor of some Christian infantry units that the triumphal Ottoman riders reined in at the Fords of the creek.

The tired Turk horsemen returned to their camp after a few volleys from the enemy's cannons. In the meantime, the Tatars got around the Christian's camp and got mixed with the fleeing enemy, slaughtering and pillaging them until dark. Although their camp was well-fortified and would have been absolutely suitable for re-organizing their troops nobody was able to issue such orders. The wagons were being detached from each other and many of the mercenaries tried to salvage as much as they could carry by plundering their own camp in the terrible havoc. Seeing this, the Archduke did not even dare to enter his camp.

In addition to this, the evening brought a dense fog and the Fieldmarshal Schwarzenberg got lost in it. The Transylvanians did not seem so frightened. They were quite indifferently packing their belongings and left the camp with their wagons in good order. Only General Pálffy remained in the camp and he made a war council at midnight with the remaining officers. Seeing the disintegration of the army, they could do nothing except collecting their most important possessions and leave the camp in silence.

During this time, the Sultan's units on the other side of the creek did not look like a victorious army. They were feverishly packing and disassembling their camp and nobody thought of chasing the Catholics and no military actions were made. The commanders of the Sultan could regain the full control over their army only when the Christians had left the battlefield. The Ottomans were not able to take away the several hundreds of wagons which had been abandoned by the enemy and lots of the enemy's supply and cannons were left on the field as well.

The losses of the Sultan approached 30,000 and the number of casualties has been growing. It was easy to tend a wound caused by swords or pikes but nine out of ten soldiers perished because of infections who had been injured by a musket. The enemy suffered less than half of this number, most of them fell during the plundering of the Turkish camp and when the second line broke and fled. The most numerous casualties came from the Swabian, Bayern and the two Czech contingents who ran away in panic, trodding each other to death.

The Catholics have almost won the battle of Mezőkeresztes but finally, they were the ones who had to leave the field. Their failure had a rather a spiritual and political consequence than tactical or strategic. It is quite undeniable that the initial action had always been in the hands of the Christians. They had chosen the battlefield and they were in a better position. Who were the victors of all the clashes if not them? Were they not rolling the Ottoman cavalry before them with their tremendous artillery fire at their will? Did not they deploy their troops and sweep the Turks off the battlefield as artfully as if it had been written in military books? There were five different kinds of Christian soldiers, western and eastern infantry, three kinds of cavalry and who knows how many nations together, all acting quickly in unison, showing excellent discipline and carrying out difficult orders. Were they not able to cover continuously each yard of the battlefield before them with the lethal fire of their surprisingly mobile artillery? Why did the mightier Ottoman army accept a battlefield where they were not able to make full use of their strong cavalry? Why was the Sultan's army so slow to make camp and receive orders with such a great delay?

It is a miracle indeed that the exhausted Turks could draw their sabers and the horses could run this much at all. On the top of this, the battle order of our Muslim friends was quite old-fashioned which was easily torn into two by the heavy cavalry wedge of the enemy. Although the Ottomans had twice as many cannons as the Christians, they could not take advantage of this, either. No wonder, that despite the official celebration of the battle, there is a gossip in the Seray and certain eunuchs talk only about the "lucky escape" of Sultan Mehmed due to a single fatal mistake of the enemy. Soon after this victory, the Padisah appointed Pasha Cigala as the new Grand Vizier who had saved his life in the last minute of the battle.

As it turned out, the Catholics were unable to take back the Castle of Eger so an important fort of the frontier came under the Ottoman rule. The greatest success of the Sultan was that the Catholics' coalition fell apart and the Transylvanians hurried home. According to the latest reports, Prince Zsigmond Báthory is terrified of the possible punishment he might receive for this adventure with the Habsburgs and he is trying to make amends to the Sublime Porte.

At the same time, the idolizer Habsburg Archduke Maximilian has drawn the following conclusion from the conflict:

"This most disadvantageous clash can duly indicate that the enormous army of the pagans and their best forces can be easily beaten and defeated in a grand-scale battle with the aid of God if we keep a good battle order and attack the enemy bravely and chase them steadfastly."

In spite of my conclusion, I pray your Majesty, as soon as possible to make it manifest without allowing any doubt about the outcome of this military clash to send your congratulations to Sultan Mehmed. And if Your Majesty would deign to give me credit to go on your behalf to satisfy the Sultan of your goodwill God is my witness that I should be most faithful in serving you and the interests of the Church of England with my utmost zeal.

Your most obedient servant and Ambassador in Istanbul,

Edward Barton"

42. Tiszolc Castle   GPS: 48.676916, 19.942191

Who says that we don't appreciate the smaller ruins? Their stones can be overgrown by bushes but once they had their role in our history.

Tiszolc (Tisovec, Theissholz, Taxovia) is located in Gömör County, in the middle of the Upper Lands. The small town is 35 km to the north of Rimaszombat (Rimavská Sobota) on the border of the historical county of Zólyom and Gömör-Kishont. It is just a few kilometers from the important mining town of Breznóbánya (Brezno, Bries, Briesen).

You can see the ruins of Tiszolc Castle on the top of the 893 meter high Castlehill. The stone castle was built after the Mongolian invasion of 1241-42 on the site of the previous earthen fort. The castle belonged to Ajnácskő Castle (Hajnacka, Pirsenstein) and in spite of the distance it was controlled from that location. In the beginning, it was a German-Hungarian miner's settlement, its name comes from the German word "Theisholz" which means "Tiszafa" in the Hungarian language and is "yew" in English. The mines in its hills were renowned for the iron, magnetic ore and silver.

László, the Archbishop of Kalocsa was the owner of the town and the castle in 1334. This year was the first mention of the place in King Robert Károly's document, as "Thyzolch". The next owner was Chief Comes Tamás Széchy who inherited it from the Priest. The Bohemian Czech Hussites appeared there and took the castle in 1442 but after 1458 King Matthias drove them out. Many noble families moved into Tiszolc during the 16th century, including the Losoczy, the Guti Országh and later the Kubinyi, the Forgách and the Nyáry families.

We know that the infamous Istók Feledi was the lord of the area in 1526 and whose nickname was Iron Istók because he had so much iron ore mined and cast that he became famous for his trade, and infamous for other deeds. When Istók died, the lord of Murány Castle, an even more wicked robber knight, Mátyás Basó took it from him. He was sitting in Tiszolc Castle like a spider in his web waiting for the little flies, the travelers and traders, passing by. In the meantime, he was forging money in the dungeons. Allegedly, he had his treasures hidden in Tiszolc.

2003/ 8/ 7

The army of Ferenc Bebek attacked Basó in order to stop the illegal activity in 1548. He and the county's noble army destroyed the castle and hung the dark knight. The king had the castle rebuilt and placed a garrison there. When the Turks showed up in 1594, they sacked it and took away a Protestant priest called György as a hostage.

The Turks visited the area many times looting and burning the land and kept attacking Tiszolc. Two years later the place was mentioned as a town and it had the right to hold a market. There were 38 houses there, 3 of them belonged to peasants. The town was prospering. The Kubinyi family built a paper mill there in 1663. After the area was liberated from the Turks, the castle lost its strategic function very quickly.

The town suffered a lot in 1623 due to the plague and then there was a natural disaster in 1687 when the locusts caused major destruction. The last time the castle was mentioned was when the troops of Prince Thököly were close to its walls at the end of the 17th century, although they couldn't take the castle. Yet, it might have been on the rebel's side later because the Imperial army had to lay siege against it. The mercenaries took the castle by force and destroyed the walls to the ground. During the Revolution of Prince Ferenc II Rákóczi (1704-1711), Tiszolc was the place where the cannon balls were cast for the rebel's army as the first iron smelting factory of the Upper Lands was established there.

The plague of 1710 decimated the population and perhaps because of its role in Rákóczi's War of Independence, the town soon lost all of its privileges.

Today, while one can see only a few white cliff remnants of the castle's walls, it offers a spectacular view of the Valley of the Rima River.

43. The Wasps of Tiszolc Castle (1597)

The Turks of Gömör and Kishont counties were busily trying to extend the borders of the Padishah's Empire further to the north. They were attacking the city of Rozsnyó or Dobsina regularly. Unfortunately, the Valley of the Rima River never escaped the looting and plundering. Mainly it was the Pasha of Fülek Castle and the Pasha of Eger who thusly entertained the Hungarian and the Saxon people of the land.

It was a nice summer day when the guards of Tiszolc Castle saw the Turks suddenly appear in front of the walls without the usual music, barely stirring any dust on the road.

"The Turks of Eger Castle!" cried the guard in the tower and sounded the alarm. Indeed, the enemy was right there, bringing cannons, sacks of gunpowder tied on camels, and with lots of proud Janissaries equipped with shining rifles, waving their flags adorned with horse-tails at their tips. In the blink of an eye, they made camp, deployed the breach-breaking cannons on a small hill and began to shoot the walls at once. The visitors were no less than two-thousand strong, while only one-hundred defenders received them. Bey Hassan was the leader of the attackers and Lieutenant Balázs Darázs was the sworn Castellan of Tiszolc.

However hard Bey Hassan bombarded the castle, the walls proved to be too strong and firm. After some successful days, he decided to send a messenger to the gate with a white flag. The Turkish soldier blew his horn three times and exclaimed:
"Surrender the castle, you cannot hold it for long, anyway."
"You had better bugger off." came the answer.

A Christian castle besieged by Ottomans

Bey Hassan took the insult to heart and became angry. He had ladders, ropes and explosives brought out and sent one-thousand of his men to scale the walls. The soldiers of Balázs Darázs beat them back and the Janissaries had to turn back with bloody heads. Despite the valor of the defenders, the

Turks succeeded in setting many roofs on fire and the explosions blew some gaps into the walls. The siege was going on and on, assault followed assault each day. There were many wounded men after the attacks within the walls, and they were getting short of food, too. The Bey again sent his messenger,

"Surrender the castle, open the gates and you all can have mercy and leave."

"Never," cried the lieutenant, on behalf of the others as well, "We will never do so, even if we all perish here!"

Bey Hassan's face went red with anger. He had lost one-thousand of his troops already. The number of defenders was also decreasing. Castellan Darázs had only fifty men left by now.

"Shoot the walls! No stone must remain on a stone." raged the Bey, encouraging his soldiers either with words or by whips and ordered that the flag of the Majestic Padisah be carried to the walls again and again. The cannons were roaring and black smoke covered the attacking Turks who were desperately crying "Allahu Akbar" which subdued the "Jesus, Jesus" cries of the defenders. Two-hundred more Janissaries fell and there were only twenty exhausted Hungarians rising and striking their swords on the ramparts.

It went on like this the next day, too. The cannons were throwing iron and fire, the walls were crumbling and the ladders were broken by the axes of the defenders. Finally, the gate was in shreds and collapsed. The entire castle of Tiszolc was a smoldering ruin, and indeed, there was not a stone lying upon a stone anymore. The Turks rushed into the castle yard with triumphant cries, jumping over the broken piles of stones and pushed the surviving defenders to the blackened ruins of the collapsed chapel where they made their last stand. Three injured, sweaty men in bloody armor and broken swords, the fourth of them was Balázs Darázs, not giving up their lives easily. They killed five more Janissaries before they were disarmed and captured. They were led before the Bey with a rope around their necks and pushed to their knees.

There was no more clamor of battle. A great silence fell on them, only the moans of the dying and the wounded were heard. The four smoky and dusty warriors did not ask for mercy and proudly looked into the eyes of the Turkish commander without any hope.

The Bey said nothing, just watched them for a time and hemmed and hawed. Castellan Darázs lost his patience at last and said fiercely,

"What are you looking at so much, Bey? Why do not you just take our heads right now?"

Finally, the Bey answered him, with pity in his voice,

"By Allah, I am not planning such a thing with you, valiant warriors. Rather, the bird of peace is smiling on you for I will set you free. Had you surrendered when you had twenty-five men, I would have tied you to the tail of a horse to die slowly because you had made me angry mightily. But I saw you fight with the last broken sword and you have proven your worthiness. Let a horse be given to each of you and you may leave in peace."

Balázs Darázs could barely believe his good fortune. He sighed and rose to his feet with his swaying men. Bowed deeply and addressed the Bey with respect,

"Thank you, noble Bey, for your true knightly decision. In exchange for your kindness, I will tell you the secret of Tiszolc Castle. If you follow my words, you could be rewarded by miraculous things. I know that you are going to rest your men here for at least three days until you bury your dead warriors. There will be a full moon three days later, the perfect time when a wondrous spring will surface from the rocky side of the castle hill. Leave behind your weapons and take nobody with you just go and follow the Furmanec Stream upward the hill when the moon is high. Count your steps, noble Bey, and stop after three-thousand steps. You will notice the deep sounds of bubbling water on your left side. Water is springing up every hour and fills into a small basin where you can bathe your body. When the moon is showing midnight, wash your eyes with this water and you will have such clear eyesight in the future that you will be able to see clearly all the wisdom of the worlds and all the trouble and joy around you. When you see the water coming up from the hill for the second time, wash your limbs in it. Your arms are going to be strong and your legs will never feel tiredness in all of your life. When the cock crows and the water come up for the third time, take a handful of it into your palm and look into the rising sun and drink it. You will have eternal life if you do it right. And now, farewell, may God be with you."

Balázs Darázs and his three soldiers were given horses and they rode away towards Murány Castle without glancing back at the sorrowful remains of Tiszolc Castle which buried so many valiant men under its stones.

Bey Hassan wondered if the story was true, but finally he followed the Castellan's instructions and did everything as it had been said to him. Three days later, having completed his evening prayers to Allah, he took his prayer rug under his arm and strolled down to the Furmanec Stream where it flowed into the Rima River. He counted exactly three-thousand steps and then he stood in the deep silence of the forest. Nothing happened.

He was returning home when he heard the gurgling sound and in the silver light of the Moon, he discovered a flow of water between two cliffs. The Bey quickly leaned down and washed his eyes in the crystal clear water.

Then he sat down on his Persian carpet and sank into his meditations. Unearthly ease filed his mind and he felt the water cleansing his thoughts, and his senses became sharper than ever before in his entire life. After an hour passed, the gurgling sound was heard again and the Bey pulled his boots and shirt off and splashed into the small basin, washing his arms as well. When he was finished, the water disappeared again. Strength and vigor engulfed him and he praised Allah for the magic effects of this enchanted spring. Now he waited intently for the end of the next hour. "The water of eternal life!" he kept repeating this sentence in awe and when the cock crowed, the water was bulging up as it was promised. Hassan could hardly wait to get a handful of it into his two palms and while he was lifting it to his mouth, he looked into the rising Sun. He opened his mouth but there came a small angry wasp which was accidentally stirred up. The wasp flew into his mouth and stung the middle of the Bey's tongue.

Hassan had never feared sword or musket but this attack took him by such surprise that he cried up and the precious water fell to the ground. He dropped onto his praying carpet with tears in his eyes, saying to himself: "I can be clever, I can be strong but the water of eternal life could not be mine. It must have been Balázs Darázs who had sent this wasp here." he sighed because he knew that in the Hungarian language "Darázs" meant "wasp".

While going back to his camp, he realized the true wisdom that man cannot yearn for the water of Eternal Life, because only Allah can grant it, and it can never be acquired by magic.

"A mere man can never be as mighty as God," he thought when he arrived among his soldiers with a spring in his step.

44. The Castle of Osgyán   GPS: 48.374675, 19.890918

The castle of Osgyán (Ozdany) is 10 km from Rimaszombat to the west in Gömör County. It is hard to find the way there, but once you have arrived you can see how the majestic renaissance corner bastions and the leaking roofs fight their unbalanced last battle against the attacks of bushes, thorns and human neglect.

Osgyán was first mentioned in the 13th century when the initial castle was built. The Hungarian Queen Erzsébet called the Bohemian Czech Hussite mercenary soldiers of Jan Giskra into the country after 1440 in order to protect her son from the usurpers. They became fond of the country and decided to stay and seized huge territories in the middle and eastern parts of the Hungarian Upper Lands. It was during this time that they also took

Osgyán. The army of King Matthias took these lands back between 1459 and 1462 by either beating the Bohemian Hussites in battle or hiring them as mercenaries.

The ruins of Osgyán Castle before the fire of 2019 (Photo: MirecXP)

The previous owners, the Orlay (Orlle) family, were re-established in Osgyán around 1462. It is assumed that it was Miklós Orlay who turned it into a fortified castle around 1550 because it was close to Fülek castle and the Turks were heavily raiding the area. We don't know whether Osgyán was ever taken by the Ottomans, but it is almost certain that it had to withstand their attacks. The settlement lay on the northernmost fringe of the Ottoman Empire and the inhabitants lived every day in danger.

János Bakos was the next person who gained the castle in 1590. This lord had the feudal right to hold a blood court in Osgyán. It meant that he had the right to execute criminals on his own land.

At this time, it was already an agricultural town. Bakos was a learned man and when the Turks took Fülek castle, he gave a home to the high school of Fülek in Osgyán at the beginning of the 17th century. We know that the castle used to be in the hands of the Szakál, Vajna, then the Korponay and the Luzsénszky families in different periods.

The present Renaissance look of the castle came from its construction during the first part of the 17th century on the foundations of the earlier fort. The castle became famous for the Battle of Osgyán when General Giovanni Basta of the Habsburg king, defeated the forces of Prince Bocskai's captain, Balázs Németi in 1604.

Baron István Orlay owned Osgyán in 1631 when he was appointed as Chief Comes of Gömör County. He held this office until his death, in 1641.

The Transylvanian Prince György I Rákóczi and Habsburg King Ferdinand III made peace in Linz in 1645 and Osgyán was given to Gábor Bakos who became loyal to the Habsburg monarch for this. A Diet in 1647 decided in Pozsony (Bratislava, Pressburg) that as the Ottomans were still in the neighborhood, the castle had to be reinforced as protection against them. Later, the king took the castle back in 1666 because Gábor Bakos died without an heir.

Soon, the Géczy family took ownership. Osgyán was on Vienna's side when it was attacked in 1678 by the Hungarian Kuruc rebels, but we do not know the outcome of that clash. All we know is that the fort had to be reinforced again in 1681 against the rebelling Hungarians, according to the ruling of the Diet.

During the War of Independence of Prince Ferenc II Rákóczi, (1704-1711), Osgyán's overlord was Zsigmond Géczy. His daughter was Julia Géczy who later became the wife of the Kuruc captain, János Korponay. Julia was the legendary "white woman" of Lőcse city.

At least the castle of Osgyán escaped the fate of so many Hungarian forts and the Habsburgs did not have it totally destroyed after Rákóczi's revolution. Inevitably though, the outer walls were pulled down and the moat was filled up later by the new owners.

The castle was seriously damaged in WWII and the renovation only began in the 1970s. The castle got a new roof in 2003 but the rest of the Renaissance building was still in ruins in 2006.

Osgyán castle

45. The Battle of Osgyán (1604)

By the first years of the 17th century, it became clear that nobody would be able to win the 15 Year War which began in 1591. The fighting Muslim and Christian forces had become equally exhausted. The Turkish and the Tatar raiders had pillaged and destroyed Transylvania and Upper Hungary beyond all imagination.

Yet, Emperor Rudolf I (1576-1608) wanted to carry on the war at all cost. As his treasury was empty, he tried to get money from his Hungarian noblemen. As a result, many aristocrats were accused of treason. Mostly the Protestant ones were targeted.

In the autumn of 1604 the wealthy Protestant Lord, István Bocskai, was the next target. Bocskai had been great supporter of the anti-Ottoman war and as the man of the Transylvanian Prince Zsigmond Báthory, he had a leading role in the Habsburg-Transylvanian alliance against the Turks. Also, he won a decisive victory over the Muslims at Gyurgyevó in Wallachia.

Despite this, the Chief Captain of Emperor Rudolf, Belgiojoso, launched a campaign against Bocskai and besieged his castles. At the same time, the Hajdú soldiers left the Emperor and sided with Bocskai who was able to successfully resist and defeat the foreign mercenaries at Diószeg, on 15 October 1604.

This victory triggered a whole-scale rebellion against the Habsburgs. Belgiojoso fled to Kassa (Kosice, Kaschau), but the second greatest town of the Upper Lands closed its gates before him. His army dispersed and it was further scattered by the Hajdú soldiers of Balázs Lippay and Balázs Németi.

On the other hand, Bocskai was welcomed in Kassa and he received the authorization of Sultan Achmed I which made him the Prince of Transylvania. Bocskai's first order was to send Lippay after the fleeing Belgiojoso to the Szepesség (Zipt Land). Then, he sent Balázs Németi with 1,000 Hajdu soldiers and 3,000 badly armed peasants (other sources talk about 4,000 Hajdus and 4,000 peasants) to defend the road to Kassa at Osgyán castle. When the Emperor's general, Basta heard of this, he quit the siege of Esztergom in November and soon he was near to Osgyán.

Balázs Németi was not willing to withdraw to Kassa but took up positions to beat back the four times larger imperial army. His officers tried to dissuade him, but it was in vain. Basta was marching towards them with his 18,000-20,000 mercenaries and with numerous cannons. The general had a fearsome reputation because he was the one who had devastated Transylvania with his army just a few years before, with bestial cruelty.

The Hungarians took themselves into the castle of Osgyán and into the small agricultural town which was surrounded by a weak palisade. Németi had some trenches dug on the higher grounds but most of the troops were deployed behind the palisade and in the castle. There was a creek separating them from the advancing enemy, Németi placed his only cannon at its bridge. We know the cannon's name it was called "Sólyom", Hawk. The Battle of Osgyán began in earnest on 14th November.

Németi set out with 300 Hajdú riders to entice the vanguard of the Imperial army which was led by Friedrich von Hollach. Németi withdrew his unit under constant combat and heavy fire. The Hajdu soldiers maneuver worked well, but seeing the riders galloping home, the undisciplined peasant soldiers became frightened and began to run towards the castle, leaving behind "Sólyom" without firing it. The German mercenaries were on their heels, mercilessly cutting down the laggers. Németi jumped off his horse and gathered his hardened men, trying to cover the withdrawal of his remaining soldiers but soon he also had to take shelter in the castle. Behind its walls, he trusted his big old hook-guns or arquebuses and hoped that Basta would not start a siege.

Hajdú soldiers

After seeing the gates shut ahead of him, General Basta had two mortars positioned in front of the castle. Its weak fence and walls were destroyed in a very short time. Soon, Németi had only 500 Hajdús left in the castle and had attempted to break out several times. When the tower of the castle was blown up by the cannon fire, the captain had only 400 men remaining.

Basta offered them safe conduct in surrendering and it was accepted. Yet, he couldn't stop his mercenaries when the Hajdús came out to lay down their arms. Most of them were slaughtered on the spot and only a few got away. According to German sources, the rebels lost more than 3,000 men while the imperial troops suffered 700 casualties.

Németi was shot in his left arm and taken into captivity. Basta took him with the army and marched on towards Kassa. There, at Edelény, the general defeated the troops of the other Hajdú captain Balázs Lippay as well, towards the end of the month. Basta celebrated both his victories on the last day of November.

The execution of Balázs Németi was part of the program. The general wanted to know more about Prince Bocskai's army, so he had Németi hung upside down on a tree for two hours but the tough captain betrayed nothing. Then, he was led to his execution, his hands tied before him. He was scorned and cursed while being led to the executioner's platform. Nobody would have expected him to attack the executioner and take away his two-handed sword with his hands roped together. But this was the very thing that happened. The Hajdú captain seized the great sword and cut down many German mercenaries in the throng before he went under their blades.

In spite of his victories, General Basta was not able to stabilize his position in the Upper Lands. He did not even try to besiege Kassa and was forced to withdraw during the winter of 1604-1605.

In the meantime, Prince Bocskai was able to gather not only the smaller noblemen around his flag but the more powerful aristocrats as well. Soon, he occupied the larger portion of Royal Hungary and instead of the title of King, he chose to remain only Prince of Hungary. He wouldn't accept the crown from the hand of the Sultan.

46. Pozsony Castle   GPS: 48.144147, 17.108708

Pozsony (Bratislava, Pressburg) was once the Capital of Hungary, now it is the Capital of Slovakia. The castle was a fort owned by Count Braszlav before the coming of the Hungarians who took it in 902 A.D. The famous battle of Pozsony is considered to be the last step of the Hungarian's 'Home Taking' (it is called "Honfoglalás" in the Hungarian language) and it took place on 4 July 907. This victory was a major success and guaranteed Hungary's independence against the Holy Roman Empire and the west. The first mention of "Poson" is from 1002. During the interregnum in 1042, after St Stephen's death, the castle was taken for a short time by a Czech prince called Bretislaw, which is why Pozsony is called Bratislava now. This castle stood on a strategic point on the bank of the Danube River and it guarded the land from a hill.

Holy Roman Emperor Heinrich III tried to take the castle by siege in 1051 but his boats were sunk by the Hungarian, Kund the Diver, and his men. The Eastern Germans and the Austrians had always wanted to seize Hungary and Pozsony blocked their way. Yet, the city was in Austrian hands for a short time in 1146.

The next threat from the West came when Frederick Barbarossa, the Holy Roman Emperor, was gathering his troops at Pozsony whilst he was on his way to the Holy Land in 1189. But Béla III, the Hungarian king, let him pass through Hungary. He even gave food to the Crusaders and guides seeing them through the Balkan so they did not have to pillage food. Not all Germans were hostile though. Peaceful German settlers from Bavaria arrived there in the 13th century and they became dominant in the city, as in so many Hungarian towns.

Pozsony was one of the lucky forts that were not taken by the Mongols in 1241, which was an outstanding deed.

The town was always in the middle of the action. King Béla IV was defeated at Pozsony by his son, István, in 1262. The Austrian Prince, Ottokar took the fort twice in 1263. It happened because of the city's strategic location. It was King István V who later made his truce with Prince Ottokar in 1270, but the prince took the fort the next year in spite of the truce. Soon, he returned it according to a new truce. Next, the Austrian Prince Albert took it in 1287; but it was promptly retaken. Later, the Hungarian King Endre III gave privileges to Pozsony in 1291. The famous Miklós Toldi, the legendary strong Hungarian warrior was the captain of Pozsony in 1354.

Pozsony is known as the City of Diets which is where the Hungarian Noble Estates met to decide on the important questions of the Kingdom. The first Diet was held in the city in 1402 by King Zsigmond. He began reinforcing the fort in earnest because of the Hussites' threat. When he became Holy Roman Emperor, he summoned the Imperial Council to Pozsony in 1429. Thus, Pozsony became the capital of the Holy Roman Empire for a while.

Initially, the town was under the authority of the Chief Treasurer of Hungary. Perhaps this was because of the famous mining towns of the Upper Lands which produced an immense amount of gold and silver for the king, or for the debtors of the king. The town grew according to its importance. Its university was established by King Matthias in 1467.

Monarchs and rulers met in this important city. Pozsony was the place where the Hungarian King Vladislav (Ulászló) II and the Holy Roman

Emperor Habsburg Maximilian II agreed, in 1491, that after the end of the Jagiellonian dynasty, the Habsburgs were to inherit the throne of Hungary. This was the agreement upon which all of the Habsburg rulers have based their claims for the Hungarian throne ever since. Later, this contract was broken by the decision of the Hungarian nobles who supported King János Szapolyai.

Pozsony (photo: Peter Zeliznak)

Eventually, the treaty of 1491 paved the way for the Dual Kingship when King Ferdinand and King János Szapolyai tore the country in two while the Ottoman Empire slowly gained ground amid their debate. The town was taken for a short time by the Austrian Maximilian I in 1506.

Owing to Ottoman advances into Hungarian territory, the city was designated to be the new Capital of the Kingdom of Hungary in 1535, marking the beginning of a new era. When Buda fell in 1541, Pozsony emerged as the new capital. Pozsony was a formidable obstacle on the Danube and it was able to block the Turk's advances on Vienna. The Turks had besieged and damaged Pozsony but had always failed to conquer it.

The city became a coronation town and the seat of kings, archbishops (1543), the center of nobility and all major organizations and offices. There were 43 Diets held in the city altogether during the 16th century. The reconstruction of the castle in the Renaissance style took place after 1552. The Hungarian Holy Crown had been held there and many members of the

Pálffy family were in charge of it. The wealthy Pálffy family also gained the hereditary title of the Comes of Pozsony County. This Lord and his family members fought the Ottomans very effectively. Between 1536 and 1830, eleven Hungarian kings and queens were crowned in St. Martin's Cathedral.

During the time of the Habsburg-Transylvanian wars, Pozsony had always been rather loyal to the Hungarians from Transylvania in spite of its German Burghers. The army of Prince Bethlen took the town in 1619 and he made his peace with the Emperor in this city in 1626.

As for culture, the beginning of the Hungarian baroque period is around 1630, first appearing in territories here near Austria. It is during this time that the reconstruction of the royal palace of Pozsony began in 1635 in the Baroque style.

The fort guarded the Danube River with its cannons so it remained the greatest roadblock before Vienna. Unfortunately, the Habsburgs alienated a Hungarian aristocrat, Imre Thököly, who rebelled against the king and soon the Sultan made him Prince of Transylvania and Northern Hungary. Thököly knew that the Turks needed Vienna. However, they could never set their feet on his territories, so he let the Turks go towards their desire, the Golden Apple, Vienna.

The Austrian capital was reached in 1683 by the Ottoman Empire because Pozsony had opened its gates for the rebel Prince who let the Turks pass unhindered towards Vienna. He thought; let them kill each other. Yet, his dreams were soon broken. He was arrested by the Sultan's man at Nagyvárad (Oradea) and the Turks were defeated by the Polish King Sobieski's Hussars. It was at this point that the Western powers realized that, without the Polish, they would not be able to withstand another Ottoman onslaught, nor a Hungarian uprising. So they decided that, after a 150-year hesitation, they must drive the Turks out of Hungary.

Pozsony was where the Diet accepted the Habsburg's right to inherit the throne of Hungary.

In 1687 the Hungarian Estates decided to hand over unrestricted power in exchange for their help in driving the Turks from the country. The famous "Article Number 31" of the Golden Bull was thrown out. This article had authorized the nobility to resist against tyranny and banish such kings as who would not uphold the Hungarian Constitution of the Golden Bull of 1222. Thus, Hungary was "liberated" and all of Thököly`s soldiers joined the Crusade against the Ottomans.

This is how Hungary was conquered by the Habsburgs. Some historians say that this last war of "liberation" caused greater destruction and more casualties than the previous Ottoman occupation altogether.

The old Pozsony Castle from the 16th century

47. The Transylvanian Prince takes Pozsony (1619)

When the Protestant Czech noblemen in Prague turned against Emperor
Ferdinand nobody thought that the rebellion would eventually lead to the
Thirty-Years-War. The rebels knew that they would not be able to beat the
Imperial army of the Holy Roman Empire alone, so they decided to ask the
Protestant Gábor Bethlen, to ally with them. Their choice fell on him
because this prince had greatly improved the wealth of Transylvania in
only a few years and, most importantly, he organized a very strong army.
Bethlen did not hesitate to aid the Czech and he was ready to make war
against the Habsburg Empire. He did it because he knew that the
Hungarian nobles who lived in Royal Hungary were beginning to give up
their trust in the Habsburgs just as their Czech neighbors had.
He set a goal for himself of re-establishing the union between Transylvania
and Hungary under his rule. Before throwing his troops headlong into the
war, the prince prepared his campaign by entering into an intricate
diplomatic game.
First, he gained the Sultan's approval to launch his campaign against the
Germans. Bethlen never forgot the fact that he had been installed on the
throne of Transylvania in the shadow of Turkish swords. By now, his
power had increased so much that the Turks did not pose an immediate
threat, but he paid heed not to anger them. In the west, he was nicknamed

"Turkish Gabor" but in reality, he was far from being a vassal of the Sublime Porte.

Secondly, he needed the Transylvanian Székely's cunning to deceive those Hungarian lords who were on Ferdinand's side. Quickly, he sent a message to András Dóczy who was both the Chief Captain of Upper Hungary and Captain of Kassa. He reassured him that his campaign was targeted against the rebellious Czech and he was just supporting His Majesty, the Emperor with a strong Transylvanian army.

Lord Dóczy was so pleased that he sent lots of wagons of gunpowder to Bethlen so he would have enough ammunition against the treacherous rebels. How surprised Lord Dóczy was when a young nobleman called György Rákóczi appeared at the gates of Kassa with his Hajdu soldiers on behalf of Prince Bethlen. When he realized the plot, and gave the order to fire the cannons at them, it was too late. The Burghers of Kassa rebelled and the second largest city of Upper Hungary fell to the Transylvanian ruler without a fight.

In the meantime, Bethlen had been busy writing countless letters to the greater and lesser Lords of Royal Hungary. This propaganda brought him tremendous success because almost all of them received his message with great pleasure. Bethlen's troops marched into Debrecen, his army was constantly growing, and when he entered the Castle of Sárospatak in Royal Hungary thousands celebrated him as a liberator. The strongholds, castles and walled cities of Upper Hungary were opening their gates before him and he led his men as far as Érsekújvár and Nagyszombat at the Bohemian border.

He knew that the Trans-Danubian castles in the South were waiting for him. Yet, there was just one obstacle, a city on the banks of the Danube. It was Pozsony, the capital of Royal Hungary. The town and its formidable fort were not far from Vienna so the Emperor had it well guarded.

Prince Bethlen's army took some rest in Nagyszombat after their long march from Kassa. They then moved a bit to the south and made camp at Szenc, not far from Pozsony. One day, the Prince was having his dinner when a man from his bodyguard reported an urgent letter from Pozsony sent by the Burghers of the city had arrived. The letter went like this: "Your Majesty, today, two-thousand Imperial mercenaries have arrived with three cannons, led by Rudolf Tieffenbach. The Burghers of the city did not open the gates before them, so they made camp on the banks of the Danube, digging trenches around them. They were feasting and merriment, boasting that each of them would cut down at least ten Hungarians. Now they are just about to get down to go to sleep."

Prince Gábor Bethlen

This was enough information for the Transylvanian commander. Bethlen immediately summoned his officers and put to them a question:
"Should we attack the Germans right now or not?"
The officers began to find excuses, puffing up their cheeks like Székelys do. One of them said it would be ill-advised to attack in such rain, while another said the soldiers were too tired in the evening. All agreed that the roads were soaked and muddy. Could they dishearten the Prince? By no means.
Gábor Bethlen was famous for his wisdom and for asking the advice of his many counselors. Then, he finally decided after weighing everything.
"It is no good to let the Germans build more trenches and dig in. So let the drums sound the march and let the troops move on right away. It is my command."
There was nothing to do. The grumbling soldiers had to march through the night. They reached the town of Pozsony at sunrise and attacked the Germans without the least delay. The Imperial mercenaries had been so sure that they were safe that they failed to post sentries. They were frightened by the sudden attack. But, being well-disciplined troops, they quickly regained their senses and made their stand. The muskets and cannons were throwing fire at the advancing Hungarians and there was a hard fight.

At last, the Hajdú soldiers of Bethlen climbed the trenches and that was the moment when the Germans began to run for their lives. However, they did not get far.

The Chronicle says that "...the Hungarian cavalry fell on them, screaming and yelling at the top of their lungs and not many could escape out of the fifteen-hundred Germans. They were cut down all."

It was how Pozsony was taken by Prince Gábor Bethlen of Transylvania.

48. Murány Castle   GPS: 48.734282, 20.045237

Murány Castle (Muránsky Hrad) was perhaps the most formidable of all the forts in the Upper Lands of the Hungarian Kingdom because it is situated on the steepest and highest cliffs of the Carpathian Mountains. The place was first mentioned in 1271 when King István V gave it to Comes Gunig. This means that the castle was probably built right after the Mongolian invasion in 1241-42. The Ilosvai family owned it in the 13th century and the Bebek family seized it from them around 1401. We know that the village under the castle was called Murányalja and that it was paying taxes for 24 houses in 1427.

It was King Zsigmond who affirmed this ownership of the Bebek of Pelsőc family by giving the taxing places of Murány and the castles of Jolsva and Fülek to them in 1435. Legend says that they were the ones who built the stone castle on the rock, while others say that the castle was built by the Ilsva (Ilosvai) family, or by the Czech Jan Giskra.

It is true, that Hungarian Queen Elisabeth of Luxemburg gave Murány, among other castles, to the Czech robber knight and mercenary leader Jan Giskra. As for the Hussites, they indeed built some forts during their stay. It was István Szapolyai, the commander of King Matthias' army, who took Murány Castle back for the king. The Tornallyai family owned it around 1500, then, we find it in the Habsburg king's hands in 1549.

As the Royal Court was always in need of money, Murány was offered for sale to Prince Zsigmond Rákóczi for 40,000 gold Forints in 1600. But then, Johann Rottal, the Chief Advisor of Hungarian Affairs in the Secret Council of the King, took the transaction into his hands. Finally, Murány landed in the hands of Baron Jakab in exchange for 100,000 gold Forints. There was a huge domain attached to the castle, so the Court decided to buy it back in 1608, according to a decision of the Diet from the same year. As the king had no money, the next year a wealthy Hungarian aristocrat, Tamás Széchy paid Baron Rottan a token amount to acquire Murány Castle and its lands.

The heyday of the castle began with the Széchy family. Tamás Széchy had a son, György, but instead of the castle going to him, the ownership went to his wife Mária Homonnay. Later, Mária purchased it from her father-in-law. She and György Széchy made Murány one of the most important centers of the Protestant spirit and culture in 1613.

Murány Castle

György Széchy opposed both the Catholic King Ferdinand II and the Protestant Prince Gábor Bethlen of Transylvania knowing no lord over himself. When he suddenly died in 1625, the ownership of the castle had reverted to the king. However, his widow bribed the Viennese court with 22,000 gold Forints so she could become the castle's owner again. She had to swear an oath that neither she nor her heirs would ever yield it to the Transylvanian princes or anybody on their side. She received the king's approval in 1626. Before her death, the relentless mother forced her daughter, Mária, to give up her rights in favor of her sisters and their husbands. Maria went to court against her mother, but nothing could be done. When the strict widow died all of her daughters took the side of Prince Rákóczi in spite of their mother's oath.

As it turned out, in the 1630's, two daughters owned the castle, Éva and Kata. Maria was just a barely tolerated person when she stayed there as you will read. Mária lost her first husband in 1631 and remarried a Transylvanian nobleman called István Kun in 1634. Kun was the Chief Comes of Szatmár but he was a violent man and Mária divorced him three years later. When she fled from him to Déva Castle Kun besieged the fort with his 250 men to take her back. Luckily, Mária was able to get home to

Murány Castle, as much as she could call it her home. She was less than welcome.

The famous legend of Murány tells the story of how Mária Széchy tricked everyone and gained the castle for her fiancée, Ferenc Wesselényi in secret. Wesselényi happened to be on King Ferdinand's side, so this was how the fort returned to the king in 1644 without him having to pay or fight for it.

Wesselényi had been a talented and valiant, but not very rich nobleman. He was the Captain of Fülek Castle, not very far from Murány. When he wed Mária Széchy he became prosperous and his career rose higher and higher. Eventually, he was appointed as Palatine of Hungary, the second person in rank after the king. He had been fighting against the Turks all his life. But when the great poet and general, the Hungarian-Croatian Count Miklós Zrínyi died in 1664 (some say because of the assassination of the king), Wesselényi became deeply disappointed in regards to the Habsburg's good intentions about saving Hungary. He organized a conspiracy against the Court in which almost all of the highest aristocrats were involved. Sadly, they were betrayed and his friends were executed. Wesselényi died in 1667 before his trial.

Maria would not give Murány Castle up so easily, though. Duke Charles V of Lotharingia had to bring his army and lay a proper siege on it in 1672. Maria Széchy was personally leading the defenders. But despite how heroically she fought, she had to surrender the fort. Maria Széchy had to leave Murány Castle and died in 1679 whilst in exile in Kőszeg. Duke Charles found certain documents in Murány castle that revealed many details of the earlier conspiracy. The Court did its best to take revenge on the Hungarian noblemen of Royal Hungary, regardless of their involvement. This led to growing restlessness and later to the so-called Kuruc rebel wars of Prince Imre Thököly and Prince Ferenc II Rákóczi in the following decades.

During the new Habsburg-Hungarian conflicts, Murány Castle changed hands often between the Imperial forces and Thököly's men. There was a great fire in 1702 which caused severe damage to the castle. Miklós Bercsényi, the famous general of Prince Ferenc II Rákóczi, took the fort in 1706 and considered it safe enough to guard the Holy Crown of Hungary within its walls. After the end of Rákóczi's War of Independence, Murány lost its strategic role and the Habsburg King Charles III gave it to Count Koháry in 1720.

At least, this stronghold was not exploded by gunpowder because of the fear of the rebellious Hungarians.

49. The story of the Venus of Murány (1644)

It was not for nothing that Mária Széchy, a proud and free Hungarian lady was called the Venus of Murány castle. Her beauty was renowned in the whole country and she was either envied, or loved, for her love of independence and her brave and straightforward character.

Unfortunately, her own mother and two sisters, Kata and Éva, were among those who disliked her behavior and personality. It also did not help that she loved rich and extravagant dresses and she rode horses astride, as in men's fashion.

Her mother, the widow of György Széchy, was particularly angry regarding her great love of jewelry and expensive horses. Éva and Kata were living in Murány Castle with their husbands and they were afraid that Mária would spend all of the family money, so they kept instigating their mother against her. Their gossip was just to the widow's liking and she did not have to be persuaded to cut Mária off without any money. Mária did not want to cede everything to her malicious sisters and their greedy husbands, but her mother closed her in a room and did not let her out until she signed the document in which she accepted the disinheriting.

Maria Széchy (1610-1679)

János Lisztius and Gábor Illésházy, her brothers-in-law, were happy to take over control of the impregnable Murány Castle and the immense domains belonging to it. Mária tried to attack her mother's verdict in court, but it was in vain.

When Mária returned to Murány Castle after divorcing her second husband her mother was no longer alive. Éva and Katalin had to allow their sister to stay with them, but all control over the castle was in the hands of Gábor Illésházy, Éva's husband. Moreover, against the oath of the late widow, Illésházy left King Ferdinánd behind and took the side of Prince György I Rákóczi. Why did he do that? When he was asked, he just shrugged, saying that the Transylvanian prince had just conquered the Upper Lands of Hungary and he was closer than the Habsburg king. King Ferdinand was in despair seeing that his Hungarian vassals were turning their coats one by one. How happy he was that he found a loyal and decent Hungarian nobleman who did not go back on his word. This was Ferenc Wesselényi, the young captain of Fülek Castle, not far from Murány. Wesselényi had trusted the Habsburgs and at this time he fully believed that they would help Hungary to drive the Turks out. The young man was already renowned for the deeds that he had won in one hundred fights against the Muslims.

At once, the king ordered him to take Murány Castle back, by force or by trick. Wesselényi was scratching his head hard when he got the royal command. He knew that the walls of the fort were towering high on the top of those sharp cliffs and that even birds became tired flying over them. Yet, he was aware of the plight of Mária Széchy and had heard a lot of her beauty. He was a widower himself and thought that he might try and gain the castle and the heart of a unique woman at the same time. But first, he had to somehow find a way to her.

Wesselényi sat down and penned a poetic letter to Mária, gently offering her his adoration and help. He expected that the lady might consider him as an ally against her bullying relatives. When ready, he summoned his most cunning Hajdú soldier, János Nagy, and said to him:

"Look, my son, here are seventy pieces of gold Forints in my hand. They can be yours if you deserve it."

"My lord, please, command me, who should I kill for it, whoever he might be."

"No, there is no need to kill anyone. Can you bring a letter into the castle of Murány and deliver it to Lady Mária without being caught?"

János nodded and immediately set out on the quest. The shrewd servant dressed up like a peasant and bravely walked up to the gate of Murány Castle carrying a great basket full of sizable cucumbers. He was thoroughly searched but no-one could find the secret letter that he hidden inside of the longest cucumber that had been carefully hollowed out before. He was free to go to Lady Mária now. The lady was surprised to see the strange gifts but János told her quietly:

"Please, my Lady, eat this one first, but do not blush when you find something inside."

With that, János was gone and Mária was soon reading the letter. Instead of blushing, she came to like the idea of romance. Not many days later, she was ready with her reply. She had a trusted old servant called István Kádas carry her letter to Fülek Castle.

Captain Wesselényi was overjoyed. He gifted Kádas with one hundred gold pieces and sent a valuable present to the Venus of Murány, a fine clock adorned with precious stones. He invited her to a secret rendezvous in the deep forest under the Murány Castle.

The whole countryside was a battlefield between the Austrian king and the Transylvanian prince but nothing could stop them from the meeting. They fell in love with each other at the first meeting and agreed that they would tie their lives together forever. Wesselényi promised to marry her three days after taking Murány Castle and assured her that she would be the only rightful owner of it. Mária said to him:

"If God is willing, I will be your faithful wife with a true heart and you may hang up the king's flag on its tower too. But you must know that there are six hundred soldiers guarding the walls, and every night the Castle gate's key is with my sister Éva, the wife of Castellan Illésházy. Yet do not despair, I will send you word soon, just keep your men in readiness."

Mária returned home and she set herself to work at once. She had just a couple of trusted men, but she could send them to the village to buy her rope. It took some time until it was smuggled into the castle and was hidden in the attic right above Mária's room. She measured the height of the walls with strings when nobody was watching and then they constructed twenty-yard-long rope ladders in the attic at night. Finally, the old Kádas showed up in Fülek Castle with Mária's message.

"Be at the foot of the northern wall next Thursday at midnight and look up to see candlelight in a window above your head. There you will find the rope ladders hanging down."

When Wesselényi's men heard that they would attack Murány Castle at night, their courage left them and it was hard to find twenty of them to volunteer. The rest of Wesselényi's soldiers were told to wait near the castle and rush to the gate when they would see a signal. When the time came, the small unit was waiting at a given place, balancing on the sharp rocks but there was no candlelight in the window. They were about to leave when they heard the whisper of the old Kádas from the foot of the wall:

"Here, come here. The rope ladders are here but we did not light a candle out of fear."

Wesselényi crossed himself and followed Kádas with his pale-faced men.

COM FRANCISCVS VESZELE,
NV de Hadio Perpetuus de Murany nec non
Partium Superioris Regni Hungariæ Gene-
ralis et Prorndy Elchienis Administrator ac S.
CRgM. Cammarius et Consiliarius

Ferenc Wesselényi (1605-1667)

Finally, all of them were in the bed-chamber of Lady Mária who said to them:

"Hurry up, there are just a few guards at the gate and I have given some sleep-inducing wine to the rest who are on duty at night."

So saying, she summoned the castle's officers into her quarters one by one. The first was Illésházy and how surprised he was when he saw the Captain of Fülek in front of him! He was arrested and the officers were made to swear fealty to the king. One of them was sent right away to fetch the key to the gate from Lady Illésházy. There was nothing to do, the key had to be given to Mária. She opened the gate herself and gave the signal to the hiding troops to enter. When the defenders woke, they discovered their weapons had been taken away and the castle had fallen to the men of Wesselényi.

The wedding of Mária Széchy and Ferenc Wesselényi was held as promised, three days later on the 8th of August 1644 in the chapel of Murány Castle. Mária's sisters took no part in the merriment, they were released, along with their husbands, to tell everyone how Murány Castle fell into the Habsburg King's hand because of the hatred and jealousy in their family.

50. Revistye Castle   GPS: 48.521318, 18.722730

Revistyeváralja (Revištské Podzámčie) means "The village at Revistye Castle" and it is now only four kilometers from the City of Zsarnóca. The castle is located on the 314 meter high hill of the Madaras (Birdy) mountains not far from the country road and the Garam River. It is in a strategic spot where the river becomes narrow and it could defend the so-called Garam Gate from the enemy approaching from the South. On the other side of the valley is Saskő (Eagle-stone) Castle which helped to defend the road that led to the Mining Towns of Selmecbánya, Újbánya, Bakabánya for silver, and for gold, Körmöcbánya. („Bánya" means „mine" in the Hungarian language.) The place was first mentioned in 1228 as "terra Ryvcha" and its castle later was also known as Ricse Castle.

Revistye Castle (Photo: Patrik Kunec)

The castle was built in the second part of the 13th century by the cupbearer of the king, Bés of the Miskolc clan who were the ancestors of the Vezeklényi family. They could keep the castle only by swearing fealty to the great oligarch of the Upper Lands, Máté Csák. After the death of this high lord in 1321, the Vezeklényi family became loyal to the king and as a result of this they could keep Revistye. The castle went into the king's possession in 1331 and Queen Maria got it as her "needle-money" in 1388. King Zsigmond gave Revistye to László Sárói, Comes of Temes County in 1391. He was the ancestor of the Lévai Cseh family who later rose into the circles of the wealthiest families.

The Czech Giskra's men took it from the Lévai Cseh family around 1442 and they appointed Péter Kollár as castellan there. King Matthias was able to drive them out in 1462 by making a treaty with Giskra. The Czech mercenary leader ceded all of his castles, including Revistye, in exchange for the castles of Lippa and Solymos in Arad County and 25,000 gold Ducats. His soldiers were employed by the king who created the core of his Black Army from them. The king gave the castle to his Queen, Beatrix, in 1477. In 1479 the Dóczy family had Revistye. They were so rich that their wealth rivaled the Mining Towns. They built a 22 acre fish pond next to the castle. The Nagylúcsei family owned the castle after 1490. They were relatives of the Dóczy family and they owned Zólyomlipcse Castle and Breznóbánya city at this time as well.

There was a debate between the Nagylúcsai family and the miners of Breznóbánya over a mill. Domján, László, Gergely of Nagylúcsai and their relative, Ferenc Dóczy attacked Breznóbánya city with 600 riders, armed peasants and infantrymen on 30 April 1517. The soldiers pillaged the church and killed two of the priest's men, then burned down the church on the people who had taken refuge there. King Louis II punished the killers with a death sentence and confiscated their properties, but his rule was so weak that his verdict was just mocked. László of Nagylúcsa was the owner of Revistye Castle at that time and he did not even let the king's men enter his castle.

There was another clash with the king in 1519 when István of Nagylúcsa was the captain of Revistye. He threatened the king's men who wanted to give his two villages to the town of Selmecbánya. In spite of this, the king stopped the legal case against the family in 1523 which was just further proof of the utter weakness of his royal power three years before the Battle of Mohács.

Later, Revistye was returned to the Crown and it was controlled from Selmecbánya. Then the Nagylúcsai-Dóczy family was able to get it back. The lords of the castle carried on their rivalry with the Burghers of Selmecbánya during the 16-17th century. The castle remained a third-class private castle because it was never updated to withstand a siege against more advanced cannons.

The castle opened its gates for the Hajdú soldiers of Prince Bocskai in 1605 and to the troops of Prince Bethlen between 1619 and 1623 as well. Prince György I Rákóczi was also warmly welcomed in 1644. Three years later, the Turks were raiding and pillaging along the Garam Valley and they ambushed Revistye burning and sacking the castle. This line of the Nagylúcsai family ceased to exist in this year and the castle was taken over by Selmecbánya city. The Garam Valley and Revistye Castle witnessed the campaign of General de Souches in 1664 who took the castle of Nyitra back from the Ottomans and defeated the army of Pasha Kücsük Mehmed in the battles near Zsarnóca and Garamszentbenedek.

The Lippai family were also its owners though the Crown bought the castle back from them in 1676. During the Habsburg-Hungarian wars that took place against the rebels of Thököly the king placed strong German garrisons into the Revistye and Saskő Castles to defend the Mining Towns in 1677. When Körmöcbánya surrendered to Thököly, these guards fled and in 1678 the Hungarian rebels took Revistye.

Prince Thököly was trying to advance on with his rebel Kuruc troops, aided by French auxiliary forces but General Wrbna defeated him at Garamszentkereszt. Habsburg mercenaries had the Castle of Saskő exploded, but for some reason they kept the small Revistye Castle intact although it suffered some damage because of a fire, although it was soon restored.

The castle was still inhabited in the 18th century until it was struck by a lightning bolt in 1792 which partly destroyed it. Now you can see the one-story-high remains of its walls and four bastions. The renovation was very nicely proceeding in 2017 and the future of Revistye is quite promising.

51. The Sword with the Precious Stone (1646)

There was a great sadness in the high castle of Revistye, the Lord of the castle, old Pető Reviczky, was about to die. He was beloved by everybody because he was a straightforward and honest man, good-hearted and generous with his folks and strangers alike. When the end was near, he sent for his only son, Andorás, and told him:

"You are my only son, Andorás, your two brothers fell in battle when defending the king from the Turks. My castle will be yours along with of all my lands in Bars and in Nyitra Counties. So as to remember me, let me gift you with this bejeweled sword which I was given from the King of Poland. I have never unsheathed this blade, never cut or thrust a man with it. You may use it only if your honor, your King or Country would be in danger." and closed his eyes.

"Yes, father, I swear that I will wield it only in defense of the good case, to protect my honor, the King and my Country." muttered his son. He hung the sword with the emerald stone on the wall among the other relics of the family and hoped he would never need to use it.

Lord Andorás Reviczky turned out to have inherited his late father's character. He hurt neither men nor animals. He was loved by all of his soldiers and servants, even his peasants were content with his rule. He was respected all over in the region and because he was a good-looking man, all of the ladies of the Garam and the Nyitra Valleys were sighing after him.

There was a big Ottoman raiding party which had been lurking around for a while. They were scaring the Mining Cities; ambushing Bakabánya or Újbánya, Léva. They were fast, appearing as if they had come from the morning fog and disappearing as quickly as the dew in the dawn. Nobody was safe because of them. Lord Andorás chased them many times with his Hussars but they never stood for a battle, just skipped away.

Their leader was Pasha Kerim, a renowned and valiant warrior, a true follower of the Prophet Mohamed and an angry enemy of the infidel Hungarians. He had a beautiful daughter, the black-haired Gülike with great dark eyes and rose-leaf shaped face. She followed her father everywhere except into battles. Gülike had heard about the handsome looks and the bravery of the young Andoras Revitzky. The Turkish warriors talked a lot about their pursuer in the evenings by the campfire under the stars. It was not surprising that the enemies spoke each other's language, and knew each other by name and by reputation. She was listening to the songs and the stories so on and on until she fell in love with the mysterious Hungarian warrior without ever seeing him. Her desire grew and she wanted to meet him. As she was a brave and straight-forward girl she always carried out whatever she decided.

They happened to have a Christian captive with them, Bars, the inner slave of the Pasha. Gülike began to persuade her Dad with sweet words pleading with him to set the man free saying that he must have suffered enough already. The Pasha was not a cruel man. He smiled and finally gave in to his daughter, shrugging his shoulders, and released Bars from his service. Bars was not an ungrateful man and sought out Gülike to express his thanks to her in the tent of the women. The girl gave him ten gold pieces and whispered to him:

"Listen to me, Bars, you used to be a warrior yourself, so go now go and stand before Sir Andoras Revitzky in Revistye Castle and offer him your sword. Tell him about my love and my desire to meet him. Hurry on."

Bars was happy to walk away. He went to the first Hungarian town he came across and bought himself fine new clothing and hung a saber on his belt. Then he went to find Sir Andorás in Revistye Castle. He was greeted warmly and they quickly found him a place among the guards. At the first opportunity he had in which he could talk to the young Lord in person he, at once, shared the words of the beautiful Gülike. Lord Andorás just stared open-mouthed because of the surprise.

"How is it that this Turkish girl could feel like this when she has never even seen me?"

"Sir, she said she sees you in her dreams all the time."

Sir Andorás was shaking his head.

"Is she ugly?"

"She is nice, like a dewy rose."

"Is there a problem with her size? Is she a dwarf or perhaps round like a barrel?"

"No, Sir, she is like a reed, she is slim and slender. She walks like a deer and her voice is like the nightingale's. Her honor is like the snow."

"I cannot understand this. I must see this girl for myself." concluded the Captain.

When Bars told him that Gülike had given instructions as to how and when they should meet he was given ten gold Forints for his good job. The man thought he could suffer such captivity every week.

The next day, as he had been instructed, Sir Andorás dressed in the clothes of a shepherd and walked straight into the Ottoman camp in the evening with a long stick in his hand and with an Eagle's feather in his hat. There were many shepherds coming and going there and only his feather distinguished him from the rest. Gülike caught sight of him and Sir Andorás saw a veiled-face girl who brushed by him. He quickly followed her to a small grove where there were no Turkish guards around.

"I am that Turkish girl" she whispered "and I love you dearly, Knight."

"Please, let me see your face, I would like to get to know you."

"I am not allowed to do so, but I will show it for a minute, for you." and so she did.

Under the countless stars in the sky, The Captain was amazed by her beauty from what he could see well in the light of the campfire.

"You are beautiful. How did I deserve your love? Come with me to my castle. We will be happy there."

"I cannot go," shook her head sadly, "I just wanted to find out whether you looked like the same that appeared in my dreams."

"And what now? Am I the one you thought of?"

"Yes, you are!"

They would have whispered for a long time but Gülike heard the Pasha was looking for her so they parted. Yet, Sir Andorás visited her next day and on the third day, he brought a peasant girl's attire for her.

"Now, my love, I will not go away without you, you must come with me, if you love me."

The girl was not reluctant this time and pulled the drab clothes over her silk dress, tied her hair and they slid out of the Turkish camp together. When the cock crowed, they were safe and sound behind the closed gates of Revistye Castle. Pasha Kerim could not find his daughter anywhere. He would have torn his hair out, if he had had any under his turban. He was raging:

"Go and find her, search the villages, pull the trees to the ground, dry out the waters, but bring my daughter here dead or alive."

Three days later his servant, Hassan, appeared in front of the curtain of his tent, bowing deeply. Hassan was a "pribék", a Christian previously, who had embraced the Muslim faith of his own free will. He followed Pasha Kerim wherever he went.

"Your daughter, most merciful Pasha, is in Revistye Castle. She fled with Andorás Revitzcky and she became a Christian because of him."

Poor Pasha Kerim's face turned red and he was cursing in his black mood. After his rage left him, he just stared at Hassan.

"I have no daughter anymore. What shall I do now?"

Hassan did not tell the Pasha that he wanted Gülike for himself and she was the reason why he had originally become a Muslim. Yet, the girl never ever cast a look on him. Hassan was equally angry and he was seething like rainwater heated on glooming embers. He wanted to take revenge on the lovers so he told Kerim his plan:

"I will go up to the castle and tell to Revitzky that I had left behind the Muslim faith and would like to repent and take the Christian faith again. I swear I will help Gülike to escape from there."

"What if she does not want to come?"

"I will poison the Captain and then I will make him eat my dagger."

The Pasha agreed, but told him not to give a lethal dosage of poison to him, just enough that would slow him down.

"When you see him getting dizzy, whisper in his ear that I would wait for him on the field for a duel at noon."

Hassan made haste and did everything as they had agreed. He was warmly accepted in the castle and nobody suspected anything about him. The next day, when the sun had not yet fully reached the middle of the horizon, Hassan appeared in the dining room before Sir Andorás who was in a very good mood, swimming in happiness. He offered some wine to the renegade who has returned from his stray ways and stepped to the window to take delight in the gorgeous view of the Garam River's valley in its spring splendor. Behind his back, the "pribék" quickly poured the sleep-inducing powder into his goblet. Andorás turned back and smiled at the man, then said:

"Let us drink to your homecoming." and they emptied their cups.

It took less time than saying a Lord's Prayer that the Captain began to wilt and his legs grew heavy. Hassan leaned over to him and whispered in his ears:

"Sir, make your haste, your enemy is waiting for you in the field on the bank of the Garam. Tie up your sword and answer the challenge, otherwise, he would take away your lovely bride."

As if in a dream, Sir Andorás snatched a sword that was hanging on the wall of his hall and stumbled down the stairs. Hassan saw him climb into the saddle and ride out of the gate without any escorts. The renegade grinned widely and followed him.

Pasha Kerim was waiting for him already. His stallion was nervously pawing the ground under the fidgeting bloodthirsty warrior, armed to the teeth, and determined to kill. When he saw the deceiver of his daughter coming, he gave out a roar and spurred his horse to gallop. Kerim held a saber in his right hand and wielded a curved khanjar in his left, ready to extinguish the candle of Andorás' life.

Gülike appeared unexpectedly on the banks of the river and saw with horror what was going to happen.

"Father, do not hurt him!" she screamed, but Hassan stepped up to her and dragged the girl aside, revengefully:

"Slow down, Gülike, Andorás now will get what he asked for. And you will be mine."

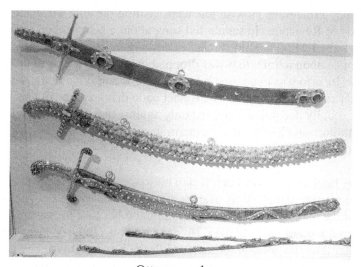

Ottoman sabers

Andorás did not realize that he had brought the renowned sword of his father that was studded with emeralds. He just drew it to evade, instinctively, the strike of Kerim. A strike, that was never finished. When the Pasha raised his hand to deliver the lethal blow, his eyes fell on the enemy's sword. His hand stopped in mid-air and Kerim gave out a sharp cry "Bismillah!" and reined his mount in, making it dance on its hind-legs. He stared at the sword and exclaimed:

"The sword with emerald, the weapon of the old Sultan!" he said "It is banned to fight against it, I recognized the sword from the jewels. You won, Revitczky. My daughter is yours and I will not demand her back anymore. But I do not want to know the two of you in this life."

Hassan approached him and put his hand on the bridle of Kerim's stallion. "What happened to you, great Pasha, that you do not defend the honor of your daughter?"

The Pasha turned to him and poured all his rage on him, saying:

"Woe to the traitors, you are full of lies and demons dwell in you!" and thrust his khanjar into the heart of the "pribék". Looking sadly once more at his daughter, he spun his horse back toward his camp.

As Sir Andorás slowly came back to his senses he was just looking at his father's sword with blank eyes. He then took his bride onto the saddle in front of him and slowly walked his horse back to Revistye. This was how Gülike became his lady wife, and later the mother of his children. They heard no more of Pasha Kerim. He disappeared like the wind of the hot deserts of Asia and never came back to this northern fringe of the Sultan's Empire.

Years later, a traveling Turkish musician visiting the area was welcomed in the Castle of Revistye. He sang a sad song about a heartbroken father and a sword adorned with emerald stones. According to his story, there was a sword, once upon a time, that was dropped by the Prophet from the highest Heavens. Its grip was decorated by magic spells and ornaments, studded with clear emeralds. The mighty Prophet bade that it can be unsheathed from its equally decorated scabbard only against those who are evil and wrong, traitors and hypocrites. Its razor-sharp blade would never be able to scratch the good and the noble-hearted.

As it was bidden, the sword could stay no longer than seventy-seven years with one warrior and all of its bearers must be loved by Allah. The first owner of the magic sword was Sultan Mahmud because he was an exceptionally good and true man. He gave it to his Grand-Vizier who was none other than the great-grandfather of Pasha Kerim. This ancestor of the Pasha left it for the Polish king. From there, the rest of the sword's story was obscure. According to a dream of a wise Mufti, the sword was inherited by a true Hungarian warrior.

Pasha Kerim saw its blade flash in the hand of his enemy as the fate of Allah was willing it. When the Pasha realized what sword it was, he humbled himself before Allah. Alas, he realized his sin at once, because this sword was the sign of his wrongdoing. Had not he wanted to have his enemy poisoned just to take his revenge easier on him? Yet, the Pasha found his peace in the knowledge that Allah is the most merciful and he knew that this sword will one day be inherited by his grandchildren.

As it was promised by the Prophet, whoever owns the sword, must be an honest and good person otherwise the blade will disappear into thin air.

52. Nyitra Castle   GPS: 48.300032, 18.066939

Nyitra (Nitra, Neutra) is 92 km East of Pozsony (Pressburg, Bratislava), laying on the northern fringe of the Hungarian Small Plain, in the Valley of the Nyitra River. You can see the Northwestern Carpathian Mountains towering above the city and its castle, which was built in the 11th century, on a 60-meter-high hill at the ford of the Nyitra River. It belonged to the Hungarian kings who often stayed there. As Nyitra was also the Hungarian prince's place, the unfortunate Prince Vazul was blinded there in 1037 by the order of the German Queen Gizella, wife of King István I. It was Queen Gizella who had a chapel built in the castle what she devoted to Saint Emmeram, the Patron Saint of Regensburg.

Emperor Henrik besieged Nyitra in 1074 but could not take it. King Könyves (Bookish) Kálmán established the Bishopric of Nyitra in 1113 and gave the place to its bishop. The Castle's church was finished in 1158. The gothic cathedral of the Bishop was built in the 13th century and you can see the sculptures of two Hungarian kings, Saint István and Saint László, on the main altar. Nyitra Castle was among the few forts which were able to withstand the siege of the Mongolians in 1241-42.

Nyitra was given a new privilege in 1248. It became a Free Royal Town. The Czech King Ottokár II took the castle between 1271 and 1272 and it was heavily damaged. The Czech raids also damaged the Bishop's property and therefore, as compensation, Nyitra was put under his administration in 1288.

In the conflict between the king and the oligarchy of Máté Csák the bishop of Nyitra remained loyal to the king. In 1313, the king confirmed bishopric privileges and extended them to include the right to administer not only Nyitra but the whole of Nyitra County. Yet, the powerful Máté Csák of Trencsény took it in 1317.

It was taken and sacked by the Hussites in 1440. In this period, the members of the Stibor family tried to defend Nyitra against them. The Polish King Kázmér IV got the castle in 1471 but King Matthias took it back a year later. After the defeat at the Battle of Mohács in 1526, Nyitra was under threat of Ottoman attacks.

In 1563, the town became the seat of the Captaincy of Lower Hungary. The Turks failed to take it three times but Prince Bocskai's man Rhédey was able to take it in 1605, with Turkish help. Prince Bethlen also took it in 1620 and held it for a while. The Franciscan monastery and church date back to 1630.

Nyitra Castle (Photo: XMetov)

The Battle of Vezekény took place not far from Nyitra in 1652 where 1,200 Hussars of Chief Captain Ádám Forgách defeated a three times larger Ottoman army in an open battle. Among other things, this battle was famous because four members of the high aristocratic Esterházy family died in the fight.

The castle fell into the Turk's hands without a fight in 1663 because János Terjén, the tax-collector of Zala County and the Castellan of Nyitra, surrendered it. The city became a center of the Nyitra Sanjak.

It was retaken by the army led by Jean-Louis Raduit de Souches and István Koháry in 1664 when the Ottomans surrendered after a two-week-long siege.

When the Hungarian rebels were gone in 1683, the garrison of Nyitra and Léva castles opened their gates for the army of General Rabatta and the Palatine.

According to the 1702 Act of Emperor Leopold I, in which most of the Hungarian castles were doomed, Nyitra Castle was ordered to be pulled down as well. It was due to the efforts of the Bishop of Nyitra, László Mattyasovszky, that the castle remained finally intact.

Nyitra Castle fell to Prince Rákóczi in 1704 but in 1708 the town burned down during the fight against the Habsburgs.

Today, the outer fortifications are gone but you can find most of the old buildings of the city in a nice condition. In case you are permitted to enter the old library you can see 80 books from the 15th century and about 1,500 from the 16th century.

53. The Battle of Vezekény (25 August 1652)

Count Miklós Zrínyi parried the rapier with his dagger and attacked with a fine cut at the left side of his opponent. It was a half-hearted blow and Signore Angelo deflected it with ease.

"Sir, it is not a saber, it is a rapier. Thrusts, not cuts, with respect."

The Count withdrew, hastily saluted, and tore his fencing mask off his face. He shook his long dark curly hair with distress and hung his rapier back in its place on the wall of his knightly hall of Csáktornya Castle.

He spoke with his fencing master in fluent Italian; perhaps it was with a rather Venetian dialect, as Signore Angelo di Fiore thought. Of course, his name was a made up name after the fashion of the renowned fencing master from the old times. He was actually just an impoverished elderly nobleman with steel muscles and firm blue eyes. An adventurer, who sold his rather good skills with the rapier to this immensely rich Hungarian-Croatian magnate.

The Signore sensed the unease of his lord and considered today's practice done. He bowed elegantly and prepared to leave the arched hall. It was a late October afternoon and suddenly he thought he could use some hot, spiced wine. His lord shook his head and motioned him to sit down at the small table where refreshments were placed on a silver tray.

"Signore Angelo, do not despise the saber that much. Sit here and let us drink some wine together, please. With my saber, I have sent many Turks to the seventh Paradise in the last thirty years. I killed the first in 1632 when I was sixteen. True, it is not an elegant blade for playing around in a hall where the paintings of my ancestors are peering down from the walls. Life is nastier than that."

Nyitra Castle in the 17th century

They were sitting on cushioned chairs and enjoyed the beams of the October sun as they shone through the colored windows. Zrínyi went on and poured out what was in his heart as the Signore was expecting. The Count raised his cup and gave a toast:

"Let us drain our cups in tribute to the fallen heroes."

They drank in unison. In his heyday, the Signore had visited the battlefields of half of Europe and he had many comrades to think of.

"Bad news, Sir?" he asked.

"Always, Angelo." he replied and added: "My dear friend Pál Esterházy sent me a letter in which he has given an account of the Battle of Vezekény in August."

"Was the victory of Captain Forgách, wasn't it?"

"A victory of Phirros, I would say. You certainly have heard of the famous Esterházy family? Miklós Esterházy is the Palatine of the Kingdom, the second in rank after the king. Four members of his clan died in that battle."

"Unbelievable," slurred the Signore then bit his lip. He was shocked because the sons of the wealthy very rarely lost their lives in a battle, at least as far as he had experienced..

"I tell no lies," exclaimed Count Zrínyi and his black eyes flashed dangerously. Then, he added in a softer tone,

"Signore, let me tell you the story of this battle, you might even learn one or two things about how the Hungarian aristocracy differ from those of the west."

"Sir, forgive my bluntness and please, do tell me the story."

Zrínyi lay back and began to relate it in his deep, resonant voice. The Signore remembered that his lord was not only a celebrated military genius, but a recognized poet as well.

"The battle itself was not remarkable because these kinds of fights have occurred countlessly all over our poor homeland, from Croatia up to Upper Hungary during the last one hundred and twenty-six years since the Battle of Mohács was lost. Five thousand Ottomans against one-thousand-two hundred Christians - this rate has been quite commonplace, too. The sad uniqueness is the fact that there are not many examples of the loss of four so highly born persons in a single battle according to the historians of this land."

"Did the outcome of the battle change anything in the flow of the war, Sir?"

"No, Signore, it was a common Turkish raid, like here in the south, around Csáktornya. If you saw one you have seen all."

"Where is this place, Vezekény, My Lord?"

"It is to the north, near Érsekújvár. It is the area where the castle-ring of the Hungarian forts is going around Vienna and it is close to the rich Mining City District where lots of copper and silver are being produced. This is the area where my late father, György Zrínyi fought against the Swedish and the Turks under the flag of General Wallenstein in 1626. You know, Signore Angelo, Wallenstein was the one who had him poisoned out of jealousy."

"Yes Sir, it is a sad story which I had happened to hear."

"So, the Turks have frequently tried to take those lands, but so far in vain because the Chief Captain of the Mining Towns, Ádám Forgách has valiantly been repelling their attacks, so far."

"Was he leading the Hungarian flags this time?"

"Oh yes, he was. He had been informed by his spies in advance that Bey Mustapha, alias the Robber Bey, would set out from Nógrád Castle with four-five thousand riders."

"Was heavy cavalry among them, Sir?"

"Yes, there were the Sipahis and their men, but we are usually talking about lighter cavalry in case of raids like this. Here, in Csáktornya, you can meet with riff-raff irregular raiders every other day. Like the ones I had hung on the castle's gate a few days ago. In the north, you can more often run into Asabs and Deli riders."

"Who are the Deli riders?"

"Mounted berserkers, with eagle wings attached to their shields. Despite the lack of armor, their battle-frenzy can be very dangerous to the morale of our soldiers."

"Did Count Forgách go to meet them or did he wait behind walls, Sir?"

"Signore, it has been the quick action of constantly moving units which could work well against the Turks. Of course, he set out against them, but did not want to risk a frontal attack in an open battle."

"He was outnumbered almost five to one, wasn't he."

"Yes, indeed. Count Forgách warned the countryside and decided to let the Turks wander around and intended to ambush them on their way back. It is also an old trick of the Valiant Order."

"What is the Valiant Order, Sir? Is it like the Order of the Templars had been?"

"No, not really," Zrínyi smiled for the first time "they are not even all of them noble born warriors. Yet, they fight to preserve the Christian faith, even the Protestant ones. They value all the honorable principles which can be worth dying for, for a knight. Their unwritten law has firm rules for duels, sharing the booty and taking care of the widows and orphans of the fallen. In most cases, they elect their own captains and officers and they keep themselves to their other one hundred habits and customs. If you are familiar with them, you can learn the rank, origin, reputation, as well as the social status and the martial skill of a Hussar warrior from the first glance of his dress by seeing the colors he is wearing, the numbers of feathers in his hat and so on."

"Thank you, Sir, for explaining it to me."

"It is interesting that even the Turks are regarded as the part of this Valiant Order because they roughly share the same rules. Perhaps they differ only because of the religion. Sometimes you can distinguish them from each other only because they wear turbans on their helmets. But let's get back to the battle. As I said, Forgách was waiting for his chance. He also wanted to free those hundreds of people who were rounded up by the pagans to be sold on the slave market. The Captain placed his troops in a strategic spot where the Turks were expected to come through. He had a strong wagon fort built by chaining together many carriages. These wagon forts are very effective against cavalry if you have good muskets. It was where he deployed his 150 German musketmen and his 150 Hajdú soldiers who also had their rifles with them."

"Are the Hajdús as good as the Germans?"

"Yes, many western generals appreciate their steadiness. Germans are more disciplined and skilled, but the Hajdú soldiers are more savage in the melee."

"Were there any German riders as well?"

"He had 600 good Hungarian Hussars, heavy cavalry in their flexible armor, and there were also 150 German heavily armored riders on their huge horses. When the riders of Bey Mustapha appeared, these horsemen crashed into them like lightening into the mast of a ship, cracking and tormenting it. Unfortunately, it did not have the anticipated shock effect so as to scatter the lighter Turk cavalry. They withdrew and the Turks began to attack the wagon-fort, wave after wave. A particularly bloody and fierce fight had been taking shape. Bey Mustapha suffered very painful losses in the next two hours due to the fire from the footmen. In the end, the attack of the heavy German cavalry decided the battle, aided by the Hussars who we should consider as half-heavy cavalry, compared to them. Many high-ranked Turkish officers were slain, for example, the Bey of Hatvan Castle. The tragedy of the Eszterházy boys happened in the last phase of the fight."

"My Lord, why did they throw themselves into the melee like a commoner?"

"Alas, Signore Angelo di Fiore, you know very little of the people of this land, yet. Poor László Eszterházy, he was just 26, but already the Chief Captain of Pápa Castle. He was a member of the Imperial Chamber and also a Secret Advisor to the king. After bleeding from his many wounds, he died of a cut aimed at his head. His brother, Ferenc was beheaded next to him. Tamás and Gáspár perished along with their bodyguards who tried to defend them in vain. Their deaths caused such a shock to the Christians that albeit winning the battle, the surviving Turks could escape, pillaging and burning the countryside all the way home."

Miklós Zrínyi / Nicholas Zrínski

"What a fight, Sir. I am deeply saddened to have heard that, Dio mio," said Signore Angelo, seemingly touched by the story. Count Zrínyi lifted his cup again.

"Hail to the Eszterházy clan.They had actively taken their share from defending the Homeland throughout these centuries."

Draining their cups, the lord of Csáktornya finished his story by unfolding a sheet of paper. He stood up and read a part from Pál Eszterházy's letter by the light of the setting October sun filtering through the blue and red colors of the window.

"These are the words of my friend, Pál Eszterházy:

"...my brother lord's army was pushed back by about two-thousand Turks although they were firing back at them very fiercely. Many Turks fell there, but eventually the Hungarian's order was loosened. There was my brother lord on his horse called Zöldfikár - the one he had promised to give me - and he was riding together with my lord János Eszterházy and his page called Marci, along with twenty horsemen of his. They were forced into a muddy stream and his horse fell. He was fighting for quite a long time and could even cut down two Turks. Finally, weakened by his many wounds, he gloriously put down his life along with his servants fighting around him. It happened between six and seven in the evening, God rest them in His heaven. The next day, they found my poor brother lord together with the bodies of Ferenc, Tamás and Gáspár Eszterházy who all fell valiantly for their God and Homeland. There were altogether forty-five of my poor lord brother's servants who fell with him in that fight and many more were wounded. All the bodies were found stark naked, the body of my poor lord brother had only a shirt and trousers on. There were twenty-five wounds on him, cuts, gashes, and bullet wounds."

Signore Angelo di Fiore piously crossed himself and bowed his head in respect to the heroes. Yet, he felt a more genuine sorrow for the followers and servants of these great lords. Perhaps because he himself was not a high-born knight, just a lowly adventurer, he reasoned to himself.

54. Érsekújvár Castle   GPS: 47.985466, 18.157982

The Ottoman peril had been reaching up to the northern lands of the Hungarian Kingdom ever since the middle of the 16th century. The Turkish raiders broke into the Valley of the Nyitra River in 1543. Vienna and its battle-zone, the Hungarian borderland, had to be protected by a new line of castles. Many old ones were reinforced but a few new ones were also constructed.

Érsekújvár (Nove Zamky, Neuhäusl) Castle was just such a fortress, built to oppose the Ottomans on the site of an older settlement. It was Pál Várday, Archbishop of Esztergom who placed the first stone on this marshland to protect his domains in the years 1545-46. His work was continued by the next Archbishop of Esztergom, Miklós Oláh, who had the first palisade fort rebuilt between 1573 and 1581. The word for "Archbishop" is "Érsek" in the Hungarian language while "újvár" means "new castle". So this is why the fort is called Érsekújvár. To begin with, it was also called "Oláhújvár", after its builder.

A town developed quickly around the fortress giving shelter to many churchmen and refugees from the south. The huge new fortress was one of the most modern fortresses in contemporary Europe. It was a prime example of a star fortress which was considered to be adapted according to the advancements made in artillery in the preceding centuries. The earthen ramparts and bastions provided better deployment for the cannons and were not easy to breach unlike the old-fashioned thin, high castle walls built in gothic style. It was Cardinal Péter Pázmány who had the archbishop's palace built there in 1620 in order to fight Protestantism. He consecrated a Franciscan church and monastery there in 1631.

Érsekújvár was considered a strategic place near the Bohemian border and became the target of many Ottoman attacks. The Turks attempted but failed to conquer it six times (except for Turkish rule between 1566–1595 and 1605–1606). But in 1663 they managed to do so, despite the efforts of the castle's Captain, Ádám Forgách. There is even a saying about the insistence of the Ottomans that went like this:

„Strong as a Turk in front of Érsekújvár`s Ghiaurs" which means working with determination and stability, reflecting upon the memory and determination of the Turks who wanted to have the fort so badly. The castle's final fall was a tremendous loss to the Christians. The town was made the center of a Turkish Vilayet in Upper Hungary. We know much about this period thanks to the famous Turkish traveler Evliya Celebi (1611-1682).

In 1685 the castle was re-conquered by the imperial troops of Charles V, Duke of Lorraine. All over Europe, it was considered to be a huge victory and its day was celebrated for many years. Six years later, the settlement received town privileges from the Archbishop of Esztergom. The town also played an important role in many anti-Habsburg uprisings in the northern parts of Royal Hungary in the 17th century. It was in the hands of the Emperor when Prince Ferenc II Rákóczi seized it in 1704 and kept it in high esteem. He issued his famous Memorandum from there in 1706, demanding liberty and independence for Hungary.

Nowdays, you can find no trace of the once famous fortress. Emperor Charles VI wanted to prevent potential further insurrections which could use the fortress as their base, so he had it razed to the ground in 1724–1725.

55. The Taking of Érsekújvár Castle (1663) according to Evliya Celebi

"It happened 1,106 years after the Run of the Prophet Mohamed, in the year 1663 according to the infidel's calendar. The Grand Vizier Köprülü Achmed and his glorious army set out from Istanbul to make the Ghiaur Hungarians country, Üngüristan, bend the knee before the Padishah. He crossed the Danube River at Esztergom and took the small mouse-hole called Castle of Párkány. Then he appeared before the walls of Érsekújvár in a blink of an eye. This Újvár had already been standing there for a hundred years or so. It was built against us by a Ghiaur priest who dared to resist us. He had this hexagonal fort built at the confluence of the Nyitra and the Zsitva rivers and this castle had been blocking the way of our shining armies to reach Vienna.

This is the reason why the glorious Ottoman Empire wanted to twist it from the infidel's hands, besides the Hussars of Újvár had saddened us on lots of occasions as well. The soul of the Prophet Mohamed had spurred our warriors of the True Faith to go around the water of the Nyitra River and try to take the castles of Léva and Nyitra and occupy the Mining Towns.

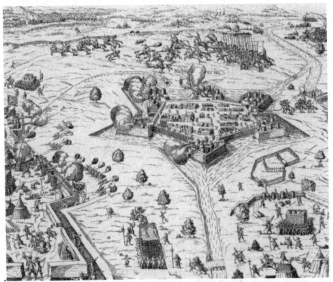

Érsekújvár Castle in 1685 (Source: Péter Pogány)

Ádám Forgách was the Hungarian's captain in Újvár. He was like all the Hungarian chief warriors and captains; he preferred action and battles instead of sitting idly at home. These Hungarians all have a desire to run to the battlefield, they are like restless pretty girls who always like to dance. Alas, Ádám Forgách did the same, he and his Hussars danced before us to Párkány. There he almost lost all of his men and could barely retreat back behind the walls of Újvár. It made the Grand Vizier-Pasha satisfied because he understood that Újvár has already fallen into his lap.

Allah aided his warriors so we could surround the castle of Újvár and manage to lead away the water of the Nyitra River from its moats. Those who were sitting inside the castle were whimpering like dogs. The Archangel appeared in my dream and foretold me that I am going to sing the Ezan, the song of victory, in the market-place of Újvár.

It was a warm summer. This is the weather when our glorious warriors of the True Faith like to make war against the Ghiaurs. But sadly, the rain began to fall and did not cease pouring for forty days. The whole Üngür country was soaked through and all the roads were turned into muddy streams. Allah had them dried up only after forty days and we were able to get our cannons pulled there by bison and oxen through the fields. We had to hurry up with the siege of Újvár because the Worshipful Pasha wished to reach Vienna soon.

Finally, we could start the siege of Újvár in earnest at the end of the summer. It also lasted for forty days. We were able to take the fort in the autumn and we were glad that General Montecuccoli did not send any reinforcements to assist Ádám Forgách during this time. When the news about the fall of Újvár reached them, the inhabitants of Vienna became so frightened that they all escaped from their town and our Tatar riders were galloping around Pozsony and Vienna after them. But it was not a lack of bravery in Ádám Forgách or in the Hussars of Újvár that helped us to gain victory.

To our fortune, there were many thousands of German, Walloon and Spanish mercenaries there who were howling in fear of our soldiers. They forced Forgách to hang out the white flag. We have decently let them go and they did go away on the tunes of their music. After they left, we marched in triumphantly, with drums and whistles, raising the horse-tailed flags high. The Pasha was riding in front of his Janissaries, our dervishes were dancing joyfully. The Grand-Vizier Pasha summoned me and told me:

"My Efendi, Evlija, you are a respected Hodja and Hadji. You had asked me before that in exchange for your efforts and troubles that you are permitted to sing the Ezán of victory in this Ghiaur nest. So behold. I bid you sing the prayer of victory tomorrow for those heroes and martyrs of

Mohamed who have gone up to Paradise. But first, we have to throw out those dark idols and pictures of their saints from the infidel's church and quickly cover the paintings with whitewash in order to turn it into a Mosque of the Worshipful Allah. Just to make you sing with merry heart, I will appoint you the Chief Imam of this rat-nest that has now become a famous castle of the Ottomans. You are now the high priest here."

Hearing this, I spread myself on the ground before the legs of the mighty and merciful Pasha and kissed the top of his slippers and the edge of his kaftan. He kissed my shoulder and gifted me with a new, splendid kaftan. Then, I felt great happiness.

After this, I climbed up into the tower and from the terrace of this tower I looked around and saw the extended plains of the Zsitva, the Nyitra and the far away Danube rivers. This land, blessed by Allah and given to us until the end of times.

The statue of Evliya Celebi (1611-1684) in Eger, Hungary

Then, I began to sing beautifully in a silvery voice:

"Allahu la illáh, Allahu Akbar! You have opened the gate of annihilation ajar before the infidels and you have sprinkled the dust of decay into their faces. Our heroes, the Rumelian warriors sent the Ghiaurs into the land of darkness, into the hell of decay with the strikes of their swords that were shining like falling stars. Gratitude to you, worshipful Allah, gratitude to you, Mohamed Prophet, the eagle bird of glory, thanks to you for all of this! You turned the world into darkness with the black smoke of the Muslims' cannons and guns so that the ugly eyes of the Christians could not see anything. The world is shining only for us. Allahu Akbar! Allahu illáh!"

The Grand-Vizier was very satisfied with me and allowed our warriors three days of free plundering, but he banned the Tatars from the town because their cruelty was too much even for him. The rains of autumn have returned and the Pasha remained in Újvár. We sent envoys to the camp of General Montecuccoli and demanded to have the castles of Léva and Nyitra, but the infidels ceded only Hollókő and Gyarmat. The tombs of our martyrs who gloriously sacrificed their lives for the True Faith were danced around with sweet-smelling joss sticks and we were singing laudatory songs above them. But they were already sitting in seventh heaven at the feet of the Prophet and they were being served by the souls of the infidels killed in the battle.

The honorable Pasha dismissed me mercifully a week later, upon having gifted me richly. He gave me new horses and new servants and two Christian slaves as well as a golden kaftan, a silk dress and two bags of gold. Not forgetting a silk turban and a scimitar adorned with precious stones.

I was singing once more, during the lunch of the Pasha. Finally, he let me depart with this message:
"The shining steel of your voice is still the same, its silver is glittering, my Evilja. The position of the Chief Imam will forever be yours in Újvár. Anytime you return here, the main mosque will be yours. You will receive a regular salary for it, too. But you have to come here to get paid. I cannot send it to you because it will be stolen. Now, take your leave and may Allah bless the dust beneath your feet."

With that, I kissed the hand of the Pasha and rode away happily. Upon leaving the city, I let the two Christian slaves go home, though."

56. Léva Castle   GPS: 48.215030, 18.600427

The name of the town and the castle of Léva (Levice, Lewenz) is usually associated with the name of its captain, György Thury, the greatest Hungarian duelist of the Turkish wars.

Léva castle stands on a cliff and in the past it was surrounded by marshlands. It was very effective in guarding the seven mining towns of the Kingdom where an immense amount of gold and silver was being produced. No wonder the Turks always wanted to take them.

The castle watches over the valley of the Garam river just 34 kilometers from the rich mining town of Selmecbánya (Banská Štiavnica, Schemnitz).

The walls were built on top of a strong Celtic fort and the town was first mentioned in 1347 as "Leua". Next to the city on a hill called Baratka, the remains of an old church and another fort from the 12th-century can be found.

Léva had been a royal castle owned by the Hungarian kings and built in the 13th century. The Czech King, Ottokár II, tried to take it by siege in 1270, but failed to do so. Later, when royal power had weakened, Mate Csák, the great feudal lord of the northern lands, seized it. The king was only able to take it back in 1321 and the stronghold was so important that the ruler turned it into the administrative center of the County of Bars.

When King Karoly Róbert and his queen were the targets of an assassination attempt by a bewildered nobleman, Felician Zách, the king took cruel revenge on him and had the entire family of the nobleman killed in 1330. The Castle of Léva had to witness as the king had Sebe, the daughter of Felicián Zách, beheaded. After the execution, the king gave Léva to his Queen, Erzsébet, who had lost two of her fingers in the assassination attempt.

Léva Castle (Photo: Péter Schoeller)

During those 150 years when the Ottoman attacks became daily realities in the northern lands, Léva's role became more important. In the days between 1400 and 1542, the surrounding lands of Léva had been in the hands of the Lévay family. Then, the infamous but valiant, robber knight, Menyhért Balassa, gained the castle through a marriage. In spite of his reputation, Balassa heroically defended the walls of Léva in 1544 against the Turks although later the Captain was accused of treason. (He changed sides nine times in his life.) The grim army of King Ferdinand I besieged the fort and soon Balassa had to flee for his life to Transylvania.

Its other famous Captain had been the legendary György Thury, the duelist. Some years later it was commanded by István Dobó, the hero of Eger Castle, who was made Comes of Bars County in 1561. Dobó was aware of the Ottoman threat and had the place reinforced along with building a gorgeous renaissance palace at the foot of the castle. These buildings were completed a year before he died there in 1572.

As Léva remained in Habsburg hands, the Transylvanian Prince, István Bocskai, laid a siege on it during his campaign against the king. The Prince could not take the castle, so he burned the city instead in 1605. When the second clash took place between the Habsburgs and Transylvania, Prince Gábor Bethlen proved to be more successful and took the fort during his campaign. However, Léva was returned to the king after Bethlen's death. The City was so in the throat of the enemy that it ceased to be the center of Bars County in 1621 and the noble Estates of the county moved their seat to the safer Aranyosmarót.

The merriest days in Léva were in 1635 when the pompous wedding of Ferenc, the son of Palatine Miklós Esterházy, and Erzsébet Thurzó took place. There was even a knightly tournament held in celebration of the newly married high aristocrats of Hungary.

The new lord of the castle became László Csáky in 1640; the peasants of the area blessed his name. Later, the Castle opened its gates to the huge Ottoman army appearing in front of it in 1663. Pasha Csatra Patra Ali was appointed as its new commander.

General De Souches took the castle back the following year, but died doing so. It was taken and retaken periodically by the rebel aristocrat, Prince Imre Thököly, in 1678 and 1685. The Eszterházy family became the owner of the castle in 1688 and they remained its lords until 1867.

Although, the Castle changed hands three more times during the War of Independence of Prince Ferenc II Rakoczi's struggles in the early 18th century.

When the rebel Kuruc troops of Rákóczi suffered a major defeat at Trencsén in 1708, the Prince didn't take risks. Rákóczi didn't want to cede Léva to General Heister and had the Castle destroyed, its walls pulled down and its moat and well filled up. A year later, the remains were finally and utterly destroyed by General Heister. The point is that its town suffered beyond imagination. Presently, there is a beautiful exhibition among its remaining walls.

57. The White Geese of Léva Castle (1664)

The legend of Léva castle reaches back to the time when the Turks were its lords. The commander of Léva at that time was Pasha Köprülü and he was having a good time in it. His only problem was that he felt lonely and his harem was empty. He was fortunate to have a scribe called Ali who was a shrewd renegade originally called Pali. Ali kept whispering into the ears of the fat Pasha who finally offered him one hundred gold coins if he could come up with a good idea.

Within a very short time, and on behalf of the Pasha, the scribe wrote a letter with his copper writing stick to the Hungarian city judge of Léva town.

"Behold, you judge of Léva. I send you my command that you are to send into the castle fifty snow-white geese within three days from now. Each must be carried in by a young and pretty maid. If you fail to obey my words, I will have you impaled, and your twelve town advisors will be beheaded, too. Otherwise, I send you my greetings, may the peace and good will of Allah be known by you and your foot would never step on a thorn on your path, and may the Prophet bless your entire family."

The judge and the city leaders of Léva were frightened and without advice. The fathers, husbands, and fiancées were holding a council from evening to morning, but they had no idea how to save the girls from peril. They were about to decide to defend them by taking up arms when the door of the council room opened and Veronika, the beautiful daughter of the judge, entered with a proud confidence in her eyes.

"My lords, take heart and never despair. Trust me and the other maidens. We are going to take care of the fat Turkish pig. Yes, we will go up to the castle, all fifty of us, each holding a white goose. All we need from you is a sharp dagger to hide under our skirts. Your job is to be armed and come near the castle gate in secret. When you see the geese flying away, hurry into the castle with unsheathed swords."

There was nothing to do, Veronika couldn't be discouraged and finally, her plan was accepted. The next day the girls set out at dawn to go and present them to Pasha Köprülü as it was commanded. The gate was opened before them and they entered the castle in twos, holding their snow-white geese tightly. The Pasha had sent most of his troops to raid the countryside because he didn't want so many hungry men watching the girls join his harem.

Ali, the scribe was grinning when he led the fair and slender Veronika to the Pasha. His palm was itching for the prize he was anticipating for his brainy plan.

"You are going to be my first wife!" exclaimed the Pasha with cow eyes "Just put down that bird and hug me, let me kiss your rosy cheeks." Veronika cast her eyes down obediently and released the goose that immediately took to its wings and flew away. Did the Pasha care about that when he was about to be kissed and pampered like he would be in the heavens? Veronika did hug him and with the same move of her shapely hand, she slit the throat of the Turk with her father's dagger.

That was the sign. All the other geese went flying with a great noise into the air and the blades of long knives glittered in the girls' hands. The renegade was the second to fall and those twenty or thirty lazy soldiers in the yard were surprised and slaughtered in a blink of an eye.

The lads and burghers of Léva had not much work left when they rushed into the castle. Once they were in, they secured the gates and loaded the cannons on the bastions with nails and musket balls.

When the raiding Turks returned they were greeted by a hailing rain of hot iron from the throats of their own cannons. They had to run away. Perhaps they are fleeing still, even to this very day, from those walls.

58. Zsarnóca Castle   GPS: 48.481612, 18.721584

Zsarnóca (Zarnovica, Zarnovia) is not far from the Castle of Revistye and it is only 17 kilometers from Selmecbánya City, on the right bank of the Garam River. The settlement was first mentioned in 1332 as „Zanog" and „Zirnog". Its church was dedicated to Saint Nicholas.

There was a ferry at the ford of the Garam River where fees and taxes were collected. Zsarnóca belonged to the Castle of Revistye and it was mentioned as „Sarnocza" in 1389. The Dóczy family became its owner in 1479. They built the three-story castle on a rocky hilltop, in late gothic style, between 1480 and 1485, surrounded by strong walls. Zsarnóca became a town in 1563 and was allowed to hold markets in 1681. The meetings of the local Noble Estates of Bars County were held in the city during the 17th century.

The army of Prince István Bocskai made its camp next to Zsarnóca in 1605. The first Battle of Zsarnóca took place next to the castle in 1644 where an Ottoman army was defeated. The Turks attacked again in 1647 and killed Zsigmond Dóczy and took away his wife. As the Dóczy family had no more male heirs, the Treasury seized the castle in 1647 and placed it under the authority of Selmecbánya. The Turks attacked it during the same year and caused lots of destruction. The City of Besztercebánya belonged to the king, so it took over the administration of Zsarnóca in 1662.

The second Battle of Zsarnóca took place on 16 May 1664, when General de Souche and his Imperial Army defeated the army of the Pasha of Várad. The city was totally destroyed in the battle.

The mercenaries of the king ceded Revistye Castle to the Hungarian rebel Kuruc troops in 1677 who sacked the area.

The first guild to be established in the agricultural town was the Furrier's Guild in 1696. The Burghers were famous for their wood products, and for their beer, which they could sell easily in Selmecbánya.

The castle is still intact but seems empty, and we know little about its present conditions.

59. The Battle of Zsarnóca (16 May 1664)

"Did you say it was Pasha Kücsük Mehmed from Várad Castle who had set out against me?" General Jean-Louis Raduit de Souches asked of the dust-covered messenger, a trusted Hungarian Hajdú of his. The Hajdú called Balogh, was a thin, sinewy man. He was dwarfed by the well-built and tall French man. The General entrusted nobody else to carry his personal messages to his good friend, Count Miklós Zrínyi who had just finished his famous campaign in the southern Borderland of Hungary. His Croatian-Hungarian friend had just burned the famous bridge of the Sultan at Eszék in February.

De Souche had come to like these Hungarian Hajdú soldiers for their steadiness in battle. He had seen, not once, how they perished under the enemy fire with that indifferent eastern look in their eyes, fighting until the last man. Not all his fellow generals loved them, though. General Raimondo Montecuccoli, Zrínyi's lethal rival, hated them for their allegedly cruel and savage ways. De Souche allowed his messenger to sit down in his spacious tent. And while the thirsty man was being served by his attendants, he thought of his last encounter with Montecuccoli in Vienna.

"You never know when they will slit your throat from behind," Montecuccoli used to say "they always separate themselves from the rest of the decent troops in camp. When they drink and dance they give out unearthly cries like beasts from the underworld to the music of that damned Turkish clarinet. It should be banned because one day it will turn them into rebels. But, they are even more baleful when they are just sitting around their fires and wordlessly peer into the flames saying nothing for hours."

How he cursed Zrínyi, and how he tried to discredit him, calling him a traitor and a secret conspirator against the crown. It was due to Montecuccoli's propaganda that Emperor Leopold did not take advantage of Zrínyi's victory and sent no reinforcements. And this was why his Croatian-Hungarian friend's efforts evaporated in vain; the military engineers of Grand Vizier Köprülü Achmed had recently rebuilt the great bridge and a forty-thousand strong Ottoman army presently is said to be crossing the capricious Dráva River unhindered, according to the report of Balogh.

Zsarnóca, the Mansion of the Dóczy family

De Souche looked at the unrolled map on his camp-table and sighed. "Now," he thought, "I have taken the Castle of Nyitra after two long weeks of siege, but Zrínyi and General Hohenlohe have been trying to take the formidable Kanizsa Castle,however, they will not succeed without the Emperor's reinforcements. Grand Vizier Köprülü Achmed will most likely chase them away and no one has enough troops to stop him in the Trans-Danubian Region. As a result, the Vizier will end up here, in the north. I must not let him join the forces of Pasha Kücsük Mehmed. Damn Montecuccoli. He dissuaded the Emperor from helping Zrínyi because Zrínyi was given the desired Golden Fleece from the King of Spain sooner than he." he mused and hummed.

Yes, reputation was everything. Rank and privileges could always be purchased from the Emperor in exchange for offering a generous loan to the Treasury. And he, De Souche, has been raised into the highest aristocrats of Hungary this way. He had urged his promotion with an extra one-thousand freshly minted gold Forints just like Montecuccoli, Salm, Caprara and others did. As for his own career, De Souche made the Pasha of Várad responsible for spoiling his good luck four years ago.

The General pursed his lips while recalling the unfortunate incident. Pasha Ali and Kücsük Mehmed were cunningly waiting until the Hungarian Captain of Várad left his castle leaving behind less than nine hundred defenders. The Turks immediately besieged the city, which was the Gateway to Transylvania, while De Souche and his ten thousand men were idly staying at Rakamaz not very far from them. Did not the poor Burghers of Várad send an envoy to him, pleading for help? They begged for the sending of only three or four hundred good musket-men and a few skilled artillerymen because they could not use their cannons. Did not he agree to send them? Yes, he did, and asked them to swear fealty to Emperor Leopold and obey the captain he would send. The poor fellows accepted his terms, but in the end, he could send them no help at all. He received strict orders from his ruler not to give any help so he had to go back on his word. Várad Castle fell forty days later and half of Europe blamed him for not having aided his Christian brothers. He had to live with this shame attached to his name.

Now that Palatine Wesselényi had allowed him to take the Ottoman castles in this western corner of Upper Hungary, he had a chance to make amends for his fault. He turned to Balogh who was already standing at attention.

"How many people does the Pasha have, and where is he now?"

"Sir, he has fifteen thousand men and he is making haste. He can be here in ten days."

The General dismissed his man and issued his order to strike camp and prepare to meet the enemy on a proper battlefield that was more to his liking.

It was not easy to snare the Turks into his trap and it took several days to reach the flooding Garam River where he pretended to make his army ready to cross it. There, he let the scouting Turk irregular riders come close and count his troops. He had less than eight-thousand, and five-hundred Austrian soldiers, most of them footmen, and he knew how the Turks despised the Christian infantry. In fact, the lay of the land in Hungary was not favorable because one could not fully use the advantages of the infantry. The terrain was frequently divided by thickets, higher or lower hills, marshlands and dense forests where the light cavalry could gain more success. Proper battlefields were rare, but De Souche knew of one. He wanted the Turks to follow him there, making them place their trust in their overwhelming numbers. His heart was on fire with the desire for revenge.

By the time the army of Kücsük Mehmed suffered itself across the river, De Souche was already deploying his army on a long gradually rising slope. He carefully placed his rested musket-men on the higher ground. Three or four lines could easily fire above each other's heads then run behind the next three lines to reload their weapons. The slope was narrow enough so that the attacking cavalry had to be thronged because the left and the right sides were impenetrable thickets and marshlands. Behind the

Austrians was the Garam River, with the only usable ford, in case of a retreat. It was called the Ford of Zsarnóca.

General Jean de Souche

De Souche had ropes tied across the ford to prevent accidents and posted a few sentries there to conduct the withdrawal if it was needed. The City of Bakabánya was not very far and could offer a very good fortified shelter at any time. Yet, he wished he had just a handful of Hussar riders with him. De Souche prayed to God that the Pasha would bite the bait. He knew that further Ottoman units were coming from the north, sent by the Pasha of Érsekújvár, and the Bey of Esztergom had launched his troops as well. His prayers must have been answered because he did not have to wait more than a day.

It was the 16th day of May when the Ottomans realized they could not get around him and decided to launch an attack. The formidable "Allahu Akbar" roar filled the air and thousands of hooves shook the land. The Ottoman musicians were trying to be heard over the clamor and the enemy wanted to trod them into the harsh green grass of the slope. As they rode on, the terrain became narrower as if it was a huge triangle laid on the ground.

De Souche stood out from the midst of his men and excitedly shouted: "Fire!"

His officers had been thoroughly informed of what their duty was to be, and the Austrian war-machine came swiftly into motion. This hellish grinding device of subsequent rows of musketeers swallowed the newer and newer waves of Turk attacks. The Asab riders were shocked and simply could not believe why they could not reach the Austrians.

The Turks were more frightened of the rage of their Robber Bey than from the throats of the muskets and desperately fought on until the Pasha himself was shot. After the death of Kücsük Mehmed, the Ottoman officers sent no more riders up the steep and slippery killing ground. Some tentative moves were made to prepare their retreat without losing face.

This was the perfect time to launch the counter-attack. De Souche ordered his soldiers to drop their muskets and draw their side swords. He led the infantry on foot like one of them, and they ran down the remains of the Ottoman army pushing them into the flooding River of Garam. The heart of General Jean de Souche swelled with joy.

He wished he had just a handful of Hussars, or a few hundred mounted Hajdús, to make his victory complete.

60. Likava Castle   GPS: 49.104787, 19.311307

Likava (Likavka) was built on the top of a tall protruding cliff overlooking the valley of the Vág river. It is clearly visible from the road and it appears to be really huge. It guarded the road towards Poland. The Ikavka Stream flows at the foot of the hill.

The Castle was built at the end of the 13th century by the Chief Comes of Liptó County, Master Dancs, the ancestor of the Balassa family. The Castle was a center of a huge domain as well. In the beginning, it was a royal castle, then King Robert Károly gifted it to Master Dancs in 1312. The Castle was in the hands of Bebek, the infamous robber knight, at the end of the 14th century but King Zsigmond took Likava away by force in 1399. King Zsigmond gave Likava and the Chief Comes post of Liptó County to Palatine Miklós Gara. The Castle burned down in 1431 and it was rebuilt in 1440.

Likava fell into the hands of Jan Giskra`s Bohemian Hussites who placed the fearsome knight, Péter Komorowsky, there. It was King Matthias, the second most famous member of the Hunyadi dynasty who was able to take it back again. The king liked to dwell in Likava because he took pleasure in hunting in the enormous forests around it. King Matthias made his natural son, János Corvin, the Duke of Liptó and gave him Likava Castle among other domains. He tried to make his son strong in order to inherit his throne, but it was in vain. After Matthias' death, Likava was taken in 1496 by Palatine István Szapolyai, the father of the next king of Hungary. The curved coat of arms of the Hunyadi family was still clearly seen in the Castle during the 18th century.

The ruins of Likava Castle (Photo: PetiPeton)

The Dual Kingship was a time when the forces of King János Szapolyai and King Ferdinand I were fighting each other in the area. It was during this period that the Habsburg's General Katzianer burned Likava. The outer castle and its buildings were constructed in the 16th century. The Castle changed hands between the Thurzó, the Pekry, the Báthory and the Illésházy families. It was György Illésházy who sold it to István Thököly in 1650.

The heyday of the Castle was during the twenty years these mighty upstarts, the Thököly family, owned it. Sebestyén Thököly was involved in the Wesselényi Conspiracy against the king so General Heister laid a siege on Likava and had it halfway ruined.

After 1670, taken by the Imperial Army, Likava Castle was used as a prison until 1707, the year of its demolition by orders of Prince Ferenc II Rákóczi.

In our day, the Castle is being restored, and perhaps one day, the black raven holding a golden ring in its beak - the symbol of the Hunyadi dynasty – will return to the walls of Likava.

61. The Treasure of the Thököly family (1670)

István Thököly gained his way into the circle of the wealthiest Hungarian oligarchs through the hard work of a long life. He acquired his fortune by selling wine to Poland and by herding gray cattle to Nurnberg City. His men traded broad-cloth between Krakow and the Transylvanian Máramaros. He invested his money in countless forests and fields, vineyards and sheep-herds, dense forests and full-packed storehouses all over the Upper Lands of Hungary and Transylvania. He had everything, except a castle. A strong fortress was needed where he could hide his immense treasure behind thick walls on the top of a high cliff. Likava Castle was just perfect for this purpose.

Did György Illésházy want to sell his castle? He was not a fool. But the Lord of Likava liked to spend gold beyond limits and István Thököly was always ready to offer him a loan. Soon, the day came when Illésházy had to take his leave and cede Likava Castle to its proud new owner, István Thököly. Sir Thököly was a good owner and turned the old castle into a shining and magical home. He had green gardens planted in the dusty castle yard and he reinforced the water system with a bastion so its huge stones were able to protect the incoming fresh water against all kind of artillery attacks. He had a new well dug which reached fifty yards down into the rock where the Vág River was flowing. He bought unique foreign plants to grow in the hanging gardens which contributed to the splendid looks of the place. Outside, the walls and the towers were freshly whitewashed with a mixture of fine sand and white of eggs and honey melted in wine and thick cottage cheese. One could see the whiteness of the castle from a distant land.

There were fabulous treasures piled up in the vaults of Likava and Árva castles; all the precious stones, and metals that the Thököly family was busily gathering in the markets of six countries. But everything comes to an end, even for the rich. Count István Thököly passed away and left behind a child of 13, Imre Thököly. Who thought that this young lad would become Prince of Hungary and Transylvania one day?

General Heister was the commander of the Imperial forces at this time and he took a fancy to these castles; all the more reason as their hidden treasures had raised his interest. As the Emperor was also the King of Hungary, he permitted his trusted man to take the castles away from the child, if he was able.

Heister waited for nothing and laid siege on both Likava and Árva castles. He did not know that he would alienate Imre Thököly from the Emperor for a lifetime, gaining him a mighty and talented adversary. The young boy was already the Count of Szepes and Chief Comes of two counties making him the wealthiest heir of Upper Hungary. An educated and clever boy who spoke equally well in Hungarian and German along with Slovakian and Latin. He was brought up as a soldier and borderland warrior of the Valiant Order. Still, he was just a child with only a very few men-at-arms.

Likava Castle in the 17th century

There was more gold than cannons in Likava and Heister's army was strong and menacing. The siege was going on systematically, the German cannons and muskets spread their missiles over the castle with precision. Heister wanted to ruin the water-supply line but it was too well-built to his liking. Eventually, the enemy was already at the gate and only a handful of defenders remained alive. In the evening, it was just a question of a few hours and the castle was doomed to fall. Mátyás Péterfi, the castellan of Likava hurried to Imre's room and woke him:

"My young Lord, you must flee for your life." said the old warrior and added, "The men of the General will have the gate broken in by the morning and you will be captured and taken to Vienna."

"What is your plan, then?" asked him the lad, without fear because he was taught not to fall into panic when in any danger.

"Shame or not, you will have to dress in girl's clothing and we will smuggle you out through the secret tunnel of the castle."

Imre went pale because of the humiliation, but there was nothing to do, skirts, scarves, and dresses were already being brought to him. He bid farewell to his faithful castellan who was preparing for his honorable last stand approaching with the new dawn.

The secret tunnel led him out of the castle to a hidden grove where only two silent horses and a stableboy waited for him. The shoes of the horses were fixed backward so that when they rode away the tracks would show only two incoming riders. The stable-boy skillfully guided him past the fires of the besiegers. They were getting away through roadless roads and ravines, hiding in the valleys of the snowbound Carpathian Mountains. They rested during the day and traveled by night until they reached the pass that led them to the White-Vág River which was already Szepes County, the domain of the Thököly's. It took them one more day and night to get to Késmárk Castle where Imre could change from his disguise and put on his normal clothes, back to boots and sword. Yet, he kept the girl's dress as a reminder.

In the meantime, the mercenaries of General Heister had pushed the gate of Likava in but to their greatest dismay, the Thököly heir was gone. Heister was raging and gave the strict order to find the tracks of the fugitive but they found no signs indicating that anyone had left the castle.

"The lad must have a Devil in his service," fumed the General. "Mark my words; he will play many nasty tricks on us once he grows up."

He was right because Imre Thököly became a military genius and rose to the throne of Transylvania and opened a channel for the Ottoman army to lay siege on Vienna in 1683.

And, what happened to the vast Thököly treasure? Heister left no stone unturned and had the whole castle turned upside-down in search of it, but all his work had been in vain. Nobody knew anything, no hard beating of the Castle's servants nor the most severe threats could give him a hint.

Finally, the mercenaries caught a young man in the pub of the village and dragged him before the General,

"Sir, this man was mumbling something strange while drinking himself numb. Something like 'if I was allowed to speak, I would tell things . . . 'and so on."

The young man was becoming sober and threw himself before the feet of Heister, trembling in fear. He was covered with spots of whitewash and sand.

"What is your job in the castle?"

"I was a mason, Sir."

"What is your secret? Did you wall in something, perhaps?"

The lad was threatened with torture and a painful death unless he opened his mouth. No wonder that he gave in, hoping to get some of the treasures himself.

"How much reward shall I have if I talked?"

"The quarter of it will be yours."

The mason boy hurried to admit that he and his team had hidden the strongboxes of the Thököly's in secret chambers behind covering walls of Árva and Likava Castles. He was sent to Árva Castle with some soldiers and returned with two wagons full of huge iron-bound wooden boxes. At once, he was put to work in Likava, too. When the lad opened up a hidden part of the cellars, the seasoned soldier, Heister was shocked to see the fabulous treasures.

When the gold and silver items were unpacked in the dining hall of the Castle, the General was amazed at how many ornamented swords and weapons stuffed with priceless stones, and goblets, cutlery, jewelry, and daggers were laid out on display. The noble materials, the carpets, the paintings and the embroidered golden dresses and belts were piled up next to the books whose covers were shining with rubies and emeralds. The General had seen a lot of booty in his long life, but nothing compared to this. His eyes were taking in the sight with joy. He exclaimed,

"A third of it is the king's, the second third is my part and the rest will go to the soldiers who took part in the siege."

"Sir, and what of my share? You promised me a quarter of it!" The mason boy's eyes grew wide.

"Your head is exactly a quarter of your body. So I will keep my word and I let you have it stay on your shoulders, as a present for betraying your liege-lord," answered Heister with a small smile.

The mason boy did not need to be told twice, he ran away as fast as he could and he did not stop until he found himself out of the country.

62. Kassa   GPS: 48.710167, 21.222256

Kassa, (Kosice, Kaschau) was the key city of the Eastern Upper Lands of the Kingdom of Hungary, presently it is twenty kilometers to the north of the Hungarian border. The City has always been very important in the Kingdom, but especially so in the 16th and 17th centuries, so its history has to be told in more detail.

As for its central location, there is an interesting legend, that the huge bronze bell of Kassa's Cathedral could be heard as far as the city of Eger, 100 kilometers away.

The City's strategic function was due to the main trade route which crossed between Poland and Hungary. The Valley of the Hernád is about two-kilometers wide at Kassa, while it is twice as wide at Szikszó City which area provided good lands for the inhabitants. The Valley of the Hernád, fringed by rich forests, was connected with the Vág River and with the Sajó River as well, not to mention the Bodrog River and the upper part of the Tisza River. As a result of this, military units could easily reach in all directions from Kassa.

The town of Kassa was born in the middle of the 12th century. According to the first mention of the town in 1230, its inhabitants were Hungarians at that time. This early settlement was destroyed by the Mongols in 1241 who killed everybody in it.

King Béla IV invited Saxon settlers to Kassa. They were traders and also produced lots of wine as well. We know of Hungarian nobles who also owned lands around the city. The first walls around the town were built in this period and they enclosed a 36-acre area. These walls were thin and several towers were guarding them. The City was growing and the king awarded it with privileges in 1249. The inhabitants owned five-thousand acres of land in the Valley of the Hernád River in 1255 and they were allowed to hold a market on each Thursday. The City was permitted to have a judge and jury men in 1270 and they began to mint silver coins in 1290. The first church was called Saint Elisabeth and there was a hospital in 1283 which belonged to it.

The Burghers of Kassa swore fealty to the new King, Robert Károly of Anjou. They helped him fight the oligarchs Amádé and Máté Csák with the help of the Saxon soldiers of the Zips cities of Upper Hungary in the Battle of Rozgony which became a milestone in Hungarian history.

The battle was decided by the onslaught of the Burghers of Kassa who received many privileges from the king in exchange for that. They received the same coin-minting rights as Esztergom and Buda, thus becoming one of the ten biggest cities of the Kingdom. On top of that, the king granted them tax exemption in Abaúj and in Zemplén Counties in 1319. King Róbert Károly met the Polish Kazimir III and the Czech King John in 1335 in Visegrád where they agreed in using the trade route of Kassa-Lőcse - Krakow. As a result of this, Kassa was flourishing even more during the 14th century. It became a Free Royal Town in Hungary in 1347 when King Róbert Károly's son, King Louis I awarded Kassa with the same privileges as the town of Buda.

In 1361, Kassa was granted the right to stop all of the merchants traveling through the city. In 1368, there was a new trade treaty born between King Louis I and the Polish King Kazimir III. It was not surprising as to why the Burghers of Kassa were so happy in 1369 when their city was given a Coat of Arms from the king containing the symbols of the Anjou Dynasty. The Anjou kings loved this city, King Louis I even held a Diet there in 1374.

The next King, Zsigmond of Luxembourg, was always short of money so he sold his royal palace of Kassa in 1392. The good times came to an end when Queen Elisabeth brought the Czech Hussite mercenaries into the Kingdom in 1440. She appointed their leader, Jan Giskra, as the commander of Kassa. Giskra put his subordinate, Captain Talafúz, in charge of the city. The Hussites gradually took huge territories of the Upper Lands under their control. King Ulászló's Captains, Jan Czapek and Imre Bebek, tried to take Kassa back in 1441, but the Hussites proved to be stronger. It was also at Kassa that Giskra defeated the army of Tamás Székely in 1449.

The city of Kassa, 1900

The unfortunate King Ulászló died in the Battle of Várna against the Ottomans and this was how Jan Giskra became one of the seven Chief Captains of Hungary. As a result of this, he was able to remain in Kassa until 1461. King Matthias was the monarch who hired Giskra and took Kassa back. The king highly appreciated the City and made the Burghers pay extra military taxes several times during his rule. It was the period between 1474 and 1477 when the main altar and the 48 Gothic pictures of the Saint Elisabeth Cathedral were painted.
After King Matthias' death in 1490, Prince Albert of Poland broke into the Country and laid a siege on Kassa.
After a half-year-siege, the Black Army of the late king drove them out of the Kingdom. During the first year of the Dual Kingship, the Austrian mercenaries defeated King Szapolyai in several battles and the City had to open its gates for King Ferdinand I in 1527. The local Saxon Burghers

were celebrating the Habsburg king's victory by lighting bonfires in the City squares.

Military fortune returned to King Szapolya in 1536 when his man, Sir Lénárd Czeczey, ambushed the City with his men-at-arms and took it in a surprise attack. During the following decade, the Hungarian noblemen took over the majority in the city council and many Saxons had to leave the town. Soon, there were four times as many Hungarians as Germans in Kassa because many noblemen fled there from the southern lands where the Turks had become the masters.

Sir Czeczey had all the gates walled in, except for the main entrance of the city. He decided to keep Kassa at all costs; he even had his own fortified house built in the city. Sir Czeczey remained firmly in his position for 15 years. Meanwhile, he had the walls of the city reinforced and had lots of supplies and ammunition piled up in the storehouses. He was a renowned military leader who surprised the army of the Habsburg king in 1539 and scattered them in a bloody battle. As a result of this victory, King Szapolyai's men were able to take the Saxon cities of the Upper Land under control. King Szapolyai died in 1540 but Sir Czeczey managed to hold the City for Queen Isabella, the widow of the late king. He even had twelve more cannons cast, which he baptized with honest Hungarian names.

Czeczey invited to his court the most famous Hungarian singer, lutist and chronicler of the age, Sebestyén Lantos Tinódi in 1544. The artist was given citizenship in Kassa and he lived there until 1553. As Queen Isabella resigned in 1551, Kassa went under the rule of King Ferdinand I. Soon, the men of Ferdinand took over control of the city council. The Habsburgs had realized the strategic importance of Kassa and as a result of this, they sent the best western military architects there to update the city's defenses.

The engineers built round bastions, along with Italian bastions, in both the old and the new fashion. The new walls with the added eight large bastions already surrounded a 50-acre area. The Captaincy of the Upper Lands of Hungary was established and Kassa became its seat.

In 1556 there was a great fire in the city allegedly caused by the men of the robber knight, György Bebek. According to a report in 1558, the walls were close to collapsing in some places and the city council was made responsible for the neglect. As it turned out, the Burghers had spent only 401 gold Forints for the needed repairs of the 2,000 coins dedicated for this purpose.

Chief Captain Schwendi, the leader of the Captaincy, set out with his army from Kassa and eliminated the power of the robber knight György Bebek, taking the Castles of Krasznahorka, Szendrő, and Szádvár in 1566-1567. When the Turks occupied the Castle of Eger in 1596, the Catholic

Bishopric of Eger fled to Kassa. Tensions grew between the Catholics and the Protestant Saxons.

It was General Belgiojoso, the Chief Captain of Kassa in 1604, who took the Saint Elisabeth Cathedral away from the Lutherans by applying force and gave it to the Catholics of Eger. In answer to that, the delegates of the Free Royal Cities of the Upper Lands agreed that they would defend their Protestant faith even with arms if it was needed. This time soon came because Prince István Bocskai of Transylvania launched his war in defense of Protestantism and of the rights of the Hungarians. Bocskai's hajdu soldiers defeated the men of Belgiojoso at Álmosd and the Burghers of Kassa shut the city's single gate to the fleeing Habsburg General. Of course, the gate was happily left ajar for the Transylvanian Prince who placed his headquarters there.

When the Empire fought back, General Basta defeated the Hajdú troops in two battles but he was not able to take Kassa by siege and had to withdraw his army. Bocskai died in Kassa in 1606, his Hajdú soldiers slaughtered his advisor, called Káthay, on the spot as he had been accused of poisoning the Prince. According to the new peace treaty, Kassa returned to the Habsburg-ruled Kingdom of Hungary. In 1607, the Emperor garrisoned it with 400 Hussars, 30 Hajdú soldiers, 500 German infantrymen and with 51 artillerymen.

It was György Rákóczi, the strongest supporter of Prince Gábor Bethlen of Transylvania, who took Kassa with a sudden ambush in 1619. The rather shameful execution of three Jesuits (István Pongrátz, Menyhért Grodecz and Márk Kőrösi) took place right after the taking of the city in spite of the promise which had been made that they could leave freely. Neither the 23-year-old Rákóczi nor Bethlen knew about the murders.

Allegedly, Péter Alvinczi, the Protestant preacher of the city, had demanded the Jesuit's heads, along with the death of all the Catholics of Kassa. Alvinczi was the greatest Reformed preacher of the period and he was the legendary enemy of the famous Cardinal Péter Pázmány. One of the executed priests was Pázmány's dear friend. The savage Hajdú soldiers tortured the Jesuits to find out where their gold was and who might have been members of a Catholic conspiracy. After two days of starving them they were offered some raw liver to eat before their execution - but being a Friday, they could not accept this kind of food. Two of them were beheaded, the third, thought to be dead, was thrown into the cesspit where he died twenty hours later.

A half a year later the peace talks between Prince Gábor Bethlen and Palatine Zsigmond Pálffy took place in the same house where the Martyrs had been executed. Upon reaching an agreement they held a great feast and

Prince Bethlen asked the wife of the Palatine, Katalin Pálffy, for a dance. She was willing to dance only under the condition that the martyred priests were allowed to have a decent burial. It was grudgingly agreed to, provided that the burial would happen at night. In 1905 the Martyrs were canonized by the Catholic Church as the Martyrs of Kassa. Their day on the Catholic calendar is September 7, the day they were killed.

Kassa in 1617

We know that Bethlen made further compensation in 1626 when he wed the young Catholic Catherine of Brandenburg who married him under the condition of bringing justice in this case. Catherine arrived in Kassa for her pompous wedding with 340 riders and 40 carriages, accompanied by the 2,000 noblemen sent by her fiance. The merry-making and wedding festivities lasted for a week, but the wife and the husband could barely communicate as they spoke different languages.

When Bethlen died in 1629, Kassa again returned to the Emperor. He appointed Miklós Forgách as the Chief Captain of Upper Hungary. He set out from Kassa in 1632 and scattered the uprising peasants of Péter Császár. We know that the Jesuits had a mission house in Kassa in 1630 which was due to the Catholic Habsburg's influence.

Prince György I Rákóczi's army appeared in front of Kassa's walls in 1644 and the City welcomed him. Hearing this, all of the cities of the Upper Lands opened their gates before the Prince. The Emperor sent his army against Kassa, led by Palatine Miklós Esterházy, to take the rebelling city back. The Palatine's efforts failed because the troops of the Transylvanian, János Kemény, hurried to relieve the city and defeated him. Enmities ceased to exist with the death of the Transylvanian Prince in 1648, and according to the Treaty of Linz, Kassa obediently returned to the Emperor as usual.

During the time of the Wesselényi Conspiracy in 1670 the Habsburgs had a modern citadel built in the southern part of the city so as to supervise the rebellious Burghers whom they no longer trusted. The Battle of Enyicke took place not far from Kassa in 1672 in which the Hungarian rebels defeated the Imperial army in a fight which was an interesting military clash of the 17th century as told in the following chapter.

Chief Captain Strassaldo led his mercenary army from Kassa in 1675 against the agricultural town of Debrecen that lay to the south. He punished and sacked the town because it had been supporting Hungarian rebels. Similarly, the Viennese Military Council ordered General Cobb in 1677 to extend the punishment of the Hungarian rebels to their family members as well. Cobb gathered 60 Hungarian soldiers, peasants and noblemen and executed them in the main market of Kassa, either beheading or impaling them. In answer to that, the rebels captured 32 Imperial officers and impaled them, nailing their hats into their heads.

The new Chief Captain of Kassa, Count Herbenstein, and his 80-man retinue could not reach his assigned post because the Kuruc soldiers of Prince Imre Thököly captured them in July 1682. One night, not too many days later, the rebel Prince's men, led by the Chief Captain of Ónod Castle, Pál Semsey, and his mixed army of 1,500 Hussars and infantrymen, approached the German's citadel in Kassa in utter silence. They scaled the walls with ladders and surprised the sleeping garrison. The rebels managed to take the fort slaughtering all of the defenders in a pitched battle. However, the rest of the town remained in the German's hands and they surrendered it in August.

The city was only taken back by the Imperial troops after a two-week siege in 1685 when Péter Fajgel surrendered it to General Caprara. Most of Fajgel's men joined the army of General Caprara as the war against the Turks was coming.

The Habsburgs began to oppress the Protestant inhabitants of the city by again taking away their churches through force. The darkest times took place in 1687 when Dávid Feja, Chief Judge of Kassa was beheaded. At this time there were 3,700 inhabitants living in the 388 houses of the city.

Prince Ferenc II Rákóczi took the town in 1704 and it became the finest jewel in his Princedom. When you visit Kassa, remember to bring a flower to his tomb where he and his mother, Ilona Zrínyi, were buried in the Saint Elisabeth Cathedral.

Kuruc-labanc (Hungarian-Austrian) fight in the 17th century

63. The Battle of Enyicke (14 September 1672)

05 September 1672

The sun was scorching the trees of the River Tisza's flood area but the nights were getting colder in the first days of September. Birds were getting ready to find their nests and proclaimed their claim of territory with their loud evening songs.

The lonely horseman was heading towards the northern hills where black clouds lay before him. Only his mood was darker. Thick foam covered the mouth of his stallion and the time had come to dismount unless the poor beast stumbled and fell. The man was a robust Hajdú lad in a torn and bloody kaftan which had obviously been pulled from a Turkish cavalryman. He slowly slid from the ragged blanket he used as a saddle and gently stroke the sweaty head of his horse.

"At least we can see who is following us, Csillag, while you take a rest," he whispered into his ears. Standing in the cover of his animal, the lad quickly checked his matchlock pistol which was in a clean and shining condition. It was always loaded because his life could depend on it. The Trans-Tisza Region had been infested with a new-born generation of villains and outcasts since the Emperor decided that he would not pay the warriors of the Hungarian borderland anymore. He cocked the delicate spring in readiness and primed the weapon from a small wooden container that was hanging around his neck on a leather string. The other rider caught up with him and reined in keeping a safe distance.

"Come closer if you have good intentions or good riddance." the Hajdú lad let out a loud warning towards him. After a little hesitation, the other shrugged and lifted his weaponless arms up, asking his horse to step where the lad stood. The young lad slightly lowered his pistol and took a closer look at the soldier-like stranger. "His horse is a noble kin, it looks at first glance. After his waxed mustache and red velvet dolman and hat, he must have been a lord as well, yes a lord on the run." he thought and carefully un-cocked his weapon and struck it into his once-white broad silk-belt. The first stars of the evening found them silently sitting around their campfire and roasting brown mushrooms on sharpened branches. They were past the first rites of introduction and quickly decided to travel together until they reach the camp of the rebels who were gathering near Kassa.

Farkas Nagy, the Hajdú lad did not have much to say. He had been a castle guard in Tokaj, just like his father, grandfather and their ancestors before. They fought, raided, ambushed the Turks or were being raided or ambushed by them, in short, they had lived the life of the Valiant Order of the Borderland for five generations. When the Habsburg Emperor made Gasphar Johann Ampringen the Governor of Hungary, he dismissed the Hungarian warriors from one hundred castles of the Borderland, claiming them to be unreliable folks who could not be trusted. Foreign mercenaries were placed in the garrisons who became the curse of the land. They systematically robbed the villages of North-East Hungary, alienating not only the Hungarians but all the Slovakian, Ruthenian and Wallachian commoners they met. The peasants suffered more from these unpaid soldiers than people living under the Ottoman's yoke a bit down to the South. Their misery cried up to the sky in vain.

Farkas did not trust his new companion enough to tell him how he was chased away from home when he tried to protect the house of their Reformed preacher nor how the starvation forced him to cut Turkish throats near Debrecen. His last hope lay in joining the forces of the rebelling Hungarians. After the disastrous Wesselényi Conspiracy fell the rebelling noblemen just did not want to accept the tragic loss of the leading high aristocrats who were all executed in Vienna. The Emperor's revenge just stirred the humiliated and deprived people up.

Some weeks ago, eight-hundred horsemen rode out, led by the Captains István Petrőczy, Gábor Kende, Pál Szepessy and Mátyás Szuhay. They were aided by some French gold and by Bey Hassan, the commander of Várad Castle, who offered his sword and his five-hundred Asab riders to them. The Reformed preachers welcomed the Turks and convinced the

Hungarians easily that even the ancient enemy, the Muslims, were better than the henchmen of the Catholic Holy Roman Empire.

Farkas' companion was a nobleman, indeed, a Captain called Benedek Serédy. He was on an errand, sent from the direction of Transylvania and carried good news to the rebelling Lords. All who didn't want to change religions or were accused of treason had fled to the border near Transylvania. They found each other in numbers and assembled in the hills, and the hidden valleys and they could hardly wait for a spark that would ignite the gunpowder. Now, they were on the move and wished to meet the rebels near Kassa.

Sir Serédy was more than willing to hurry ahead of them with the good news, the list of the newcomer Lords and the number of their units was sewn into his red velvet hat. Thousands of seasoned Hajdú soldiers and hardened Hussar warriors were marching in nice order to join forces with Petrőczy's and Szuhay's troops. Serédy told nothing about these things to the Hajdú lad but took him into his service. By the time they met the rebels, Sir Serédy had recruited thirty more Hajdú soldiers in his retinue and this is how Farkas Nagy was promoted as their lieutenant.

10 September 1672

General Paris von Spankau, the military commander of Upper Hungary, signed his name on the document in which he issued an order against the riff-raff Hungarian villains who dared to upset the order. He adjusted his white wig with his inky fingers and absent-mindedly stroked his intricate lace collar, then helped himself into his dove-grey coat.

The General had no doubt that his two-thousand well-trained and disciplined German musket-men in Kassa would be able to scatter the rebels, but he was persuaded to summon the more than eight-thousand mercenaries from the castles of the Borderland to his aid. He knew that General Wolfgang von Cobb would come immediately to Kassa which was obviously the target of the approaching Hungarian scum. According to the reports, the rebel army was marching through Debrecen and Kálló having already crossed the Tisza River and was past Tokaj, and now reached Ónod, not awfully far from Kassa. Spankau walked to the door of his spacious working quarters and motioned for his officer to come in.
"By God, they have grown in numbers reaching 15,000 of them!" he said, rolling his eyes and making a funny face at his Lieutenant-Colonel Soyer, a strongly-built commander of his dragoons.
"Sir, would you like me and my 300 dragoons to chase them back to the tent of the Sultan?" "By all means, but let us wait for General Cobb to join

the merry-making. Have this dispatch sent to him at once. He had better get here in a few days if he does not want to miss the duck-shooting game." The Lieutenant-Colonel looked adoringly at the small plump man, saluted and hurried away.

13 September 1672

Benedek Serédy and his Lieutenant, Farkas Nagy, riding in the vanguard of the army, were silently watching as the small patrolling Imperial cavalry unit turned tail after being sighted. The rebel army made camp south of Kassa, between the tiny villages of Enyicke and Buzinka. The sky was overcast and it was misting on them. Farkas spat on the ground and cursed the wretched weather. Sir Serédy sent him a reprimanding look, saying: "Lieutenant, have manners."
"Yes, Sir, sorry, Sir. How lucky we are that we have not single cannon to get wet."
Captain Serédy sent Farkas to assess what kind of newcomers had been enlisted recently under the flag of his rapidly growing regiment.

Nagyvárad Castle before the Ottoman siege

"So far so good," he thought, because the armed men who had joined their flags had come from the Valiant Order. They were the ragged but toughened knights of the Borderland. He cast his eyes on the neighboring camp where the men of Bey Hassan were busily erecting their Ottoman-made tents and he shook his head. He would have never imagined that one day he would drink wine with the Pasha of Várad, as it had happened last evening. Bey Hassan spoke as fluently in Hungarian as Serédy in Turkish and they were recalling the days when Várad, the gate of Transylvania was taken after a bloody siege by the Ottoman army. It was no more than twelve years ago, he recalled the date. Serédy was not there but he had heard of the valor of the 850 men and women who held the castle for forty-five days against the 50,000 seasoned warriors of Pasha Ali. Although the Pasha had a wicked reputation, he recognized a heroic deed when he saw one. The surviving handful of defenders, mainly untrained students and peasants who were so unskilled that they were unable to use their cannons, finally had to surrender.

Ali let them go unmolested. They were even allowed to carry away the disassembled printing machine of their school. To Serédy's inquiry as to what had happened to the huge bronze statues of Saint László and the other giant statues of the ancient Hungarian kings, Bey Hassan told him that they were all broken up and used as prime quality material for casting new cannons for the Sultan.

"Except the head of Saint László", he added, "because they could not make such a hot furnace to melt it."

The Hajdú soldiers and castle-warriors had been eyeing the Turks for a while, but soon they mingled with them. It was not difficult since half of the Turks spoke the Hungarian's tongue and many Ruthenian and Slovakian Hajdu soldiers could make themselves understood with the rest of the Turks whose original mother tongue had been Serbian.

The second column of incoming troops, some 8,000 men from Transylvania, were expected at any minute and as Captain Petrőczy and his fellow-captains had no idea how many Imperial troops are in Kassa, they decided to wait for a few days.

14 September 1672

Paris von Spankau had the city's gate opened and gave his order to advance. Colonel-Lieutenant Soyer's heart swelled with pride and agreed with him. Why should they cede victory to General Cobb? What a sight it will be when Cobb's army arrives just to see how Von Spankau had crushed the eight-times stronger enemy. The General was not an idiot, though. On the contrary, the small plump man was a clever and fearless soldier who knew that the rebels are being led by five leaders at the same time so they would not be able to mobilize their whole army, just a fragment of it. Besides, his infantry with up-to-date rifles and muskets was able to humiliate any cavalry, anytime. As for the dragoons, they had swords, but they were equipped with short-barreled muskets and a pair of pistols as well. Soyer was rather proud of their training and discipline.

"For Heaven's sake, it is not the Dark Ages. The rapid musket-fire will rule over the onslaught of the barbarian hordes with their ancient weapons." Soyer thought as he was leading his 300 dragoons. He was to find out the enemy's number so they rode a mile ahead of Spankau's soldiers. The General and his 2,000 men took up position in the village of Bárca and waited patiently.

In the rebel's camp the alarm was sounded and Sir Benedek Serédy and his men were told to join the units of Captain's Szuhay and Petrőczy. More than 1,200 horsemen thundered on the road that led from Pest to Kassa to attack the vanguard of the Austrians. They were stopped by savage musket fire and the falling horses slowed them down. When the Hussars reached the enemy, the pistols were fired into their faces and the shocking force of the half-heavy cavalry was broken. The dragoons wore only a breastplate on their chests and a steel helmet on their heads, but they proved to be a formidable match to the Hussars. Yet, the sheer numbers decided the first clash and the dragoons were gradually pushed back to the village of Enyicke. Soyer knew that he was playing the role of the bait so he quickly ushered his men into the small palace of Enyicke which was a fortified stately home of a local nobleman.

There, they had been able to withstand the overpowering force for several hours as was expected from Soyer's experienced, trained and well-equipped soldiers. Captain Petrőczy tried to lay a siege and beat him out but he was losing more and more men. The Hajdus dismounted and used their muskets with equal skill, but the dragoons fired at them from the windows and behind the cover of the low wall around the building.

At noon, Spankau's musket-men arrived at last and began to systematically shoot the Hungarians to shreds.

"Captain Serédi, where is the rest of our army?" cried Farkas Nagy from the cover of a tree busily reloading his musket. There was no answer. His superior was away, trying to help in placing the men in new positions to answer the new enemy's challenge. The Austrians outnumbered them already. Just as Spankau had anticipated. Yet, he did not count on the steadiness of the Hajdú soldiers who were able to withstand the Austrian musket fire from two directions for more than three hours. Only well-trained and seasoned warriors were able to do this. They were far from a bunch of villains and cut-throats. Many Imperial troops paid with their lives to learn this fact too late.

Petrőczy encouraged his men and the Hussars took to their horses and charged the infantry of Spankau. The fearsome battle-cry of the Hungarians filled the air and they threw themselves on the footmen. More and more German screams were heard and the uniformed mercenaries began to waver. Von Spankau ordered the reserve to fire volley after volley. The small plump man drew his rapier and led the counter-attack in front of them. Serédi saw his new lieutenant fall from the saddle with glassy eyes. More and more horses ran past him in the white smoke of the guns with empty saddles. The charge was broken, the Hussars retreated behind the covering rifle fire of a handful of Hajdu marksmen.

Who knows what would have befallen them if the 1,500 Hussars of Captain János Szőts and the 500 Asabs of Bey Hassan had not appeared a few minutes later?

Now, the lack of a central command became visible, because altogether only 4,000 people were able to be mobilized out of the 15,000-strong army. Spankau's gamble was almost successful, but it was just not good enough. On top of this, the sky joined in the battle by pouring a terrible shower down on them soaking the muskets through. No more shots were heard in the battle.

The cries of "Jesus, Jesus" by the Protestant horsemen were mixed up with the "Allahu Akbar" roar coming from the Muslim's throats. The attackers regained the ground and Von Spankau had to sound the retreat. Soyer sallied out with his few remaining men and joined him.

The General was pale. His life was saved only by his white wig which deflected a saber cut and now it was covered with blood. Soyer half-carried him until they could reach the gates of Kassa with the wreckage of their army. The Lieutenant-Colonel wondered what sort of soldiers they had just encountered in this battle, and shook his head.

„I swear to God, they could overrun the City of Kassa at any time if they were led by a good strict German officer like Von Spankau instead of six quarrelling Lords," he muttered to himself and with that, they closed the iron gates behind themselves, knowing that while they had lost the battle they were not beaten into submission as they still held the City of Kassa.

64. Fülek Castle   GPS: 48.269974, 19.823365

In our day, Fülek (Filakovo) and its castle can be found very close to the Hungarian border. The first written document that mentions this castle on the boundary of Nógrád and Gömör counties is from 1242. The Castle crouches on a huge basalt rock and looks over the broad valley of the Ipoly River from there. It was an infamous robber knight, Fulko, who was the castle's first owner. He was forging money within its walls. The Castle was named after him. His evil deeds reached the ears of King Béla IV who took the castle away from him in 1246.

The fortress had many owners, it was in the hands of the mighty Máté Csák around 1300, then the Ráskay, the Perényi, and Bebek families followed suit. The walls were reinforced when the war broke out with the Czech Hussites in 1435. The role of Fülek and its small town became very important only in the 16th century because of the Turkish peril. After the Battle of Mohács its Captain was Ferenc Bebek as he had married the daughter of Balázs Ráskai. Bebek had the castle reinforced with the help of the Italian Alessandro da Vedano in 1551. He built the lower castle and a huge tower for deploying his cannons. This tower is still proudly standing and you can see it from a distance. Although Fülek was an important and well-guarded borderland castle, the Turks took it from Ferenc Bebek. The Castle fell not by the sword but by deception.

The Ottomans had owned it for 39 years and Fülek was the gateway to raid the Hungarian mining towns. Szokoli Mustafa built many new buildings in the town and in the castle, including a minaret. The garrison consisted of 49 Janissaries, 177 riders and 89 Asab soldiers between 1556 and 1557. Ten years later they had 59 Topcus, artillerymen, in the castle. There were ten Beys between 1554–1593 who led the castle: Kara Hamza (until 1556), Velidzsan (1562–1564), Arszlán (1564), Mehmed (1575), Hasszán (1576), Mahmud (1579), Korkud (1579-1590), Ali (1591) and Juszuf (1593). From Fülek, the Turks could reach the area around the Castle of Murány in 1562. Bey Ferhard Haszán would occupy the lands near Miskolc and Krsznahorka.

The Turks used Fülek as a basis to take as many borderland castles as they could. This was how the Castle of Salgó was taken by the Ottomans in 1554. The opposing Castle, Somoskő, resisted for 22 years but it also had to be yielded after a short battle by its Captain, Miklós Modolóczi. The Castle of Várgede would resist from 1560-1571. The Turks of Fülek took it when the number of the garrison was decreased and ruined it shortly after. Hajnácskő Castle also fell to them in 1566. When the people of Dobsina denied paying taxes to them in 1580, the Bey of Fülek set out with his marauders and sacked and burned their city in 1584. He took away 350 people who were sold in Fülek's slave market.

General Tieffenbach Kristóf and General Miklós Pálffy took the castle back in 1593 when the Ottoman Captain, Bey Ofressus, was not at home. After a fierce but short fight, the Turks surrendered the Castle to the 4,000 strong Christian armies. The settlement used to be a Sanjak, a district center, and it had a larger Turkish population. When the Christians took over the City, three-hundred Turkish families decided to stay. The Castles of Salgó and Somoskő were also retaken. Mihály Sörényi was Fülek's Captain in 1598, then, the title was given to Honorius Tonhauser in 1599. The heyday of the Castle was in the 17th century. Fülek remained one of the most important Borderland castles of Upper Hungary until the end of the Ottoman wars.

During the revolt of Prince Bocskai, Ferenc Rhédey's men took Gömör County in 1604, but Fülek was too strong for them. The Ottoman Janissaries helped Bocskai's troops take Fülek Castle away from the Habsburg king in the following year. The fortress went back to the Habsburg king in 1606 and its next famous Captains were the Wesselényi and Bosnyák family members. It was the Bosnyák family's property from 1607 and during the 1630's. Fülek had been the center of Nógrád County and the noblemen from the surrounding areas regularly assembled there.

Fülek Castle

A terrible fire destroyed the city and the castle in 1615 and they were able to rebuild it only by 1619. The construction was hardly finished when Prince Gábor Bethlen of Transylvania took Fülek in 1619. After the storms of the Prince's campaign, the castle was soon retaken in 1621 by the Habsburgs with the help of György Szécsi. Their quick success was due to Fülek's Captain who betrayed Prince Bethlen. The cowardly Captain won his reward. Having surrendered the castle, he died the following day. The renowned soldier, Rhédey, took the castle from György Szécsi and he repelled Prince Bethlen who returned to retake Fülek with 10,000 men. This was during the time that the Hungarian warriors of Fülek ventured deep into the Ottoman Occupied Lands to raid as far as to the south of the

City of Szeged. Their leader, Benedek Balogh, became famous for his adventure of tricking the Bey of Szeged.

King Ferdinand II gave the Castle to Judit Bosnyák in 1630. The huge Evangelical Church was built at that time and the town also boasted of having two public baths as well. The Evangelical High School also opened its gates at that time. Sadly, most of these buildings perished before 1682.

The Castle's Captain was Ádám Wesselényi between 1650 and 1664; however, the Chief Captain became Baron István Koháry from 1657. Wesselényi ordered over 197 German infantrymen, 300 Hussars, 150 Hajdu soldiers, 25 artillerymen to the castle in 1652. The Koháry family reinforced the castle in 1672 out of fear of the Thököly revolt. Prince Imre Thököly tried to take it in 1678, but it was in vain. The Prince laid a second siege in 1682 and this time he had Ottoman auxiliary troops as well. The Castle was defended by 4,000 soldiers (including the inhabitants) and was attacked by 60,000 warriors.

Thököly paid 20,000 Thalers to a peasant called András Braka who promised to set the Castle on fire but the man was caught and brutally executed. Finally, Koháry's men yielded the place against his will. After the siege ended the Turks had the castle exploded because Thököly did not let them pillage it.

Fülek was where Prince Imre Thököly of Transylvania was elected King of Hungary in 1682; however, he never accepted this title. He had Count István Koháry imprisoned in his strongest fortress, Munkács Castle. When the sun of the Prince was setting, Koháry returned to Fülek and took it over again. Koháry had a nice and comfortable palace built below the castle where he spent his last years peacefully.

These days the renovation of Fülek Castle is proceeding steadily and there are historical festivals within its walls every summer.

65. Prince Thököly and Fülek Castle (1682)

Young Imre Thököly was a wealthy Lord from the Upper Lands of Hungary with high ambitions and hopes, blessed with bright military talent and bravery. He was the bitter enemy of the Habsburg king as the Viennese Court had devoured his immense domains around Trencsén Castle like a mighty serpent swallowing a tasty piglet.

"The Austrians are the true enemy of my poor country, to drive them out I had better have the help of the Turkish Sultan. The Sultan does not have the power to render me a mere vassal and so eventually I will take care of the Ottomans, too. If the Austrians liberated the country, we would surely lose all of our independence." he reasoned. He recalled the death of poor

Miklós Zrínyi, the poet and General, who was killed by a boar in 1664. "That boar spoke in German." he mused. He was so happy that Ilona, the daughter of Zrínyi, had accepted his proposal and became his wife. "Was not Péter Zrínyi, Ilona's Uncle beheaded by the executioner of the Emperor? Has not the Court accused of treason all of the rich Hungarian Noblemen of the Upper Land? No wonder that everybody lost faith in the Habsburgs."

Fülek Castle in 1664

Ilona was already a widow and a few years older than Thököly, but she looked great and was not only educated, but also a brave woman befitting the Zrínyi family. Her late husband, György Rákóczi, left behind a boy who inherited the immense wealth of the Rákóczi family. Ferenc was his name, the boy was the second to wear this name among the Rákóczi clan members.

Suddenly, Thököly's domains multiplied because all of the Captains of the Rákóczi's castles swore fealty to him. Now he could muster enough power to launch his war against the Habsburg king. The towns and forts of the Upper Lands have always greeted those Hungarian Lords and Princes who turned the heads of their horses against Vienna.

The gates of Kassa, Eperjes, and Lőcse were quickly opened before him. Thököly's rebels took Szepesvár and Szendrő and gained hold of the Castle of Tokaj as well. The western Hungarian towns yielded power to the new Lord from the east with joy and with tremendous relief just as they had done when the Transylvanian Princes, Bocskai, Bethlen and György Rákóczi made war against Vienna during the last seventy years. Did they care that this new warlord, Thököly, had the help of the Turkish Sultan? Well, the crescent moon of the Ottomans' was obviously declining and they were not the invincible enemy who used to freeze the blood of the Burghers with terror anymore. Yet, they still had military strength and their relentless enemy was Vienna, the much desired Golden Apple.

"Let the Devil give them Vienna, just let me have control over my homeland." thought Thököly and the alliance was made with the Sultan. Yet not every fortress welcomed Thököly, some Hungarian Captains still placed their hope in Emperor Leopold, the anointed King of Hungary. István Koháry, the Captain of Fülek Castle remained loyal to him and he greeted Thököly and Bey Ibrahim, the Turkish commander of his auxiliary forces with cannon balls. Koháry was a high born and well-educated aristocrat who valued a foreign Christian ruler higher than a Hungarian upstart backed by Muslim swords.

"You, traitor of Christ, you will never have his Majesty's stronghold so long as I wield a sword!" shouted Koháry from the ramparts when Thököly rode there to ask him not to shed Hungarian blood and surrender the castle. There was no point in arguing, the siege began in earnest. The huge cannons were throwing iron balls and exploding bombs at the walls and into the city. It was sad to see how the flourishing town was consumed by the storm of flames. Not many days later, the walls of the town were breached and the Janissaries launched the first assault. After bloody combat, the defenders emptied the town and withdrew behind the walls of the inner castle. Thököly hoped he could avoid more bloodshed and suspended the assaults and the bombardment for three days hoping that Koháry would change his mind. When it was over, Bey Ibrahim sent an envoy, Bey Ulman, to the castle.

"Noble Captain, surrender the castle and save your men," said Bey Ulman to Koháry. The Captain said nothing, just showed the envoy around the castle. The Bey could see with his own eyes how many soldiers and how much supplies and gunpowder he had and how the cellars were packed full of food. At last, he addressed Bey Ulman with these words:

"Go and tell your commander: if he lives on the field, we live in houses in our castle. If he has his drums sounded, we will do the same. If he is not afraid, neither will we be afraid."

The siege was re-started with renewed force. The losses of the Turks soon amounted to four-thousand men and Koháry lost many good soldiers as well. It did not matter how many times Thököly had tried to ask them to yield the castle, it was always refused. Surrendering the Castle was out of the question. Bey Ibrahim was desperately sending his men against the walls. He tried at night. He assaulted the castle during three consecutive nights, and yet again he was beaten back.

Captain Koháry fought like a hero, but his men began to give up hope. He had sent secret envoys from the besieged castle to the Palatine and the king nine times, but there was no help coming. There was a point when the defenders realized how futile further fight would be, but Koháry had made up his mind and would never give up the king's castle. All of the women and children of the castle gathered around him and were begging and pleading with tears to have mercy on them, but the captain turned a deaf ear to them. Then, a soldier of the guards became angry and exclaimed: "Men, listen to me. If the Captain does not give in, I will throw him down from the bastion."

Prince Imre Thököly

When Koháry realized that his soldiers were serious about doing so, he ground his teeth, but finally surrendered Fülek Castle. Upon coming out of the gate the bewildered Janissaries wanted to tear him to pieces. He was able to escape only because Thököly and a Turkish officer were defending him with drawn swords on his left and right side. Thököly was blaming him:

"Why did you have to waste so much blood, what was it good for?"

"I did not want to surrender the castle" replied Koháry "for I had sworn fealty to Emperor Leopold at its gate that I would defend it until my last breath. It was not me, but my soldiers who surrendered."
"You should have sided with us rather than with the Austrians," Thököly said reproachfully. But, István Koháry was a steady man and would have never changed his word, whatever the cost. He was sent to Regéc Castle in chains and was not released for any ransom for a long time.

Having taken Fülök Castle, Thököly did not allow Bey Ibrahim to sack the city. The Janissaries were angry at that, but the Bey did as he had been instructed and proclaimed Thököly as King of Hungary. The Ottoman Pashas gave him nice coronation jewelry and he was gifted with the ceremonial kaftan of the Sultan. Bey Ibrahim told him:
"Imre Thököly, take this kaftan that has been sent to you by our majestic and invincible Sultan as a symbol of your royal power. Let it be known, that whoever dares to take this robe from you, it would be regarded as if he had torn it off from the own shoulder of the Sultan."

When Thököly returned to his tent, he told to his Hungarian followers that he would not use the royal title as he felt not worthy to do so. He said he would suffice with the title of Prince of Transylvania and Lord of the Castles of Hungary.

66. Munkács Castle   GPS: 48.437224, 22.719615

Munkács (Ukrainian: Мукачеве, Ruthenian: Мукачово, German: Munkatsch) Castle is in a strategic location which is now part of Ukraine. The Castle is built on an enormous rock and overlooking the town and the Latorca River. It was controlling the road to the Eastern Passes of the Carpathian Mountains. Due to the strategic importance of this castle, its story is long as everyone wanted to take control of this stronghold.

The first wooden tower was built by the Hungarians in the 9th century right after they invaded the country led by Chief Árpád. The initial stronghold was enlarged after the Mongolian invasion as it was first mentioned in 1263. The domains belonging to the Castle were mostly impenetrable forests during the time of King Béla IV who gave the area to his daughter, Konstancia.

It was seized by the King of Halics, Leo, in the first part of the 14th century, but he had lost it by 1311. The founding cornerstone of the castle was laid down some years later by the members of the Hungarian noble family, Aba, and Munkács was an important fortification of the Kingdom of Hungary throughout the centuries.

The area became more developed during King Róbert Károly's reign who settled more people here. The king's foreign policy was active towards Poland and Holics so the role of Munkács increased. Tamás, Chief Comes of Bereg County was in charge of the castle in 1321. The Anjou king gave Munkács to his Queen, Erzsébet.

Munkács Castle

In 1397, King Zsigmond gifted the castle to the Lithuanian Todor Korjatovics, the Prince of Podolia, in exchange for obtaining rights over the Podolian part of the Lithuanian Principality. The Castle was rebuilt in a European style according to the fashion of the western knights during this time. The construction of the nunnery was ordered by Korjatovics and his wife, Olga. After their deaths, the castle returned to the Hungarian Crown and Zsigmond passed it on to Máté Pálóci, the Comes of Bereg County.

István Lazarevic, the Serbian Despot, made a contract with the king in 1432 wherein he obtained Munkács, among other domains, in exchange for the key fortress of the Hungarian Southern Borderland, the Castle of Nándorfehérvár aka Belgrad. Lazarevic became one of the most trusted of Zsigmond's men and he was even rewarded with membership in the Order of the Dragon. Lazarevic heir was György Brankovics who was in charge of Serbia as well.

As he was allying himself with the Ottomans, the Jagiellonian King, Ulászló I, confiscated Munkács from Brankovics and gave it to László Pálóci, the Judge of the Country. King Ulászló I was slain by the Turks in the Battle of Várna 1444, and Munkács was taken over by János Hunyadi, Governor of Hungary. The great General visited Munkács several times and after his death it was Erzsébet Szilágyi, his widow, who controlled the castle and the area. King Matthias of Hunyad tried to strengthen the position of his illegitimate son, János Corvin, and gave him Munkács in 1484. Unfortunately, János Corvin was not able to gain power after Matthias' death and his domains were divided among his enemies.

The Castle and the vast domains belonging to it were owned by Bishop Ernuszt Zsigmond of Pécs and then by a Transylvanian priest, Bishop László Geréb, for a short time. This was how Munkács ended up in the hands of the Bishop's brother, Péter Geréb of Vingárt, the Judge of the Country who owned it until 1499.

Then it returned to the Crown, and King Ulászló II pledged it to György Drágfy of Béltek in 1504. Munkács was given to the Queen in 1505 and later it was given to the next Queen of Hungary, the wife of King Louis II, Queen Habsburg Maria in 1522. It belonged to King Szapolyai in 1528. He traded Munkács with István Báthori in exchange for the Cities of Szatmár and Németi in 1529. Báthori did major construction work in the castle, particularly reinforcing the inner castle.

The following year Munkács went back to King Szapolyai. But it was Mihály Büdy, Habsburg Maria's man who was, in fact, the commander within the walls in 1537.

According to the peace treaty of 1538 between King Szapolyai and King Ferdinand, Munkács was returned to Szapolyai. Unfortunately, after his death the widow, Queen Isabella, gave the castle back to Ferdinand in 1540.

By now, we can see that Munkács Castle had to stand on a very important spot because it had changed hands so frequently. When Queen Isabella finally had to leave the country in 1552 Munkács was given to Péter Petrovics, Duke of Temes. He was the foster-father of Szapolyai's son, King and Prince János Zsigmond. When Duke Petrovics died, his fosterling inherited the castle.

The Habsburg troops led by Lázár Schwendi, the Chief Captain of Upper Hungary, would take Munkács in 1567 through a siege. Emperor Maximilian appointed Gáspár Mágóczhy as the Captain in Munkács in 1573 in exchange for 42,000 gold Forints. Mágóczhy was a renowned soldier having previously been the Captain of Torna, Gyula and Eger Castles, loyal to the Habsburgs through and through.

Later, Zsigmond Rákóczi came into possession of Munkács through a marriage. Zsigmond Rákóczi was among the wealthiest noblemen. His annual income was about 97,936 gold Forints. There were 260 houses in the area which paid taxes, and the new landlord had Wallachian and Slavic settlers brought in to cultivate more lands. The money coming from the huge domain around Munkács Castle was almost entirely spent on the maintenance and the improvement of the castle.

Prince István Bocskai took the castle in 1605 and kept it until his death. In 1608, we find the castle again in the hands of Ferenc Mágóchy, Chief Captain of Upper Hungary and Chief Comes of Torna and Bereg Counties. When he died in 1611, his widow, Orsolya Dersffy re-married. She gave her hand to a Lieutenant of Munkács Castle, a young man called Miklós Esterházy. This was the beginning of the rise of this family who became magnates through this marriage. The Habsburg king appointed Miklós Esterházy as Chief Comes of Bereg County in 1617, but Munkács had to be ceded to Prince Bethlen of Transylvania in 1620, according to the Peace Treaty of Nikolsburg. As compensation, Esterházy was given Fraknó Castle by the king.

Gábor Bethlen arrived in Munkács only in 1623 and he posted János Balling as his Castellan. Balling was the one who had the fort improved up to the contemporary military standards in 1629. The Castle had 14 bastions at that time. Prince Bethlen died during the same year and his young Queen, Catherine of Brandenburg, was trying to cede as many castles and lands to her lover, Pál Csáky, as she could during her one-year reign in Transylvania. The Governor of Transylvania was István Bethlen, the younger brother of the late Gábor Bethlen. He strongly disapproved the Queen's Habsburg orientation so he began negotiations with a wealthy Hungarian magnate, György Rákóczi, and invited him to the throne of the Principality. While he was negotiating, the Noble Estates of Transylvania made the Queen resign and elected István Bethlen as their prince.

Catherine of Brandenburg claimed that Munkács had traditionally always been the property of the queens and she went there to persuade Balling, the Castellan, to cede the castle to her. Balling was a steady man and he was willing to let her enter, but only without Csáky and his men. When she failed to simply take over control the castle, Catherine went to Rákóczi and tried to obtain Munkács by making different offers.

Instead of István Bethlen, György Rákóczi was the next Transylvanian Prince and Balling let him enter Munkács in 1631. At this time there were four agricultural towns and 148 villages belonging to Munkács Castle. The

Prince held his court here. He received the ambassadors from Poland, France, and Sweden within its walls. After his death in 1648, the castle went to his widow, Zsuzsanna Lorántffy who moved there to live.

Munkács Castle

His son, Prince György II Rákóczi, also received the envoys of the Cossack Hmelnickij in this fort between 1649 and 1656. He aspired to the throne of Poland and Munkács lay in the best location. Unfortunately, the Prince's Polish campaign resulted in a disaster and the troops of the Polish Hetman Lubomirsky broke into the country burning and pillaging the land. Zsuzsanna Lórántffy found shelter in Munkács but she was eventually captured by the Poles.

When the enemy was gone and she was released, she immediately began to reinforce the fort and it was transformed into an impregnable fortress by her French engineers. The inner castle, the middle castle and the outer castle were distinctly separated as can be seen today.

Munkács was inherited by Zsófia Báthory who was the widow of the unlucky Prince György II Rákóczi. She passed it on to her sister-in-law, Ilona Zrínyi in 1680. The castle did not cease to remain the traditional eagle's-nest of the Rákóczi's, though. Prince Ferenc I Rákóczi of Transylvania also lived here. He wed Ilona Zrínyi and their son was the famous Prince Ferenc II Rákóczi, the hero of a later war of independence against the Habsburgs between 1703 and 1711. But that was yet to come. Munkács had to witness more wars and fights before that. After Prince Ferenc I Rákóczi's death, Ilona Zrinyi re-married and became the wife of Imre Thököly in 1682. Thököly had the fort's palisade repaired and reinforced the castle where it was not yet strong enough and held a rich court there.

The Habsburg Emperor's General, Aeneas Caprara, took the Castle of Ungvár and besieged Munkács while Thököly was imprisoned in Belgrade by the Turks. His wife, Ilona Zrínyi heroically defended the fort from November 1685 to 1688 with her Hungarian, Slovakian, Rusyn and German soldiers. She lost 24 men altogether during the siege but the Austrian's losses were many times higher than this. The young Ferenc II Rákóczi was alongside his mother with his little sister. This siege of Munkács is the most recalled historical deed of the heroic Ilona Zrínyi. As for Ferenc II Rákóczi, he grew up and became Prince of Transylvania. His first order of business was to lay a siege on Munkács which lasted from 1703 to1704 when he successfully took it back. He made the castle his natural headquarters during the War of Independence. He received the envoys of Russan Tsar Peter I within its wall. The Rusyn and Slovakian people living in the area have always supported the Hungarians during these centuries of war. It was Munkács Castle again, which was the last to fall into the hands of the Habsburgs when Rákóczi's freedom fight was put down in 1711. Munkács Castle is the symbol of two centuries Habsburg-Hungarian struggles.

67. The Legend of Munkács Castle (1685)

The lucky star of Prince Imre Thököly was falling but his wife, the brave Ilona Zrínyi, was fiercely defending their last stand, the Castle of Munkács. She pulled chain-mail over her womanly dress and took the defense of the fort into her own hands. Knowing that the enemy was coming, she had the storage rooms filled with food and supplies, doubled the guards, and waited for the attack with keen eyes. She did not have to wait long because General Caprara soon arrived, along with his drums and guns.

However, Caprara was not willing to waste his men on hasty assaults so he tried to get the castle without a fight. He knew well that Ilona Zrínyi was in the castle with two of her young children, Julianka and Ferenc. So he sent a letter to the mother, that he would save the lives of the two children if she surrendered Munkács. He reasoned that their lives would be of more importance to her than the stones of the castle.

Lady Ilona did not despair for a moment. She was ready to risk her life, and the childrens' future, because she felt herself obliged to keep the castle for the rebelling Hungarians. She wrote her reply with these words to Carpara:

"I am the mother of the orphans of Prince Ferenc I Rákóczi and took shelter in this fortress which I am to keep, as it is their inheritance. Neither I, nor my small children, caused any harm to the Emperor, why are you taking our castles one by one, then? I make enemy with no-one but I will resist those who attack me. If the Emperor wants to turn his weapons against a mere woman and weak orphans, I do not think that this kind of war will increase the glory and the reputation either of His Majesty or of his General."

Carpara came to see that there was no more room for bargaining. He had his breach-breaking cannons deployed and began the bombardment of the castle. More than fifty huge bombs fell on the Castle every day but the walls were massively filled with earth which swallowed the heaviest cannonballs. Some of the bombs exploded in the halls of Lady Ilona, smashing the furniture and igniting the carpets but they had stored water in the attic just for these cases. The small Ferenc made more trouble for his mother than did the bombs, he was always slipping away and showed up in the midst of the greatest peril. Ilona Zrínyi did not cease to encourage the defenders and as a sign of her determination, she had red flags of rebellion planted on the fifteen bastions. Her envoys were already on their way to find her husband and ask for his aid.

The bravery of the Lady seemed to have cast a spell on her soldiers who were valiantly beating back the assaults. The siege was lasting longer and longer, the besiegers were losing heart. One day, forty-nine of them deserted the Habsburg's army and tried to get into Munkács to serve under Lady Ilona. Some of them reached the safety of the walls but Carpara would catch twenty-nine of them. He decorated the trees with them around his camp.

When summer came and the wheat became ripe, the soldiers begged Lady Ilona to go out to harvest. It had been the way of life since the Turks came in more than a hundred summers ago; when the wheat was ripe, the soldiers became peasants and gathered the blessed crops. Was it leniency, or unwritten law, that the Turkish and the Hungarian warriors did not attack each other during the harvest?

Lady Ilona had to let them go, but she sent them armed. It was a wise precaution because the German mercenaries fell on them twice - it was luck that only one warrior was killed before they repelled the attack. It was a bloody harvest, people died and the Germans burned some of the wheat-fields but a goodly amount of crops were brought into the granaries safely. "May God be their judge!" swore the defenders, because burning the wheat was the biggest sin they could imagine. General Carpara was almost about to give up the long siege when things took an unexpected turn.

Prince Thököly was hurrying with a reinforcing army but he suffered a heavy defeat by the Tisza River. He could only send a letter to his wife, written in a secret, coded language. The Prince was explaining his plans that he would ask for the Pope's help and Lady Ilona should do the same. The Pope would certainly aid them if they could somehow convert the Lutherans back to the Catholic Church.

Was it a wise plan or not, but it sealed the doom of Munkács Castle. As it happened, Lady Ilona's Castellan was a devoted Lutheran called Dániel Absolon. He knew the secret code very well and was taken aback by how his liege-lord would betray his faith. Sir Absolon decided to turn against Ilona Zrínyi in a cunning way. He began to waste the food and the supply that had been paid for with the harvester's blood. The granaries were getting low and after a time, food became scarce. In addition to this, Sir Absolon hid lots of the supply away or simply covered them with empty boxes. After this, he showed the storages to Lady Ilona:

"My Lady, now you can see with your own eyes that we have no food left. The castle must be surrendered."

What was to be done? Lady Ilona had to open the gates for the proud General Carpara after long years of siege. Her children were taken to Vienna as hostages and the small Ferenc was given such an education so as to grow up as a loyal subject of the mighty Emperor.

How could anyone in Vienna think for a minute that the offspring of the steadfast Thököly, Zrínyi and Rákóczi clans would never draw a sword in defending the liberty of his beloved country?

Bibliography:

Kálmán, Benda: "Magyarország történeti kronológiája" (Akadémia Publishing House, 1983)

Károly, Dely: "Vártúrák Kalauza" (Sport Publishing House, 1969)

Klára, Hegyi: "Egy világbirodalom végvidékén" (Gondolat Publishing House, 1976)

Dénes, Lengyel: "Magyar mondák a török világból" (Móra Publishing House, 1975)

Gábor, Lipták: "Amiről a kövek beszélnek" (Móra Publishing House, Budapest 1972)

Alajos, Mednyánszky: "Regék és mondák" (Európa Publishing house, Budapest 1983)

Katalin, Péter: "A magyar romlásnak századában" (Gondolat Publishing House, 1979)

Viktor, Szombathy: "Száll a rege várról várra" (Madách Publishing House, 1979)

Viktor, Szombathy: "Szlovákiai utazások" (Panoráma Publishing House, 1980)

Sándor, Takáts: "Bajvívó magyarok" (Corvina Publishing House, 2000)

Zsuzsanna, Újváry: "Nagy két császár birodalmi között" (Gondolat Publishing House, 1984)

J.János, Varga: "A fogyó félhold árnyékában" (Gondolat Publishing House, 1986)

Gábor Szántai has a historical fiction novel that is also available for sale:

The Ring of Kékkő Castle
(Hungarian-Ottoman War Series Book 2)
Edited by Suzanna Lahner King

„In the tumultuous year of 1634, Bálint Felföldi starts a quest to find the lost Ring of King Matthias Corvinus in the wild lands of the Hungarian Borderlands where the remnants of the once great Hungarian kingdom mix with the Habsburg and Ottoman Empires.

At the center of this tale of adventure and intrigue is Bálint, the son of a Hungarian mother of the Székely frontier guards of the Carpathian Mountains and Scottish soldier-of-fortune who came to Hungary to serve the Prince of Transylvania.

On his quest, he has adventures and overcoming obstacles, hardships, and foes that seek to undermine his efforts.

The novel wishes to pay tribute to the Hussar and Hajdú warriors of the Hungarian Valiant Order of the Borderland who had been gloriously blocking the Ottoman Empire's expansion into Europe for centuries."

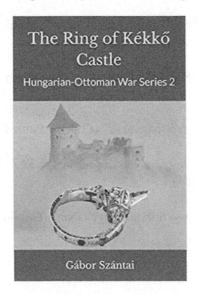

Made in the USA
Las Vegas, NV
16 December 2024

14446606R00154